# The King's Evil

# ANDREW TAYLOR

HarperCollins*Publishers*

HarperCollins*Publishers* Ltd
1 London Bridge Street,
London SE1 9GF

www.harpercollins.co.uk

This paperback edition 2020
4

First published in Great Britain in 2019 by HarperCollins*Publishers*

Prelims show image of Clarendon House © Antiqua Print Gallery/
Alamy Stock Photo

A catalogue record for this book is available from the British Library

ISBN: 978-0-00-811919-5 (PB b-format)

This novel is entirely a work of fiction.
The names, characters and incidents portrayed in it are
the work of the author's imagination. Any resemblance to
actual persons, living or dead, events or localities is
entirely coincidental.

Set in Fournier MT by Palimpsest Book Production Limited,
Falkirk, Stirlingshire

Printed and bound in the UK by CPI Group (UK) Ltd, Croydon CR0 4YY

MIX
Paper from
responsible sources
FSC C007454
www.fsc.org

This book is produced from independently certified FSC™ paper
to ensure responsible forest management.

For more information visit: www.harpercollins.co.uk/green

Praise for *The King's Evil*

'A masterclass in writing for the genre'
  Ann Cleeves, author of the Shetland and Vera Stanhope series

'An absolute treat from start to finish – a hugely engaging,
atmospheric historical thriller'
      Antonia Hodgson, author of *The Devil in the Marshalsea*

'This is a novelist of consummate skill at the absolute peak of
his power'        Manda Scott, author of *A Treachery of Spies*

'Taylor's mantelpiece already groans under awards . . . and this
latest is as striking as anything he has written'
              *Financial Times*, Crime Books of the Year

'Few historical novelists write with more authority and a greater
sense of authenticity than Andrew Taylor'      *Sunday Times*

'This is historical crime fiction at its dazzling best'    *Guardian*

'Vivid and compelling'                    *Observer*

'A novel filled with intrigue, duplicity, scandal and betrayal,
whose author now vies with another master of the genre, C. J.
Sansom'                            *Spectator*

'Glorious'                        *Sunday Express*

'Another fine outing from one of the best historical novelists
around'                          *Sunday Times*

# Praise for Andrew Taylor

'If you like C. J. Sansom, or Hilary Mantel, you'll love Andrew Taylor'
*Peter James*

'Effortlessly authentic . . . gripping . . . moving and believable. An excellent work'
*C. J. Sansom*

'A breathtakingly ambitious picture of an era' *Financial Times*

'This is how historical crime should be written, with rich authenticity underpinning a twisting plot' *The Times*

'One of the most reliably enjoyable of historical novelists'
*Sunday Times*

'Taylor brings the 17th century to life so vividly that one can almost smell it' *Guardian*

'Once again, Taylor combines his detailed research with a deviously twist-laden storyline' *Observer*

'This is terrific stuff: intelligent, engrossing and . . . wonderfully plausible' *Daily Telegraph*

'Thrilling . . . Gripping, fast-moving and credible' *Spectator*

'Finely wrought and solidly researched . . . The novel's plot is fiendishly complex' *Sunday Telegraph*

# The King's Evil

Andrew Taylor is the author of a number of crime novels, including the ground-breaking Roth Trilogy, which was adapted into the acclaimed TV drama *Fallen Angel*, and the historical crime novels *The Ashes of London*, *The Fire Court*, *The Silent Boy*, *The Scent of Death* and *The American Boy*, a No. 1 *Sunday Times* bestseller and a Richard & Judy Book Club Choice.

He has won many awards, including the CWA John Creasey New Blood Dagger, an Edgar Scroll from the Mystery Writers of America, the CWA Ellis Peters Historical Award (the only author to win it three times) and the CWA's prestigious Diamond Dagger, awarded for sustained excellence in crime writing. He also writes for the *Spectator* and *The Times*.

He lives with his wife Caroline in the Forest of Dean.

@AndrewJRTaylor
www.andrew-taylor.co.uk

By the same author

*The Fire Court*
*The Ashes of London*
*Fireside Gothic*
*The Silent Boy*
*The Scent of Death*
*The Anatomy of Ghosts*
*Bleeding Heart Square*
*The American Boy*

*A Stain on the Silence*
*The Barred Window*
*The Raven on the Water*

THE ROTH TRILOGY: FALLEN ANGEL
*The Four Last Things*
*The Judgement of Strangers*
*The Office of the Dead*

THE LYDMOUTH SERIES

THE BLAINES NOVELS

THE DOUGAL SERIES

*For Caroline*

To that soft *Charm*, that *Spell*, that *Magick Bough*,
That high Enchantment I betake me now:
And to that Hand (the Branch of Heavens faire Tree)
I kneele for help: O! lay that hand on me,
Adored *Cesar*! and my Faith is such,
I shall be heal'd, if that my King but touch.
The Evill is not Yours: my sorrow sings,
Mine is the Evill, but the Cure, the KINGS.

        Robert Herrick, 'To the King, to cure the Evill'
                       (*Hesperides*, 1648)

# THE MAIN CHARACTERS

*Infirmary Close, The Savoy*
James Marwood, clerk to Joseph Williamson, and to the
  Board of Red Cloth
Margaret and Sam Witherdine, his servants

*The Drawing Office, Henrietta Street*
Simon Hakesby, surveyor and architect
'Jane Hakesby', his maid, formerly known as Catherine
  Lovett
Brennan, his draughtsman

*Whitehall*
King Charles II
James, Duke of York, his brother
Joseph Williamson, Undersecretary of State to Lord
  Arlington
William Chiffinch, Keeper of the King's Private Closet
George Villiers, second Duke of Buckingham
John Knight, the King's Surgeon General

*Clarendon House*
Edward Hyde, Earl of Clarendon, the former Lord
   Chancellor of England
George Milcote, a gentleman of his household
Matthew Gorse, a servant

*Others*
Olivia, Lady Quincy, formerly Mistress Alderley
Stephen, her footboy
Mr Turner, a lawyer, of Barnard's Inn
Mr Veal, of London
Roger, his servant
Rev Dr Burbrough, of Cambridge
Rev Richard Warley, of Cambridge
Mistress Warley, his grandmother
Frances, a child
Mr Mangot, of Woor Green
Israel Halmore, a refugee

# THE ROYAL FAMILY

September 1667

Charles I = Henrietta Maria of France      Edward Hyde,   = Frances Aylesbury
d. 1649                              Earl of Clarendon   d. August 1667

Charles II = Catherine of Braganza      James, Duke of York = Anne Hyde

Mary b.1662          Anne b.1665

# CHAPTER ONE

HE COULD NOT help himself. In one fluid movement, he stepped back, twisting to present his side to the enemy. His right leg was slightly bent at the knee, the foot pointing towards danger. In that instant, he was perfectly poised, as his fencing master had taught him, ready to thrust in tierce, ready to spit the devil before him like a fowl for the roasting.

As he moved, he heard a sharp intake of breath, not his own. His right foot was on solid ground. But the left ('at right angles to the body, monsieur, for stability and strength') was floating in the air.

'God's—'

In that same instant, he stared at the figure in front of him. Dusk was pouring through the grimy windows of the basement like a noxious vapour. He wanted to beg for help. No words came.

He flung out his arms in front of him in a violent attempt to restore his balance. His fingers stretched, groping for a hand to pull him back. Steel clattered on stone.

He fell with no more choice in the matter than a poleaxed ox. His head slammed against the coping. Pain dazzled him. He cried out. His arms and legs flailed as he fell. The damp, unyielding masonry grazed his fingers.

Nothing to hold. Nothing to—

His shoulder jarred against stone. The water hit him. The wintry chill cancelled all pain and drove the breath from his body. He opened his mouth to cry out, to breathe. The cold flooded his lungs. He choked.

Fiery agonies stabbed his chest. He sank. He had always feared water, had never learned to swim. His hands scraped against unyielding stone. His boots filled, dragging his legs down.

His head broke free. He gulped a mouthful of air. Far above him, he glimpsed the shadowy outline of a head and shoulders.

'Help me,' he cried. 'For the—'

But the words drowned as his body sank again and the water sealed him into its embrace. The purest in London, that's what her ladyship claimed. His fingernails scrabbled against the stone, trying to prise out the mortar to find handholds. His limbs were leaden. The pain in his chest grew worse and worse. It was impossible that such agony could exist.

Despair paralysed him. Here was an eternity of suffering. Here at last was hell.

The pain retreated. He was no longer cold, but pleasantly warm. Slowly, it seemed, every sensation vanished, leaving behind only a blessed sense of peace.

So this, he thought, this is—

# CHAPTER TWO

*One Day Earlier*

O N FRIDAY, I was watching the King healing the sick in the Banqueting House at Whitehall.

'Don't look round,' Lady Quincy said softly.

At the sound of her voice, something twisted in my chest. I had met her last year, in the aftermath of the Great Fire, during an episode of my life I preferred not to dwell on, which had left her a widow. She was a few years older than me, and there was something about her that drew my eyes towards her. Before I could stop myself, I turned my head. She was staring at her gloved hands. Her hat had a wide brim and a veil concealed her face. She was standing beside me. She had brought someone with her, but I could not get a clear view. Someone small, though. A child? A dwarf?

'Pretend it's the ceremony that interests you,' she murmured.

'Not me. Or I shall have to go.'

We were on the balcony, and the entire sweep of the hall was laid out before us. My eyes went back to the King. In this place, the largest and by far the grandest apartment in the palace of Whitehall, Charles II was seated on his throne below a canopy of state, with the royal arms above, flanked by crowds of courtiers and surpliced clergymen, including his personal confessor, the Clerk of the Closet. His face was calm and very serious. I wondered whether he could ever forget that his father had once stepped through the tall window halfway down the hall on to the scaffold outside, where a masked executioner had been waiting for him with his axe. As a child, I had been in the crowd that had watched as the old king's head was struck from his body.

'Say nothing,' Lady Quincy said. 'Listen.'

The Yeomen of the Guard marshalled the crowds in the body of the hall, their scarlet uniforms bright among the duller colours worn by most of the sufferers and their attendants. Many of the courtiers held handkerchiefs to their noses, because ill people did not smell agreeable.

'I've a warning,' she went on. 'Not for you. For someone we shan't name.'

I watched the sick. Most of them had visible swellings, great goitres that bulged from their necks or distorted their features. They suffered from scrofula, the disease which blighted so many lives, and which was popularly known as the King's Evil, because the King's healing hands had the power to cure it. There were at least two hundred sufferers in the hall below.

'I had a visitor on Wednesday.' Lady Quincy's voice was even softer than before. The hairs lifted on the back of my neck. 'My stepson, Edward Alderley.'

One of the royal surgeons led them up, one by one, to kneel before the King. Some were lame, hobbling on crutches or carried by their friends. There were men, women and children. There were richly dressed gentlemen, tradesmen's wives, peasants and artisans and beggars. All were equal in the sight of God.

There was a reading going on below, something interminable from the Prayer Book; I couldn't distinguish the words.

'Edward was in good spirits,' she went on. 'Full of himself, almost as he used to be when his father was alive. Prosperous as well, or so he would have me believe.' There was silence, apart from sounds of the shifting crowd below and the distant gabble of the reading. Then: 'Do you still know where to find his cousin Catherine? Just nod or shake your head.'

I nodded. The last time I had seen Edward Alderley, he had struck me as an arrogant boor, and I knew his cousin would not welcome his reappearance in her life.

'Good. Will you take a message to her from me?'

'Yes,' I said.

'He told me that he knows where she is hiding. He said it was a great secret, and I would know everything soon.' Lady Quincy paused. 'When he has his revenge for what she did to him. He said that he and his friends would see Catherine Lovett dead and he would dance on her grave.'

'His friends? What friends?'

She shrugged and was silent.

I was surprised that anyone might want to make a friend of Edward Alderley. He was a bully and a braggart, with a dead traitor for a father. After his father's disgrace last year, Lady Quincy had lost no time in reverting to the name and title she had used when married to her first husband.

In the hall below, the King was stroking the neck of the kneeling patient with his long fingers, while someone in the crowd was weeping and the clergyman was praying in an inaudible monotone. The King's face was grave, and his heavy features gave him an air of melancholy. He was staring over the head of the kneeling woman. It seemed that he was looking up at me.

'Do you think Alderley was telling the truth?' I said.

Lady Quincy stirred beside me, and her arm brushed mine, just for an instant. 'He came to . . .' There was a pause, as if she needed a moment to decide what to say. 'He came in the hope of impressing me, perhaps. Or . . . Or to make me afraid of him.'

'*Afraid?*' I looked towards her again, but her face was still invisible. 'You? Why should you be afraid of him?'

'Warn Catherine for me,' she said, ignoring the question. 'Promise me you will, and as soon as you can. I don't want her death on my conscience.'

'I promise.'

'I believe Edward would kill her himself if he could.' She paused, and then abruptly changed the subject. 'I shall listen to the sermon at St Olave's on Sunday morning. Do you know it? In Hart Street, on the corner of Seething Lane.'

I nodded. It was not far from the Tower, one of the few churches in the walled city that had survived the Great Fire.

'Will you meet me there? Not in the church but afterwards – wait outside in a hackney. I wish to be discreet.'

'Very well.' I felt a stab of excitement. 'May I ask why?'

But she had already turned away. She slipped through the crowd towards the door, followed by her small attendant, who I now saw was a lad with dark hair, presumably her footboy though he wasn't wearing her livery. He was wrapped in a high-collared cloak that was too big for him.

Disappointment washed over me as Lady Quincy passed

through the doorway to the stairs. The footboy followed his mistress. In the doorway he glanced back, and I saw that the lad was an African.

After Lady Quincy and her attendant had gone, I waited for a few minutes to avoid the risk of our meeting by accident. I left the balcony and went down to the Pebbled Court behind the Banqueting House. The sky was grey and the cobbles were slick with rain.

The public areas of the palace were packed, as they always were when the King was healing. The sufferers did not come alone: their family and friends came too, partly to support them and partly to see the miracle of the royal touch. It was unusual to have a big public healing ceremony in September, but the demand had been so great that the King had ordered it. Charles II was a shrewd man who knew the importance of reminding his subjects of the divine right of kings. What better way of demonstrating that God had anointed him to rule over them than by the miracle of the royal touch?

I crossed to the opposite corner of the court, passed through a doorway and went up to the Privy Gallery. Mr Chiffinch was waiting in the room where the Board of Red Cloth held its quarterly meetings; I was clerk to the board, and he was one of the commissioners. He was alone, because the other commissioners had already gone to dinner. He was sitting by the window with a bottle of wine at his elbow. He was a well-fleshed man whose red face gave a misleading impression of good nature.

In his quiet way, Chiffinch wielded more power than most men, for he was Keeper of the King's Private Closet and the Page of the Backstairs, which meant that he controlled private access to the King. It was he who had told me to wait on the balcony in the Banqueting Hall until Lady Quincy approached me; he had said it was by the King's order, and that the King relied on my discretion. He had also said that I was to do whatever her ladyship commanded.

'Well,' he said. 'What did she want?'

'I'm not permitted to say, sir.'

He shrugged, irritated but clearly unsurprised by my answer. He disliked being in a state of ignorance; the King did not tell him everything. 'You didn't attract attention, I hope?'

'I believe not, sir.'

'I'll tell you this, Marwood: if you put a foot wrong in this business, whatever it is, we shall make sure you regret it. The King does not care for those who fail him. And he's not in a forgiving mood at present, as my Lord Clarendon is learning to his cost.'

I bowed. A few weeks earlier, the King had removed Lord Clarendon, his oldest adviser, from the office of Lord Chancellor in one of the greatest political upheavals since the Restoration of the monarchy seven years before. But removing Clarendon from office had not made him politically insignificant. His daughter was married to Charles II's own brother, the Duke of York. Since the King had no legitimate children, and Queen Catherine was unlikely to give him any, the Duke was his brother's heir presumptive. Moreover, the next heirs in the line of succession were Clarendon's grandchildren, the five-year-old Princess Mary and her infant sister, Anne. If the King were to die, then Clarendon might well become even more politically powerful than he had been before.

'These are dangerous times,' Chiffinch went on. 'Great

8

men rise and fall, and the little people are dragged up and down behind them. If my Lord Clarendon can fall, then anyone can. But of course a man can rise, as well as fall.' He paused to refill his glass, and then went on in a softer voice: 'The more I know, the better I can serve the King. It would be better for him, and for you, if you confided in me.'

'Forgive me, sir. I cannot.' I suspected that he was looking for a way to destroy the King's trust in me.

'It's curious, though,' Chiffinch went on, staring at the contents of his glass. 'I wonder why my lady wanted to meet you in the Banqueting House of all places, at one of the healing ceremonies. She so rarely comes to Whitehall these days. Which is understandable enough. It takes more than a change of name to make people forget that she was once married to that bankrupt cheat Henry Alderley.'

I said nothing. Edward Alderley's father had committed a far worse crime than steal other people's money, though few people other than the King and myself were aware of that. I had done the King good service at the time of Henry Alderley's death, which was when I had also had dealings with Lady Quincy. I kept my mouth shut afterwards, which was why he trusted me now.

Chiffinch looked up, and I saw the flash of malice in his eyes. 'Did Lady Quincy get a good look at you, Marwood? Did she see what's happened to you since she last saw you?' He turned his head and spat into the empty fireplace. 'It must have come as quite a shock. You're not such a pretty boy now, are you?'

# CHAPTER THREE

L ATE ON FRIDAY afternoon, the rain dashed against the big windows of the Drawing Office at the sign of the Rose in Henrietta Street. It had grown steadily heavier all day, whipped up by a stiff, westerly wind. If it grew much darker they would need to light the candles.

Apart from the rain, the only sounds were the scratching of Mr Hakesby's pen and the occasional creak of a floorboard, when Brennan, the draughtsman, shifted his weight from one foot to another. He was working on the detailed elevations for the Dragon Yard development by Cheapside, which was the main commission that Mr Hakesby had in hand at present.

Catherine Lovett was standing at a slope placed at right angles to one of the windows. Her neck and shoulders ached. She had spent the last half-hour working on another job. She was inking in the quantities and materials in a panel at one side of the plan for one of the new warehouses by the docks.

The careful, mechanical lettering was dull work, and the warehouse was a plain, uninteresting building, but Cat was thinking of something quite different – the garden pavilion project at Clarendon House, where she and Mr Hakesby had been working this morning. Mr Milcote had visited them to discuss the basement partition. Milcote was acting for his lordship in the matter, and she could not help thinking that their lives would be much more pleasant if all their clients were as agreeable and straightforward as that gentleman.

She rubbed her eyes and stretched. As she was dipping the pen in the ink, there was a tap at the door. She laid the pen aside and went to answer the knock. That was another of her more tiresome duties, along with keeping the fire going, sweeping and scrubbing the floor, filling inkwells and sharpening pens.

Cat found the porter's boy on the landing, holding out a letter. It was addressed to Mr Hakesby in an untidy scrawl. She took it over to him. He was sitting huddled over the fire, though it was not a cold day, with a board resting over the arms of his chair so he had a surface for writing and drawing, when his hands were steady enough.

Hakesby broke the seal and unfolded the letter. It trembled in his liver-spotted hands. There was another letter inside. He frowned and gave it to her. Her name – or rather the name she used in Henrietta Street, Mistress Jane Hakesby – was written on it in the same hand as the outer enclosure.

'What is this?' Hakesby said, his voice petulant. 'There's nothing for me here. Do you know anything of this?'

Brennan looked up. He had sharp hearing and sharp wits.

'No, sir,' she said in a low voice.

She concealed her irritation with Hakesby, for he was increasingly peremptory with her now that he had a double reason to expect her obedience. She opened the letter and scanned its contents.

*I must see you. I shall be in the New Exchange tomorrow afternoon, at about six o'clock. Look for me at Mr Kneller's, the lace merchant in the upper gallery. Destroy this.*

The note was unsigned and undated. But there was only one person who could have written it. She dropped the paper into the glowing heart of the fire.

'Jane!' snapped Mr Hakesby. 'Take it out at once. Who's it from? Let me see.'

It was too late. The flames licked the corner of the paper and then danced along one side. The letter blackened. For an instant, Cat saw one word – 'destroy' – but then the paper crumpled and fluttered and settled among the embers.

## CHAPTER FOUR

O N SATURDAY AFTERNOON, as chance would have it, I was kept later than I had expected at Whitehall. There was a crisis in the office. Much to Chiffinch's irritation, I spent the majority of my time working under Mr Williamson, the Undersecretary to Lord Arlington, the Secretary of State for the South and one of the King's most powerful ministers. Mr Williamson's responsibilities included the publication of the *London Gazette*, the government's newspaper. Under his direction, I shouldered much of the day-to-day burden of editing the material, seeing it through the press and ensuring it reached its readers.

In London, the *Gazette*'s distribution relied heavily on a group of women who carried the newspapers to the taverns and coffee houses of the city, and also delivered them to the carriers who took them the length and breadth of the kingdom. Over the last few weeks there had been problems of late delivery or even no delivery at all. These were probably due to the usual causes of death, disease, drunkenness and simple unreliability. There was also the fact that we paid the women a pittance, which was often weeks in arrears. But Lord Arlington wasn't interested in the reasons. He blamed Williamson for the failure, and Williamson blamed me.

When at last I was able to leave the office, I took a boat from the public stairs at Whitehall – fortunately the tide was on the ebb – and went by water to Charing Cross. The sun was low in the sky, slanting through a gap in the clouds.

Outside the New Exchange, the Strand was packed with waiting coaches and sedan chairs, reducing the flow of traffic in both directions to fitful trickles. Aggrieved drivers struggled towards the City or upriver to Whitehall or past the Royal Mews towards Hyde Park. Those on foot were making better speed.

The clocks were already striking six as I entered the building. Since the lamentable fire last year, which had destroyed the shops of Cheapside, the old Royal Exchange in the City and so much else, the New Exchange was busier than ever. The world came here to buy and sell. Everything the heart could desire, the proud boast went, could be found under one roof. You could purchase all the luxuries of the globe without having to get your feet muddy, your clothes wet, or your ears assaulted by the vulgar cries of the street.

I forced myself to slow down – people sauntered in the New Exchange: to hurry was to draw attention. The shops were arranged in long lines that faced each other on two floors. I made my way to the stairs. The upper galleries were even busier than those on the ground floor.

Mr Kneller's shop was larger than most and equipped with a wide mullioned window, the better to allow customers to inspect the wares for sale. Much of his stock was imported from France and the Low Countries.

I hesitated on the threshold. The last of the sunlight slanted through the panes in broad stripes that brought to life the silks and lace in its path. The shop was thronged with people, men and women; the air was heavy with perfume, and filled with the murmur of voices and the rustle of skirts. The proprietor's wife, a pretty woman of about thirty, was showing a delicate spray of lace to a richly dressed gentleman with a face like a horse. The gentleman was more interested in her than in her lace. For an instant her eyes flickered towards me and then returned to her customer.

'You like the look of her, don't you?'

My head jerked to the left. Cat was at my elbow, looking up at me. She wore a light cloak and a hat that shaded most of her face.

'Nonsense,' I said, instantly defensive. 'I was looking for you.'

'You're a liar, sir,' she said. 'Like all men.'

# CHAPTER FIVE

C AT ALLOWED MARWOOD to lead her to a quieter corner, partly shielded from the rest of the shop by the projecting counter on which the apprentices were laying out the larger pieces of lace. She had last seen him three or four months ago. She glanced surreptitiously at him, and found he was doing the same to her.

He looked more prosperous than before, and somehow older. He was wearing a new periwig, finer and more luxuriant than his old one. His face was plumper – the last time she had seen him, pain and laudanum had sharpened his features.

It was important to be natural: they were a man and a woman idling away an hour in the New Exchange, enjoying the pleasures of shopping. She took up a piece of lace. 'Is this Bohemian work, I wonder?'

'I need to talk to you,' he muttered. 'It's urgent.'

'Yes. And while you do, we need to look as if we are here to look at lace.'

She glanced up at Marwood's face, tilting her head to have

a better view of the left side of his neck. To her surprise, he gave her a sardonic but not unfriendly look.

'Well?' he said. 'How do you find me?'

'Better. As far as I can see, that is. Your wig and your collar hide the worst of it.'

He shrugged, dismissing his disfigurement, dismissing the memory of what the fire had done to him. He said softly: 'Your aunt talked to me about you.'

Cat's eyes widened. She raised her voice. 'Come to the window, sir, and let me see this piece properly.'

They stood in the embrasure. The lace spilled over her arm like a frosted spider's web. She held it to the glass and pretended to examine it.

'Lady Quincy?' she said. 'What does she want, after all this time? I'm surprised she still has an interest in me. She did nothing for me when she was married to my uncle, and when we lived under the same roof, nothing when I most needed help.'

'She wants to help you now.'

'I'm sure she told you that, sir.' Cat felt irritation rising like bile inside her. 'But then you would believe anything she says. You always had a – what shall we call it? A tenderness for her.'

'I don't know what you're talking about,' he said coldly. He bent down, bringing his lips closer to her ear. 'Your cousin Edward Alderley called on her,' he said slowly. 'He told her that he has discovered where you are hiding. He plans to have you brought to the gallows.'

'Perhaps my cousin was lying,' she said. Marwood was growing angry, she thought, which pleased her. 'Edward never let truth get in his way.'

'You can't take that chance. She believed he was telling the truth. There's still a warrant out for your arrest on a charge of treason, on the grounds that you aided and abetted your father, a Regicide. It's never been withdrawn.'

'But what could I do?' she said. 'He was my father, whatever he had done. Besides, I had as little to do with him as I could.'

'Alderley also told Lady Quincy that he has powerful friends, and they will help him destroy you.'

'I thought no one would give Edward the time of day after my uncle's disgrace.'

'It appears you were wrong,' he said. 'Lady Quincy believed him, and she wanted to warn you, from the goodness of her heart.'

'Goodness? From my Aunt Quincy?'

'You should leave Henrietta Street. At least for a time. It's not safe.'

She flared up: 'Why should I run away from Edward? I've had enough running.'

Marwood glanced at the nearest apprentice, who had heard this. He moved nearer to Cat, turning and shielding her. 'For your safety.'

'I'll tell you something.' She touched his sleeve. 'Do you know what my cousin did to me?'

'Yes, of course – he helped his father cheat you of your fortune, and he attacked you and—'

'He raped me.'

'What?' Marwood stared aghast at her. 'I don't understand.'

'What's there to understand? In his father's house, he came to my bedchamber by night. He took me by force. Is that plain enough for you, sir?' She lowered her voice. 'That's why I took out his eye and ran away from Barnabas Place. I thought I had killed him when I stabbed him. I wish to God I had.'

The apprentice advanced and gave a little cough. 'Sir – mistress – may I show you some more pieces? We have some particularly delicate work newly brought from Antwerp.'

'Not now,' Marwood said.

'Sir, I can promise you—'

'Leave us,' Cat said, raising her voice. 'Go.'

The sounds of the shop died away. Half the customers were staring openly at them. So was the shopkeeper's pretty wife.

'Later,' Marwood said to the apprentice.

He took Cat's arm and marched her out of the shop. So much for their attempts to be inconspicuous, Cat thought. She said nothing as he led her to the stairs and down to the ground floor. The movement made the curls of his periwig swing away from his face. For an instant she glimpsed what remained of his left ear.

When they reached the street, Marwood turned abruptly towards her.

'Why didn't you tell me what that damned knave did to you?' he said.

'Why should I have done? What's it to you?'

He tightened his lips but said nothing. The last of the sun had gone. Grey clouds blanketed the city.

'One day,' Cat went on, in a dull voice as if mentioning a future event of no importance to her, 'one day, I shall kill my cousin.'

'Don't be foolish. What would that achieve except bring you to the gallows, which is exactly what he wants?'

'You forget yourself. You have no right to tell me what I may or may not do.'

Marwood looked away from her. 'In any event, we must assume, for your own safety, that Alderley has found you again. That means you must leave Mr Hakesby, leave Henrietta Street. Even better, leave London for a while.'

'I can't.'

'You must.'

She shook her head. 'There's too much work to do. Mr Hakesby depends on me. I have a meeting with one of our clients in less than an hour. I must go. Besides—'

'If it's a question of money, I can help. I've brought five pounds with me.'

That was generous, and the offer touched her.

'You don't understand, sir,' she said, in a gentler voice. 'If I need money, I shall ask Mr Hakesby. I'm betrothed to him. He will soon be my husband.'

After a good week at the Drawing Office, measured by the entries that Cat made into Mr Hakesby's accounts, they had fallen into the habit of supping together on Saturday evening. Hakesby was careful with money but not ungenerous. There was plenty of work at present, as half of London had turned into a building site after the Fire.

Hakesby was a creature of habit, which was why he always entertained Cat and Brennan in a private room at the Lamb in Wych Street. The tavern was a shabby place, but the people of the house knew him: they valued his custom and treated his habitual ague, however bad it was, as nothing out of the way. Usually these were cheerful occasions when even Mr Hakesby allowed himself to take a glass or two of wine, though it tended to make his symptoms worse.

A few months ago, Cat would not have believed it possible that she would spend an evening in Brennan's company. At the start of their acquaintance, she had disliked intensely both the fact that Brennan had dared to court her affections and the manner in which he had approached this impossible task. But she had dealt with that, and so had he, and she had come to respect his skill as a draughtsman, his reliability and his kindness to Mr Hakesby.

Brennan had come to Henrietta Street armed with a glowing letter of recommendation from Dr Wren, and time had justified the praise. Hakesby paid him a regular wage now, rather than using him as a piece worker. Someone, she suspected, was looking after him, perhaps the motherly young woman who worked in the pastry cook's in Bedford Street.

On this evening, they supped later than usual, at nearer nine o'clock than eight. It was not a cold evening, but Cat was chilled to the bone. It was hard to concentrate on what the men were saying. The thought of her cousin Edward kept forcing itself into her mind. She wondered if she could ever be happy again.

At first, Hakesby and Brennan failed to notice her silence. Both of them were elated, partly from wine and partly because Hakesby had received an unexpected stage payment for the Clarendon House commission, which had allowed him to pay Brennan a bonus. Despite his political troubles, Lord Clarendon remained an influential client, the sort who led where others followed. Hakesby had been concerned about the work on the pavilion, as her ladyship, who had taken such a particular interest in it, had recently died. There was also the fact that his lordship was not only in disgrace at court but rumoured to be short of money. Nevertheless, the payment had been made. They probably had Mr Milcote to thank for that.

As the meal went on, however, Cat noticed that Hakesby was shooting worried glances at her. He was growing more and more dependent on her, she knew, and that could only increase as his ague worsened. Their marriage was fixed for the end of October; next month, they would start to call the bans. The marriage was to be a private affair in the new-built church in Covent Garden.

'The building is a pure Inigo Jones design,' Hakesby had said with satisfaction. 'Not one of those crumbling medieval hotchpotches the Papists built.'

After supper, as they were going downstairs to the street, he touched Cat's arm and said quietly, 'Are you well? Are you sickening?'

'No, sir. It is nothing, a woman's matter.'

Hakesby shied away from her, turning to take Brennan's arm. In the street, he said he would not take a chair back to his lodgings; he felt perfectly capable of walking. Brennan and Cat exchanged glances, silently accepting the necessity of accompanying him. The three of them walked slowly towards Three Cocks Yard off the Strand, where Hakesby lodged on the first floor of one of the new houses. Brennan took him into the yard and up to the house, while Cat herself lingered in the Strand.

Brennan was only gone for a moment or two. When he returned they walked back the way they had come. She would have been content to go by herself – in the past year, she had learned to cope with the streets. She always carried a knife, and was not afraid to show it. But it would make Hakesby unhappy if she walked alone after dark, so she accepted Brennan's company. Walking back with her to Henrietta Street did not take him far out of his way.

'What's amiss?' he said as they passed St Clement Danes. 'You hardly said a word during supper.'

'Nothing,' she said automatically. Then she came to a sudden decision and changed her mind. 'No. That's not true. I – I have a difficulty. I need to go away for a while. And no one must know where I am. Even Mr Hakesby.'

'Why?'

'I can't tell you.'

'Where will you go?'

'I don't know.'

'You can't be so foolish,' he said. 'Is it something to do with that letter you had?'

She nodded. 'It's urgent. I must go, and the sooner the better.'

They walked past Somerset House. The Savoy, where Marwood lived, was not far away to the west and she pulled up her cloak to shield her face.

Brennan misinterpreted the action. 'Do you think someone might be following you?'

'Perhaps.'

A solitary woman always attracted attention, she thought, usually the wrong kind.

'Would you – would you need comfort?' Brennan said.

She stared at him, her anger flaring up. 'What?'

'If there were somewhere you could hide, I mean,' he said hastily. 'But somewhere the conditions were mean and poor, where they weren't suitable for . . . you.'

'Why?'

'I know somewhere you could go for a week or two, longer maybe. It wouldn't cost much.'

'As long as I was safe, I wouldn't need a featherbed. Or a maid to wait on me. If that's what you mean.'

'In that case,' he said, 'I have a notion that might help.' He hesitated. 'Though what I have in mind would hardly be fitting for one such as you. But no one would find you there. No one would even think to look there.'

'Where is this?'

'A few miles outside London. It's a refugee camp, and it's on my uncle's land. He used to farm it, but everything's gone to wrack and ruin since his son died.'

# CHAPTER SIX

WHEN CAT AND I had gone our separate ways, I walked down the Strand to the Savoy. My house was here, in Infirmary Close, which lay deep in the warren of crumbling buildings that made up the former palace and its immediate surroundings. The Savoy was still owned by the Crown, though its precincts were given up to a variety of purposes. I was lucky to have even a small house to myself – lodgings of any sort were in short supply, especially since the destruction of so much of London in the Great Fire. My master Mr Williamson had spoken on my behalf to the clerk who handled these royal leases.

I was not in the best of tempers. When my manservant, Sam, let me into the house and took my cloak, I swore at him for his clumsiness, though in truth he was as graceful as a man with only one whole leg can be, and more nimble than many with two of them.

Margaret, his wife, brought me my supper. She lingered by the table as I began to eat. 'Your pardon, sir, but is it the *Gazette* women that's troubling you? My friend Dorcas says they're all at sixes and sevens and she's worked off her feet.'

I felt ashamed of my ill humour to the servants, who were hardly in a position to answer back if they wanted to keep their places. I said, in a gentler voice than before, 'That and other things.'

'It's only that perhaps I could help. If you need someone to do a few rounds for a week or so, then I will, if you permit me. Or I could share Dorcas's load. I've done it before.'

It was a kind offer. Margaret had been one of the newspaper's distributors before she came to work for me, and she was still friendly with several of the women she had worked with. She knew the routine. I also knew that she had disliked the work intensely, for the younger, more comely women often attracted unwanted attentions.

'Thank you,' I said. 'But I need you here.'

I dismissed her. In a way it was useful that Margaret and Sam should think that I was out of sorts because of problems with the *Gazette*. Better that than the truth.

Afterwards I sat by the window, which looked out over roofs and walls. Slowly the daylight slipped away from the evening while I thought about Catherine Lovett and her ingratitude. Couldn't the woman understand that I was trying to save her life? Why was she so headstrong? Why so foolish? Or was I the fool to put myself out on her behalf for no good reason whatsoever?

I worked myself up to a sullen rage and encouraged my sense of ill-usage to burn steadily within me. What had really upset me was the knowledge that Edward Alderley had raped Cat. And also the fact that she had betrothed herself to Simon Hakesby, a man old enough to be her father, possibly her grandfather.

I should have felt an abstract outrage that Alderley had forced himself on an unmarried cousin living under his father's roof. As for the betrothal, I should have felt an equally abstract pleasure for Hakesby and Cat, for he would bring her security and she would bring him the vigour of a young woman.

But there was nothing abstract about my outrage. The very thought of these things made me feel inexplicably injured. So, desperate for a diversion, I fell to thinking of my Lady Quincy instead, though I found little consolation there. Tomorrow I would see her again, but I could not begin to understand why she wanted me to collect her from church in a hackney. Was it to do with her stepson, Edward Alderley, and the warning she had asked me to pass on to Cat? The possibility unsettled me. I wanted nothing further to do with Edward Alderley in this world or the next.

Something else unsettled me: the thought of seeing Lady Quincy again. Despite the difference in our stations, I had desired her once. It had been folly then, and it would be worse than folly now. Besides, as Chiffinch had reminded me, who could desire a man like me?

# CHAPTER SEVEN

C AT MADE HER preparations. A strange calmness possessed her, a sense that her fate had already been decided and that nothing she could do would materially alter it.

In her closet she found the canvas bag she had brought with her when she came to Henrietta Street. She packed a spare shift and stockings. She would wear her old cloak. She took half a loaf that remained from breakfast. She wished she could take her Palladio, a dog-eared copy that Mr Hakesby had given her, but that was impractical: though the four books of *I quattro libri dell'architettura* were bound into one volume, it was a large and cumbersome folio that was hardly appropriate for a fugitive. As a consolation, she packed her notebook and a miniature travelling writing box that included a pen, ink, a ruler, a brass protractor and pencils. She had nearly thirty shillings in her purse so at least she wasn't penniless.

Through the open window, she listened to the church clocks striking eleven. Her mouth was dry. She had spent too much of her life running away, and she did not want to do it again. She fastened the cloak over her shoulders, picked up the bag and looked around the Drawing Office. The candlelight made it insubstantial, a place of shadows and dreams. She had been happy here and she did not want to leave.

She snuffed all the candles. The only light came from the small lantern they used when they went up and down the stairs in the evening. On the landing, she locked the door behind her and slipped the key into her pocket under her skirt, where it knocked against the knife she always carried.

The light of the lantern preceded her down the stairs, swaying drunkenly from side to side. The porter had been dozing on his cot but he stirred as she reached the hallway.

'Going out, mistress? At this hour?'

'Didn't I say?' she said. 'I'm to spend the night with an old friend. She and her father are waiting for me. Will you unbar the door?'

He shot back the bolts, one by one, and lifted up the bar. 'It's very late, mistress.'

'Not really. They've been supping with friends and they're waiting in Covent Garden for me.' Cat found sixpence in her purse and gave it to him. 'Would you do me the kindness of not mentioning to anyone that I've gone out? Especially Mr Hakesby. He'll only worry, and there's no need.'

'Don't you worry, mistress. Your secret's safe with me.' He smiled at her in a way she did not care for. 'I'll be silent as the grave.'

Late though it was, the arcades of Covent Garden were brightly lit and crowded with brightly dressed crowds of theatregoers, revellers and the better class of whores; among them, like lice in a head of hair, moved the thieves, the pedlars and beggars, plying their trades.

Cat had grown familiar with this world of pleasure-seekers in the last few months, and she navigated its perils with confidence. The small, forlorn figure of Brennan was waiting for her in the entrance court of the King's Theatre in Brydges Street. He darted forward when he saw her. A link boy was beside him, the flame of his torch flaring and dancing in the breeze. By its light she saw that Brennan's face was pale, and his sharp features were drawn with anxiety.

'You've come – I wondered if you'd change your mind.'

'Of course I've come,' Cat said. 'Were you successful?'

'Yes. It's all arranged. Have you got the money? If not, I can lend it—'

'I've got the money.'

'We'd better walk there.' He hesitated. 'Do you mind? Would you like to take my arm?'

'Of course,' she said. 'Can we manage without a link boy to light us?'

He nodded. 'I know the way well enough.'

At first they had little need of a link, for their way took them up Bow Street and into Long Acre, which were almost as busy as Covent Garden itself. Up by St Giles's Fields, though, it was a different story, with long, unlit stretches; it was muddy underfoot and there was the constant danger of stumbling into the gutter. But Brennan was as good as his word and guided her safely, though she grew increasingly irritated by his habit of enquiring regularly how she was managing or whether he was going too fast for her.

'I do very well, thank you,' she snapped at last. 'I'm not made of glass. But I'd rather save my breath for walking.'

'Would you like me to come with you tomorrow? It's Sunday – I'm not needed at the Drawing Office. I could walk back afterwards, when I know you're safely there.'

'No,' she said. 'It's best I go alone. And what if Mr Hakesby finds me gone? He will send for you at once. You must be there to reassure him. Tell him you don't know where I am but I'd said I was seeing a friend.'

The inn was a small, low building near the church of St Giles-in-the-Fields. They went through the central passageway to the yard, where there was a long range of stables.

'Uncle Mangot doesn't trust them,' Brennan said in a whisper. 'It's not his horse, you see. It's hired from a neighbour and he can't afford to have it stolen. Anyway, it's cheaper to sleep in the yard, and just as safe as inside after the gates are barred.'

They found Brennan's uncle at the end. The horse was in its stall and the old man was in front of it, sitting in a small covered cart in the yard outside. It was difficult to see him clearly. A rushlight in an earthenware pot hung beside the cart, but his face was little more than a blur against the surrounding darkness.

Brennan hung back, touching Cat's arm. 'I almost forgot: if my uncle asks about me, it's best not to mention that we've been working at Clarendon House.'

'Why?' Cat whispered.

There was a rustling of straw, and a man's voice quavered, 'Who's that?'

'Uncle Mangot,' Brennan said. 'It's me. I've brought her.'

The man in the cart leaned towards them. 'You're late. Is this the girl? You'll have to sleep here tonight, with me. We leave when it's light.'

'Very well,' Cat said.

'She's my friend, Uncle,' Brennan said. 'You'll treat her well, won't you? You'll let her sleep in the house? She can pay for everything.'

'If you wish.' The old voice sounded papery and uncertain, as if its owner rarely used it. 'But there's nothing to buy. She can work for her keep, eh? A long time since I had a servant.'

'No one must know she's with you,' Brennan said. 'Promise to keep her safe.'

Mangot spat over the side of the cart. 'I won't blab if she don't and you don't.' There was a wordless sound in the darkness which might have been laughter. 'She'll be safe enough, Nephew. We don't get many visitors. The refugees frighten away the ungodly.'

Cat came forward into the glow of the rushlight. 'Five shillings,' she said. 'For one week. That's what your nephew told me.'

'And a room on her own,' Brennan put in.

Mangot sniffed. 'You didn't mention that before. Seven shillings.'

Brennan tried to argue but the old man was obdurate. Cat put an end to it by taking out her purse and finding the money.

'One more thing,' Mangot said to her as he counted the coins in the palm of his hand. 'You'll have to share the cart on the way back.'

'Who with?' Cat said.

'His name's Israel Halmore. He used to be a glover. Before the Fire, he had a shop on Cheapside, and now he's got nothing.'

Mangot's Farm was a few miles outside London in the direction of St Albans. It was on the outskirts of a village called Woor Green.

True to his word, Mangot set out from the tavern at dawn. Cat had spent a chilly night, huddled in her cloak and half-buried beside a pile of sacks containing flour. She had shivered almost continuously, though that had not been solely because of the cold. Israel Halmore had arrived at some point in the early hours, waking her from a light sleep. He had been a long way from sober and he had fallen asleep almost at once.

As well as the flour, the cart was laden with rolls of canvas that smelled strongly of fish, and with bags of nails. Mangot was equipped with a pass signed by a magistrate, which permitted them to travel on a Sunday. The streets were quieter than usual and they made good time through the outskirts of London. Halmore woke up and insisted on their stopping so he could relieve himself against a tree. Afterwards, he sat up with Mangot and took the reins from the old man. In the daylight, he was revealed as a gaunt giant of a man, with strongly marked features and a shock of grey curls. His fingers were twisted and swollen with arthritis, which must have made it impossible for him to carry on his trade.

In the back of the cart, Cat pretended to doze while the two men talked together in low voices. Her mind was full of her own thoughts, which were bleak. Unless there were a miracle, she could not see how she could safely return to her old life in Henrietta Street. Once the hue and cry had died down, perhaps her best course would be to flee abroad, to Holland, perhaps, or even to America, where many of her father's friends had found refuge.

She was distracted by Halmore saying, more loudly than before, 'Well, I wasn't going to say no, was I? Not when the Bishop was buying ale for anything on two legs.' Mangot started to speak, but Halmore overrode him: 'Clarendon's a greedy rogue, master, and he's in league with the Papists.'

'May God damn him,' Mangot said.

'Aye. The Bishop's doing God's work in his way.'

'But it was dangerous,' Mangot said. 'Notwithstanding the cause is just. You could have been arrested.'

'No. Not me. When I was there, we were just standing outside Clarendon House and shouting and booing. I threw a few stones, but only when the light was going and no one could see who it was.'

'Who's this Bishop then?' Mangot asked. 'What's his real name?'

'I don't know. But he carries a deep purse and he's open-handed. That's what matters.' Halmore had a low, resonant voice that carried easily, even when he spoke quietly; a preacher's voice. 'We all had half a crown apiece, as well as the ale. Know what they're saying? He's the Duke of Buckingham's man. That's where the money comes from, and that's why the Bishop said we don't have to worry about being arrested. The Duke will see us right. He's always been a friend of the people and a good hater of Papists. As for Clarendon, a pox on him. He deserves all we can give him. And I tell you one thing: he's going to get a lot more before the Bishop's done with him.'

Mangot glanced at him. 'Meaning?'

Halmore shrugged. 'I don't know. Only that what they're planning will strike him where it hurts.'

# CHAPTER EIGHT

S T OLAVE'S WAS on the south side of Hart Street, not far from the sprawling buildings of Navy Office in Seething Lane. On Sunday morning, I waited outside the church in a hackney. It was a fine day, and I had pulled back the leather curtain so I could feel the sun on my face and watch the church door.

When the congregation emerged, I saw several men I recognized, mainly clerks from the Navy Office or the Tower. I stepped down from the coach and waited for Lady Quincy. The church was crowded, and she was one of the last to emerge from the porch. She was veiled, and flanked by her maid on one side and the footboy on the other. The maid was a prim-faced woman who avoided looking at me.

I bowed to her ladyship, and she nodded to me as she climbed into the coach and sat down, facing forwards. The boy scrambled after her, and she drew him down beside her. Despite the warmth of the day he wore the thick, high-collared cloak I had seen on Friday. I waited for the maid to follow her mistress but she walked away in the direction of Mark Lane.

'Where to, madam?' I asked.

'Tell the coachman to go to Bishopsgate Street beyond the wall. I will give you further directions when we are there.'

I gave the man his instructions and joined her inside the hackney. The boy was huddled beside her. I faced them both, though I automatically turned my head a little to the right to conceal the disfigurement on the left side of my face. Lady Quincy moved aside her veil, and for the first time I saw her face clearly. I felt a pang of sadness, almost a physical pain.

Here was the reason I had put on my best suit of clothes this morning and had my periwig newly curled. Olivia, Lady Quincy, was a gentlewoman a few years older than myself; she had fine, dark eyes, a melodious voice and a full figure that her sober dress could not entirely conceal. But the living creature was not the same as the one who had played such a dramatic role in my mind for nigh on a year. She was well enough, I told myself, but one glimpsed a dozen like her every day at Whitehall, and many more beautiful.

The hackney jolted over the cobbles, and she winced. 'Let the curtain fall,' she commanded.

I obeyed, causing an artificial dusk to fill the interior of the coach. 'I did what you asked me, madam. I passed on your warning to a certain young lady. But she was reluctant to flee from her cousin.'

'She was always headstrong.'

I was tempted to tell Lady Quincy of Cat's betrothal but I kept quiet. It was not my secret, any more than the fact that her cousin Edward had raped her.

'Where is she? Is she somewhere safe?'

'I don't know,' I said.

'She's a fool if she stays. Her cousin won't leave her alone, you know. Edward nurses his hatreds as if they were his children.'

We sat in silence for a minute or two while we rattled through the noisy streets, listening to our coachman swearing at those who blocked his way.

'Where are we going?' I asked.

Lady Quincy looked up. 'To see Mr Knight. He is one of the King's Sergeant Surgeons.'

I looked sharply at her. 'Mr John Knight? The Surgeon General himself?'

'Do you know him?'

'By reputation, yes.'

Knight was one of the King's most favoured medical attendants; he had proved his loyalty during the civil war and afterwards when the court was in exile. Last year, he had corresponded frequently with Mr Williamson about the health of the Navy, which was how I had come across him. But Sunday morning was an unusual time for a consultation with a physician or surgeon, let alone one of Mr Knight's eminence. It was yet another hint that the shadowy influence of the King was behind this.

'Where are we meeting him?' I asked. 'I thought he lodged in Russell Street, not near Bishopsgate.'

'He is visiting his wife's cousin, and he has agreed to see us there before they dine.'

Lady Quincy took a purse from her pocket and handed it to me. 'He will expect his fee afterwards – would you see to it for me? And the coachman will need his fare; you must ask him to wait for us while we are with Mr Knight. By the way, there's no need to mention who I am, particularly in front of servants. You may introduce me as your cousin, Mistress Green. Our appointment is in your name, and you would oblige me if you give him the impression that Stephen is your servant.'

'Mine?' I stared at her. 'Madam, it would help if I knew what we're about.'

For a moment she said nothing. Then: 'Pull aside the curtain.'

I did as she bid me. Light poured into the hackney.

'Stephen? Show the gentleman what you are.'

The boy sat forward from the seat and pulled open his cloak. For the first time I saw him properly. He was richly dressed, as such African boys usually were when they served wealthy ladies; for they were kept as toys or pets as much as servants. He was handsome enough, in his way, with regular features and large eyes fringed with long lashes. But it was his neck that drew my gaze. If you kept a blackamoor as a personal attendant to serve you in public, it was fashionable to adorn the neck with a silver collar – a nod to the fact that he or she had been brought to England as a slave, and of course a sign of the owner's wealth. This boy didn't wear a collar, however. His neck was disfigured and bloated by swellings. He was suffering from the King's Evil.

'As you see, he has scrofula,' Lady Quincy went on. 'You must not be concerned – I believe there is no risk of infection. I took him to Whitehall to see the King touching the afflicted, to show him that there were others like himself.' She glanced at the boy and added, 'God has granted the King the ability to heal, as a token of his divinely ordained right to rule over us.'

'How charitable,' I said. I felt guilty for my earlier self-consciousness about my own blemishes, caused by a fire a few months before: if I compared them with this child's neck, what had I to complain of?

In some small, cynical part of my mind, I thought that Stephen's scrofula had provided perfect cover for our meeting when she had asked me to pass on the warning to Cat.

'I wanted Stephen to see the ceremony of healing,' she went on. 'To reassure him. He is superstitious, you see, like all these savages, and he thought it might be a sort of witchcraft.' She spoke as if the boy were not there.

'And Mr Knight? Do you hope he will cure Stephen?'

Lady Quincy shook her head. 'No – only the King can do that. But as Sergeant Surgeon he is qualified to issue certificates of scrofula, as well as the tickets for sufferers to attend the public healing ceremony. Besides, I wish to know more about the illness.' She swallowed suddenly and her fingers made small, convulsive movements on her lap. 'About its symptoms. And its causes.'

'But my lady – why do you want me to escort you? Why is the appointment in my name? Why all this secrecy?'

'Because I desire that my interest in scrofula should not be public knowledge, or not at present. That's why I wore a veil when we met at the Banqueting House, and that's why the appointment is in your name.' Lady Quincy paused, and moistened her lips. 'I have my reasons, and perhaps one day I shall confide in you. But, in the meantime, I know I may trust you to be discreet.'

The house was old and large, with many rooms and passages that seemed to have been acquired at random over the last three or four generations. It looked comfortable enough but everything was a little old-fashioned, a little shabby. There was a shop on the ground floor, though it was closed. Mr Knight's cousin imported furs from Russia. He clearly prospered in his dealings but felt no need to advertise the fact to the world.

We were shown into a small parlour on the first floor. The servant offered us refreshments, which we declined. Mr Knight did not keep us waiting long. He brought with him a hint of wine on his breath, and the scent of cooking. The surgeon was a man who had lived much at court, and it showed in his stately manner. Though he was too polished to show impatience, I guessed that dinner was not far away and he did not want to prolong this interview any longer than he needed.

After we had introduced ourselves, I told Stephen to come forward and expose his neck.

'So this is the boy,' Mr Knight said. 'How interesting. I believe I have never seen a blackamoor afflicted with the disease. I must make a note of it.'

He beckoned Stephen closer and examined him. His long, deft fingers were surprisingly gentle. Lady Quincy, her face veiled, leaned forward in her chair to watch.

'Is it the King's Evil?' she asked.

'Oh yes, mistress. There's no doubt about that. And in an advanced state. The inflation is at present mainly in the neck, with the characteristic rosy colour. Tilt your head back, boy. Yes, I thought so. The hard tumours are propagating vigorously under the jaw and about the fauces . . .'

Knight straightened and turned towards us. 'There will be no difficulty about providing you with a certificate stating that he has scrofula. And, in the circumstances' – he gave a little bow, perhaps in respect of the King's possible interest in the matter – 'I will also write you a special ticket of admission for the next public healing ceremony. Otherwise the boy would have to present himself with his certificate at my house in Russell Street before the ticket can be issued. That can sometimes take months, because there is always such a crowd of sufferers.'

'Thank you, sir,' I said.

'Tell me,' Lady Quincy said. 'How is the disease caused? What is its nature?'

He took a chair and leaned back, steepling his fingers. 'These are most interesting questions. As Hippocrates observes, he who knows the nature of the disease can be at no great loss for the properest method of cure. But I regret to say we don't fully understand scrofula, not completely. Generally it is characterized by an indolent tumour or – as in this case – several tumours.' He prodded Stephen's neck, and the boy recoiled. 'Yes, the struma yields. This one – the one on the left here, under the jawbone – will probably degenerate into a stubborn ulcer within the month.'

'And the causes, sir?' she prompted, and again I saw the curious flutter of her fingers on her lap. I wondered at her agitation.

'Well – let me enumerate some of them, or rather the conditions that may lead to the disease. We find it particularly in children descended from parents who also are disfigured by it. (What a pity we usually cannot examine them.) Or in those suckled by nurses who were themselves diseased. Or who have lived much in humid air.' He poked Stephen again. 'Africa is humid, is it not?'

The boy stared blankly at him, his eyes wide and fearful.

I guessed he didn't understand the word. I said, 'The gentleman means damp, Stephen. Was it damp where you lived before you were brought to England?'

He twitched his head like a nervous horse confronted by something he does not understand. Mr Knight took this as assent.

'There you are,' he said. 'I'm not surprised. Another cause is undoubtedly diet – viscous, crude, farinaceous aliments, in particular, or unripe fruit. Or lack of healthful exercise. Or the possession of a frigid or phlegmatic temperament.' He frowned. 'The boy certainly looks phlegmatic. Is his bile inert, by the way?'

I've shrugged. 'I've no idea.'

Knight hurried on, anxious to smooth over an awkwardness. 'External injuries – luxations, for example, or strains – or even catarrhs and fevers may lead towards scrofula. Or drinking stagnant water. There are some physicians who hold that a mother who has looked much upon a scrofulous person may, as it were, imprint the disease on her own child.'

Lady Quincy made no comment. I said, 'These are underlying causes, if I understand you correctly, sir. Are there factors that incite an outbreak of the disease in a person already predisposed towards it?'

'Well, sir – here there is some debate in the profession. Most of us, I think, would agree that the proximate cause is probably the obstruction of the small vessels by a viscid, inert humour. There are some, however, who attribute it rather to a particular acidity of the blood, which causes it to coagulate and then harden.'

'What is the best method of treatment, sir?' Lady Quincy asked.

Mr Knight smiled condescendingly. 'There is none of proven efficacy apart from His Majesty's touch. By God's mercy he has cured thousands of sufferers. Why, by my calculations, he must have stroked some thirty thousand of his subjects. No wonder the people love their King and venerate God. We are blessed indeed.'

'Indeed,' said Lady Quincy drily. 'Thank you for your advice. I believe you and Mr Marwood have a little business to transact. I shall wait here while you do it.'

Mr Knight and I left her alone with Stephen. At my request, he ordered a servant to bring our hackney to the street door. He took me into a small room overlooking the street. It was furnished plainly as a counting house. There was a terrestrial globe in the corner. A map of Muscovy had been unrolled on the table, its corners held down with pebbles.

While the surgeon was writing Stephen's certificate of scrofula and his ticket of admission for the next public ceremony, I stood at the window and stared idly down at the street. A tall and very thin man in a long brown coat was standing on the far side of the road. He was plainly dressed – he might have been a merchant in a small way. But what caught my attention was the fact that he wore a sword, as if he were a gentleman or a bully from the stews of Alsatia: yet he looked neither a rogue nor a man of birth.

He glanced up at the windows of the house. Perhaps he saw me, though he could not have made out more than a shadow on the other side of the lozenges of distorted glass. He strolled away. I forgot him for the moment as soon as Mr Knight spoke to me.

43

'There, sir. The next ceremony will probably be at the Banqueting House, unless the King goes down to Windsor. If there is any difficulty, give my name to the Yeoman on duty at the door.'

I thanked him, and paid his fee. With great ceremony, he escorted us downstairs and handed Lady Quincy into the hackney, where the maid was already waiting. Stephen and I followed her.

Sitting in near darkness, with the leather curtain drawn across, we rattled down the street towards Bishopsgate. Lady Quincy's perfume filled the confined space.

'Thank you for your help, sir,' she said. 'You will not speak of this to anyone, I'm sure.'

'You have my word, madam.' I wondered whether she would ask me to accompany her to her house in Cradle Alley, and perhaps offer me some refreshment.

'And I will not trespass further on your time. I shall put you down by the Wall.'

'Of course,' I said, telling myself firmly that the less I saw of her the better. 'That would be most convenient.'

# CHAPTER NINE

IT WAS RAINING again on Monday morning, and harder than before. I stood by a window in the Matted Gallery and looked down on the Privy Garden. The hedges and statues had a bedraggled air, and large puddles had formed on the gravel paths. Only two or three people were in sight, and they were in a hurry, using the garden as a shortcut.

The gallery ran on the first floor between the garden and the river. When I had first come to Whitehall, I had despaired of ever finding my way around such an ill-arranged and confused cluster of buildings. Gradually, though, I had realized that there was a certain logic to the place. At its core were the Royal Apartments, the King's and Queen's, both public and private. From these, two long ranges extended at right angles to each other, enclosing two sides of the Privy Garden. The old Privy Gallery ran westwards to the Banqueting Hall and the Holbein Gate. Here were many of the offices and chambers of government, such as the Council Chamber and Lord Arlington's offices. The Stone Gallery, with the Matted Gallery above, ran south towards Westminster.

The apartments of many favoured courtiers clustered about it. Those of the Duke of York were at the far end.

On this wet morning, the gallery was crowded with courtiers, officials and visitors. Gentlemen strolled up and down, and the air was full of whispered conversations and smothered laughter. It was a popular place of resort, a place to see and be seen, especially when the weather was bad. It had the added convenience of giving access to so many private apartments.

Today there was an air of suppressed excitement. The story was circulating that the Duke of Buckingham, one of Lord Clarendon's greatest enemies, had been restored to his many offices yesterday and was once again riding high in the King's favour. Buckingham was a hero to the common people and had wide support in Parliament. He had been the King's intimate friend since childhood, having been brought up with the royal family, and he was extraordinarily rich. Nevertheless, until recently he had been held in the Tower: it had been alleged by his enemies that he had commissioned an astrologer to cast the King's horoscope, which was a form of treason since predicting the King's future inevitably imagined the possibility of his death.

I was waiting for Mr Chiffinch again. He had sent a note to the office this morning, summoning me to attend him here on the King's business. Mr Williamson had let me go with reluctance, muttering that the *Gazette* would not publish itself. While I waited, I could not help thinking of Cat Lovett and Lady Quincy. They were not happy thoughts. They matched the weather.

There was a sudden stir by the entrance to the King's private apartments. The doors were flung open. The guards straightened themselves, and the crowd fell silent. The Duke of York, the King's brother, strode into the gallery, flanked by two of his advisers.

Ignoring the bows of courtiers, who bent towards him like corn in the wind, he marched towards his own apartments. The Duke was a fine-looking man, but today his face was red and his features were twisted with rage. When he left the gallery, the whispers began again, with an edge of excitement that they had previously lacked.

I moved from the window and instead examined a painting of a lady that hung nearby. She wore a richly embroidered silk black gown with ballooning sleeves and a gold chain around her neck. She stared past me, over my right shoulder, at something only she could see. The embroidery of the gown looked like writhing snakes. Behind her, a group of women were entering her suite of rooms through a distant doorway.

Ten or fifteen minutes slipped past before the King's doors opened again. This time it was Chiffinch who emerged, pink-faced like a well-fed baby, nodding and smiling to those nearby whom he considered worth cultivating. He didn't linger, however. He came over to me.

'How interesting to find you here,' he said, his eyes sliding past me to the painting.

'I don't understand, sir.'

'That lady you were looking at. The widow in her black gown. She has a look of Lady Quincy, don't you think?'

I shrugged. 'Perhaps a little, sir. But her ladyship is not so sallow, I think.'

It disturbed me that Chiffinch had mentioned her. He had a genius for finding a man's weak spots. I wondered if he had sensed my interest in Lady Quincy.

'Her ladyship's lips are fuller,' Chiffinch said, pursing his own.

'Who is it?'

'I've no idea. Some long-dead Italian princess, probably. The Dutch gave it to the King at the Restoration.' He turned away from the painting. 'Come with me.' He led me into the Privy Gallery and took me into a closet by the King's laboratory, which overlooked the garden.

'Close the door,' he ordered. 'Sit.'

He pointed at a chair by a small table underneath the window. He sat opposite me and leaned over the table, bringing our heads close together.

'I've a commission for you, Marwood. Do you remember Edward Alderley?'

I was so surprised I couldn't speak.

'Alderley,' Chiffinch said irritably. 'For God's sake, man, you can't have forgotten. That affair you were mixed up in after the Fire with my Lady Quincy's second husband. Edward Alderley was the son by his first wife. He used to be at court a great deal.'

'Yes, sir. Of course I remember him.'

'He's dead.' He paused, fiddling with the wart on his chin. 'I daresay no one will shed many tears.'

I felt shock, swiftly followed by relief. What a stroke of luck for Cat. 'How did he die?'

'Drowned. But it's not that he is dead that matters. It's where his body was found.' Chiffinch's forefinger abandoned the wart and tapped the table between us. 'In Lord Clarendon's well.'

I began to understand why the Duke of York had been in such a rage. Lord Clarendon was the Duke's father-in-law. 'In my lord's house?'

'In his garden. Which comes to the same thing. But mark: this is a confidential matter. Breathe a word of it to anyone, and you will regret it. Do you understand?'

'Yes, sir. But are you sure that I am the man best suited to a matter of such delicacy?'

'You wouldn't be my choice for the job, I can tell you that. It's by the King's command. I suppose he chose you because you know a little of the man and his family.'

Then there was no hope for me. 'What do you want me to do?' I asked.

'Go to Clarendon House and look into the circumstances of Alderley's death. The body is under lock and key. Lord Clarendon knows, of course, and so does one of his gentlemen, Mr Milcote. Alderley was discovered this morning by a servant, who has been sworn to secrecy. We don't want the news made public yet. Not until we know more. That is essential.'

'Was the death accidental, sir?'

Chiffinch flung up his arms. 'How in God's name would I know? That's for you to find out. Report back to me as soon as you can.'

'Mr Williamson——'

'May go to the devil for all I care. But I shall see he's informed that the King has given you a commission. He can hardly object.' Chiffinch glanced piously in the direction of heaven. 'After God, our duty is to serve the King. We would all agree on that, I hope.'

I nodded automatically. The more I thought about this, the less I liked it. I had been long enough at Whitehall to know that when the great ones of our world squabbled among themselves, it was the little ones who tended to be hurt.

Chiffinch drew a paper from his pocket. 'Here's your authority, with the King's signature.' He held the paper in his hand, but did not give it to me. 'Remember. My Lord Clarendon is no longer Lord Chancellor, but he still has many friends who would like to see him restored to the King's favour. And one of them is the Duke.' He paused, which gave me time to reflect on the fact that the Duke of York was the King's heir presumptive, and that the Duke's daughters – Clarendon's grandchildren – were next in line to the throne. 'So for God's sake, Marwood, go carefully. And if you see my lord himself, try not to anger him. He has had much to cope with lately. Bear in mind that his wife has hardly been a month in her grave.'

He sent me away. With my mind heavy with foreboding, I walked slowly through the public apartments, through the Guard Chamber and down into the Pebble Court. It was still raining, even more heavily than before.

I was to go immediately to Clarendon House, but on my way I had to call at the *Gazette* office in Scotland Yard to collect my cloak and my writing materials. I was tempted to scribble a note to Cat, care of Mr Hakesby, while I was there, to give her private warning of her cousin's death. But I dared not ignore Mr Chiffinch's prohibition until I knew more of the matter.

Besides—

A thought struck me like a blow in the middle of the court. I stopped abruptly. Rain dripped from the brim of my hat.

How could I have been so foolish? Not two days earlier, I had told Catherine Lovett that her cousin had found her out. And she had told me that he had raped her when she lived under her father's roof, and that she meant to kill him for it.

50

From any other person, that might have been merely an extravagant way of speaking, a way of expressing hatred. But not from Cat. She was a literal-minded creature in many ways, and a woman of great spirit. I had seen what she was capable of. And now Edward Alderley was dead.

I faced the dreadful possibility that Cat had somehow contrived to kill her cousin. Worse still, that I had played a part in causing the murder, by warning her that her cousin had found her.

# CHAPTER TEN

T HE OFFICIAL NAME of the road was Portugal
Street, in honour of our Queen, Catherine of Braganza,
but everyone persisted in calling it Piccadilly. It was an old
route west to Hyde Park and then towards Reading. Long
ago, some of the land nearby had been owned by a man who
had grown rich in the manufacture of those large old collars
of cutwork lace named piccadills, and somehow the name
had been transferred to the road. In recent years, the mansions
of the rich had sprouted like monstrous mushrooms among
the fields. The greatest of them all was Clarendon House.

It was a vast building of raw, unweathered stone surrounded
by high walls and tall railings. It faced Piccadilly, looking
south down the hill to St James's Palace, which seemed diminished and even a little squalid in comparison with its
magnificent new neighbour. I had heard Mr Williamson say
that the King was not pleased that the house of a subject
should so outshine his own palaces.

Most Londoners hated it, too. Here was Lord Clarendon
in the splendour of his new house, while thousands of them

had lost their own houses in the Fire. People called it Dunkirk House, for they said that the former Chancellor had profited hugely and corruptly from the government's sale of that town, one of Cromwell's conquests, to the French king.

Though it was broad daylight, the main gates were barred. The gateposts were still blackened in places. During the riots in June, the mob had lit bonfires here and burned the trees that used to line the street outside. They would have burned the house itself if they could.

The mob blamed him for all our ills, past and present, including the Queen's failure to give the King an heir. They believed Clarendon had purposely found a barren wife for him so that his own grandchildren by the Duke of York would one day inherit the throne. They blamed him for our crushing defeat at the hands of the Dutch navy in the Battle of the Medway. They blamed him for everything. According to popular belief, no form of corruption was too large or too small for Lord Clarendon. It was even said that he had stolen the stone intended for rebuilding St Paul's after the Fire and used it for his mansion.

It was a house in mourning – not for Alderley, of course, but for Lady Clarendon. Her funeral hatchment hung over the gateway. Two manservants, both carrying arms, waited inside the gates under a temporary shelter. I presented my credentials and asked to be taken to Mr Milcote. His name was enough to allow me into the forecourt. One of the servants escorted me to a side door in the west side of the house and brought me to an antechamber draped with black. It was so large you could have fitted the whole of Infirmary Close into it, from kitchen to attic. I was left to wait under the suspicious eye of a porter while yet another servant went to find Mr Milcote.

I heard his rapid footsteps before I saw him. He appeared in a doorway leading to a flight of stairs.

'Mr Marwood – your servant, sir.'

We exchanged bows. He was a tall, quietly dressed man in his thirties. His periwig was fair, and his complexion suggested that the natural colour of his hair was not far removed from the wig's. He too was in mourning.

'I hope they haven't kept you waiting. We have not been able to be as hospitable here as my lord would have liked, unfortunately.' His mouth twisted. 'Recent events, you understand.'

I nodded. There was an openness about Milcote that I liked at once, and also a sort of delicacy too, a sense of what was fitting for a situation. I said quietly, 'I'm come on the King's business.'

He glanced at the waiting servants, took my arm and led me outside. 'You mustn't think me rude but it will be better if we talk outside.' He looked up at the grey sky. 'At least the rain is slackening.'

We walked down the flagged path. The side of the house rose above us, austerely regular, blocking much of the light. We came to a gate of wrought iron, which Milcote unlocked to let us pass, and entered the garden at the back of the house.

'I assume you have come about our . . . our recent discovery?' he said.

'Yes, sir.'

'My lord has much to occupy himself,' he went on. If he had noticed the scars that the fire had left on the side of my face and my neck, he was too well bred to show it. 'He may not be able to see you today.'

'He knows I'm here?'

'Oh yes. The Duke sent word that someone would come.'

We paused at the corner of the house, looking out over the garden. It was on the same scale as the house – at least five or six acres, and surrounded by high walls. The paths had been laid out, and many shrubs had been planted. But there was an unfinished quality to it all: some areas were covered in old canvas sails, much patched and faded; and the paths were rutted and muddy. Oblivious to the weather, teams of gardeners were at work. Against the far wall were two pavilions, which were only partly built. One of them lacked a roof. Between them, a gap in the wall was blocked by a heavy wooden palisade.

'It will be the greatest garden in London when it's finished,' Milcote said. 'The designs are Mr Evelyn's. It's a pity that this . . . this accident should happen here.'

'Where, exactly?'

He pointed to the left-hand pavilion, the one with a roof. 'Shall we go there directly?'

Milcote guided me to a path running parallel to the side wall. Halfway down, he paused to command a gardener to keep himself and his fellows away from this part of the garden. I glanced back at the front of the house. I saw a white blur at the first-floor window nearest to the south-west corner. Someone was watching us, his face distorted and ghostly behind the glass. We walked on.

'I've sent the builders away,' Milcote said.

'They arrived after the body was found?'

'Yes. They could have continued on the other pavilion, but I thought it wiser that we should have as few strangers here as possible while we deal with this.'

'Then who knows about it?'

'Besides me, I believe only the servant who found the body, one Matthew Gorse, and Lord Clarendon himself.'

'But the rest of the household must be curious?'

'I put it about that we had discovered the roof to be unsafe, and nothing could be done there until new tiles arrived.' Milcote frowned. 'And I sent a message to the builders telling them not to come today. But we can't keep everyone in ignorance for long.'

The pavilion was of two storeys above a basement, with a balustrade masking the roof. Though the wall facing the garden was of stone, dressed similarly to the stone of the mansion, the wall to the side was of crumbling, dirty red bricks, which looked out of place in this setting. Near the ground was a small mullioned window set in a stone frame and protected by iron bars.

Milcote climbed a shallow flight of steps and unlocked the double door. I turned to see if the face was still visible at the window.

'We are not overlooked?' Milcote said.

'I think someone was watching us from the house.'

For an instant alarm flared in his eyes, but he suppressed it. 'A window? Which one?'

'At the end to the right, on the first floor.'

'My lord's private apartments are there.' He smiled, adding with obvious affection, 'He may be old, but he likes to know what's what.'

He pushed open one leaf of the door just wide enough to let us pass. I found myself in a room with brick walls, to which islands of old plaster still clung. It was lit by two tall windows, one facing the mansion and the other, at right angles to it, facing the other pavilion at the opposite corner of the garden. The flagged floor was uneven and stained with age. In one corner was a pile of planks and newly cut stones. The air was very cold.

'The body's downstairs in the kitchen,' Milcote said, closing the door behind us and throwing the bolt across. 'Through there.'

In the wall to the left, a door led to a lobby containing a staircase with worn treads.

I glanced up. 'Where does it go to?'

'The main apartment. After that, to the viewing platform.'

I followed Milcote down to the basement. It was the same size as the room above, and much gloomier, for the two barred windows were small and set high in the wall. It had a large fireplace with two ovens beside it. There was no furniture of any sort apart from a wooden contraption tucked into a corner, with a pile of scaffolding poles beside it. It was almost as high as the barrel-vaulted ceiling.

'There,' Milcote said, pointing at the floor in front of the empty fireplace where a long shape lay like a vast boar hound across the brick-lined hearth. It was draped with a horse blanket.

I took a step towards it but he caught my arm to stop me.

'Have a care. The well is there.'

Ahead of me, a yard or so in front of the wooden contraption, was a wooden disc about five or six feet in diameter. It was countersunk into the floor, which was why I hadn't noticed it before.

'I wouldn't trust my weight on the cover,' Milcote said. 'Just in case.'

I skirted the well and knelt by the body. I pulled back the blanket. My stomach heaved. I had seen too many dead bodies in the last few years. During the Plague they had been piled in the streets. But I'd never grown used to them.

This was Edward Alderley: there was no doubt about it.

His single eye stared up at me. The face was almost grey. The features were heavier than I remembered. His mouth was open, showing blackened teeth. He had lost his wig, and the dome of his skull was speckled with stubble. There were drops of moisture on his skin.

I drew back the blanket to the waist and then down to the knees. A drawn sword was lying on the floor beside the body. The tip of the blade winked in the light from the lantern. The sheath, which hung from the belt by two thin chains, had entangled itself with the legs. The leather was black from the water.

Death had made Alderley look ridiculous, as death is apt to do. Frowning, I touched his collar and then his coat.

'He's soaking wet.'

'Didn't they tell you?' Milcote said. 'The poor man fell in the well and was drowned.'

I glanced at the cover. 'But how? The cover's on.'

'It wasn't over the well this morning. It was leaning against the wall.'

'When did this happen?'

'It must have been after Saturday afternoon. That was when work stopped. So between then and first thing this morning when the servant came to unlock the pavilion.'

'Perhaps he was here on Saturday with the builders,' I suggested. 'And they locked him in by accident.'

'It's possible.' Milcote shrugged. 'But unlikely. The surveyor in charge of the works is a sober man, very thorough. He was on site on Saturday – I saw him myself.' He hesitated. 'Between ourselves, there's some doubt as to whether the work will continue. Mr Hakesby is understandably concerned, as he's already retained the builders.'

I swallowed. 'Did you say – Hakesby?'

'Yes. The surveyor-architect. An experienced man, highly recommended.' Milcote looked curiously at me, and I knew my face must have betrayed the shock I felt. 'I'll question him, of course, but I'm sure he would have ensured the well was covered up when he left, and the building secure. He has his own key.'

'Yes,' I began, 'or I will talk to him myself.' I tried to mask my confusion with a change of subject. 'Who identified Alderley?'

'I did. I was a little acquainted with the gentleman, and he's visited Clarendon House in the past.' Milcote hesitated. 'But I had no idea he was here, or how he got into the pavilion.'

I was about to ask how he knew Alderley when there was a hammering above our heads. Both of us swung round as if surprised in a guilty act. The sound bounced off the walls, filling the empty spaces between them with dull echoes.

Milcote swore under his breath. He took the stairs, two at a time. I followed. He unbolted the door. I glimpsed a manservant through the crack.

'It's my lord, master. He wants to see you in his closet. And the other gentleman.'

The old man sat by the window wrapped in a quilted bedgown. His bandaged legs rested on a padded stool. Clarendon was a martyr to the gout, Milcote had told me on the way up here, so much so that even the staircases in the house had been designed with exceptionally shallow treads to make them as easy as possible for him to climb.

A brisk fire burned in the grate, and the room was uncomfortably warm. After the grandeur of the stairs and the outer rooms, I had not expected this closet to be small. It was full of colours and objects – paintings, sculptures, rugs, pieces of china, curiosities and books – always books, more and more books.

My warrant from the King lay on Clarendon's lap. He had insisted on examining it himself, even holding it up to the light from the window, as if the very paper it was written on held secrets of its own.

'Marwood,' he said. He looked half as old as time, but his voice was clear and hard. 'Marwood. Was there once a printer of that name? Dead now, I think.'

'Yes, my lord. My father.'

Clarendon's memory was legendary, as was his command of detail. His small eyes studied me, but to my relief he did not pursue the subject. 'You're from Whitehall, yes?'

'I work for Mr Williamson on the *Gazette*.'

'The *Gazette*?' His face grew suspicious. 'Does that mean that Lord Arlington has a finger in the pie, as he usually does?'

'No, my lord.' I heard a creak as Milcote shifted his weight beside me.

'Did you see the King? Or the Duke?'

'No – Mr Chiffinch gave me the warrant and sent me here.'

Lord Clarendon sniffed. 'Does Chiffinch often give you errands, eh?'

'Sometimes – I'm also clerk to the Board of Red Cloth, and he's one of the commissioners.'

'We know what that means,' Clarendon said tartly. 'The Board does nothing for the salaries it receives. Its commissioners oblige the King in less official ways. And therefore so does its clerk.' He turned to Milcote. 'Well, George. We must cooperate, of course, which means we must give Mr Marwood all the assistance in our power. Was Alderley murdered?'

Milcote shrugged. 'We haven't examined the body yet, my lord, but it's hard to see how he could have fallen into the well of his own accord. If it was dark, he might have stumbled into it. But what was he doing there in the first place?'

'How did you know him?' Clarendon paused and glanced at Milcote; I had the sense that a silent message had passed between them.

Milcote cleared his throat. 'I had some acquaintance with him years ago, my lord – in the years of his prosperity.'

'Before his father's downfall, you mean. A more treacherous rogue never existed.'

'Whatever his father was, Edward Alderley was kind to me then.' Milcote cleared his throat again. 'When I met him a few months ago, his condition was sadly altered. I believe he had tried to improve what was left of his fortunes at the tables.'

'A gambler.' Clarendon's voice was harsh. 'The most stupid of all mankind.'

'He was trying to change his ways. He wanted to improve his condition by wiser means – he asked for my help.'

'So, like the fool you are, you lent him money, I suppose?'

'Yes, my lord – a little – enough to pay his most pressing debts.'

'You're too soft-hearted, George. You've seen the last of that.'

Not just soft-hearted, I thought, but gullible enough to be taken in by a rogue like Edward Alderley.

'He told me he was searching for some respectable form of employment,' Milcote went on. 'I promised to look around for him. I would have asked you, but I knew you would have no time for him.'

'So you are not altogether a fool.' Clarendon didn't return

the smile but there was a touch of warmth in his voice. 'And what was he doing here? And in the pavilion?'

'I don't know.'

'My lord,' I said, growing a little impatient. 'I understand that the only other person who knows of this man's death is the servant who unlocked the pavilion this morning and found the body.'

Clarendon looked sharply at me. He did not take kindly to those who spoke before they were spoken to. 'First things first. Have I your word that you will be discreet? I can't afford a scandal at this time.'

'Yes, my lord.'

'If the news gets out, I shall know who to blame.' He looked steadily at me. 'You would not like to be my enemy.'

I refused to allow him to intimidate me. I had the King's warrant. 'May I have your permission to speak to the servant?'

'Of course.' Clarendon glanced at Milcote. 'Who was it?'

'Gorse, my lord.'

'I don't know him. Have him brought to me.'

'Unfortunately he's not here.' Milcote lowered his voice. 'The mourning rings.'

'You may know,' Clarendon said to me in a flat voice purged of emotion, 'my wife died last month.'

'Gorse is delivering mourning rings for my lady today,' Milcote explained. 'Mainly to former dependants and acquaintances. So he will be here and there all over London. He should be back after dinner. But I don't know when.'

'Is he trustworthy?' Clarendon said.

'I believe so, my lord – I knew him in his old place, and suggested him to the steward.'

'I want this riddle solved,' Clarendon said, still looking at me. 'Do you understand? For my sake as well as the King's. You may make what enquiries you need to in my house, but Milcote must accompany you at all times, inside and out.'

I nodded. 'As you wish, my lord.'

'My late wife was fond of that pavilion,' he went on, his voice softening. 'It was an old banqueting hall – she remembered it fondly from her youth. I wanted to tear it down and build it anew to match everything else. But she pleaded with me, and in the end I agreed to preserve at least part of it, though I insisted on its being remodelled to match the rest of my house and garden.' He paused, staring at me. 'Are you married, Mr Marwood?'

I shook my head.

'No? If you ever are, you will find that it is a matter of perpetual compromise.' His voice trailed away, and he turned his head to look out of the window.

'Alderley's body was found in the well, my lord,' I said. 'Was that part of the old building?'

'Yes.' He looked at me again, and his eyes were brighter than before. 'Lady Clarendon was particularly attached to its water. She said it was always cold, even on the hottest day, and that the spring that feeds it is unusually pure. Indeed, she believed it to be the purest in London.' His voice changed, and I knew without knowing how that he was furiously angry. 'This body has sullied my wife's well, Marwood. It has polluted the spring. Tell the King that I want this made clean for her sake.'

# CHAPTER ELEVEN

NOW CAME THE worst part, which I had been dreading from the start. Milcote and I returned to the pavilion to examine the body more closely. I postponed this unpleasant necessity by examining a wicket gate in the back wall of the garden. It was set in the temporary palisade that covered the place where the garden gates would eventually be installed. The wicket was locked and bolted. Milcote said it was rarely used, except occasionally by gardeners and the builders during the day.

Next I went up to inspect the main apartment on the first floor of the pavilion. The work was more advanced here than it was below. The windows were glazed and barred. At the top of the stairs was the door to the viewing platform. It too was locked and bolted.

At last I could no longer delay the inevitable. In the basement, Milcote and I stripped off Edward Alderley's outer clothing. It was no easy matter, even with two of us, to manoeuvre his body. Alderley had always been a big, overweight man and, since I had last seen him, he had become even grosser.

Intimate contact with the dead, I thought, this prying into the consequences of death, should be growing easier for me since the events of the last twelve months. But custom had not yet formed a callus over my squeamishness; perhaps it never would.

'How did Gorse know that someone was in the well?' I asked as we were tugging Alderley's arms from his sleeves.

'The cover was off,' Milcote said. 'And he stumbled on Alderley's hat, which was on the floor. He had the wit to look down the shaft.'

'Why was he in the pavilion at all at that hour? Was that usual?'

'No. But Mr Hakesby was expecting a delivery of lime, and he couldn't get here himself until later. So I sent Gorse instead. He unlocked the garden door and then he came down to the basement to open the windows. The atmosphere is damp, and we try to keep the place aired. It was still dark down here, and he had a lantern.'

The body's legs flopped on to the stone floor, and a long, lingering blast of wind erupted from the corpse's belly.

'God's heart,' Milcote said. 'What a job is this. Does one ever get used to it?'

'Probably not,' I said curtly. How did he think I spent my days, I thought – laying out corpses?

I noted that the body was not in that phase of rigidity that corpses pass through after death. Perhaps the coldness of the well water had delayed its onset. If only, I thought, there were an exact way of measuring temporal gradations of decay, we should be able to deduce when Alderley had drowned, or at least to narrow down the time when it had happened. All we knew at present was that he had died between Saturday evening, when Hakesby and the builders had locked up, and this morning when Matthew Gorse had come to unlock the pavilion for the early delivery.

I suppressed the uncomfortable thought that there was another possibility: that Cat had been there with Hakesby on Saturday, and that Alderley had died before they had gone home for the night.

It took two of us to remove each of the boots because the leather was so saturated with water. Despite our labours, I was cold. The temperature in the basement seemed to drop lower and lower. The water chilled my hands and splashed over my clothes.

'Who has a key?' I said, panting, when Alderley's feet were bare, exposing untrimmed nails like pale talons.

Milcote lobbed a boot into the corner. 'Mr Hakesby. I have a set, too – I have all the household keys. My lord has another set, though those are never used and lie locked in his closet. Then there's the steward's – Gorse would have used the pavilion key from there.'

'And the house and garden?'

'Locked as tight as a drum. We take no chances, not after those attacks on my lord. During the night, the mastiffs are loose in the garden, and watchmen make an hourly circuit. There are two porters awake in the house, and lanterns in the forecourt.'

'Then how did Alderley get here?' I asked.

Milcote shrugged. 'It's a perfect mystery. Unless he came during the day, while the men were here. And he was already dead when they locked up.'

This was an echo of my own thoughts, and it led me back to Hakesby and Cat. I turned to Alderley and unstrapped his belt. The breeches were almost as hard to remove as the boots had been.

Death makes a man small as well as making him ridiculous. When we had stripped Alderley to his shirt, he looked shrunken and as vulnerable as a child. Milcote held up the lantern and I examined the body as best I could. There were grazes on the forearms and shoulders, and much broken skin on the fingers. They told their own grim story of a drowning man struggling in the water, enclosed by the sheer walls of the well. I felt the skull and found a bruise on the forehead.

Had he hit his head as he was falling down the well? Or had someone hit him beforehand?

Crouching, we rolled him on to his back again. Milcote watched closely as I turned my attention to the pockets. Alderley had been carrying a purse containing nearly thirty shillings in silver and two pounds in gold. That was a small fortune to most people; but poverty was a relative condition.

There were also two keys on a ring. One was made of blackened iron and had a long shank. The other was much smaller, and far more delicate: it appeared to be made of silver, and had a finely wrought ring at the top that contained what looked like a monogram. I held up the second key to the light of the window, but the letters were so entwined and so clogged with delicate arabesques that I could not even distinguish whether there were two or three of them.

Next, in an inner pocket, I found a sodden bundle of papers. I tried to separate the leaves from each other but the paper tore.

'Have you a pouch or bag I could use?' I asked.

'What?' Milcote dragged his eyes away from Alderley's possessions. 'A pouch?'

'I'll take these with me. I need something to put them in.'

He nodded. 'Of course.'

He went away and came back with a small bag of coarse canvas, its top secured with a drawstring. 'Will this do?'

'Admirably.'

He opened the bag, shook out its contents, a dozen or so newly forged nails, on the floor, and passed it to me. I put the papers, the key and money into it.

'He used to live in Barnabas Place in Holborn,' I said. 'A big place – you could house an army in it. Was he still there?'

'No. He had to sell it and most of the contents to pay his own debts. But he retained an interest in another house nearby, and he was living there. In Fallow Street.'

'Did you ever go there?'

Milcote shook his head. 'We met at a tavern or he came here. He grumbled about how small his lodgings were. And it was mortgaged, too, and he'd had to let part of it to a carpenter.' He gave me a rueful smile. 'I think he was ashamed. He didn't want me to see how mean his condition had become. In truth, I didn't know him that well, but I felt sorry for him.'

I turned back to the body. Alderley's mouth had fallen open. I took up the sword. It was a narrow blade of fine steel. Two silk ribbons, one red and one blue, had been knotted around the hilt. Perhaps some lady had given them to him to wear as her favour. A design had been engraved on the blade just below the hilt. I held the sword up to the light and recognized the form of a pelican eating its young, the Alderley crest.

'It's an old Clemens Horn,' Milcote said. He stretched out his hand and touched the blade with lingering respect, as a man might touch the hand of a beautiful woman who did not belong to him. 'German. Must be nigh on fifty years old, but you won't find a better sword.'

'I should like to see the well,' I said.

It was a relief to move away from the body. Milcote and I lifted off the cover and laid it on the floor. It moved easily. A man could have removed it by himself, if necessary. Or, for that matter, a woman.

Milcote crouched on the edge and held the lantern over the void. I could see nothing beyond its light. At my request, he took a rope and attached it to the ring at the top of the lantern. He lowered the light into the well. It glistened on cleanly cut masonry – the shaft was lined with stone, not brick.

Another thought struck me – and again I kept it to myself. I liked what I had seen of Milcote but he and I served different masters.

The lantern twisted and turned as it descended. It seemed to take weeks for it to reach the water.

'Mr Hakesby measured it,' Milcote said. 'It's about forty feet to the water level. And the depth of the water is another twenty feet, more or less.'

I remembered the bruises and scrapes on Alderley's body. Could he swim? I imagined him thrashing about in the well, desperately trying to find a handhold, a toehold, on that smooth, curved masonry. And all the time, the water drawing him down into its cold embrace.

I could not afford these thoughts, and I seized on a distraction. 'How did you get the body out?' It was such an obvious question that I was ashamed that it hadn't occurred to me before.

'Gorse and I used the hoist.' Milcote waved his free hand in the direction of the wooden framework I had noticed in the corner of the cellar behind the well, beside a pile of scaffolding. 'It's the masons'. They used it when they were repointing the well. Gorse went down, and he got a couple of hooks in Alderley's belt.'

'He must be a capable man,' I said. 'Rather him than me.'

'He's seen worse, I daresay,' Milcote said. 'He told me he was once apprenticed to a butcher, though he and his master did not suit. But before he left his indentures, he must have moved his fair share of carcases.'

The lantern was swaying a few inches above the black and oily surface of the water.

'Dear God,' I cried. 'What's that?'

Something was moving on the water, something dark and glistening, something alive.

Milcote laughed. 'It's Alderley's periwig, sir.' He laughed again, and it seemed to me there was an edge of hysteria to his mirth. 'What did you think it could be?'

'I scarcely know.'

'Shall I send Gorse or someone down again to fetch it?'

'As far as I'm concerned, you can leave it there to rot.'

'Someone will want it. It must be worth a few pounds.'

Milcote hauled up the lantern. 'I wonder,' he said, turning aside to drape the coil of rope over the hoist. 'I believe that perhaps Alderley's death was an accident after all.' He faced me again and went on in a low, rapid tone, 'Suppose he came here of his own accord during the day – bribed his way into the garden – and hid himself here, meaning to rob the house when all was quiet. And then in the dark, he stumbled . . .'

70

His voice trailed away. What of the mastiffs, I thought, the night-watchmen, the bolts, the bars, locks and all the other precautions that Clarendon took to keep his palace safe from intruders?

'You must know, sir,' Milcote went on with sudden urgency, 'Lord Clarendon has many enemies. If someone like the Duke of Buckingham heard of this, he would find ways to use it against him – perhaps even accuse him of arranging Alderley's murder. Surely it would be better for everyone – for the King and the Duke of York, as well as my lord – if the body weren't here?'

'What do you mean?' I said, my voice cold.

'Lord Clarendon is the last man to wish to stand in the way of justice, but Mr Alderley is dead, and we can't change that, either by accident or by his own design.' He gestured at the dead man, shrouded in his long shirt. 'Couldn't he be found somewhere else? It would be an innocent subterfuge, which would harm no one, least of all him. Indeed, it would protect Alderley's reputation. Otherwise men might say that he intended some knavery by coming here.'

He held the lantern higher, trying to make out my expression, and waited for me to speak.

'And it would protect Lord Clarendon, too, in this difficult time,' he rushed on. 'The poor man has enough troubles already without this. I wish to spare him the addition of this one. He is a good man, sir, and an honourable one, whatever his enemies say.'

'I don't doubt it,' I said.

'All we would need do is move Alderley out of the garden and leave him in one of the market gardens near the Oxford road.' Milcote followed me out of the basement. 'Perhaps in

71

a pond, to explain the water . . . Then it would look as if he had been robbed and murdered by thieves. No one could say any differently.'

I said nothing. We replaced the cover on the well and climbed the stairs in silence. At the door, I waited for Milcote to find the key.

He shook his head as if reproving himself. 'Forgive me, sir. You must think my wits are astray. Pray forget what I said. I hardly know what I'm saying.'

After we had searched the body and examined the rest of the pavilion, I dined privately with Milcote in the steward's quarters. He did not press me further with his arguments for moving the body. I had the impression that part of him was ashamed of having suggested it. Not that I condemned him – indeed, I honoured him for it in one way, because I realized that his loyalty to Lord Clarendon lay behind it.

I scarcely noticed what I ate, and we had little conversation. My mind was full of what I had learned in the last two hours. Our inspection of the pavilion had made it clear that the lower windows were barred and the upper ones were secure. The roof appeared intact. There was a viewing platform at the top, but the door to it, which was at the head of the staircase that had brought us down to the basement, was bolted and barred from the inside.

In other words, the door from the garden appeared to be the only point of access. And there were – as both Milcote and later the steward confirmed – only four keys to it: Lord Clarendon's, the steward's, Milcote's – and Hakesby's.

Before we left the pavilion, I had examined both the lock and Milcote's copy of the key. I was no expert but I could see that it was a modern lock; the wards of the key were designed to turn four levers within the lock, and each was a different size from the others. To copy a key like this, I suspected, would require the services of a skilled locksmith. There was no sign of the mechanism having been forced.

To add to the mystery, the garden was full of people by day and overlooked from the house. No stranger could have passed through unobserved. By night, the garden gates were locked, the dogs let loose and the night watchmen patrolled at regular intervals.

True, I had solved another, lesser mystery to my private satisfaction, or at least discovered a plausible solution to it: if Hakesby had been here to work on the pavilion, then Cat might well have accompanied him at least some of the time. Alderley could have caught sight of her on one of his visits to Milcote.

Time was running out. The body could not be kept a secret for long, not in a world where the Duke of Buckingham and his allies were working so industriously against Lord Clarendon. The Duke of York was determined to avoid Alderley's corpse becoming an embarrassment to his father-in-law, and therefore to himself. The King seemed equally determined, though as ever his motives were difficult to discern; perhaps he simply wanted to oblige his brother, or perhaps he had his own reasons for not wanting to lend ammunition to the enemies of Lord Clarendon, his former Lord Chancellor and his loyal companion and adviser during the long years of exile.

From Clarendon's point of view, there were only two outcomes that would help him: the first was discovering how Alderley had died and bringing his killer, if there had been one, to justice in a way that completely absolved Clarendon himself; the other was far simpler – Milcote's suggestion of moving the body elsewhere. If the King ordered the latter, it would be done. But not otherwise.

What worried me most was this: if, as seemed probable, Alderley had been murdered, then the most likely killer was Catherine Lovett. As I knew only too well, she was a woman who had few scruples when her passions were engaged, and Edward Alderley had given her every reason to hate him.

I would not betray her – or not willingly, for we had survived too much together for that. But if anyone else stumbled on the Clarendon House connection between her and Edward Alderley, then I would not give much for her chances – or indeed for my own, for I had already concealed what I knew of her.

If they hanged the daughter of a Regicide for Edward Alderley's murder, would it not be convenient for everyone except Hakesby and myself? Moreover, I had given Cat forewarning that Alderley had somehow found her. Might that be construed as making me an accessory to his murder?

As the meal neared its end, I discussed at least some of this with George Milcote. He could not have been more helpful, though he was careful what he said when our conversation touched on anything that might affect the honour of Lord Clarendon. I liked his loyalty to his master, and I regretted that the circumstances obliged me to lie to him, at least by omission.

'When did you last see Alderley?' I asked.

'Last week. We met at the Three Tuns at Charing Cross.'

'He seemed as usual?'

'Yes. He was in a good humour. We were discussing an

investment of mine. I have a small share in a privateer, and he'd offered to buy it.'

I remembered the purse we had found. 'He wasn't that poor, then?'

'No. I gathered that his affairs had taken a turn for the better.' There was a ghost of a smile on Milcote's face. 'He paid for our wine.'

'I must speak as soon as possible to the servant who found the body,' I said. 'Gorse, was it?'

'Yes – Matthew Gorse. Will you come back here in the evening, or shall I send him to you?'

'I shall need to come back here at some point,' I said with more certainty than I felt. 'Don't let him leave until I've seen him.'

To maintain the fiction that I had never heard of Hakesby, I asked Milcote who he was, and whether he was to be trusted.

'Mr Pratt vouched for him,' he said. 'In fact it was my lady – the late Lady Clarendon, that is – who suggested him.'

'Pratt?'

'Mr Roger Pratt – the architect. He designed the house for my lord, but he was unable to take on the pavilions.'

'How did Lady Clarendon know of Mr Hakesby?'

'I don't think she ever mentioned it.' Milcote shrugged. 'No reason why she should have done, of course. The important thing is that Mr Pratt vouched for him. I understand that he has worked with both Dr Wren and Dr Hooke, and they speak highly of him too.'

'Where can I find him?'

'Henrietta Street – he has a Drawing Office at the sign of the Rose. He handles the overseeing of the builders as well as the surveying and designing. I own I was a little concerned when I first met him – he has a palsy or ague, poor man – but it seems not to affect the quality of his work. He has able people working under him. I know my lady valued his willingness to indulge her desire to retain so much of the old banqueting house in the new building. Will you go and see him now?'

'Yes,' I said, with intentional vagueness, 'I must see Mr Hakesby. And as soon as possible.'

But I had other things to do first. There was no reason to mention that to Mr Milcote.

It was still raining. I decided to take a coach.

I walked along Piccadilly in search of a hackney, trying to avoid the spray from passing vehicles and horses. Perhaps it was because of the rain but I couldn't find a coach for hire at the nearest stand. I went on, pulling my hat down and huddling into my cloak.

William Chiffinch had sent me to meet Lady Quincy. And it was also he who had sent me here. But he was the King's creature in all he did, for there lay his best chance of advancing his own interest. Was the King behind both these commissions? Did that mean they were somehow connected?

Opposite the Royal Mews, liveried servants were opening the great gates of Wallingford House, where the Duke of Buckingham lived when he was in town. I stopped to watch. Outriders appeared, followed by an enormous coach, which was decorated with golden lions and peacocks and drawn by six matching horses. Afterwards came four running footmen, who held on to the straps behind the coach and splashed through the puddles, careless of the filth thrown up on their clothes.

Now that he had been freed from the Tower, the Duke had no intention of hiding his presence in London. The coach drew up outside the front door, which opened immediately. The Duke himself appeared at the head of the steps. He was a tall, florid gentleman in a blond periwig and a plumed hat. He was dressed in a silver coat and blue breeches, with the matching blue of the Garter ribbon across his chest, and the Garter star itself gleaming over his heart. He waved at the small crowd that had gathered, tossed them a handful of silver and climbed into the coach.

The crowd cheered him as he drove off towards Whitehall. I walked on in the direction of the hackney stand by Charing Cross.

The contrast between the Duke and Lord Clarendon could not have been more clearly illustrated – the one a hero to the common people of London, the other a villain. It seemed that even the King was throwing his weight behind Buckingham. But if His Majesty had decided to throw Clarendon to the wolves, to Buckingham and his enemies in Parliament, why had he sent me on a mission that seemed designed to protect Clarendon's reputation? Was it the Duke of York's influence? Or did he have some other, deeper motive?

# CHAPTER TWELVE

T HE COACHMAN DROPPED me by Holborn Bridge. 'Phugh!' he said, covering his nose with his sleeve. 'Smells like a whore's armpit.'

Fallow Street ran north–south on the east side of the bridge over the Fleet River. The river was choked with rubbish. There was a tannery nearby, and nothing made a neighbourhood stink worse than tanning leather.

The street was straight and narrow. The southern end had been destroyed by the Fire. The ruins had been cleared, but nothing had been rebuilt yet. People were living there, nevertheless, in makeshift shelters that looked as if a puff of wind would bring them down.

The southern end of the roadway had recently been partly blocked by the collapse of a long wall that had once marked the outer boundary of a building destroyed by the Fire. Someone on foot could work their way along, but the street was impassable to wheeled traffic.

I paid off the coachman and picked my way up the street. It was busy enough at the undamaged northern end. I found the carpenter's shop by the sound of sawing and hammering that came from it. Since the Fire, there had been a great demand for carpenters and a chronic shortage of suitable timber.

The shutters were open. The master and his apprentice were erecting the frame of a simple bedstead, helped rather than hindered by a small boy of about ten or twelve, who was probably the carpenter's son. The joints wouldn't fit together properly – hence the hammering and the sawing and the palpable air of frustration.

I stood outside, sheltering from the rain and blocking some of their light, until the carpenter paused in his work and glanced up. His shoulders were hunched forward, and he had a big, narrow face and a very small forehead. He looked like a Barbary ape.

'What is it?' he said curtly. He belatedly assessed my clothes and my air of respectability, and added, 'Sir.'

'I'm looking for Mr Alderley's lodgings,' I said.

He pointed at the ceiling. 'Up there. But he's away.'

'I know that. I have a key.'

The carpenter shrugged.

'I also have a warrant that permits me to go inside.' This was not strictly true. 'You may have a sight of it.'

The carpenter came into the doorway and examined the paper I showed him.

'That is the King's signature,' I said, pointing. 'And that is his private seal.'

He squinted at the warrant and said, in a slightly uncertain voice: 'It doesn't say you can come into my house, does it?'

I lowered my voice, because there was nothing to be gained from shaming the man in front of his inferiors, and said, 'It's not your house. It's Mr Alderley's. I can come back with a magistrate and a couple of constables if you'd prefer, and I'll also see you in court for obstructing the King's justice. Or you can save yourself some trouble and show me where Alderley's door is.'

He licked his lips. 'Did you say you've got a key?'

'Of course.' I showed him the keyring with Alderley's two keys. 'And the warrant allows me to use it.'

'All right. Hal – look sharp, take the gentleman round to Mr Alderley's door.'

'One moment. What's your name?'

'Thomas Bearwood.'

'When did you last see Mr Alderley?'

'I don't know. Last week sometime? The wife might know.' The small boy came out to join us, wiping the snot from his nostrils with the back of his sleeve. His father cuffed him. 'I said look sharp.'

The boy let out a howl as a matter of form, though he seemed unharmed. He led me to a passage at the side of the shop that led to the main house. Behind us, the sawing resumed. Without a word, the lad indicated a door with his hand.

I pushed the larger key into the lock and twisted. The wards turned. The boy stared up at me, and I knew he was trying to get a better look at the scarring that the fire had left on my face. He caught my eye and ran off the way he had come. I glanced up and down the passage. No one was in sight. I opened the door and went inside.

There was a tiny lobby with a flight of stairs going up from it.

I shut and bolted the door. I climbed the stairs. They were

steep and narrow and let out a creak at every step. At the top was a landing, with three closed doors. The air smelled powerfully of stale urine, which was unremarkable in a house so close to a tannery.

The nearest door led to a chamber almost entirely filled by a finely carved bedstead. The curtains were drawn back and the bed was unmade. Beyond it was a closet full of clothing, either hanging from pegs on the wall or spilling from a large press. I saw at a glance that these were a rich man's clothes, a man who liked lace and ribbons and satin. Some showed signs of wear and dirt. But others were new. I touched the sleeve of a velvet suit and wondered how much it had cost Alderley.

One of the other doors from the landing led to another, much larger closet, this one stuffed with household goods, probably salvaged from Barnabas Place: rolls of tapestries, curtains and carpets; chairs and tables stacked one upon the other; and an iron-bound chest secured with two padlocks and three internal locks. Four swords hung from a wood peg which had been hammered into a crack in the wall – why would any man need more than one? Everything in this room was covered with a layer of dust.

The third door opened into a large square room at the back of the building, though it seemed smaller because it contained so much. The walls were panelled and hung with many pictures. Alderley had obviously used the chamber as his parlour or sitting room. On the table were the remains of a meal and two empty wine bottles.

I searched the place as well as I could among such a confusion of objects. What made it more difficult was that I had no idea what I was looking for, other than something that might explain why Alderley's body had been discovered in the well of Lord Clarendon's half-built pavilion. I kept my eyes open for boxes and cabinets and the like, but I found nothing with a lock that matched Alderley's small silver key.

I paid particular attention to a large desk set in an alcove. The drawers were stuffed with papers – bills, notes of gambling debts and letters. Some of the letters were in a hand I took to be Alderley's, for several memoranda of debts were in the same writing. These letters were drafts and copies, most of which concerned attempts to raise money by one means or the other. But, on the pile in the right-hand drawer, there was a note in a clerkly hand that stood out from the rest by its neatness. It was dated last Monday, exactly a week ago.

*Sir*

*The deeds of your property in Fallow Street are ready for collection from my*

*chambers at any reasonable hour convenient to both parties.*

*J. Turner*

*No. 5, Barnard's Inn*

Milcote had said the property was mortgaged. But this letter suggested the mortgage had been redeemed. I had no idea of the size of the loan that a house like this might command, but it might well be substantial; since the Fire, all the remaining property in London had increased in value. I made a note of Turner's name and address and returned the letter to where I had found it.

I knew by the light outside that the afternoon was sliding towards evening. Nothing I had found in these overcrowded apartments hinted at a previous connection between Clarendon House and Alderley. Nor had I found any mention of Milcote. The only oddity was the unexpected signs of recent affluence – the new clothes, for example, and the letter from J. Turner of Barnard's Inn.

As I was closing the drawer, a picture hanging on the wall above the desk snagged my attention like a rock in the current of a stream. I stopped and stared at it. I felt a momentary chill.

The painting was a small portrait of the head and shoulders of a gentlewoman in a plain but heavy frame. The woman was Catherine Lovett.

Except, of course, it wasn't Cat at all. This woman belonged to another time, at least twenty or even thirty years ago. She wore a dark green gown with puffed sleeves and a necklace of pearls. Her hair tumbled in ringlets to her white neck.

In the background of the painting was a house whose outlines were familiar to me. It was called Coldridge, and I had visited it last year. It had once belonged to the family of Cat's mother, and she had lived there with an aunt for several years when she was a child. It should have been hers but her uncle and Edward Alderley had cheated her out of it.

There was something wrong with the picture. I drew closer and stooped towards it. The eyes in the portrait were unnaturally large and blank. Then I saw why. Someone had gouged out the pupils of both eyes, probably with the point of a dagger.

A series of thunderous knocks sounded below.

I went back downstairs. 'Who is it?' I said.

'Mistress Bearwood. Open up.'

I unbolted the door. The carpenter's wife barely came up

to my elbow but what she lacked in inches she more than made up with force of character. She pushed past me into Alderley's lobby. She glared at me, her hands on her hips. To all intents and purposes, she felt herself mistress of the situation.

'And who are you?' she demanded. 'What are you doing, poking around where you've no reason to be? Is there any reason I shouldn't call the constable?'

I showed her my warrant, which she read attentively.

'It doesn't say in black and white that you can come into my house,' she said grudgingly. 'Not in so many words. But I suppose it's all right. You'd think Bearwood was born yesterday. He's as innocent as a newborn baby, and just as stupid. I'm sorry, master, but you could have been anyone.'

'No bones broken, Mistress Bearwood.'

But she wouldn't let it go. 'I could have found you stripping the house bare, and him and the boy none the wiser. (Takes after his father, Hal does, more's the pity.) He can't even read properly, so your warrant made no more sense to him than Sunday's sermon.' She looked me up and down with an unflattering lack of interest, and then shifted her ground slightly to get a better view of the damage that the fire had done to my face. 'And you don't exactly look like a courtier, neither.'

'That's because I'm not,' I said. 'I'm a clerk at Whitehall. But I'm glad you're here, mistress, because I want to ask you some questions.'

For a moment it hung in the balance: her anger – with me, with her husband, with the whole world, perhaps – struggled with the suspicion that it would be foolish to offend me if I was really who I said I was.

'When did you last see Mr Alderley?' I asked.

'It's not our place to blab about him.'

'It's not your place to disobey the King, either. And I promise you, on my honour, nothing you can tell me will in any way harm Mr Alderley.'

She stared up at me with black button eyes. 'Saturday evening,' she said. 'He'd been home most of the day but he went out around eight o'clock.'

'Was that usual?'

She shrugged. 'He stays out all night sometimes, if he has a mind to. Or he lies abed all day. Or he's up with the lark. Nothing to do with me. I've got work to do, sir, and—'

I cut her off with a wave of my hand. 'Have you known him long?' I asked.

'Nigh on eighteen months. He rents out the shop and ground floor to us. He don't have a servant, so I keep his apartments clean and send out the boy for his dinner or whatever he wants.' She paused, and I had the sense that she was making lightning calculations behind those round black eyes. 'Do you know him?'

'Oh yes,' I said. 'I knew him last year when he lived in Barnabas Place.' Where he attacked Cat Lovett and raped her on her own bed. 'Does he have any visitors?'

Mrs Bearwood shook her head. 'Only the Bishop.'

'The Bishop?' Amazed, I stared at her. 'The Bishop of London?'

'No, sir.' She looked pityingly at me. 'It's just a nickname. He's one of Mr Alderley's friends. If you're such a friend of his too, you—'

'I'm not a friend of Mr Alderley's. I'm acquainted with him. When was this bishop last here?'

'Friday,' she said. 'He brought Mr Alderley home.' She sniffed. 'Mr Alderley was in liquor again. He could hardly stand. He could talk all right, more or less, but his legs wouldn't work. Bearwood and the Bishop had a terrible time getting him up the stairs.'

I threw in another question without much hope of an answer. 'Do you know where this man lives?'

Mrs Bearwood was edging away from me, tired of my interrogation. 'I don't know. Watford, maybe?'

'Watford? Outside London? Why do you think that?'

'Because Mr Alderley opened the window and called down to the Bishop as he was leaving. He bellowed like a bull – I even heard him in the kitchen, and the window was shut – and he mentioned Watford. Maybe the Bishop was a preacher, though he didn't look like one, not with a sword at his side.'

'A preacher?' I said, feeling as if I were drowning.

'Well, perhaps. It's just that Mr Alderley shouted something about "When you get to Watford, be sure to tell them about Jerusalem."'

'Jerusalem?' I repeated.

'Jerusalem. As I hope to be saved.'

# CHAPTER THIRTEEN

O N MY WAY to Whitehall, I was tempted to call at Henrietta Street and warn Cat Lovett of what had happened to her cousin. But prudence prevailed. I didn't want to risk advertising the connection between us. Besides, I was in a hurry to make my report.

They were the excuses I made for myself. Really, though, I was mortally afraid that she might already know of Edward Alderley's death, that she had known ever since the moment it happened. The words she had said two days ago in the New Exchange haunted my memory: 'I wish I had killed him.'

I ran into Mr Williamson when I returned to Whitehall – almost literally, for he was coming out of the Court Gate into the street as I was going in. I had to jump aside to avoid colliding with him.

'Marwood,' he snapped. 'When will you be back?'

'I'm not sure, sir. When the King and Mr Chiffinch—'

'How can I be expected to carry on the business of the *Gazette* without your assistance?' Irritation had scraped away the polish that Oxford and London had given Williamson's voice, revealing the uncompromising vowels of his northern upbringing. 'I have my own responsibilities, as you know, without troubling myself with those damned women of yours.'

It took me a moment to realize that he meant the women who trudged the streets of London with bundles of the *Gazette*. I had pushed the problems with our distribution network so far into the back of my mind that I had almost forgotten they were there.

'For reasons I don't understand,' he went on, warming himself at the fire of his own eloquence, 'the day-to-day conduct of the newspaper seems impossible without you, as well as other routine tasks in my office. Why this should be, I cannot tell. It is insupportable that Mr Chiffinch should have you at his beck and call whenever he wishes, disrupting the work of my department. I shall take steps to remedy it. But, in the meantime, I require your presence in Scotland Yard as soon as possible.'

I bowed. 'Yes, sir. Believe me, I wish it myself.'

He sniffed, gave me a curt nod and swept out into the street to hail a hackney.

I made my way to the Matted Gallery. There was a door from here that led to the King's Backstairs, the province of Mr Chiffinch. I asked one of the guards to send word to him that I was here and hoped to speak to him.

While I waited, I studied the picture of the Italian widow again, and decided that she looked nothing like Lady Quincy. But I did not want to run the risk of Chiffinch finding me in front of the painting, so I walked up and down for a quarter of an hour until a servant approached me. He conducted me to the gloomy chamber off the Backstairs where Chiffinch and I had met once before, earlier in the year. The small window was barred and had a view of the river. The rain was beating against the glass and the room smelled of sewage. It was an uncomfortable place that in my limited experience of it existed solely for uncomfortable meetings.

Chiffinch was already there. It was not yet dark, but he had had the candles lit. He was sitting at the table with the window behind him and a pile of papers and the usual bottle of wine before him. He listened intently while I told him of what I had learned at Clarendon House and Fallow Street.

I described Alderley's body, and the unresolved mystery of how he came to be in the locked pavilion in the garden, and the ambiguous circumstances of his death. I gave him an account of my conversation with Lord Clarendon, mentioning both my lord's anger at this desecration of his late wife's pavilion and his wish to avoid scandal. I added that his gentleman, Mr Milcote, had hinted that it might be to everyone's benefit if the body could be moved elsewhere.

'Ah,' Chiffinch said. 'Interesting.' He waved his finger at me. 'Proceed, Marwood.'

When I came to what had happened in Fallow Street, I told Chiffinch no lies but I rationed the truth. I mentioned the unexpected signs of recent affluence. I told him about the so-called Bishop, Alderley's visitor on Friday evening, whom Alderley had advised to go to Watford to tell them about Jerusalem. But I omitted the painting of the woman whose eyes had been gouged out: the woman in old-fashioned clothes who looked like Cat Lovett.

Chiffinch said nothing while I talked, which was unlike him. When I finished, he still did not speak. He ran his finger around and around the rim of his wine glass. After a while, a high wavering whine filled the air, growing gradually louder.

I shifted in my chair. 'Should I send to Watford tomorrow, sir, to enquire about newly arrived preachers? I could write directly to Mr Williamson's correspondent there. And I myself could call on this Mr Turner at Barnard's Inn about the mortgage. Also, I have arranged to go back to Clarendon House to question the servant who—'

Suddenly the whine stopped.

'Hakesby,' Chiffinch said.

I stared open-mouthed at him.

Chiffinch regarded me coldly. 'Hakesby,' he repeated, wrinkling his nose. 'I know the name is familiar to you because you yourself mentioned the man to me not a year ago. The surveyor-architect who has an office near Covent Garden. Well respected by his peers, I understand. And, as you and I both know, a man who has previously been of interest to me.'

I recovered as quickly as I could. 'Yes, sir, I remember him well.' I was on dangerous ground for Chiffinch had helped to arrange my meeting in the Banqueting House with Lady Quincy. He might reasonably expect that it had jogged my memory about Hakesby as well as Cat. He had known that Cat had found a refuge with Hakesby at the end of last year.

'Did you know that this man was the architect working on Lord Clarendon's pavilion?' Chiffinch said in a silken voice.

'Yes, sir. Mr Milcote – Lord Clarendon's gentleman – chanced to mention it this morning, but I thought it—'

'Did it not occur to you that there might be a connection?' Chiffinch's tone was heavy with sarcasm. 'We already knew the Lovett woman was working under an assumed name as Hakesby's servant, and that the King was content it should be so as long as she didn't make trouble. He is not a vengeful man.

When Lady Quincy told him that Alderley was threatening Mistress Lovett again, he was even content that you should warn her of the fact. Some might think that he's too tender-hearted, but it is not my place to question his decisions.'

I tried to put the matter in the best light I could: 'I thought it unlikely Mr Hakesby would take a woman to a site where he was working.'

'This woman is the daughter of a Regicide: and by all accounts, she's a fanatic like her father – a madwoman who hates her cousin Alderley so much that she stabbed him in the eye. He was lucky to escape alive. And she tried to burn down the house about their ears as her uncle and aunt slept.' For once in his life, Chiffinch sounded genuinely shocked. 'That a woman should do so foul a thing to her family, to the cousins who sheltered her,' he went on. 'Why, it beggars belief and turns it out of doors. And her cousin Alderley is now found drowned, probably murdered, in the very place where Hakesby is working. Does it not strike you as significant?'

'I grant it's a curious coincidence, sir.'

'A coincidence? Would you have me think you a fool or a traitor, Marwood? There's only one possible conclusion.' He opened the folder before him and took out a sheet of paper. 'I received a letter this afternoon.'

He slid it across the desk to me. He watched me, sipping his wine, as I read it. There was neither date nor address.

*Honoured Sir,*

*Mr Edward Alderley lies drowned in Lord Clarendon's new Pavilion at Clarendon House. He was murdered by his Cousin, Catherine Lovett, the Regicidal Spawn and Monster of her Sex. You will find Her hiding in the*

*House of Mr Hakesby in Henrietta Street, by Covent Garden. Mr Hakesby*

*has often been at Clarendon House of late, and the She-Devil with Him.*

*Hakesby holds the Keys to the Pavilion.*

    *A Friend to His Majesty*

The handwriting was clumsy but by no means illiterate, as if the writer had sought to disguise it, perhaps holding the pen in his left hand. I turned the letter over. There was nothing on it except Chiffinch's name. The person who had written it had known to address the letter to him, not to a magistrate or some great man charged with public order. Outside Whitehall, few people knew of the importance of Chiffinch, the man who arranged the King's private affairs. And fewer still could know that the King had charged him to look into the death of Edward Alderley.

'It was handed in at the gate,' Chiffinch said. 'I have enquired, but no one knows who brought it.'

There was a ringing in my ears. 'Is the woman Lovett in custody, sir?'

'Unfortunately not,' Chiffinch said. 'Officers went to arrest her this afternoon, but she had gone. Her flight is as good as a confession of guilt.'

I nodded, as if in agreement. Dear God, I thought as the implications sunk in, this damnable letter taken together with her flight could bring her to the gallows.

'They've brought in Hakesby,' Chiffinch was saying. 'But he's not much use to us or to anyone else. Doddering old fool. We'll find her, of course, and it won't take long.'

From my point of view, the situation was growing worse by the moment. 'Can we find out who wrote the letter?' I asked.

'How do I know?' Chiffinch snapped. 'But it doesn't much matter. Once we lay hands on Catherine Lovett, we have the evidence to hang her. Perhaps Hakesby, too, as her accomplice. It's possible that he arranged for her to disappear, or even had a hand in Alderley's murder himself. After all, she must have needed help. She may be a she-devil but when all's said and done she's only a woman. She probably hired ruffians to do her dirty work for her.'

He didn't know Catherine Lovett as I did. I bit back the retort that if all women were like her there would be some doubt as to which was the weaker sex.

Chiffinch refilled his glass and leaned closer across the table. 'On the other hand, Marwood,' he said in a lower voice, 'there's another side to this. The King desires that the matter should not cause a stir. Lord Clarendon's future is much on his mind, and a scandal of this nature could upset a number of delicate negotiations he has in train. And there are people who would seek to make mischief if they could. It's no secret that the Duke of Buckingham, for example, is no friend to Lord Clarendon, or to the Duke of York. He would use this scandal to further his own ambitions.'

He paused to drink. He set down his glass and stared at me. There was worse to come. His frankness was an ill omen.

'So,' he said, silkier than ever, 'there are two things you must do to serve the King. One is to see to it that the Lovett woman is laid by the heels as soon as possible. And the other is to move Alderley's body away from Clarendon House and its garden.'

I felt as if I were falling, with no more control over my destination than an unborn baby has. 'But where to? How?'

'Better if I leave that to you, and to Lord Clarendon's gentleman. Milcote, I think you said. A capable man, I'm told, as I would expect – my lord doesn't suffer fools gladly. I should encourage him to play the principal part, if I were you.' He opened a drawer, took out a purse and tossed it to me. 'Use that if you need money, though you must account for it afterwards.'

'Sir, do I understand that you—'

'Understand this, Marwood: move that body. It must not be an embarrassment to Lord Clarendon. Or to the King. Put it in some discreet spot where anyone could have gone. Mark you, the needs of justice will still be served, and the woman will still pay the price of the murder she has committed, either by her own hand or through hired instruments. It's merely that we shall arrange the circumstances a little more conveniently for other people.'

'But if Alderley's body is moved elsewhere, what will connect it to Catherine Lovett?' I said.

'Come – you're being obtuse. Someone must have killed him, eh? And, as I've already said, it's well known that she hates him, and that she tried to kill him in his own house last year. And her flight is a tacit admission that she was responsible for his death. Besides, once the judge hears who her father was, there will be no difficulty in the court reaching the right verdict.'

Chiffinch gave me leave to go. But as I reached the door, he held up his hand.

'One moment. You know the old proverb – "the more a turd is stirred, the more it stinks"? Take care not to stir this one too much. Or the stink will overwhelm us all.'

# CHAPTER FOURTEEN

TOWARDS THE END of her second day at Mangot's Farm, Cat sat by the window of her chamber, looking out over the sloping fields behind the house. The light was fading, and the tents and cabins below were mercifully less obvious than they were in the daylight.

It was a chilly evening. No more than two or three fires were burning, though scores of people were living there, for firewood was scarce after all these months. It was quieter than it had been earlier in the day when, under Israel Halmore's direction, the men of the camp had been building further shelters and strengthening the existing ones, using the nails and canvas that he and Mangot had brought from London. There had been ground frosts already, and the refugees realized that winter would soon be upon them.

Cat's casement was open, and she heard the sound of singing from one side of the camp; some of the men gathered here in the evening and drank a raw grain spirit that they distilled in one of the ruined outhouses in the farmyard. The smell of smoke drifted towards her, mingling with the smells from the stream the refugees used for a latrine. Once upon a time, Mangot's Farm had prospered, but that time was long gone.

This refugee camp was not like those that the authorities had established on the outskirts of London in the immediate aftermath of the Great Fire, such as Moorfields and Smithfield. These, almost all closed now, had been relatively well-administered affairs with makeshift streets neatly laid out and lined with temporary shops, and with access to markets and to the jobs that had sprung up as the city began to grow anew from its own ashes. This camp, by contrast, was small, isolated and chaotic. The only authorities its inhabitants recognized were Israel Halmore, who dominated the others by force of personality, and Mr Mangot, who let them use his land because he could no longer work it himself, and because he believed that God had commanded him in a vision to expiate his sins and those of his dead son by providing a home for the home-less.

It was warmer in the kitchen, but she preferred to be up here, alone in the little chamber under the eaves that had once belonged to the old man's son. The door was solid, and she could bolt herself in. Besides, there was nothing to attract her in the rest of the house, which was gradually turning into a ruin, and only a fool would venture into the camp itself unless they had no choice in the matter.

She felt sleepy, and her mind drifted back to the commission at Clarendon House. Modernizing an old building like the pavilion was a tricky matter, as Mr Hakesby had pointed out to my lord; it would have been far simpler to pull it down altogether and rebuild it from scratch to match its near twin in the opposite corner of the garden. However well they did it, the result must be a mongrel building, particularly from the rear and side elevations, neither one thing nor the other. On the other hand, she thought, the mansion itself was a mongrel building, for all the money that had been spent on it. It was classical in its pediment and its symmetries but, in the native English manner, it lacked classical orders. Should they ever look down on it from heaven, Andrea Palladio would shake his head and Vitruvius would throw up his hands in disgust.

The pavilion was a matter of sentiment, Cat had understood, a gift from an old man to his ailing wife. At the start, they had occasionally seen her ladyship herself. Later, when her health worsened, Lord Clarendon, wincing at the pain from his gout, had sometimes shuffled down the garden on the arm of Mr Milcote to inspect the works. But then Lady Clarendon had died, and he had come no more. Mr Milcote, my lord's gentleman, came in their place.

Cat's mind shied away from Mr Milcote. She was increasingly worried by the conversation she had overheard in the cart yesterday morning, on their way to the farm. If Halmore had been right, the Duke of Buckingham was orchestrating the attacks on Clarendon House. Who was the Bishop, who was acting as the Duke's agent? It had sounded as if he planned something else to harm Clarendon, something much worse. Perhaps he would incite the mob to break down the gates and set fire to the house itself. He might even attack Clarendon in person.

She had liked Lady Clarendon, and she respected the Earl; good clients, who took an informed interest in the work and paid Hakesby's bills on time, were few and far between. The house itself might not be architecturally perfect, but she had no wish to see it damaged. She wished there were a way to warn them.

A woman screeched somewhere in the camp, reminding Cat that she could not stay here for ever – it was time for her to prepare the old man's supper, if one could call the meal that. This was part of the price she paid for his hospitality.

She went slowly down the creaking stairs, avoiding the third tread from the bottom, which was rotten, and went into the kitchen. Mr Mangot was already there. He was reading his Bible by the faint, evil-smelling glow of a rushlight, running his finger slowly along the lines of words. He still wore his smock, which was made of unbleached linen and too large for him. He was painfully thin and always melancholy.

Cat made up the fire and set the pan of soup to warm. There seemed to be nothing else to eat here, apart from stale bread which they dipped in the soup to soften it. She had given Mr Mangot another five shillings this morning in the hope that he would buy more food.

Outside in the yard, one of the dogs barked. The other dog took it up. Then they fell silent.

'Is someone coming here?' she whispered, slipping her hand into her pocket, where the knife was.

'The carrier, probably,' he said, without looking up. His voice sounded creaky with disuse. 'They bark differently if it's a stranger. He'll see Israel first, then he'll come here. He calls for orders on Monday evenings. He's a pedlar, too – always got something to sell.'

'Food?' Cat asked.

He shook his head, his finger still moving across the page.

'Could he take a letter to London for me?'

Mangot raised his head from the book. His eyes were so filmy that she wondered he could read at all. 'A letter? You can ask him. Who's it to?'

'Your nephew.'

He snorted. 'Are you his sweetheart?'

'No.'

'Just as well.'

She glanced at the pot on the smouldering fire. The soup would take another quarter of an hour to heat through, at least. 'I won't be long.'

She took a rushlight upstairs to her chamber and wrote a few lines to Brennan.

*Beg H to warn Ld C that the D of B bribes the mob outside CH, through a man they call the Bishop, who is their leader. The Bishop intends some future move against him that will cause C particular pain. H could write a letter, saying he'd heard tavern talk about it.*

She left the note unsigned. She folded the paper, torn from her notebook, and wrote Brennan's name on the outside. She had nothing to seal the paper with. She wondered if it would do any good, even if it reached Brennan: he would have to persuade Hakesby to take it seriously – no easy task – and Hakesby would have to warn Lord Clarendon. It might be better if he went instead to Mr Milcote. She hesitated, wondering whether to unfold the letter and add a postscript. Then she frowned. There was unfinished business with Milcote; wiser not to involve him.

There was a hammering on the door downstairs. She put the letter in her pocket and went down to the kitchen. The carrier was showing Mangot a packet of newly printed chap-books, sermons and pamphlets. He looked up as she entered, revealing a wall eye, and appraised her swiftly, before turning back to the farmer.

While the men were talking, she wiped the table and set out the wooden platters and cups. She stirred the soup, willing it to heat up more quickly. Mangot bought a pamphlet about a Papist plot to murder the King with a poisoned dagger as he was going to his devotions in Whitehall.

When the carrier was packing up his stock, Cat asked him if he would take a letter to London for her. He agreed to deliver it to Henrietta Street in the morning. He charged her two shillings for the service, which they both knew was an extortionate price.

'I want you to put it in the hands of a particular man, not a servant or anyone,' she said. 'He works for Mr Hakesby, at the sign of the Rose, and his name's Brennan, and he has a thin face and ginger hair. He's Mr Mangot's nephew.'

The carrier smiled at her, revealing a toothless mouth, and spat into the fire, narrowly missing the pot with the soup. 'Then that'll be an extra shilling.'

She paid him reluctantly. As the carrier turned to go, the back door opened. A current of cold air swept into the kitchen, followed by the tall figure of Israel Halmore.

A rabbit dangled from his right hand. It was already skinned and gutted. He tossed it on to the table, where it lay, lolling, in a parody of ease. 'For the pot, master.'

# CHAPTER FIFTEEN

A FTER I LEFT Whitehall, I went home. Margaret served my supper. I stabbed and slashed at the boiled mutton. I agreed with Chiffinch about one thing at least: Alderley had been murdered. How could he have reached the basement of the pavilion without someone's help? Who had removed the cover from the well? Moreover, his naked sword had been lying on the floor. It had been perfectly dry. So had the ribbons around its hilt. The sheath, on the other hand, had been as wet as its owner and had clearly gone down the well with him.

Which suggested that Alderley had drawn his sword before he had fallen, or been thrown, down the well. And why would a man draw his sword if not to defend himself or to attack someone?

When I had eaten, I lit more candles and took the canvas bag that George Milcote had given me from my pocket. I laid out the contents of Alderley's pockets: the two keys, the money, which was in a flat gambler's purse lined with silk, and the bundle of wet papers. The papers were less saturated than I expected – the heavy wool of Alderley's coat must have given them some protection from the water. They consisted of perhaps five or six sheets of no great size, folded once and held together with a ribbon. The outer sheet was blank.

I cut the ribbon and tried to separate the papers. One of them instantly tore. I gathered them up and took them down to the kitchen, where Margaret was clearing away the supper things and setting the room straight for the night. She glanced warily at me as I entered, for I had snapped at her earlier.

'How hot's the oven?' I said.

'It's not – I haven't used it since this morning.' She wiped the sweat off her forehead with the back of her arm. 'I've banked up the fire, master. Do you want me to break it open?'

The oven was set in the wall within the fireplace, on the left-hand side. I leaned over the fire and put my hand inside. The bricks that lined the recess were dry and slightly warm to the touch.

'No,' I said. 'Leave it as it is. These papers are damp. I'll put them here overnight.'

'What shall I do with them in the morning?'

'Take them carefully out before you open up the fire. Put them somewhere safe.' I glanced about the shadowy room. 'In that bowl on the dresser.'

I wished her goodnight and went back to the parlour, where I spent a few minutes examining the silver key by the light of the candles.

Judging by its size and the quality of the workmanship, it had been designed for the lock of a small box or perhaps for the door of a cupboard set in a piece of furniture. I had seen nothing of that sort at Alderley's lodgings, but then I had not searched his crowded apartments thoroughly enough to inspect all his possessions. I peered at the monogram again, but still could not come to any conclusion: the entwined letters were so twisted and ornamented that they could have been almost anything. Was that an 'S'? Or a 'P'?

I went to bed. But the events of the day came between me and sleep. Threaded among these were troubling thoughts of Olivia, Lady Quincy. I lay on my back in the darkness of the curtained bed and tried to remember her features. I could not. But I remembered those of her African page perfectly, and the way he had stared so intently at me as if memorizing my face.

The following morning, I was awoken at dawn by a scream downstairs.

This was immediately followed by the sound of Margaret shouting. When she paused to draw breath, I heard the deeper tones of Sam's voice. I swore, got out of bed and went out on to the landing in my shirt.

'Hold your tongues, damn you,' I bellowed down the stairs.

There was instant silence. Then I heard Margaret's footsteps pounding up the stairs. Behind her, Sam was speaking unintelligibly in an apologetic whine. When she reached the landing, her face was redder than usual. Her quarrels with Sam were not infrequent, and she usually had the better of him. She was carrying an earthenware bowl in her hand.

'The numbskull,' she said breathlessly. 'The fool.'

'What's he done?' I asked.

'I'm sorry, master. Those papers—'

'What happened?'

She stopped a step below me. 'I took them out, sir,' she said, 'like you told me, and put them on the table just for a moment while I saw to the fire, and what does that fool of a man do? He picks up one of them and uses it as a spill to light a candle.'

She held out the bowl. Some of the papers I had left in the oven were there. There were also ashes.

Sam hobbled up the stairs. 'Master, how was I to know? The silly woman just left them there, a pile of scraps. I'm not a magician, am I? I—'

'Enough,' I said. I took the bowl from Margaret. 'Go away, the pair of you. Bring me my water when it's ready.'

I went back into my chamber. While I waited for my hot water to wash in, I examined the remaining papers. They were bone dry and easy to separate. One was yet another bill, this one from Alderley's glovemaker. There was also a tavern reckoning for food and drink, the paper stained with wine and the word 'Paid' scrawled across the bottom. The other two sheets were equally uninteresting – a badly printed political pamphlet inveighing against Lord Clarendon, and a bill advertising a performance of *The Northern Lass* at the King's Playhouse last Saturday.

That left the charred fragment, all that remained of the paper that Sam had used as a spill. It was the corner of the sheet, roughly triangular, and most of it was blank. Only four letters survived of whatever had been written there: *a-l-e-m*.

Jerusalem? Here, perhaps, had been the key to Alderley's last words to the Bishop: '. . . be sure to tell them about Jerusalem.' But I was no nearer to solving the enigma because Sam—

There was a knock at the door, and Margaret entered with the jug of water. She looked as if she were about to be hanged.

'Sam's a fool,' I said. 'And so are you for leaving the papers there for him to use. And so am I for letting this happen.'

She gave me a wobbly curtsy and placed the jug on the washstand.

I glanced at her woebegone face. 'For the love of heaven, woman. We all make mistakes. It's not the end of the world. Tell Sam my cloak needs a good brush, will you?'

Margaret left the room at speed, looking as if she had been granted a last-minute reprieve. She and Sam had known the depths of poverty not so long ago, and I suspected that in the back of their minds there lurked the fear that one day I might send them back to it.

I dressed and went downstairs. After I had breakfasted, I wrote a short letter to one of Mr Williamson's private correspondents, a member of the network up and down the country that provided him with so much of his information, both publicly and privately. He was a man named Fisher, who kept a small tavern in Watford in the shadow of the church.

I had often written to him on Mr Williamson's behalf, and I knew that he would assume this letter was on my master's business and not my own. I told him I had been commanded to enquire whether any independent preachers or the like had been making a stir in the town, and in particular talking of Jerusalem.

Such men often talked of a New Jerusalem, a heavenly state that would exist in this country when all its inhabitants followed their godly paths of righteousness, as prescribed by the preachers themselves. Religion and politics were never far apart, and often, for all their sincerity, they were political agitators trying to sow the seeds of revolution.

Edward Alderley's father had once dealt with such people. It was possible that his son was doing the same thing. In which case, the affair of his death had acquired yet another unwelcome complication.

I added a postscript giving Mr Fisher to understand that the matter was urgent, and hinting that Mr Williamson would esteem it a particular favour if he replied by express.

I shouted for Sam. When he hobbled into the room, the sight of him gave me the familiar mixed sensation of irritation, frustration and, if I am to be honest, affection. He had served in the navy until a Dutch cannon ball had taken off his right leg below the knee. As a result, he walked with the aid of a wooden stump and a crutch. When he entered my employ, I had given him a respectable suit of clothes, so that he should appear before the world as the servant of a rising Whitehall clerk ought to appear. I insisted he shave once a week. But nothing I could do or say would make Sam look respectable. His hair was always awry, his clothes dishevelled and, worst of all, he had a raffish air that resisted all my efforts. He was sometimes the worse for drink but long experience had made him wily in this regard, and it was generally hard to prove this. But he had other qualities which I had come to value.

'I brushed your cloak, master,' he said. 'Not a speck of mud on it. Good as new. I've done your shoes, too.'

'Take this letter to the Post Office,' I ordered, counting out some money for express postage and for the reply. 'It's urgent.'

He said nothing but I could see from his expression that he thought the task beneath him. He held out his grubby palm for the money and the letter. He let out a melancholy sigh and left the room with them, closing the door with more force than was strictly necessary.

# CHAPTER SIXTEEN

A DOZEN OR so men and women had gathered outside
the railings of Clarendon House. They were hissing
and booing the visitors as they came and went. 'Dunkirk
House!' they shouted to me as I waited for admission at the
gates. 'Tangier and a barren Queen! Dutch traitor! Impeach
the rogue!'

George Milcote, elegant in black, came out to meet me.

'Are they always there?' I asked him as we walked across
the forecourt.

'Sometimes,' he said, glancing at them. 'We drive them
away, every now and then, but it tends to make them worse.
Anyway, they come back before you know it, like head-lice.'

'It's strange they find the time for such diversions.'

'You see the two at the back?' Milcote stopped and pointed.
'The man in a brown coat, and the fat one with the heavy
old sword? I think they are the conductors of this. And the
paymasters.'

'What do you mean?'

'I've seen them here before. Always at the back. There are

alehouses nearby where you can buy a crowd if you have a mind to it. A few drinks, a few coins will do it, with the promise of more afterwards. Then they wait to see whether their master's money has been well spent.'

I stared at them for a moment. The man in brown looked faintly familiar, though I couldn't place him in my memory. We walked on towards the house. The sun was out but it was still early and the main facade was in shadow.

'Who's paying for this?' I asked. 'The crowd, that is.'

Milcote smiled at me. 'That's the question. I don't know for sure but it's probably someone who works for the Duke of Buckingham. My lord has other enemies, but most of them would not stoop to such tactics. But the Duke has a liking for underhand methods.' Despite the smile, his voice was bitter. 'Fortune has so showered her gifts on him that he considers himself above the rules that govern the rest of us. But you'd think he and his hirelings would have the kindness to leave my lord alone in his time of sorrow.'

'Since Lord Clarendon resigned the seals of office?'

'Since my lady died.' His mouth twisted. 'But one should not look for kindness from such rabble, or from the Duke of Buckingham, any more than from brute beasts.'

I nodded, though I did not entirely agree with him. Milcote saw this from Lord Clarendon's perspective; and he himself had money in his purse; he was well-clad, well-shod and well-housed. But I could understand how the mansion's stately magnificence must seem like a slap in the face to the crowd outside, many of whom had probably seen their own houses reduced to ashes in the fire. The Duke, for all his wealth and magnificence, knew how to make the common people love him.

'Gorse is waiting for us in the pavilion,' Milcote went on. 'I thought it safer to keep him apart from the other servants so I set him to whitewashing the upper room, much against his will. He knows he must hold his tongue, but there's no harm in making sure of it.'

By this time we were walking past the side of the house towards the garden. I heard a stir in the forecourt behind us, the sounds of shouts, hooves and carriage wheels.

'That will be the Duke of York,' Milcote said. 'Another private conference with my lord.'

'He's often here?'

'Of course. Their interests have so much in common. My lord is his father-in-law, after all, and the grandfather of his children.'

It was, I thought, a none too subtle reminder that Lord Clarendon had powerful allies, and even in his reduced state was not a man to be lightly offended. He was closely linked to the royal family. As the whole world knew, if the King should die, the Duke of York would inherit the crown, and Clarendon's granddaughter, Princess Mary, would become the next heir presumptive to the throne.

We walked in silence for a moment, each wrapped in his own thoughts. There were men at work on the other side of the garden, but no one within fifty yards of us.

'A word in your ear before we go in,' I said. 'You remember the suggestion you made to me yesterday?'

Milcote drew back, and there was a look of alarm on his face. 'I spoke out of turn, sir . . . You must forgive me. Pray forget it.'

'That's what we can't do,' I said. 'We have been commanded to put it into effect.'

He stopped abruptly and stared at me. 'By whom?'

'I'm not permitted to say.'

He let out his breath in a rush. He wasn't a fool, and he must know that the King was at least aware of this, and that the Duke of York had probably had a hand in it. Perhaps that was why the Duke was here: to discuss the matter with his father-in-law.

'Well, sir,' he said. 'That I did not expect.'

'Nor I. But now we must think how best to do it.'

'Perhaps the plan I outlined to you would answer?'

Both of us stopped, as if at a command.

'Leaving the body in a pond near the Oxford Road?' I seemed to have divided my mind into two: one part which was capable of planning the illegal disposal of a murdered man, and another which threw up its metaphorical hands in horror at the thought of what I had become and the dangers that lay before me. 'It would answer very well.'

'Tonight would be best – the sooner the better.'

'How do we get him there?'

'I'd thought to strap him on the back of a horse,' Milcote said coolly, as if such thoughts came naturally to him. 'A packhorse . . . Roll him up as if he were a bale of cloth. There's a lane through the fields from here to the Oxford Road. It would be easier if there were three of us – one to lead the horse, one to walk on each side. Gorse, perhaps.'

'The servant? Is that wise?'

'Better him than bring in someone new. After all, he knows so much already – including where the body was found – that it may be best to have him with us. And he's trustworthy.'

'Everyone is,' I said, 'until they betray you.'

'If he betrays us, he betrays himself as our accessory. He's a sensible fellow. If we pay him well, he will keep his mouth closed. He's good with horses, too.'

'He mustn't know my identity,' I said. 'Or who sent me.'

'Very well,' Milcote said. 'I will talk to him privately about it today, after you've gone.'

I was still uneasy. 'Even at night, someone may see us in Piccadilly.'

'I've thought of that.'

Milcote explained that to the south-east of the garden were the stables, yards, orchards and kitchen gardens that belonged to the mansion. There was a gate, he said, that led from the Great Garden, where we were, into this utilitarian area of the domain. He would arrange with the steward that we should be allowed to and fro during the early hours, the dogs would be kept in, and the watchmen and patrols should be ordered to let us pass. It was not unusual, he said, for such orders to be given, for Lord Clarendon often had occasion to send people on private errands at nighttime. We would take the body on a barrow from the pavilion to the stables, where the horse would be waiting. From there we could slip out into the lane that ran north towards the Oxford Road and thereby avoid Piccadilly altogether.

'Sword and pistol apiece for you and me, and a cudgel for Gorse,' Milcote continued. He sounded more cheerful now that it was a matter of arranging the practical details of the body's removal. 'I know exactly where to go. I walked the lane yesterday evening to make sure it's still passable. A little muddy in places, but nothing that matters. There's a pond up there, set back from the Oxford Road. It will do admirably for our purpose.'

I admired his thoroughness. I had dealt with enough fools

to appreciate someone who left as little to chance as possible. 'What about his clothes?'

'I'll have Gorse dispose of them after you've talked to him. He can pull up the periwig from the well, too. Burn the lot if he can.'

'And get rid of the sword.'

Milcote winced. 'A Clemens Horn? Such a shame.'

'Safer. Besides, it bears Alderley's crest.'

We strolled on for a few paces. Then I touched his sleeve. 'Will you tell my lord of this, sir?'

'I must. He knows Alderley's body is in the pavilion, and he will want to know.' Milcote frowned, poking the toe of his shoe into the gravel of the path. 'But perhaps it would be better if he learned of it after it was done.'

We exchanged glances, he and I, and I guessed that we were thinking along the same lines: that both of us took orders from people who preferred not to know precisely how their wishes were carried out, especially beforehand; that sometimes they preferred to hint at their desires to us rather than speak them plainly; and that in a manner of speaking we were their left hands, which operated in the dark, so their right hands might be seen to be spotlessly clean by the unforgiving light of day.

Matthew Gorse was a well-set-up fellow with a face full of freckles and no front teeth. We found him in the upper room of the pavilion. It was a lofty chamber, designed no doubt for entertaining, with tall windows on all sides.

He was at work with a tub of whitewash and a brush. He had already covered the length of one wall to the depth of a yard below the cornice. When we entered, he pulled off his hat and gave us each a nod, the nearest a man at the top of a ladder can manage to a bow. At a word from Milcote, he climbed down, propped the brush against the tub and wiped his hands with a rag. If he felt it below his dignity to be white-washing a wall, as Milcote had hinted to me earlier, he gave no sign of it. But a good servant learned to hide his feelings.

Milcote took Gorse over what had happened yesterday morning when he discovered the body. The servant answered clearly and straightforwardly, and his account agreed in every particular with the one that Milcote had given me.

Meanwhile, I turned away and looked over the garden to the house. This side of the mansion was a perfect replica of the entrance front – the fifteen bays, the projecting side wings and the flight of stairs that swept up to the door. It was a statement about wealth and power as much as a house. But it failed to match its owner – old, lonely and gouty; sitting with his feet up in a small, warm closet full of books with his enemies baying at the gate.

'Was there any sign that someone might have broken in?' Milcote was saying.

'No, sir. Not a trace. The windows were secure, and so was the door to the roof.'

I crossed the room to the opposite wall, which looked north over the fields and orchards behind the house. Each of the two tall windows was divided by a mullion and a transom, and their two lower quarters were casements. Judging by the glass and the window furniture, they had formed part of the original pavilion, which Hakesby and his workmen were busy concealing beneath a skin of stone. I lifted the catch that secured the right-hand casement and pushed. It opened outwards.

'Have you any further questions for Gorse, sir?' Milcote asked me.

I turned to face them. 'Not at present.'

There was a flicker of emotion on Milcote's face. It might almost have been relief. 'What now, sir?' he asked.

'May we inspect the kitchen again?' I said. 'It's so easy to miss something.'

'Indeed,' he said. 'One can never be too careful.'

It was almost midday when I left Clarendon House. In the forecourt, the Duke's coach was waiting, and the horses were being walked up and down. His Highness had come with an escort, and the presence of soldiers must have intimidated the crowd of protesters, for they had melted away from the street outside.

Milcote accompanied me to the gate, and told the men there that I should automatically be admitted whenever I called. I declined his invitation to dine with him again and went out into Piccadilly.

I walked eastwards, in the general direction of St Giles and Holborn. Within a hundred yards or so, I turned left into a lane that followed the boundary wall of Lord Clarendon's stables, orchards and kitchen gardens. Milcote was not the only one who liked to make sure of his ground.

The lane had been newly surfaced as far as the gate that led to the stable yard and the kitchens. After that, however, it narrowed to barely a cart's width – less in places – and it was muddy from yesterday's rain and hollowed into the ground by the passage of many feet over the years.

The wall gave place to a hedge. Cows had walked this way before me and left ample traces of their passage. I plodded onwards, cursing mechanically as some of the filth underfoot transferred itself to my shoes and stockings. Occasionally I caught glimpses of the tall chimneys of the house.

I came at last to a gate on the left-hand side. It led into a field set aside for pasture. Its left-hand boundary was formed by the high wall of Lord Clarendon's Great Garden, with the pavilions at the corners.

Several dispirited-looking cows were huddled together in the corner under the shelter of a tree. No doubt these, too, belonged to Lord Clarendon. I opened the gate and walked along the line of the wall. The wall was topped with spikes. The gap in the centre, filled by a temporary but sturdy palisade, marked the place where the gates were to be installed in the garden's northern wall. Here was the low wicket, which Milcote had said was occasionally used by gardeners and builders. I lifted the latch but the wicket, as I had expected, was barred on the other side. The grass in front of it was worn away.

The pavilion where Alderley's body lay was at the far corner of the garden. Seen from the field, it revealed the secrets of its history more easily: the brickwork of the older building was clearly visible on this side. I ran my eyes up the walls until I reached the balustrade of the viewing platform on top of the pavilion. No attempt had yet been made to mask the old bricks with a modern stone facade to match the house. Only the cows could see it from the field, and the ground below had been churned up by their hooves.

I retraced my steps along the line of the wall, examining the ground as well as I could. A little over halfway, on the far side of the palisade, I found a footprint. Or – to be more precise – the partial print. The form was unmistakable but the detail was frustratingly sparse. I could not even deduce the size and overall shape of the footprint from the fragment; nor could I see traces of nails in the sole or other distinguishing marks.

A fragment of a footprint: nothing more. It could belong to the cowherd. It could belong to anyone.

I turned to go. I was deluding myself. What could I hope to learn from a muddy field?

# CHAPTER SEVENTEEN

I WALKED ACROSS the park to Whitehall. I had heard it said that the palace contained above two thousand rooms and was the largest in Europe. It was probably the ugliest and the most labyrinthine as well. Next door, to the north along the river towards Charing Cross and the Strand, lay the equally confusing courtyards of Scotland Yard. This was a more workaday place than Whitehall. It had its share of apartments and offices, but also sheds, coal stores, woodyards, stables and warehouses.

The office of the *Gazette* was in Scotland Yard. We conducted the routine business of producing the newspaper twice a week, in addition to the private newsletters that Williamson controlled, and the gathering of any intelligence he required.

The prison was also in Scotland Yard, a small two-storey building not far from Scotland Dock, where heavy goods were brought by river to Whitehall. Sometimes the authorities used the dock to land prisoners or to take them away, usually by night, as it was more private than the public Whitehall Stairs or the King's Privy Stairs upstream.

The building had not always been a prison. It had been adapted for that purpose during the Commonwealth, when Oliver Cromwell lived in royal state at Whitehall, a king in all but name. It was used for short-term stays. Prisoners were held for questioning before they came to trial or were released. Usually they were under suspicion of committing treasonable offences. In the normal course of things such prisoners would be lodged in the Tower. But sometimes it was more convenient, and more private, for the authorities to keep them here for a few days while they were interrogated and where their friends found it harder to find them.

When I had dined, I walked into Scotland Yard and made my way to the prison. I showed my warrant to the plump sergeant who kept the place.

His eyes flickered over the scars on my face. 'Who do you want, sir?'

'His name's Hakesby.'

'Ah. The old trembler with the empty purse.' The sergeant's moonface split into a pink grin. 'Where do you want him? Here or in his chamber?'

'If he's in a chamber by himself, I'll see him there.'

'Do you want a guard with you in case he's troublesome?'

'No,' I said. 'He'll be as gentle as a lamb. Has he had any visitors?'

He consulted a ledger. 'Only one. His clerk or servant. Scrawny fellow like a fox.'

'Brennan by name?'

'Yes, something like that – he brought him a couple of shirts and blankets, and some food. And a little money, but that's gone.'

It wasn't cheap to be a prisoner. If you wanted to be

reasonably clothed, fed and housed in this place, you had to pay for it.

The sergeant waddled in front of me down the hall, jingling his keys. Hakesby was held on the ground floor in a cell barely large enough for a pallet bed, a single stool and a pot to piss in. Most of the cells held more than one prisoner. I doubted it was through kindness that he had been put in one by himself. More likely Brennan had paid for the privilege. Either that or it was a sign that Hakesby was considered too politically sensitive to mix with others.

When I came into the chamber, I found the old man sitting on the stool, leaning against the wall. He was trying to read his Bible by the light of a small barred window set high in the wall. It was not a cold day but he had a blanket around his shoulders.

He looked up as I entered. He was unshaven and dirty. His thin face was haggard, its bones and hollows newly prominent. He said nothing but lowered his eyes to his book.

How, I thought, could Cat possibly have betrothed herself to a man like this?

'Talkative sort, ain't he?' the sergeant said. 'Mind you, if you leave them long enough they usually start talking to themselves, which saves a man the trouble of asking questions.' He threw back his head and laughed, sending a waft of stale, ale-scented breath into the air. 'I'll lock you in, sir, if you don't mind. Bang on the door when you want to leave.'

I waited until the sound of his footsteps had receded down the passage. 'I'm sorry to see you in this plight, sir,' I said quietly.

'Are you?' Hakesby cried in a high, wavering voice. 'Why should I believe that?'

'Hush. There may be eavesdroppers.' I took a step towards him. I was so close I could hear his breathing, which seemed unusually loud, as if there was some obstruction in his lungs. 'Where's Cat?'

'I don't know.' This time his voice was a whisper. 'Do you think I would tell you if I did?'

'She stands accused of Edward Alderley's murder,' I said. 'She'll probably hang unless we can find a way to help her.'

'She's innocent of any crime.'

I was by no means as sure of that as he was. 'Then we must find out who did it and, in the meantime, keep her safe. And I can't do that without your help, sir.'

'You bring her nothing but trouble, Marwood,' Hakesby said. 'You nearly got her killed a few months ago. The best thing you can do for her is leave her alone.'

'The best thing I can do for her is find out who killed Alderley.'

'Go away, Marwood. Go away.'

'Do you want to have her death on your conscience?' I snapped. 'Do you? Do you?'

That got to him. 'How can you say such a thing?' He began to tremble, and for a moment I feared he would fall from his stool.

'Soft,' I said. 'Keep your voice low, for God's sake. I don't know how much they've told you. Alderley was found drowned in the well in Clarendon's pavilion early on Monday morning. The place was locked up as tight as a drum and no one had been there since Saturday evening. His hat and his sword were on the floor, and the well wasn't covered over.'

'It was when we left,' Hakesby said suddenly. 'I'd swear to that. I check the place before locking up. Always. In fact we haven't had the well cover off since the beginning of last week.'

'Good,' I said. 'That's useful to know.'

'We intend to erect a partition to make a separate well chamber. It will be safer. Perhaps we should install a pump. I must see what Mr Milcote says.' Hakesby's voice was suddenly stronger, and his face looked younger and keener. Then he remembered where he was, and why I was asking him these questions, and he covered his face with his hands.

'Did Cat go there with you?'

'Yes, sometimes,' he said. 'We went over there most days during the last week or two – to discuss the work with Mr Milcote and direct the builders. They are lazy, incompetent fellows, and we must watch them like hawks.' His lips tightened. 'I believe they are more terrified of Cat than of me.'

'I'm told you have your own keys for the pavilion.'

'Yes. They confiscated them when they arrested me.'

'Where did you keep them?'

'At the Drawing Office, of course.'

When I had last talked to Hakesby, four months earlier, Cat had slept in a closet next to the Drawing Office in Henrietta Street, and Hakesby had gone home every night to his lodgings off the Strand. But that might have changed, now they were betrothed, a term that covered a multitude of domestic arrangements.

'And at night?' I asked.

Hakesby knitted his tangled eyebrows. 'What do you mean? My clients' keys usually stay at the office. They are perfectly safe.'

'And Cat?'

'She's there too – in her closet, for the present. I trust her entirely, Mr Marwood, and I have no fears about her honesty. You know we are to marry? The bans will be called at St Paul's, here in Covent Garden, God willing. After our wedding, I intend for us to settle in Henrietta Street. I've arranged to take a lease on the apartments below the Drawing Office.'

I nodded, ignoring my inexplicable relief that they were not already sharing a bed. But I couldn't ignore the inconvenient fact that Cat had had access to the pavilion keys at night, after Hakesby and Brennan had left the office.

'Why am I being held here?' Hakesby burst out. 'What have I done, for God's sake? Why would I wish Alderley any harm? They keep asking me where Cat is, but I don't know. I wish I did.'

I crouched in front of him. 'If I am to help her,' I whispered, 'and help you into the bargain, I must find her. Have you any idea where she might be?'

'I don't know,' he said. 'And I don't know if I trust you.'

I ignored that.

He hesitated but in the end he must have decided that his silence could help no one. 'On Saturday,' he said. 'We supped together at the Lamb. You remember – the tavern in Wych Street where we met in May? And afterwards we parted for the night.'

'Was there anything strange about her manner?'

He shrugged. 'I wasn't aware of anything. She was a little quieter than usual, perhaps . . .' Again, his depression briefly lifted. 'We talked about Dr Hooke, I remember – I heard a rumour he may design a house after the French way for my Lord Montagu.'

'And after supper, you parted directly?'

Hakesby nodded. 'She walked back to the Drawing Office, and I went to my lodgings.'

'So the last time she was seen was at the Lamb?'

'By me, yes.'

I stared at him. 'So did someone else see her after that?'

'Brennan did. He supped with us, and offered to walk back with her. He lodges near Charing Cross, so it's not far out of his way, and Covent Garden can be a sadly profligate place, especially by night.' Hakesby's eyes were anxious. 'He's done it before when we've supped at the Lamb.'

'Were you and Brennan concerned when she wasn't in the office yesterday morning?'

'No. Not at first, in any case. She had told Brennan she had some errands to run on Monday morning. It was only later, when she didn't return, that I began to grow anxious. And then . . .'

I questioned him for a few minutes more, but found out nothing of importance. He was desperately worried about Cat and also about his own plight. His inability to work hung heavily over him, and his ague seemed to have worsened since I had last seen him. But, for all his weakness, Hakesby was wary of me, and I could not be sure he was not with-holding information.

He and I had been thrown together in the past, but I was never sure he trusted me. For a start, I worked for the King and government; whereas his loyalties had been with the other side during the late disturbances and during the Commonwealth. Then there was Cat. He thought I had led her into danger last May. I could hardly blame him for that: he was right.

When I left him, I gave him ten shillings and told him to

use the money to buy better food than the mixture of grit, rancid fat and rat-droppings that they served to prisoners who had no means to pay for anything better. On my way out, I gave the sergeant a crown piece and told him to make sure that no harm came to the old man.

I tapped the side of my nose and told him in a confidential whisper, 'They want to keep him plump and in the best of health at present.'

'As you fatten a goose for Christmas, sir?'

'Exactly.' I patted my purse. 'If all goes well, I'll be back in a day or two with another crown for you.'

When I went outside, I discovered it had started to rain again. The weather matched my mood. I was not in a good humour. It had saddened me to see Hakesby in the condition he was in. I had made no substantial progress whatsoever. I didn't know who had killed Alderley, and I didn't know where Cat was. There was the nagging uncertainty about the identity of the anonymous letter writer who had betrayed Cat and Hakesby to Chiffinch. I was not looking forward to my rendezvous with Milcote and Gorse tonight, either.

Nor had I much liked my behaviour with the sergeant. The ways of Whitehall – bullying, bribery and flattery – were rubbing off on me. Indeed, I was so adept at using them that I feared they were becoming part of me.

If you touch pitch, my father used to tell me, you'll be defiled. I was well on my way to becoming as black as sin.

# CHAPTER EIGHTEEN

O UTSIDE THE GREAT Gate at Whitehall, I took a hackney coach. As I was closing the door, I glanced past it and saw someone who looked familiar among the knot of men loitering under the archway.

It was hard to be sure, but it looked like the man in the brown coat who had been at the back of the crowd outside Clarendon House this morning – one of those whom Milcote suspected of being in the Duke of Buckingham's pay. Even as I saw him, however, the man turned away and sauntered out of sight.

Suddenly, and with a sense of impending disaster, I remembered where I had seen him earlier: if I was right, he had been not merely at Clarendon House, but before that, on Sunday, standing outside the house where Lady Quincy, Stephen and I had called on Mr Knight. But what possible connection could there be between Lord Clarendon's enemies and Lady Quincy's visit to the surgeon?

I ordered the coachman to take me to Covent Garden. Now that Alderley was dead, and I was under orders to investigate both his death and Cat's disappearance, there was no reason why I shouldn't visit Hakesby's office quite openly. On the way, I tried not to let my mind dwell too much on the man in the long brown coat. I had never seen him closely, after all, either at Whitehall or in Piccadilly. I would surely have noticed him before if he had followed me all the way from Clarendon House. Perhaps I had been led astray by a chance similarity.

When the coach set me down in Henrietta Street, I knocked on the door of Hakesby's house and asked for Brennan. I looked respectable enough for the porter to admit me without question. He was about to summon his boy to take me up to the Drawing Office, when I stopped him.

'A word in your ear first. I've just seen Mr Hakesby at Scotland Yard. He's concerned about his cousin, Mistress Hakesby.' Cat went under that name here, to hide her true identity. 'Has she returned yet?'

The man's eyes narrowed. 'I can't help you, sir. I hardly know them.'

He was a bad liar. No doubt Hakesby's arrest had scared him into holding his tongue.

I showed him my warrant. 'I ask in the King's name. Have you seen Mistress Hakesby?'

The porter shuffled his feet. 'No, sir.'

'When did you last see her?'

'Saturday evening.'

I thanked him with a shilling. Then, as if a sudden thought had struck me, I said, 'You saw her when she came back after supper?'

'Yes, I saw her then.' He hesitated, his eyes straying towards the warrant in my hand. There had been a slight stress on the word 'then'.

'And?'

'And I saw her again later, sir, when she went out. She said she'd arranged to meet a friend, and she might stay the night.'

'A friend? Who?'

He was growing uneasy. 'She didn't say.'

'Was it something she often did?'

'Never, since you ask.' He gave a little shrug, as if coming to a decision. 'Between you and me, she wanted it kept quiet. Didn't want Mr Hakesby to know, or Mr Brennan – or anyone. Didn't want to worry them, she said.'

'And where did you think she was going?'

'A young woman sneaking off at eleven o'clock at night, sir?' He winked. 'Not wanting her betrothed to know? It's obvious, isn't it?'

'A lover?' I said. 'Well, perhaps you're right. And you were wise to tell me of it.'

The boy took me upstairs. I found Brennan hunched over his drawing board. He was not a prepossessing man to look at, but then nor was I.

'Mr Marwood,' he said, laying down his pen and coming towards me. 'Why are you here?'

'I come from your master,' I said.

He spat out, 'Was it you who had him arrested?'

'Of course not. I'm trying to help him. And Mistress Hakesby.'

Brennan coloured at the mention of Cat. He was in love with her, I believed, and he disliked me because the fool mistook me as his rival for her affections.

'I must talk to her if I'm to help her,' I said.

'You don't want to help her. You want me to betray her.'

I gave him credit for courage, if not for intelligence. 'Don't be a fool. I could have you arrested if I wanted, but that wouldn't help her. Or Mr Hakesby. You walked her back here on Saturday evening, after you'd supped with her and your master at the Lamb. What did you talk about?'

'Nothing.' He waved his hand towards his desk. 'Work.'

I had nothing to lose so I resorted to bluff. 'I think you know where she is. Tell her I have been here. Tell her I may be able to help but she must let me talk to her. I can do nothing for her without that.'

He shrugged and turned away.

'Otherwise,' I said softly, 'they will find her sooner or later, and they will hang her.'

Brennan caught his breath. But he said nothing.

'And it will be your fault.'

He would not budge. I cajoled him. I threatened him. I shouted at him. All the while, he stood there, pen in hand, with an obstinate expression on his face and his mouth clamped shut, tight as an oyster. They could have burned him at the stake and he wouldn't have uttered a word. I've seen how religion can turn a man into a martyr. Love can do it too.

There was a knock at the open door. The porter's boy was hovering in the doorway. 'There's a man wants you, sir,' he said, looking at Brennan.

'Who?'

'Don't know, sir – he's got something for you. He's downstairs.'

'Send him up then.'

'He won't come – he won't leave his pack and his horse.'

'What's he got for me? Can't he give it to you?'

The boy looked dumbly at Brennan and shrugged. Brennan swore and said, 'Very well, I'll come down.' He glanced at me. 'After you, sir.'

He was clearly glad to have an excuse to get rid of me. We filed downstairs. The porter was on the doorstep, talking to the pedlar or whoever he was, a ragged fellow with a pronounced squint. They stood aside to let me pass. I walked slowly away towards Covent Garden.

'What do you want?' I heard Brennan say behind me.

'Mr Brennan?' the pedlar said. 'Ginger hair, yes, I see it's you. I've a letter for you.'

I glanced back. Brennan was staring past the pedlar at me. I raised my hand, as if in farewell, and hurried away.

From Covent Garden I walked through the rain to Fetter Lane. On the way I made myself pass by Clifford's Inn, where the Fire Court sat to adjudicate disputes on the rebuilding of London. It was also where I had suffered the burns which had left me scarred for life. One must face one's devils or they grow stronger.

I came out of the inn by the Fetter Lane gate and turned up towards Holborn. Barnard's Inn, another inn of Chancery, was on the west side: which was fortunate for its inhabitants, for most of the buildings on the east side of the lane had been destroyed by the Fire last year; the area was still a wasteland of blackened ruins and the temporary shelters of the poor.

I asked at the lodge for Mr Turner and was directed to a staircase beyond the hall. Originally the inn had been intended for students of law but in recent years a number of attorneys had taken chambers here, finding it a convenient place to transact their business.

Mr Turner had a commodious set on the first floor. In the outer office, his clerk was at work at a high desk. The room was lined with deed boxes and beribboned files stacked high on shelves. The door to the inner room was ajar, and I glimpsed two men sitting in conversation, their periwigged heads so close they were almost touching.

'Frankley!' One of the periwigged heads turned. Blue eyes set in a red face glared impartially at the clerk and me. 'I told you to shut that door.'

The clerk scuttled across the room and closed the inner door. He was a small, dark man with one shoulder higher than the other. He bowed to me and asked how he might be of service.

'I wish to enquire about a mortgage which was recently redeemed. I believe Mr Turner handled the transaction.'

There was a flash of understanding in the man's face, a brief rearrangement of the muscles: it suggested that he knew what I was talking about. Perhaps the transaction had not been in Mr Turner's usual line of business, or had been memorable for some other reason.

'I'm afraid I don't know when my master will be at leisure, sir. He has a gentleman with him now.'

'The matter relates to a property in Fallow Street owned by Mr Edward Alderley. I merely want to know who held the mortgage on it.'

'I can't possibly tell you that, sir. The business of my master's clients is confidential.'

I wondered if the clerk was looking at the side of my face that had been marked by the fire. 'You would be wise to do so,' I said, more sharply than I had intended.

I showed him my warrant. His eyes widened when he saw the signature and the seal. He glanced up at me with fear in his eyes.

'I'm pressed for time,' I said gently. 'I shall apply formally to Mr Turner for the information in due course. But there is no need to disturb him if you would rather not. All I need is the name of the mortgagee. Not in writing or officially. Just the name will do, at this stage.'

He hesitated. 'Perhaps I should ask Mr Turner after all . . .' he said, looking at the closed door.

'I will not look kindly on delay,' I said, making my voice harsh. I tapped the warrant. 'And nor will my master.'

'Well, I suppose there can be no harm in it . . .'

'None in the world.'

Frankley glanced again at the closed door. He licked his lips. 'The mortgagee was my Lady Quincy, sir.'

I stared at him, unable to believe my ears.

The clerk misinterpreted my silence as irritation. 'Forgive me, I can't tell you more. Indeed there's little more I could say. Mr Turner dealt with it himself. When you apply to him, he will be—'

'Did she come here herself?' I cut in.

'No, sir. The gentleman did, but Mr Turner called on the lady at her house.'

'The gentleman? Mr Alderley?'

Frankley stared at me, his eyes wide with apprehension. 'Yes, sir. He came to discuss another matter as well as the mortgage. To do with a marriage contract, I believe.'

I came a step closer to him. 'Are you telling me that Alderley hoped to marry Lady Quincy?'

My tone made him recoil. 'Sir, I don't know – you must ask my master. I heard Mr Alderley say something about a marriage contract before the door closed. That's all.'

'Frankley!' bellowed Mr Turner in the next room. 'Here!'

The clerk stared at me. For a moment, his fear of me was perfectly balanced by his fear of his master.

I took pity on him and laid two shilling pieces on the table. 'Thank you. Go.'

I left the room and clattered down the stairs into the rain-slicked courtyard. Lady Quincy, I thought, Lady Quincy. Will I ever be rid of that damned woman? What in God's name is she doing in this?

# CHAPTER NINETEEN

B Y HER THIRD evening at Mangot's Farm, Cat's life had assumed a routine of sorts. In the mornings, she cleaned the kitchen and brought in fuel for the fire. The kitchen, the most habitable of the downstairs rooms, was in a filthy state, with years of dirt impacted into every surface. Cleaning it was a task that had no obvious end in sight, particularly because all she had to help her was cold well water and a few rags. But there was a certain pleasure in this small attempt to bring order to chaos, and it left her mind free to roam.

They ate dinner around midday, and then the afternoon was her own. She read or drew in her bedchamber, filling her notebook with fantastical designs that might one day lead to a house which Palladio or Vitruvius would not find wholly barbarous. Sometimes she ventured outside, though rarely far from the house. There was a wildness about some of the refugees, Mangot had said, especially the younger ones, and they were not to be trusted.

In the evening, there was supper to be prepared. Mangot

read aloud from the Bible both before and after the meal. The evening ended with interminable prayers; the old man prayed as the spirit moved him, which generally led him to a detailed survey of the torments that awaited sinners in the next world. For Cat, it was drearily reminiscent of the later years she had spent under her father's roof, when his religion had grown steadily darker in tone and had come to pervade every aspect of his life.

There was one other part of the routine. Before supper, Israel Halmore would appear at the back door. He entered without knocking and kicked off the heavy boots he wore about the camp. He never came empty-handed. On Sunday he had brought a hatful of wizened, bruised apples whose flesh proved to have an astonishing sweetness; on Monday it was the rabbit; and tonight a large leather bottle that contained ale.

When Halmore arrived, Mangot closed his Bible. Halmore kicked off his boots, gave the bottle to Cat without troubling to look at her, and sat down at the table. Cat brought mugs for the men and, at a nod from the old man, poured ale for them. The foul-smelling rushlights on the table cast an orange glow on to their downturned faces, making their features devilish.

Serving as his maidservant was part of the price she paid for Mangot's hospitality. It was an arrangement that suited both of them, for it gave a reason for Cat to be at the farm. While the men drank and talked, she turned aside to deal with what was left of the rabbit in the pot over the fire.

'There's more from the Bishop,' Halmore said. 'His man rode over to the camp today.'

'His man?' Mangot sounded aggrieved. 'What man?'

'A tub of lard with a big sword. Ex-trooper, I think. He was with the Bishop the other night.'

'I didn't see him.'

'He came by the drover's track along the stream,' Halmore said. 'Didn't want to draw attention. He made an interesting proposition. He's been going round all the camps, drumming up support for Buckingham. Imagine what would happen if all of us – all the refugees, all the poor, all the beggars – if all of us took it into our heads to march on London and rattle the railings of Clarendon's house.'

'More ale, girl,' Mangot said suddenly.

Cat came over to the table and refilled the mugs. Neither man looked at her. She was a woman, she thought, a servant; and to them she was scarcely a sentient being, let alone a rational one, any more than the bottle or the table it stood on.

'This deserves a toast,' Mangot said.

'Aye.' Halmore smiled. 'That's why I brought the ale. We'd tear down Clarendon House, stone by stone.'

They drank solemnly to Clarendon's downfall in this world, and then to his damnation in the next. The ale was strong; Cat could tell even by its smell; and when the first bottle was empty, Halmore produced a second from the pocket sewn into his cloak.

By this time, the stew was simmering. Cat was about to ask whether Mangot wished her to serve supper, when she realized the old man had started to cry.

Halmore patted his arm clumsily. 'Hold up, master, you'll see the knave in the gutter yet. The higher they climb, the further they fall.'

'My son,' Mangot said. 'My son. How he would rejoice if

he could hear us. He would be alive if it weren't for Clarendon. Did I ever tell you the story?'

'Aye, you did,' Halmore began, 'and a very sad story it—'

'My son would be here!' Mangot interrupted, banging the flat of his hand on the table with sudden violence. 'At this table. Drinking with us, Israel. And this farm would be as flourishing as any in the county.'

Cat lingered in the shadows while Halmore drank and the old man told his story. It was simple enough, and sad enough. Shortly after the Restoration, Mangot's son, his only surviving child, had driven four cows to Smithfield Market. Afterwards, with money in his pocket, he had dined well at a tavern in the City, and perhaps he had drunk more than he should have. In the afternoon he had set off on foot for the farm. He had been knocked down by a rider and thrown under the wheels of a passing coach. The young man had been killed instantly.

The coach had been Clarendon's, though he had not been in it at the time. At the inquest, a witness had said that the coachman was drunk, and that this contributed to the fatal accident. The coachman swore blind that he had been as sober as a baby. The coroner, unwilling to disoblige a man as powerful as the Lord Chancellor, had chosen to dismiss the evidence and the witness had subsequently changed his mind about what he had seen.

Since then, Mangot had let the farm decay, for he no longer had a reason to work. The witness was dead, so was the coroner, and so was the coachman. The only person left for Mangot to blame for his son's death and the ruin of his own life was Lord Clarendon.

# CHAPTER TWENTY

I RETURNED TO my lodgings in the Savoy and told Margaret I would have supper early. I called Sam to attend me in the parlour.

'I've another job for you,' I said. 'I want you to go out and be my eyes and ears.'

'In this weather?'

'In this weather.'

'You need a boy to run all these errands, master.' He added, with a touch of satire, 'You could dress him in your livery and have him attend you at Whitehall. It would look very well indeed.'

I ignored his attempt at wit. 'You know Henrietta Street?'

'Where Mistress Hakesby lives,' he said, and his eyes narrowed. 'Of course I do.'

Both he and Margaret had taken an inexplicable liking to Cat when she had nursed me after I was injured in the fire. I sometimes thought that they treated her with more respect than they showed me.

'There's a warrant out for her arrest. Mr Hakesby is already in custody as a possible accessory. She's gone to ground and I don't know where.'

He whistled. 'And the charge, master?'

'Murder. Keep all this to yourself.'

'God love us all. Who did she kill?'

'They think she killed her cousin. A man named Edward Alderley.'

'Money, was it?' He tapped his nose. 'It usually is, when it's family business. Root of all evil, master. Says so in the Bible.'

'It was more than that. He'd treated her as badly as a man can treat a woman.'

He moistened his mouth and glanced at the fireplace. He was resisting the temptation to spit in it. 'Good riddance then.'

'She may not have killed him. There are other possibilities.'

'I always said she had spirit. I—'

'Listen to me for a moment, will you? There's a draughtsman who works at the Drawing Office in Henrietta Street. Red-haired fellow with a sharp little face. His name's Brennan. It's just possible that he knows something. I want you to follow him this evening and tomorrow. Talk to people. See if you can find out anything that might give us a clue to where Mistress Hakesby is. Maybe have a word with the porter at the house.'

'But it's raining harder than it was, master. Could I wait until it goes off?'

'No.' I took pity on him. 'There's an alehouse opposite the Drawing Office if that's any consolation.' I took out my purse. 'One more thing. A pedlar brought Brennan a letter this afternoon – he insisted on giving it into his hand, and he knew Brennan had ginger hair; he wouldn't leave it with the porter. I'd be interested to know where the letter came from. He was a scrawny man with a squint, and he had a horse with him that had a pack on its back.'

I gave Sam a couple of shillings so he could pay his way. I listened to him clumping down the stairs to the kitchen, to tell Margaret he was going out, and why; and no doubt he would add some unflattering comments about me.

I sat beside the empty fireplace and struggled against a sense of futility that rose over me like a tide. As the silence in the parlour grew heavier, I tried to distract myself by thinking of something else. But it didn't help. The longer I sat there, the more apprehensive I became about the dangerous and unpleasant job that awaited me at Clarendon House tonight.

Meanwhile the rain beat against the window panes and the light slipped away from the evening sky.

The three of us stumbled and slithered up the cart track that meandered from Piccadilly to the Oxford road. It was still raining, though less heavily. The clouds were low, masking the moon and the stars.

Gorse was in front, carrying our only light, a dark lantern, with the reins looped over his other arm. The horse plodded between Milcote and me. Milcote was armed with a sword and pistol. He had offered to lend me a sword but I had refused.

The long canvas-wrapped bundle was slung over its back. I had the legs on my side. Every now and then the horse would sway towards me when it encountered an irregularity of the ground, and Alderley's heels would brush against my arm.

It was a slow and agonizing journey. None of us spoke. Occasionally we stopped to listen in case of pursuit behind or sounds ahead. I had my warrant, which if need be would serve as a safe conduct, but I didn't want to use it. It identified me. I could imagine what Chiffinch would say if I were later linked to Alderley's corpse being found near the Oxford road.

As the lane went north, it veered to the north-west in the direction of the road to the east of Tyburn, where the gallows stood. Together with half of London's population, I had gone there to see the disinterred and rotting corpses of Cromwell, Ireton and Bradshaw hanging in chains after the King's restoration.

We stopped a good hundred yards short of the highway. Gorse unlatched a gate and led the horse into a field. The going was easier here – the field was used for hay, which had recently been cut. By this time, my eyes had adjusted to the near-darkness. I made out the gable of a house on the side of the field nearest the road, with the low dark oblong of a barn at right angles beside it. There were no lights in the house, but a dog began to bark in the distance, and it set off others.

'Quick,' Milcote whispered. 'Those damned curs will wake the neighbourhood.'

We came to the pond. Milcote cut the ropes that tied the corpse to the horse. Now began the worst part of the evening. We laid Alderley on the ground. Gorse held the lantern while Milcote and I unrolled the canvas. The body was clad only in its shirt. It had been unwieldy in the pavilion yesterday, but in the darkness, with the dogs barking and the growing fear of discovery, it was ten times worse. It was as though the inert flesh that had once been Alderley had become charged with blind malevolence.

Milcote suggested it would be easiest to put the body in the pond if he and I took the legs, and Gorse the head and shoulders.

'Wait,' I said, wiping the rain from my face. 'We must take off his shirt.'

'We haven't time for that,' Milcote said; there was a hint of panic to his voice that hadn't been there before.

'Yes, we have.' I pawed the body in the darkness, trying to find the bottom hem of the shirt. 'Help me. It's a linen shirt worth good money. He's lost his other clothes. If he'd been picked clean that thoroughly, the robbers would never have left the shirt on his back.'

'I'll have it, sir,' Gorse said. 'I know someone who'll take it and ask no questions.'

I was surprised at the servant's tone, which I thought impertinently assured, as if he had decided he would have the shirt, and he would brook no argument about it. But Milcote didn't reprove him. No doubt he was right to hold his tongue – we could not afford to quarrel among ourselves at this point. Besides, we were all wrought up, and our situation was so strange and so terrifying that none of us was behaving as he usually did.

We tugged the shirt together, yanking so hard that I heard a seam give way. At last we got it off. The three of us lifted the body, which seemed even heavier than before. Our boots sunk lower into the mud. Water seeped into mine.

'One,' I said. 'Two. Three.'

We swung the body over the pond as far as we could and let go. There was a great splash. A spray of water hit me. I staggered back, colliding with Gorse, who swore.

'Quickly,' Milcote said. 'Let's be gone.'

We made much better time on our way back to Clarendon House. Before we reached the stable gate, we stopped. Milcote murmured something to Gorse, and the servant's deeper voice replied. I heard the chink of coin.

Milcote whispered to me across the horse's rump: 'Gorse will take the horse by the stable gate. It will be better if you and I go in by the front. Perhaps we should find a tavern and warm ourselves first.'

'I shall leave you here,' I said. 'Better that way.'

'As you wish.'

We waited in silence while Gorse led the horse away. I heard the gate open and close. When Gorse was safely inside, Milcote let out his breath in a sigh of relief.

'By the way,' he said, drawing even closer to me. 'My lord desires to see you tomorrow.'

'Why?'

'I don't know. Would you call on him in the morning at about ten? Perhaps we might talk afterwards. Among other things, we must advise about what to do with Alderley's clothes.'

'If I can,' I said.

'And there's so much we still don't know,' Milcote said. 'How did Alderley get there? How did he fall in the well?'

I bade him a curt good night and walked by myself down to Piccadilly. It was dangerous to be out on the streets so late, especially alone, and for a moment I wished I had accepted Milcote's invitation. I made my way warily down to Charing Cross, where I tagged on to a party of law clerks who chanced to be leaving one of the taverns. I walked in their company to the Strand.

The strain was telling on me. I was aware that I was wet,

tired and irritable. It seemed to me that both Clarendon and Milcote expected me to jump at their bidding. I wondered how far we could rely on Gorse to keep his mouth shut. I thought Milcote had been too ready to trust the man.

Trust. It all came down to that. Whom could I trust in this business?

## CHAPTER TWENTY-ONE

WHEN I WOKE on Wednesday morning, the memory of the previous night flooded into my mind, along with my attendant doubts and fears. I shouted for Margaret to bring my hot water. It was Sam I heard climbing the stairs, however, always a slow, laborious process. He pushed open my bedroom door with his crutch and came in, spilling some of the water. He set down the jug on the washstand and turned to face me. The puffiness around his eyes told its own story.

'Well, master,' he said. 'What's he doing with a woman's cloak, eh? That's what I want to know.'

'Who?'

'That Brennan, course.' There was no mistaking the smug expression on Sam's face. 'I did as you ordered, watched his door in Henrietta Street from the alehouse over the road. This woman came along with a bundle.' Sam spread his arms wide. 'Big, heavy thing. She knocked on the door, left it with the porter.'

'What's this to do with Brennan and Mistress Hakesby?' I said. 'Or with that letter he had?'

'I'm coming to that, master, first things first. The woman came over the road, didn't she, thought she'd have a drink to keep out the cold. Mulled ale. And I happened to fall into conversation with her.' He favoured me with a wink. 'Not a bad-looking wench, all things considered, though of course I'm a married man, I'm not one to let my hands or thoughts stray where they shouldn't, as you—'

'Get on with it,' I said.

'She says to me, after we'd been talking for a while – she works for a woman up the road, you see, sells second-hand clothes – anyway, she says what does that Mr Brennan want with a woman's cloak? He'd come early in the day, asking for a woman's winter cloak, nothing fancy, she said, good plain wool. He paid on the nail but the hem needed a touch of work, so there she was delivering it.'

'Well done,' I said. 'Anything else?'

'Maybe. She said Brennan wanted it wrapped in canvas as he was sending it out of town tomorrow by carrier.'

'Did he indeed? I don't suppose he mentioned where it was going, or the carrier's name.'

'No, master.' Sam glanced up at me, his eyes bright and cheeky as a robin's. 'But I watched him leaving the Drawing Office yesterday evening, and he didn't have the bundle with him. I take my oath no one else took it out of the house. So he left it there overnight.' He raised his eyebrows. 'Which means . . .'

'You'd better get over there now.' My spirits were rising. The cloak was almost certainly for Cat. 'Keep watch all day if necessary.'

Sam coughed. 'I'll need more money for that.'

'But I gave you two shillings yesterday,' I said.

'It soon goes, master.' He grinned at me. 'A man can't just sit in an alehouse and take nothing to eat and drink. And I had to give the woman something for her thirst. Just to be civil.'

I gave him another two shillings. In return Sam made an obsequious bow, no easy thing when leaning on a crutch, and left the room before I could change my mind.

On my way to Piccadilly, I called in for breakfast and news at the coffee house on the corner of Bow Street. The talk was mainly of the Duke of Buckingham's return to favour at Court, and what it might mean to ordinary men, here and in the City. There was mention of Lord Clarendon, too – in particular a rumour that he was to be impeached before Parliament, where Buckingham had many supporters. If Clarendon's enemies were successful, the King might be compelled to sign the death warrant of his chief councillor. But there was no news of a body found in a pond near Tyburn.

After I had breakfasted, I walked to Clarendon House. The sky had cleared overnight and the sun was already warm. There wasn't a crowd outside the gate this morning – perhaps it was too early for them. The guards recognized me and waved me through. I walked across the forecourt towards the door I had used previously.

Milcote must have been watching, for he came out to greet me. 'All well, sir?'

'Well enough,' I said. 'I called at a coffee house on the way here, and there was no news worth hearing.'

He looked relieved. 'No news is good news. Thank you for your kindness, and for your help. My lord is most grateful, and so am I.'

It was a civil speech, so I bowed in return and said it was nothing. I did not add that I would not have helped him if Chiffinch hadn't ordered it. Nor was I happy that my masters had obliged me to act illegally. But I liked Milcote, nevertheless. He struck me as a decent man, honourably loyal to his master, doing his best in a difficult situation.

'Lord Clarendon has asked me to bring you to him. He's on the terrace.' He lowered his voice. 'His gout's bad today. He may be irritable.'

Rather than go round the outside of the house, he took me through it. For the first time I saw some of the state rooms in the central block of the building. They were as grand as the King's and infinitely cleaner; they seemed as full of marble busts and columns as the entire city of ancient Rome.

We went out by a door in the centre of the house that led to a broad flagged terrace. It was separated from the garden by a stone balustrade ornamented with urns.

Lord Clarendon was sitting in a wheeled armchair, with his bandaged legs resting on a stool. He was reading a letter. The table at his elbow was piled with books and papers. We approached him but he raised a beringed hand, indicating that he wished us to wait. He kept us there, standing in silence, while he finished the letter and pencilled a few words on the bottom of it. He put it aside and nodded to us.

'Marwood,' he said as I bowed to him. 'How kind of you to call on an old man.' There was an edge of sarcasm to his tone. 'George – I don't need you at present. Only Marwood.'

Milcote looked disconcerted, but he bowed and withdrew. Clarendon watched him until he was out of earshot.

'He tells me that the pair of you moved the problem elsewhere last night.'

'Yes, my lord. With Gorse's help.'

He winced, as if the gout had stabbed him unexpectedly. 'The servant who found him? I hope he proves trustworthy. Has the body been discovered yet?'

'Not that I know of.'

'And we still don't know how Alderley came to be drowned in my wife's well.' Frowning, he peered up at me. 'Unless you bring me further intelligence on that score?'

I had plenty of information about Alderley and his movements, but none of it made any sense. I said, 'I'm not sure if this is germane to the matter, my lord, but I came across a footprint in the field beyond the pavilion. There are windows on the first floor – if one of them had been left ajar and a rope thrown down, it's just possible that a man could have got into the pavilion after dark without going through the garden. And there's also the wicket in the palisade in the back wall, though that's barred on the inside.'

Clarendon wrinkled his nose as if at an unpleasant smell. 'It seems far-fetched to me. And either of those would have needed an accomplice within, too.'

'Then there is the matter of Mr Hakesby.'

'My surveyor? The Duke tells me that he's in custody at Scotland Yard. I can't think why – he could have done nothing directly: he's almost as frail in body as I am.' He frowned. 'Besides, what could his motive have been? He has been well paid for what he does. And I find it hard to believe him untrustworthy. My wife's cousin recommended him to her, and he spoke very highly of him indeed. I've talked to him myself once or twice, and he seems a decent man, and one who knows his business.'

'And this servant of his . . . ? The woman.' It would have looked suspicious if I had failed to mention Cat.

Clarendon seized on this. 'Ah. That's another matter. Alderley's cousin, I understand from the Duke, and by all reports a most vicious, savage girl. Did you know that her real name is Lovett, and that her father was a Fifth Monarchist and a Regicide as well? I have it on good evidence that she hated her cousin and had already attacked him once before.'

'I confess I find it hard to see how she could have managed it.'

'She had access to the keys of the pavilion, because Hakesby had a set at his office. And she's gone into hiding. If that's not a confession of guilt, I don't know what is. It all seems plain enough to me. Blood will out, Marwood, blood will out.'

'Yes, my lord.'

He shot me an angry glance. 'I want more than "Yes, my lord" from you. I want you to do something about it, and so does the Duke. This is a plot by my enemies – you may be sure of that. I suspect that they are using the Lovett woman as an instrument for their conspiracy against me. This is designed to do me harm.' He beckoned me closer and whispered, though there was no one in earshot. 'It is just possible that someone of my household is involved.' He paused, and for an instant he looked not only frail but frightened. 'I trust George Milcote as much as I trust any man, but he may have made an error, or been too trusting in his friendships. He brought Edward Alderley here, after all, and without that, none of this would have happened.'

'Do you know when he first brought Alderley here?'

He gave me a sharp look. 'Not long ago. Three or four

weeks, perhaps. I believe they had some acquaintance before Alderley's father was disgraced.'

In other words, I thought, about the time that Clarendon was forced to surrender the seals of the chancellor's office, and his enemies began seriously to think of how to impeach him.

'George is always too soft-hearted for his own good.' He toyed with his pen. 'I shall tell you something in confidence that I have told no one else, apart from Milcote and my son-in-law, the Duke.' It was the fourth time this morning that he had found occasion to remind me that his son-in-law was the Duke of York, the King's brother. 'I discovered Alderley in my closet one day. Quite by himself. He said he had opened the wrong door by mistake and begged my pardon for his intrusion.'

'But what was he doing in that wing at all, my lord? I thought that part of the house was devoted to your private quarters?'

'George Milcote had brought him there to show him some of my pictures. I was out at the time, so there was no reason why he shouldn't. But then George was called away, and he left Alderley here for a moment or two. I came back unexpectedly. Alderley said he was looking for the stairs.'

At first sight, there was nothing strange in the story. It was normal enough for a trusted senior member of a household to show his friends his employer's collections.

'I asked George later, and it was perfectly true,' the old man went on. 'Some household emergency, I believe, and he was delayed longer than he thought he would be.'

'Was anything missing afterwards?'

'An interesting question.' Clarendon nodded. 'I can't find

a small box which I kept in a drawer of my desk. It's not much more than six inches wide, two inches high and four inches deep. It's made of a hard wood but covered with silver.'

'Do you think Alderley took it?'

'Perhaps. I don't know how long he had been in the closet. On the other hand, I hadn't looked at the box for months. It's possible that someone else took it beforehand, and Alderley was speaking the truth when he said that he had strayed into the room by accident.' He made a dry, snorting sound that, after a second or two, I realized had something to do with laughter. 'Or even that I mislaid it myself.'

I thought of the silver key on Alderley's keyring. 'Was it locked?'

'Yes, but the key was with it. Have you searched Alderley's lodgings?'

'Yes, my lord. But I didn't find anything like the box. What was inside?'

He looked away, into the garden. 'It doesn't matter. Just find me the guilty parties, Mr Marwood and, if you can, find me that box. But don't open it. Do that for me, and I shall be in your debt. More to the point, so will the Duke.'

# CHAPTER TWENTY-TWO

AFTER I LEFT Lord Clarendon, I didn't look for Milcote. I went out into Piccadilly. A few people had gathered outside the gates, but they were silent. The man in the long brown coat wasn't one of them, and nor was his fat friend with the old cavalry sword.

I found a coach for hire. I told the driver to take me up to Holborn. I paid him off at the bridge and walked the rest of the way to Farrow Lane.

Gradually my nose grew accustomed to the stink of the tannery. At the shop, Bearwood and his wife were dealing with potential customers, two elderly ladies. They had their backs to the street. The apprentice was sawing industriously in the workshop behind them. There was no sign of the little boy. I slipped into the passage that led down the side of the house to the door of Alderley's lodgings.

I pushed the key into the door and twisted it. It didn't move.

Had someone changed the lock? Then a simpler explanation occurred to me. I reversed the direction of the turn. The lock moved smoothly into the jamb of the door.

In other words, someone had already unlocked the door. Chasing on the heels of that realization came the next: the someone in question was probably still inside.

I took out the key, as quietly as I could, and pocketed it. I wished that I had a better weapon than my stick.

Slowly I raised the latch. I pushed the door. It swung silently backwards on well-greased hinges.

I stepped inside. I stood in the flagged entry from which the staircase rose to Alderley's apartments and listened to the sounds above. I heard slow, heavy footsteps marching to and fro. It was as if a man above were pacing the room, deep in thought.

There was nothing stealthy or secretive about the movements, which was odd. No one had a right to be up there, except perhaps myself.

Stick in hand, I climbed the stairs, tread by tread. Two of them creaked but, by the grace of God, the noises coincided with sounds upstairs. The intruder was pulling heavy objects across the floor. He was in the largest of the chambers, the one at the back of the house with the desk and the mutilated portrait of the woman who looked like Cat.

On the landing, I paused to listen. All the doors were ajar. Some of Alderley's clothes were strewn across the floor. My mouth was dry, and I was beginning to regret my folly at coming here alone.

I toyed with the idea of running downstairs and ordering Bearwood and his apprentice to come with me. But that would alert the intruder to my presence. Besides, Bearwood was slow of apprehension and by the time I came back here with him, the man upstairs would be long gone. Then there was that most potent argument of all, the one that men use to justify their rashest and most stupid behaviour: I did not want to appear a coward to myself.

I abandoned subtlety. I raised the stick, charged down the landing and threw open the door. It collided against a fallen chair. I plunged into the room, waving the stick like a madman and bellowing like a bull. Two paces later, I stopped so suddenly that I almost fell over with my own momentum.

Bearwood's boy was standing not three feet away. He was cowering from me. He wore a plumed hat which came down over his eyes and a pair of enormous riding boots. And he held a sword that was almost as tall as he was.

We stared at each other. I cleared my throat. 'Put that down,' I suggested as gently as I could. 'The sword, I mean.'

The blade wobbled in the boy's hand.

'Put it down,' I snapped. 'On the floor.'

He crouched and laid the sword on the bare boards. The movement dislodged the hat, which fell off his head. He had a triangular face with a pointed chin below a shock of yellow curls. It was hard to imagine how his lumpen parents had come to produce him. Perhaps he was a changeling, left by the fairies in exchange for the real Bearwood child. In that case, the fairies had had the worse of the bargain.

I combed my memory for the name his father had used. 'Hal.'

The lad took a step backwards as if retreating from a blow. He was still wearing the boots, which came up almost to his crotch, and he tripped and fell backwards on to the floor. He began to cry.

'Stop it,' I said. 'I won't harm you.'

I was looking about the room. The apartment had been untidy when I had last seen it. Now it was in chaos, with

Alderley's possessions on the floor and on tables and chairs, and the cupboards open and gaping empty.

'Hal, did you do this? Throw everything about? Empty the cupboards? It wasn't like this when I was here on Monday.'

'No, master, I swear it, I never did anything, it was like this when I came, and all I did was try on the hat and pick up the sword . . .'

His voice trailed away. When I was downstairs, he had been clumping to and fro in those ridiculous boots and wearing that absurd hat; he had probably been waving the sword at imaginary enemies.

'Then who did it?'

'I think it was him, sir, Mr Alderley's friend. The Bishop.'

'Why do you think that?'

Hal wriggled. 'Who else could it have been?'

I pressed him on this, sensing that he had been about to say more but had then decided better of it. I switched my approach: 'And how did you get in?'

'The door was unlocked, sir.'

'And why are you here?' I gestured towards the sword and the hat. 'To play the fool?'

His face coloured, and I knew I had been cruel. 'Mr Alderley owes me sixpence. And I thought, he might have left it for me somewhere, so there'd be no harm in having a look for it, I didn't mean—'

'Be quiet,' I cut in. 'Why does he owe you the money?'

'Because I took a letter for him to the Bishop. He promised me sixpence when he next saw me. But I ain't seen him since then.'

I hesitated, considering the matter. Hal took the opportunity to step out of the boots. His feet were bare, and very dirty.

'When did Mr Alderley give you the letter for the Bishop?'

'Last time I saw him, master. Saturday, about dinnertime.'

'Where did he ask you to take it?'

'Golden Ball, sir. Leadenhall Street.'

I didn't know the place but it sounded like a tavern. 'This Bishop,' I said, jingling the change in my pocket. 'What's he like?'

'Tall. Taller than you, sir, tall as that door, nearly. And he's all bones. Wears a brown coat.'

'A long one?'

Hal nodded.

This affair grew worse every minute. One of the men organizing the protesters outside Clarendon House was tall and thin. He wore a brown coat and carried a sword.

I tried to reconstruct the sequence of events during Alderley's last few hours in Farrow Lane. On Friday evening, he had returned, drunk as a lord, with the Bishop. Mrs Bearwood had heard him call out something about Watford and Jerusalem. About midday on Saturday, Alderley had sent Hal with a letter to the Bishop in the Golden Ball. In the evening, Mrs Bearwood said he had left the house at about eight o'clock and that had been the last time she had seen him.

'Did you hear either of them say anything about Jerusalem? Or Watford?'

'Only on Friday night, when Mr Alderley was hanging out of that window.' He hesitated. 'Only it wasn't Watford.'

'Your mother said it was.'

'Ma got it wrong.' Hal sounded more confident than before. 'She's hard of hearing, and she doesn't hear all of it or get it right. Besides, she was in the kitchen, but I was in the yard. I was nearer. And I could see him.'

'Really?' I said, trying not to sound too interested.

'He leaned out of the window so far I thought he'd fall out. And he called down to the Bishop, promising to write it all down in the morning. In black and white, he said, signed and sealed. All about Jerusalem.'

'What about Watford?'

'Sounded more like Wallingford to me.'

The implication hit me at once. I stared at him. 'Wallingford? Are you sure? Absolutely sure?'

Hal nodded. 'Cross my heart, sir. That's what he said. He said he'd send it over to Wallingford, and the Bishop says no, send it to the Ball by dinner time.'

'What else? What else did he say?'

'Nothing.'

I pounced on Hal, giving him no warning, and seized his arms. 'You saw the Bishop later, didn't you?' I gave him a shake, like a dog with a rat. 'You saw him when he came again and searched this place?'

The boy's face lost its colour. He opened his mouth to scream and I covered it with my hand.

'Gently. Tell me the truth and no one will harm you.'

He whimpered and I released him. Had it come to this, I thought, that to make a living I must scare the life out of children?

'He came on Monday evening, sir. No one else was here – they were all in the alehouse.'

'Did he talk to you?'

Hal shook his head. His eyes seemed twice as large as before. 'But he saw me looking down from my window. And he did *this*.'

He raised his forefinger to his lips. Then, still staring at me, he drew it across his neck.

*Hold your tongue or I'll cut your throat.*

It was strangely sinister to see this: not so much the gestures as the look of terror on the boy's face. I found a sixpence and dropped it into his hand.

'If I find you've lied to me,' I said, 'I'll see that you're beaten harder than you've ever been beaten before.'

His fingers closed over the coin. 'It's no lie, master. It's all true. I swear.'

I told him to leave me. Wallingford, I thought, not Watford, and the man in the long brown coat: if the boy really had spoken the truth, it changed everything, and changed it for the worse.

Hal ran down the stairs. He flung open the door to the passage and slammed it behind him.

Wallingford House, near Charing Cross and the Royal Mews: where the Duke of Buckingham lived in state when he was in London. Buckingham – Clarendon's enemy, the man behind the crowd shouting at his gates in Piccadilly, one of the leaders of the movement to impeach the old chancellor in Parliament. And I had just learned that Buckingham's man had been involved with Alderley and perhaps had had a hand in Alderley's death as well. The Bishop connected them all.

When I was alone, I walked slowly from one chamber to another. The rooms had been untidy before, and crowded with too many things; but now they were chaotic, with drawers hanging open, cupboards bare and Alderley's belongings strewn across the floor.

Alderley had left few papers behind him – or if he had, the Bishop had taken them. I had a particular desire to discover anything that concerned Alderley's marriage contract. Perhaps his new affluence had turned his thoughts to marriage.

Had he found an heiress worth wooing? Not Lady Quincy, surely? The very idea was distasteful to me. But the Prayer Book forbad a man to marry his father's wife. There was comfort in that, and in Lady Quincy's own intelligence; she was not a woman to throw herself away, though perhaps she might sell herself if the price were right. But nothing Edward Alderley could have offered her would have been enough.

The more I looked, the more the chaos worried me. The Bishop had been either in a desperate hurry or simply indifferent to the fact that he had made his search so obvious. And then another possibility: perhaps he had wished to send a message, to me or to anyone else who followed him here on behalf of Clarendon or the King: that he was invulnerable, that he had no need to make the slightest effort to conceal his visit.

A large leather satchel was hanging from a hook on the back of the closet door. It was empty. It occurred to me that Cat was probably her cousin's heir, morally at any rate, and quite possibly legally as well if Alderley had not made a will.

Wherever Cat was, and whoever found her, she would need money sooner or later. I threw into the bag any small portable items that could easily be sold: a set of silver forks in the French style with three tines; a jar containing nutmeg; two collars made of lace, finely worked; a bracket clock; one of the new pocket watches, this one in a gold case with the hands stopped at five minutes after four o'clock. Chiffinch would almost certainly disapprove of my actions, but Chiffinch need never know.

I also put in the small portrait of the woman who looked like Cat, despite her old-fashioned clothes. Perhaps she would be grateful for this reminder of both the place and woman in the painting. True, the eyes had been mutilated but someone skilled in the art of painting should be able to remedy that.

In the bedroom I knelt down to peer under the carved bedstead with its rich hangings. I found nothing but cobwebs and a chamber pot which, as I discovered when I moved it, had not been emptied for some time. I pulled myself back sharply, to avoid the flowing tide of urine.

As I stood up, the heel of my shoe came down heavily on something on the floor. There was the sound of splintering wood. I glanced down. A shawl was lying in a heap near the foot of the bed. I twitched it aside, which revealed a small silver box. I picked it up. The lid hung drunkenly from the base, attached by a single hinge. My heel had done that. But someone else had already forced the lock with a knife or a chisel.

'A small box,' Clarendon had said to me an hour or two earlier. 'Not much more than six inches wide, two inches high and four inches deep . . . made of a hard wood but covered with silver.'

The silver was badly tarnished. I moistened my forefinger and rubbed the metal. An ornate pattern began to emerge, full of curves and arabesques. I had seen it before. It was identical to the design on the key on Alderley's ring.

I took the key from my pocket, inserted it in the lock and turned. Despite the damage, the mechanism still moved, though it could not travel its full course.

Clarendon had been right: Alderley had taken the box. Now it was almost certain that the Bishop had found it. Which meant that whatever it had contained was probably in the hands of the Duke of Buckingham.

# CHAPTER TWENTY-THREE

IT WAS NOW Wednesday. I had not reported to Chiffinch for nearly forty-eight hours. I knew it would be unwise to put it off much longer.

When I left Farrow Street, I took a coach to Whitehall. As chance would have it, Chiffinch was not there: he had ridden over to his house near Windsor yesterday afternoon and had not yet returned, though he was expected within an hour or two.

A strange interlude occurred, a time of enforced inaction in the middle of the activity and anxiety of the last few days. I felt a desperate need to be active, though I had no idea how. I had a sudden memory of a singing bird that my mother had once kept in a cage. When the nights grew longer with the approach of winter, the bird stopped singing and grew desperate to escape. Instead of singing it flapped to and fro, dashing itself with blind force against the bars of its cage.

I chanced to meet one of my fellow clerks from Mr Williamson's office, who took me to a tavern in King Street for a glass of wine. To judge by his account, the *Gazette* had been plagued by one disaster after another in the last few days, caused by a combination of poorly edited copy, Mr Williamson's bad temper and the distribution difficulty, which had yet to be resolved.

When I returned to Chiffinch's lodgings, he still had not returned. So I went to see how Hakesby was faring in the Scotland Yard prison. The moonfaced sergeant was on duty again.

'I trust I find you in good health, sir,' he said, rising from his chair as I entered and beaming not so much at me as at the memory of my generosity to him yesterday.

'How does Mr Hakesby do?' I asked.

'Well, the gentleman's no trouble, sir, I give him that. But precious little appetite.' He pursed moist lips. 'I can't understand it. I've seen to it that he has the choice of the most admirable dishes, and I know that you gave him the means to pay for it. But he ignores them.'

'Surely he's eating something?'

'Scarce enough to keep a mouse alive. In fact, he's had almost nothing except the odd sip of water.'

'You've pressed him?'

Moonface put on an injured expression. 'Of course, sir. Why, I couldn't have been more particular in my attentions if he had been my own father.'

I didn't find that reassuring. 'Has Mr Hakesby said why he won't eat?'

He shook his head. 'Not a word. Not a syllable.'

'You'd better take me to him.'

The sergeant bustled down the passage in front of me, jingling his keys as a leper jingles his bell. I glimpsed other unfortunates in his charge as we walked along. Two of them called out to me, one begging for charity and one asking me to take a letter to his friends.

The gaoler unlocked the door of Hakesby's cell and stood aside to allow me to enter. The cell was gloomier than before. The window was small and high in the wall. It was at least glazed, but with tiny lozenges of old green glass that distorted the light. Thick vertical iron bars divided it into three. The air struck chill and damp.

Hakesby was lying fully clothed on the cot, his knees drawn up towards his chest and his face turned to the wall. He gave no sign that he was aware of us.

The sergeant cleared his throat, which caused a bubbling sound to arise from deep in his chest. 'I'll leave you then, sir,' he said in a voice that was suddenly uncertain. He stared down at his prisoner. 'It ain't natural, is it?'

I glanced at him and gave him a nod. I guessed that he was confused by Hakesby's behaviour. It was outside his usual experience. It disconcerted and even disturbed him.

He withdrew. The door slammed behind him; the bar scraped into its socket and the key turned in the lock.

'Sir,' I said softly. 'It's Marwood.'

There was no reply. I suppressed a spurt of irritation: I had done my best for Hakesby; I had spent good money on him; and he repaid me by behaving like a statue.

Not like a statue: a fit of trembling rippled through him. I leaned across him and looked down at his face. His cheek seemed hollower than before, and there was a drop of moisture on the end of his nose. His eyes were open. He was staring at the blank wall beside his cot, on which a previous occupant had scratched DEVIL TAKE THE PRIVY

COUNCIL TO HELL and another MAY GOD HAVE MERCY ON MY SOUL.

I touched his shoulder and shook him gently. He offered no resistance. He might have been an inanimate thing. The only sign of life was the passage of air in and out of his nostrils and the slight movements of his chest.

'You must eat, sir,' I said. 'How can it help anything if you starve yourself?'

I straightened up and glanced about me. On the stool was a jug of small beer and a covered platter. I lifted the lid and found the end of a loaf and some hard cheese.

Hakesby's Bible was on the floor between the side of the stool and the bucket that served as a privy. That was disturbing, too, for Hakesby was a serious man, and one with Puritan leanings: someone who would value his Bible above all things. I picked up the book and laid it carefully on the chair.

I returned to the bed and stooped over him again. 'You must not abandon hope,' I whispered. 'The more I look into this matter, the more it appears to touch on affairs of state which have nothing to do with Cat.'

I paused but he gave no sign that he had heard me.

'But I have to find her. I must make sure that she comes to no harm. I will discover the truth about Alderley's death and see to it that you are released, and your innocence made plain to everyone.' I squeezed his shoulder as if to demonstrate the strength of my determination, though I knew these were empty promises. I hesitated, swallowing. 'And then you and she may be married.'

I waited. The only sounds were Hakesby's breathing and the muffled cries of unfortunates in other cells.

'I can do nothing,' I said, 'unless you tell me where Cat is.'

A bout of shivering took him again. It occurred to me suddenly that it might not be the ague that caused it, or not that alone – he might simply be cold. I glanced about for something to throw over him.

His cloak was hanging on a peg on the wall by the door. I picked it up. I was about to spread it over him when I saw that it was hanging in a lopsided manner. One side was heavier than the other. I patted it, and discovered a pocket sewn into the lining on the left-hand side, with the opening at the top secured by a flap. I undid the tie and drew out a notebook.

I put it aside on the chair for a moment, and turned aside to drape the cloak over Hakesby. He gave no sign that he was aware of it.

I took up the notebook again and flicked through its pages. There were a few loose sheets among them. The handwriting was almost illegible but I made out enough to realize that the notebook contained his working notes. There were measurements, brief memoranda of meetings and decisions, and of costs and quantities. There were also rough sketches, most of them annotated, of buildings and their details.

Among the loose leaves was a letter written by Milcote, confirming that Lord Clarendon wished the old well to be retained, repointed, cleaned, and set apart from the rest of the kitchen. On a separate sheet, a carpenter had provided a list of the timber required to erect a partition for the well, together with an estimate of the cost.

Another paper was a dog-eared sketch plan in pencil of a rectangular building with a gallery running at right angles across one end. Hakesby had annotated this in ink. I struggled to read what he had written. Suddenly the marks unscrambled themselves and became first letters and then words:

*Dr Wren his Design of the new Chapel at Jerusalem.*

I glanced over my shoulder at Hakesby's back. 'Sir? What's this about Jerusalem?'

There was no answer.

I gave him a gentle shake. 'Jerusalem – what is it? The city? Or what?'

It was absurd even to entertain the possibility that some caliph or sultan or patriarch had commissioned Dr Wren and Mr Hakesby to build a chapel in the Holy Land. In that case, what could it mean?

I didn't expect him to answer, and he didn't. He had retreated so far into his quivering silence that I could not hope to have the truth from him, or not at present.

Jerusalem: on Friday evening, Alderley had called down to the Bishop, 'Tell them about Jerusalem.' It could not be a coincidence.

I was desperate to be gone. I thrust the notebook and its contents in the satchel I had brought from Alderley's lodgings. I banged on the door for the sergeant.

# CHAPTER TWENTY-FOUR

MR CHIFFINCH LEANED back in his chair and stared up at the ceiling. 'Alderley has been found drowned.'

It was a bald statement of fact. He expressed neither satisfaction nor regret.

'Really, sir?' I said in an equally colourless voice. 'I hadn't heard the news.'

'In a pond near the Oxford Road. Not far from Tyburn. He had been robbed, too – stripped of everything he had. It's a dangerous locality, of course, almost as bad as Knightsbridge. The King has made it known that he is most concerned that footpads and highwaymen should operate with such impunity so near to London.'

Chiffinch was still in his travelling clothes. He had only just returned from Windsor, he said, which was why he chose to interview me in his private closet at his own lodgings. He sat eating grapes while I stood near the door. I suspected that he was enjoying the elaborate charade that this was the first he had heard of Alderley's death. It struck me that the ability to indulge your sense of humour in the presence of your inferiors was a sign of your power over them.

'As to other matters.' He spat the pips on to the floor. 'The Lovett woman. Have you found her yet?'

'No, sir. She's vanished from the face of the earth. I've set a watch on her house.'

'That's no good. We want her under lock and key.'

'But do you in fact need her now, sir?' I said. 'If Mr Alderley was left for dead after he was set upon and robbed on the highway . . .'

We stared at each other in silence. There was an unsettling irony to the situation: Chiffinch wanted to find Cat to make her the scapegoat, and he was employing me as his instrument; I wanted to find her to save her life.

He took another grape and studied it. 'Because I'm not at all convinced of her innocence in this matter. In fact, the more I think of it, her flight seems a clear indication of her guilt. No doubt she bribed someone to do the work for her. One of those rogues who followed her late father, perhaps.' He bit into the grape and chewed. 'Not that it signifies who did the work for her – plenty of men in this city will murder a man for the price of a good supper with a whore to follow.' He spat out the pips. 'And, for that matter, plenty more will stand up in court and swear they overheard her plotting the murder.'

'I have new intelligence that puts a different perspective on this, sir.' I wanted to move the conversation from Cat as soon as I could, for he seemed determined to see her hanged by fair means or foul. 'It touches on the Duke of Buckingham.'

'Buckingham?' Chiffinch paused in the act of lifting another grape to his lips. 'I told you he would try to make mischief from this if he could.' He let the grape drop from his fingers. 'If he has a hand in this you must proceed with great care. Are you sure of your facts?'

I was sure of nothing. 'I can only tell you what I have uncovered. Alderley had a drinking companion on Friday evening, a man known as the Bishop who apparently has a connection with Wallingford House and therefore with the Duke. Mr Milcote believes that the Bishop is also one of those who arrange the demonstrations against my Lord Clarendon in Piccadilly. I've seen him there myself. I also caught a glimpse of him here in Whitehall yesterday afternoon, by the Great Gate.'

Chiffinch frowned. 'You mean he followed you?'

'Perhaps. I'd walked down from Clarendon House, and come through the park. I mightn't have noticed him – I wasn't paying particular attention to other people.' I hesitated. 'Or he was here on other business.'

Chiffinch and I looked at each other in silence. Neither of us pointed out that the Duke of Buckingham had been also at Whitehall yesterday, flaunting the fact that he had returned to the King's favour. Neither of us needed to.

'Who is this Bishop?' he asked.

'I don't know, sir. Not yet.' I rushed on before he could interrupt: 'I've also learned that Alderley had recently acquired quite considerable sums of money. Just before he died, he paid off the mortgage on the house in Farrow Lane and bought new clothes. It's possible that he was contemplating marriage, too.'

'Who was the woman?'

I shrugged. 'I don't know that, either. But the very idea that he was considering it is interesting. It suggests that he felt his affairs were more settled than they had been. I imagine he intended to pay his addresses to an heiress.'

Chiffinch nodded. I couldn't bring myself to tell him that it had been Lady Quincy who had held Alderley's mortgage, something which she had unaccountably failed to mention to me. My jealous heart suggested that perhaps she had been closer to her stepson than she had admitted to me. But would it not be unfair, I argued to myself, if I were to mention this possibility to Chiffinch before I asked the lady herself about it? After all, I should give her a chance to explain. My pulse beat faster at the thought that I had a reason to call on her.

Before it could occur to Chiffinch to enquire about the person who had held the mortgage, I said, 'And there's more, sir. You must see this.'

I unbuckled the straps of Alderley's satchel and took out the broken box I had found in his lodgings. I laid it on the table beside Chiffinch's chair. I took the key that fitted it from my pocket and put that beside it.

He said nothing but his eyes widened momentarily, a flicker of muscles. 'What's this?'

'Lord Clarendon told me this morning that he has lost a box like this. He described it in some detail. He also said that he had discovered Alderley in his closet a week or so ago. Mr Milcote had brought him up to his private apartments to see the paintings, and then had been called away. Alderley told my lord that he had lost his way.'

'Ah.' Chiffinch dropped another grape into his mouth. 'So Lord Clarendon thinks that Alderley stole his box?'

I nodded.

'Did he tell you what it contained?' he asked, and pushed in another grape to join the first.

'No. But I went directly to Alderley's lodgings to search more thoroughly. As you see, I found it. It was on the floor of Alderley's bedchamber. But I was too late. Someone had been there first.'

Chewing steadily, Chiffinch picked up the box and examined it. He lifted the lid and said, in an even tone as if the words hardly mattered to him or anyone else, 'Who forced it open? You?'

'Of course not, sir.' I did my best to look horrified, but I doubt I fooled him. 'Besides, I came across the key in Alderley's pocket when I searched his body on Monday. Why would I force the lock?'

He would not let it go. 'The box was empty?'

I nodded.

'So who opened it?' His voice was suddenly harsh. 'Are you sure it wasn't you?'

'On my oath, sir.'

He stared at me for a moment, sighed and took yet another grape. 'Then who?'

'Alderley had no need to force the lock. I believe it may have been done by the Bishop. I questioned a boy who had seen him.'

'What boy?' Chiffinch snapped.

'The son of the carpenter who leases the lower part of Alderley's house. He told me the Bishop returned on Monday evening. It was clear that the apartments had been thoroughly searched, and by someone who didn't care to be discreet. Everything was left awry. The motive can't have been robbery, or not robbery in the usual sense because many valuables hadn't been touched. I can only think that the Bishop was looking for this box. When he found it, he stole whatever it contained.'

Chiffinch wasn't looking at me any more. He had picked up the box and was tilting it this way and that, examining the design of the lid. He set it down on the table and took up the key.

'Can you make out these letters, Marwood?'

'No, sir.'

He put down the key, spat out some seeds, took another grape and popped it in his mouth. 'Nor can I,' he said casually. 'Perhaps they aren't letters at all. Just a pretty pattern signifying nothing.'

Chewing, he stared at me. His eyes were glassy and more prominent than usual. I knew he had given me a warning.

'Keep it to yourself,' he went on, speaking quickly and urgently, as if he had suddenly realized he was in a hurry. 'If you happen to see my Lord Clarendon, there's no need to mention that you've found the box. Not yet.'

'Then what would you have me do, sir?'

'Come and see me tomorrow evening,' Chiffinch said, drawing the box closer to him and covering it with his hands as if to keep it safe. 'Ask for me at the Privy Stairs at ten o'clock. In the meantime, say nothing and do nothing, unless you get a whiff of that Lovett woman and her whereabouts.' He spat. 'Leave me. Make yourself useful. Go back to Williamson and his scribblers in Scotland Yard.'

I was glad to get away from Chiffinch. It was only when I reached the open air that I realized that I had forgotten to tell him about the design for a chapel that I had found in the pocket of Hakesby's cloak. Perhaps it was as well: the discovery didn't resolve anything; it merely deepened the mystery. Better to wait until I knew more – either from

Hakesby himself, if I could persuade him to talk, or from Brennan.

One of Lord Clarendon's footmen intercepted me as I was crossing the Great Court on my way back to Scotland Yard. He must have known my face from my visits to Clarendon House because he said nothing to me; he merely bowed and handed me a letter. He stood back and waited, hands clasped.

I broke the seal and unfolded the letter.

*Dear Mr Marwood*

*Gorse has disappeared. No one has seen him since last night. Will you sup*

*with me this evening? I shall be at the Goat by Charing Cross at nine o'clock.*

   *G. Milcote*

*Clarendon House*

I folded the letter and put it in my pocket. Here was another complication. Gorse seemed straightforward enough in his way, but I had thought Milcote had been rash to trust him with our expedition last night. Had he gone of his own accord or had someone used force?

I beckoned the servant. 'Tell Mr Milcote that I shall be there.'

Like the well-trained footman he was, he bowed again and walked smartly away without a word, without even waiting for a tip. How unlike my poor Sam, I thought, in all departments.

I walked towards the archway leading to Scotland Yard, Mr Williamson's complaints and the drudgery and routine of the *Gazette*. The court clock struck four before I reached it. I stopped abruptly. After a moment's thought, I turned right and walked swiftly down to the public stairs from Whitehall. I took a boat downriver to the Savoy.

It was as if God had leaned out of heaven on a whim and touched me with a spell of madness.

When I reached Infirmary Close, I discovered that Sam had not yet returned from watching Brennan, nor sent word. Margaret, who let me into the house, was worried about him. I told her that he was a grown man capable of looking after himself, but if he returned drunk again he would feel the weight of my anger.

I swept away her reply with a string of orders: 'Send for the barber directly – I wish to be shaved. Then set a pan of water to heat. I want a jug in my bedchamber as soon as it's done. Bring out my best suit, and see that it is brushed and clean and all things neat. Also a Sunday shirt – the new one: make sure it's pressed.'

She seemed to welcome the distraction. Before I went upstairs, she gave me a letter which had been brought from the Post Office. It was from Mr Fisher, Mr Williamson's correspondent in Watford. He regretted that he was unable to help me. There were no itinerant preachers in the town at present, and talk of Jerusalem was confined to the parish church and licensed chapels, where it belonged.

No surprises there. I already knew that Watford was a blind alley. I threw the letter on the kitchen fire, where the pan of water was warming.

In my chamber, I locked Alderley's satchel in my closet. If I ever found Cat, she might find its contents useful one day. I passed the next hour and a half washing and shaving, combing and dressing, adjusting and brushing, until at last I was able to gaze at the reflection of the undamaged side of my face in the mirror with something like satisfaction.

I turned the other cheek and looked at what I saw there. I shrugged. It would have to do.

# CHAPTER TWENTY-FIVE

I HAD HAD no occasion to visit Cradle Alley, the narrow street that ran from east to west in the City by Moorgate, for nearly a year. But I had not let that trifling circumstance prevent me from going there. About once a month, or every six weeks, I would found myself strolling down the street on my way to somewhere else that lay in quite a different direction.

The reason? Lady Quincy lived there.

In that time, Cradle Alley had gradually changed. The western half had burned down in the Great Fire. As the months passed, the ruins had been cleared, and the sites of the buildings marked out. One or two houses had already been rebuilt, and temporary huts had grown up among the ashes and the weeds.

The Fire had spared the eastern half of the alley, towards Broad Street, which was where my lady lived in a house that had come to her by her first husband, Sir William Quincy. The building was one of those big, half-timbered merchants' houses which had been so common in the City before the

Fire; it was larger than most, however, and in better condition. The upper storeys jettied over the street, and their old-fashioned diamond panes glittered in the light of the sinking sun.

I own I was nervous. My unnatural finery seemed suddenly inadequate for the task in hand, a pathetic attempt to make myself seem what I was not. The closer I came to the house, the slower my footsteps and the greater my sense of my own folly.

I knocked hard on the door to give myself courage. I waited for what seemed like an age. Then there was a rattle of bolts and the door swung inwards. I told the porter my name and asked him to enquire whether Lady Quincy was at leisure.

He summoned a tall manservant I remembered from previous visits, and whispered something in his ear. The servant went away.

I waited in the outer lobby under the porter's eye. It was very quiet. All I heard was my own breathing, which sounded unnaturally loud. Time crawled like the tortoise, and my heart raced like the hare.

In stark contrast to the street facade, the lobby was flagged with marble; an archway set between columns framed a view of the inner hall and the carved staircase rising into the upper storeys. The building had been extended and refurbished in recent years. Behind its old-fashioned frontage lay a richly furnished modern townhouse whose principal apartments faced towards the garden. It was rumoured that the King had paid for these alterations, and that Lady Quincy had been his mistress when the Court was in exile on the Continent, and even now she made herself useful to him in other ways.

The servant returned. 'If you will follow me, sir.'

He led me to a small chamber on the ground floor and at the front of the house. He stood aside to let me enter. Then, without a word, he closed the door, leaving me alone.

The room was dimly lit. It was furnished simply, unlike the grand drawing room upstairs where Lady Quincy had entertained me on my visits last year. There was a desk, a chair, a stool and a heavy, iron-bound chest. A tall press stood against the wall with two locks securing its doors. The window was small and heavily barred. This was a place where valuables were stored and business was transacted.

I heard footsteps. The door opened. Lady Quincy came in, attended by her African page. I bowed.

'I am sorry to keep you waiting, sir,' she said. 'Please sit.'

She sank gracefully into the chair, leaving me the stool. The boy took up his station at her shoulder.

'Why have you come?' she said, and her tone, though pleasant enough, increased the distance between us.

'I have intelligence for you, madam. It has to do with our meeting at Whitehall.' I let my eyes travel towards the boy standing by Lady Quincy's chair. 'Perhaps you might wish . . .'

'Stephen,' she said. 'You may leave us. Close the door but stay within call. I will ring when I need you.'

He bowed, and slipped out of the room.

'It's not wise of you to come here unannounced. Have you news of my niece?'

'She's vanished, madam.'

'It seems that she heeded the warning after all. Thank God.'

'You have no idea where she might be?'

Lady Quincy was a clever woman, and her mind was busy.

'I think, sir, you may know more than you are saying. Suppose you enlighten me.'

I had to trust her, at least partly, if she was to trust me. 'There is news, but it's not yet public knowledge, though it soon will be. If I share it with you, will you keep it to yourself until it is known by all the world?'

She stared at me. 'How intriguing. Very well.'

'I hope it won't distress you to learn that your stepson is dead.'

Lady Quincy was sitting with her back to the window, and I could not see her face clearly, especially as the light outside was softening and beginning to fade. How could I ever have thought her ordinary? She radiated an allure which had no words to describe it.

'How . . .?' Her voice was scarcely above a whisper.

'He has been found drowned. The circumstances are . . . mysterious.'

'Are you saying he was murdered?'

I shrugged. 'He was discovered in a pond near Tyburn. He was naked.'

She fired a fusillade of questions at me: 'Who did it? Footpads? What was he doing up there by himself? When did it happen? Who knows of this?'

I replied to none of the questions. The silence lengthened. She sat with her fingers laced together on her lap and stared at me.

'Why do you come here to tell me this?' she asked.

'Because Mr Chiffinch believes that Catherine Lovett was responsible for his death. There's a warrant out for her arrest.'

She considered this and then gave a snort of amusement. 'That makes it plain enough. The King must have an interest in it or Chiffinch would not trouble to have an opinion on the matter. Perhaps I should ask him.'

'You'll do as you wish, madam, I'm sure.' I tried to take her off guard, saying in the same breath, 'Tell me, why did you lend Alderley money? You didn't think to mention it to me the other day.'

'Why should I have done? What business was it of yours? Besides, I told you his affairs were prosperous. That was the important point. His paying off the mortgage, and the interest he owed me, was but a consequence of it.'

'Was another consequence that he intended to marry?'

'Marry? Edward?' She raised her eyebrows. 'That's the first I've heard of it.'

'You also told me he said that he and his friends would see your niece dead and he would dance on her grave. When I asked you who these friends were, you wouldn't answer. Will you now?'

'Perhaps he didn't tell me who they were.'

It seemed to me that this strange conversation had become a dance with words, and for some reason she was allowing me to lead her, as the man does in a dance.

'Let's say that he did give you a hint about these friends,' I said, 'were they by chance connected with the Duke of Buckingham?'

'You might very well think so, Mr Marwood.' She smiled at me, which reinforced my awareness that there was nothing ordinary about Lady Quincy, and that the spell she exerted on me had not lost its power. 'But of course I cannot say. I'm but a woman, you know, and nowadays I live quite retired from the world.'

She rose to her feet in a rustle of grey silk. Automatically

I stood as well. She held out her hand. It lay warm and defenceless in mine. I desired her more than I had ever desired anything in my life.

'I'm glad we've talked,' she said. 'Perhaps we shall talk again one day.' She picked up the bell on the desk. But she didn't ring it. 'Tell me – and I hope I'm not prying – how did you come by those scars on your face?' She raised her hand and touched her own cheek, as if she were myself in a mirror. 'Forgive me if this is a painful subject to you.'

I felt the colour rising to my face. 'I was caught in a fire three or four months ago, madam.' I gave her a stiff and unconvincing smile. 'Believe me, it looks better than it did.'

'I'm sorry.' Her voice had become gentle. 'But it doesn't much matter, you know. Anyone with eyes sees the man within, not the scars without.'

Lady Quincy rang the bell. When Stephen returned, she said, 'Mr Marwood is leaving.'

# CHAPTER TWENTY-SIX

I REACHED THE Goat shortly before nine o'clock, still dazed from my interview with Lady Quincy. The tavern was by the Chequer Inn on the corner of St Martin's Lane and the Royal Mews.

Milcote rose to his feet as I was shown into his private room. 'I'm glad you could come, sir.' He waved the servant away. 'This business is driving me mad – it grows worse every day. And you're the only person I can talk about this with. I've taken the liberty of ordering our supper.'

There was a bottle of wine on the table. It was half empty. He poured me a glass as I sat down on the bench opposite him.

'You're very à la mode this evening.' He raised his eyebrows. 'Is there a lady concerned? Your mistress? Should we drink to her?'

'No,' I said, thinking that these gallant gentlemen were all the same under the skin, their minds running naturally after women and wine. 'But I'll propose a toast if you wish. To a happy resolution to our troubles.'

'I'll drink to that.'

Milcote emptied his glass and reached for the bottle. He had acquired an air of strained gaiety. His face was flushed and his movements lacked their usual precision.

'Have you heard the news?' he said, glancing at the door to make sure it was closed. 'Alderley's been found drowned in a pond near the Oxford road, not far from Tyburn.' He let out his breath in a rush and smiled. 'They say he must have been there for a while. The corpse isn't fresh.'

'No. I don't imagine it is.'

He lowered his voice still further. 'At least it's out in the open. My lord's pleased. This deserves another toast, I think.'

'What's this about Gorse?' I asked, when he was refilling our glasses.

'The rogue's fled. The steward told me after dinner. The last time I saw him was last night, with you.'

'When he took the horse and cart back to the stable yard?'

Milcote nodded. 'The watchmen said he attended to the horse and then he went back to the house.'

'Does he sleep alone?'

'No – there are three of them in the room, and he shares a bed with one of them. He was there in the morning – I'd given him leave to lie an hour longer than usual, so the others rose before him. They saw him there, fast asleep.' He shrugged. 'And after that, nothing.'

I frowned. 'You mean he simply vanished?'

'It would have been easy enough for him to leave, if he wished. No one admits to seeing him go, but there again, why should anyone have noticed? A servant about his business in his master's house is unremarkable. Besides, my lord's servants are cautious about what they say and do at present.

183

They know enemies are gathering and they begin to look to their futures.' He scowled. 'Like rats leaving a sinking ship.'

I said carefully: 'Gorse's not where Alderley was, is he? Have you checked?'

It was warm in the room and Milcote's forehead had become shiny with sweat. 'No, not there. Thank God.' He shivered. 'The well was the first place I thought to look. My lord asked me the same question when I told him that Gorse had gone.'

'Of course. And he must be worried by this – in the light of what Gorse knows.'

'Yes. Especially after last night's adventure.'

Milcote picked up the bottle, found it was empty and rang the bell violently for the waiter. He demanded another bottle of sack with more sugar to sweeten it.

'I ordered his box to be searched,' he said when we were alone again. 'We found his muddy clothes in it, and his best suit gone.'

'It looks as if he went out of his own free will,' I said. 'And he didn't mean to come back. Had he money?'

'I gave him five pounds in gold yesterday. To keep his mouth shut about last night and . . . and about the other thing. Alderley, I mean. Which brings me to the worst of it. When I—'

The servant chose this moment to enter with the next bottle, followed by the boy from the cookshop with a tray of covered dishes containing our supper. Milcote and I waited in strained silence while they prepared the table.

When they left us alone at last, Milcote stared at the food before us, a look of distaste on his face. 'I find I have no appetite, sir. But may I help you to a leg of—'

'What were you going to tell me just then?'

He looked across the table at me. 'I believe I made a terrible mistake with Gorse. I was wrong to trust the man.'

'Because he's fled?'

'No, it's worse than that. Much worse. When I searched his box, I found an old pair of shoes with holes in the soles.' Milcote put his hand around the bottle as if for support. 'He'd stuffed paper into the toes to hold their shape. I don't know why, but I pulled the papers out. One was just an old broadsheet. The other was a note of instructions from a former master, nothing of significance in itself, a list of errands. But it was signed "EA".'

'You think it was Alderley?'

Milcote nodded. 'I'm certain of it.'

'Why?'

'He had a way of putting little flourishes on the "E" and the "A" of his name. He gave me a note of hand when I lent him money, and I noticed it then.'

I rested my elbows on the table and leaned closer to him. 'I don't understand. Are you saying that Alderley had once been Gorse's master? Yet they pretended not to know each other?'

'Yes. And it was Gorse who found his body in the well, and Gorse who helped us move him last night.'

For an instant, I glimpsed another possibility, like a big fish moving in the depths of a murky pond, far beneath its smaller brethren near the surface. I said, 'Perhaps the steward at Clarendon House can tell us more about his background?'

'I've already enquired about that. One of my lady's friends had suggested him as a well-trained and trustworthy servant.'

'Who?'

'I don't know. And Lady Clarendon is in her grave.' Milcote waved his arm, as if to point out its location. 'There's no one to ask. No one. No one at all.'

'Then who is truly Gorse's master?' I asked. 'Not my Lord Clarendon, obviously, for all he paid the fellow's wages. Was it Alderley still? But you can't serve a dead man, can you? So . . .'

'He . . . He might have run away. Servants do, after all.'

'Or,' I said, 'he might have left Clarendon House because his real master commanded him to do so.'

'His real master . . .' Milcote repeated slowly.

He stared at me across the table, his handsome face flushed and haggard. I took the wine from him and refilled our glasses. We both drank.

'I've faced an enemy on a field of battle more than once, and counted it no more than my duty.' His voice was quiet and steady now, with no trace of the wine he had drunk. 'I've fought a duel over a lady, because her honour was involved, and therefore I was obliged to defend her for the sake of her good name. But this – this is different. This shapeless, creeping dread. I can't face the danger because I don't know what it is or where it lies.'

By the time we left the Goat, both of us were a long way from sobriety. Milcote seemed to have little control over his limbs, which struck him as intensely humorous.

'The truth is, my dear Marwood, I am most dreadfully foxed.'

'I can't say I'm altogether clear-headed myself. Let's summon a chair to take you back.'

*In vino veritas*, they say – when a man is drunk, you discover the truth of him; you see him as he really is, stripped of caution and calculation. From that perspective, I found much to like in Milcote: he seemed open, honourable; even when drunk, he was unfailingly courteous, and he treated me without a hint of condescension.

There was a stand for sedan chairs at Charing Cross. I summoned one and helped Milcote into it with some difficulty. I told the chairmen to take him the short distance to Clarendon House, and paid them generously in advance.

By the time this was settled, and Milcote had made his last farewells to me and dozed off on the seat inside the chair, I felt more myself again. The fresh air and the exertion hadn't made me sober but they had counteracted some of the more extreme effects of the wine. I set off home on foot – the Savoy was even closer than Piccadilly.

As I walked, my temporary good humour ebbed away with the fumes of the sack. Before he had entered Lord Clarendon's service, Gorse had worked for Alderley. Neither of them had seen fit to mention that to Milcote or anyone else. Why? It suggested that there had been a conspiracy between them.

I turned off the Strand and passed under the archway that led down to the Savoy. It was darker here, and the stones were slippery. A mist was rising from the river, its tendrils softening the shadowy outlines of the buildings. With the mist came the stink of sewage; the smells were always worse at low tide when much of the foreshore was exposed.

Here and there, lights surrounded by blurred halos showed in windows or above gateways. I walked more slowly and carefully than usual, though the way was as familiar to me as the passages and stairs of my own house. The tapping of my stick on the stones sounded muffled.

Something from our conversation in the Goat snagged in my memory, but too far beneath the surface for me to retrieve it. I struggled with it for a moment, but I could not identify what it was.

'Mr Marwood, sir?'

The voice was little more than a whisper. It came from my right, where there was a narrow passage between two buildings; it was usually the haunt of beggars during the day, especially if it was raining.

I stopped and turned towards the sound. The path was as black as a pool of ink.

'Mr Marwood?'

The voice was low-pitched and gravelly.

'Who are you?' I said, taking a firmer grip of my stick and raising it, ready to use it as a cudgel.

'A friend, sir, a friend.' The man cleared his throat. 'My master would speak with you.'

'Then let him come to me by day.'

'Now, sir. He's but a step away. He—'

The crack of a latch made him break off. The sound came from the gateway further down the alley on the left that led to that part of the Savoy set aside for private lodgings, including my own.

The wicket opened. In the dim light that hung above the gate I saw the blurred shape of a man coming out into the alley. He was carrying a small lantern. I heard the familiar tap of a crutch on the stones.

'Sam,' I cried. 'Sam — is that you?'

'Aye, master. Come to light you home.'

Relief washed over me. 'You there,' I said, suddenly bold. 'Show yourself.'

All I heard in reply were retreating footsteps.

A moment later, Sam drew level. 'Were you talking to someone?'

'Yes.' I waved the stick towards the passage. 'A man over there. He wanted to take me to his master.'

'Big man?' Sam said. 'Belly like an alderman's? Carrying a big old sword?'

'I don't know. I couldn't see him at all. His voice was full of phlegm.'

'He came to the house a few minutes ago. Wanted to see you, late though it is. An ugly fellow – I wouldn't let him in. Talked to him through the shutter.'

Sam lowered the lantern, and for a moment its light touched the butt of the pistol in his belt.

'What are you doing out here, anyway?' I asked.

He turned his head and spat. 'Came to see if you were about. I didn't take to him.'

I felt guilty for my earlier thoughts of Sam, my dark suspicion that he would return home drunk as a lord and useless to anyone. If anyone was drunk and useless, I was.

We walked back to the house in silence. Big man, I thought, with a belly like an alderman's and carrying an old sword. Sam's description sounded disturbingly like the fat man whom Milcote thought was one of those conducting the protests outside Clarendon House.

Sam knocked at Infirmary Close, and Margaret unbarred the door to us. She said nothing but her eyes moved from me to Sam and back again, inspecting us for signs of damage. Candle in hand, she followed us into the parlour.

'Are you hungry, sir?'

'No. Go to bed.' I wanted to be alone. 'Both of you.'

Sam cleared his throat. 'I've news, master.'

I wheeled to face him. 'You've found Mistress Lovett?'

He came forward into the circle of light thrown by the candle. 'Not sure. Brennan went out this afternoon, and he was carrying a sack. Big enough for the cloak. I followed him.' He glanced down at his wooden leg. 'As best I could. He went up to St Giles and left the sack at that little tavern by the church.'

I sat down abruptly. It looked as if we had been right. In the ordinary way, Brennan would surely have sent out the porter's boy to take a parcel. But not if he had been sending something to Cat, and hadn't wanted it known. 'What happened then?'

'Brennan came out of the tavern without the sack,' Sam said. 'So I went in. And there was that pedlar, the one you mentioned, who brought that letter. The one with the squinty eye. He had Brennan's sack on the floor at his feet. He was drinking, and then so was I, and he was grumbling that he had to go out of town today, and it looked like rain. A special trip, he said, and at least it paid well. God, I said, you poor devil, and Squinty said luckily he was only going as far as Woor Green, matter of five or six miles, so it could be worse.'

'Woor Green? Where's that?'

'On the way to St Albans. It's a village by the high road.' Sam paused for effect. 'I heard there's a refugee camp up there. I reckon that's where she is.'

'You've done well,' I said. 'I shall rise early in the morning. Call me at five.'

'Wait, master – there's more, and maybe it'll make you change your plans.' Sam came closer to me. 'I came back by Henrietta Street and whetted my thirst at the alehouse in case

. . . in case Brennan was up to anything else. Just as well I did. Did you know they've found Mr Alderley drowned in a pond near Tyburn? They say he'd been beaten and robbed.'

'Yes,' I said in a colourless voice. 'I believe I had heard the news.'

Sam cocked an eyebrow. 'You take it mighty calmly, sir. Phlegmatically, sir, as the learned gentlemen say.'

'Don't be impudent. I take it how I please.'

He had my measure, and he grinned. 'And I heard another thing there too, master, which perhaps you don't know. Brennan's gone.'

'What do you mean – gone? Run off?'

'No – he's been taken up for questioning. They were waiting for him when he got back to Henrietta Street. There's no one left in the Drawing Office.'

# CHAPTER TWENTY-SEVEN

THE FOLLOWING MORNING, I was up and about as soon as it was light. There was no time to be lost. Brennan had been arrested. I didn't doubt his attachment to Cat, though I disliked it intensely because I thought her far above him. But I was doubtful of his ability to withstand expert interrogation at Scotland Yard. It was probably only a matter of time before they forced him to reveal all he knew.

I hired a horse for four shillings from the livery stable at the Mitre. Williamson wasn't expecting to see me at Scotland Yard, or Chiffinch until ten in the evening. There was a fair chance that I could safely devote the day to my own business without anyone being the wiser.

The trouble was, Cat was Chiffinch's business too, for a different reason. I was playing a double game, with all the dangers that entailed. And there would have been no necessity for this dangerous expedition if Cat had taken me into her confidence.

The day was fine, with the promise of heat later on. I rode north up Watling Street in the direction of St Albans. My head was thick from last night's wine, but it began to clear once I left the stink and noise of London behind.

I didn't often ride and I lacked great skill in it. Managing the horse took up most of my attention. The keeper of the stables had assured me that the mare had a placid, biddable nature – 'Why, sir, your lady mother could safely ride her from here to John O'Groats without mishap' – and for the first few hundred yards his claim seemed justified. The beast plodded through the streets, allowing me to guide her with the utmost docility.

Once we reached the open road, however, she became altogether less manageable. She showed a tendency to shy at animals we encountered along the way, and a positive aversion to barking dogs. Moreover, her appetite grew as we left the city behind, and she would stray to the roadside for a mouthful or two of grass or anything else that took her fancy. I tugged at her reins but it seemed to have little effect; she ate what she wanted and then pottered onwards of her own accord.

After an hour or so, I suspected I had passed Woor Green without knowing it, for there were no fingerposts on this stretch of the way. I asked a man labouring in a hayfield by the side of the high road.

'Woor Green, master?' he said, leaning on his rake. 'Why do you want to go there, and you a gentleman and all?'

'What's wrong with it?' I asked, accepting his flattery and recognizing it as a discreet appeal to my generosity.

'Terrible place since the refugees came. They'd slit your throat for sixpence.'

He gave me directions, nevertheless. I had indeed missed the turning, which was a mile back. The village, he said, lay a few hundred yards west of the high road, though the cottages were so mean and scattered that you would hardly know it was a village.

'I'm looking for the camp,' I said. 'What's it like? Why's it so bad?'

After the Fire, the camps around London had housed the refugees in their tens of thousands. But most of the refugees had moved out of them now, and those that remained had become like small towns, with their own streets and regulations.

'It's not like the others, master,' the labourer told me with relish. He was a garrulous man, delighted to have an audience. He explained that the Woor Green camp was very small, with a shifting population of only a few score families. Its retired situation made it harder for the refugees who sheltered there to find work nearby, and London was too far away for them to walk there and back every day. Most subsisted on what they could scratch from the soil, or beg or steal, or on the charity of families and kindly neighbours. These were refugees who had lost all they had to the flames. In most cases, they had lost the will to improve their lot even if they could.

The camp was on land belonging to an old farmer named Mangot, who had let the place decay since his wife died. Soldiers had been billeted there during the war, and they had done a good deal of damage. Mangot had had one son who survived into adulthood, but he had died a few years ago.

I gave the labourer the wherewithal to drink my gentlemanly health and rode back the way I had come. A rutted lane led to the village, such as it was. I came across an old woman picking blackberries from a hedgerow. The eyes were sunk deep in their sockets. Her skin was brown, with a single fissure on either side of the mouth, so deep it might have been slashed with a knife. While the mare took a few mouthfuls of the vegetation underneath the hedge, I asked her where I might find Mr Mangot and the camp. She gave me a sour look and pointed a grimy forefinger further up the lane.

When the mare had eaten its fill, I rode on. The lane narrowed and sank lower between the adjacent fields. The hedgerows became more and more unkempt. The air smelled of decaying vegetable matter.

Two dogs came at me from nowhere, circling around me, snarling, snapping at my legs. The horse grew restive, backing away and weaving to and fro in the confined space. At any moment, I knew, she could rear up, and I would probably fall off the damned animal. I swore at the dogs and shouted for help.

'Here, you devils.'

The voice was a man's, sharp and high pitched. It came from someone standing above and behind me. The dogs cowered, their tails down, and slid up the bank at the side of the path. The hedge was in such poor condition that I could see through it to the outline of a thin figure on the field beside the path.

'Mr Mangot?' I said.

'Who wants him?'

'My name is' – I plucked from memory an old schoolfellow at St Paul's – 'Rawlindale.'

'Why do you want him?'

'To ask about the young woman who came to this camp a day or two ago. I want to speak to her.'

'Who?'

I didn't know what name Cat was using. I said, 'She had a cloak sent to her yesterday.'

'You'd better come with me. I'm Mangot.'

A small man wriggled through the fence and slithered down

the bank to the lane with the dogs behind him. He was a wiry fellow with a tangle of long, greasy grey hair and eyes filmed with infection. He wore a filthy smock and filthier breeches. Without a word, he fumbled at the wretched horse until he found her bridle. Limping, he led us up the lane. The dogs followed. I felt like a captive in a triumphal procession, not a visitor.

We came to an open space, where there was a tumbledown farmhouse with a sagging roof green with age; a third of it had fallen, exposing broken rafters and leaning trusses. A small pig was rooting for its dinner in the muddy, weed-strewn farmyard. There was no other sign of life apart from a nanny goat tethered to a ring set in the barn wall beside a moss-encrusted mounting block.

The man made a growling sound in his throat and the dogs lowered their tails and ran into a barn attached to the ruinous end of the house. 'There,' he said, pointing to a parcel of land behind the yard that sloped down to a stream. 'That's the camp.'

I had been to refugee camps before but nothing had prepared me for Woor Green, even the warnings from the labourer I had met on the road. Beyond the buildings of the farm was a chaotic collection of canvas tents and makeshift cabins built of wood. There were no makeshift shops or streets in this place. Wisps of smoke rose from half a dozen fires. Figures moved among the shelters. The colours – of the tents, the clothes of the inhabitants, of the ground around them – were shades of brown: the colours of sackcloth and dishwater, of mud and excrement.

'How many live here?' I said.

He shrugged. 'I don't know. Nigh on a hundred? There were more. These are just the ones that are left. The poor damned souls.'

'But what do they do?'

'They wait,' Mr Mangot said. 'Everyone's waiting in Woor Green.'

'Waiting for what?' I asked.

'For death, master. What else is there to wait for?'

He released the mare's bridle and, without a backward glance, limped into the house.

I rode slowly through the yard and into the field beyond. The mare picked her way around the perimeter of the camp towards the stream at the bottom. The refugees stood by their shelters and stared at me as if I were a being from another world, which in a way I was. They had their own dogs and these followed at a safe distance; they seemed as cowed as their owners.

When I stopped by the stream, however, a tall, gnarled man came towards me and asked me, civilly enough, what I wanted.

'Where is the young woman who came here the other day?' I asked. 'Who perhaps had a cloak sent to her by a pedlar who called here?'

'A cloak, sir?' he said, lifting his hat and scratching the halo of grey curls beneath. 'I know nothing about a cloak.'

'What about the young woman?' I snapped, my frustration bubbling over. 'She probably came here on Sunday.'

In my irritation, I must have tugged at the reins. The horse took exception. She tossed her head and cantered back up the field, with me clutching at her neck. At the gateway to the yard, one of Mangot's dogs made a run at her. She veered away along the back wall of the farmhouse. I shouted at the dog and waved my stick, which by a miracle I still had in my hand. Snarling, it backed away.

But it was only a temporary respite. The other dogs of the

camp, no longer cowed, were converging on me, and so were the human inhabitants. What made it worse was that none of them shouted or spoke, and the dogs did not bark. In silence, they advanced towards me and the mare. The tall man was at their head. He was carrying an axe. I tightened my grip on the stick and wished to God I had borrowed Sam's pistol.

A door opened behind me. I tugged the reins, trying to wheel the mare towards this new threat.

'My dear sir, what in heaven's name are you doing to that unfortunate animal?'

I almost fell off the damned horse in my surprise. Cat came out of the farmhouse, took the mare's bridle and patted her neck in a way that miraculously restored her to the placidity her owner had promised.

At the sight of Cat, the refugees and the dogs lost their menacing air. It happened so subtly, so strangely, that I found myself wondering if I had imagined their hostility.

'Thank you, Mr Halmore,' she said. 'Mr Mangot tells me this man is looking for me.'

Halmore shrugged. 'Just keep him out of the camp. He's not wanted here.'

Cat nodded. She led the horse, with me on her back, round to the yard, and brought her to a trough of water. The mare lowered her head to drink. I took the opportunity to slide from the saddle and landed with inexpressible relief on muddy ground.

'Why are you here?' Cat said. 'And how did you find——?'

'Have you heard?' I interrupted.

'Heard what?'

'Edward Alderley is dead. Almost certainly murdered.'

Cat stared at me for a moment, her face perfectly still. In

the last few days her complexion had darkened, though there had been little sun. Her hair was dressed differently and her eyes were very clear against the tanned skin. They seemed larger than usual, as though her face had shrunk around them.

'Good,' she said at length. She paused. 'Yes – good.'

Her face was unreadable. I felt the familiar frustration seething within me. Dealing with Cat Lovett would have been so much easier if I could understand her. But the more I knew her, the less I understood.

She led me into the kitchen. Mangot was sitting at the table, apparently absorbed in reading his Bible. He ignored us. Cat drew me into a passage that led to the ruined part of the house. The sky was blue and clear over our heads, beyond the fragments of beams and posts and rafters.

'Keep your voice down,' she said softly, 'and no one will hear us. How did you find me?'

'It's a long story and it's not worth the telling. You're not safe here any longer.'

Alarm flared in her face. 'Why?'

'The authorities are building a case against you for Alderley's murder.'

'I never touched him,' she spat. 'That's God's literal truth. Though by God I wish I had.'

'In their eyes you had motive enough to kill him, and more. You had opportunity, too, for he came and went at Clarendon House, just as you were doing.'

'Who told them?'

'Someone laid information against you, accusing you of the murder. And when they came to arrest you, they found you'd fled – and for them that confirmed it. It's another strand in the noose that will hang you.'

She shrugged but said nothing. After a pause she changed the subject. 'How did he die?'

For a split-second I entertained the possibility of telling her the truth, that Alderley had been found in Lord Clarendon's well. But there was still too much I didn't know about this business, and I was privy to secrets that weren't mine to share. Besides, she hadn't trusted me, so why should I trust her?

I said, 'He was discovered drowned yesterday in a pond near Tyburn. His body had been stripped, and they say he had been beaten too. They think you hired men to do it for you.'

'Edward dead,' she said. 'I still can't believe it. Are you sure? Are you truly sure?'

'Of course I'm sure,' I snapped. She seemed more inclined to rejoice at her cousin's death than fear for her own safety. 'But that's not why I am here. They took Brennan for questioning yesterday. If they haven't cracked him open yet, it's only a matter of time. And when he does . . .'

She looked momentarily guilt-stricken. Then: 'He won't talk. He wouldn't betray me.'

'Don't be a fool.'

She glared at me. I had a better idea than she did of what they could do with suspects at Scotland Yard. True, the bad old days of physical torture, of the rack and the thumbscrews, were gone. But the interrogators had other methods of making their prisoners talk, especially men like Brennan who had no one to speak for them in the right places. The draughtsman had struck me as having a hard shell, but I suspected that he was like an egg, thin and brittle on the outside; he would break easily under pressure, and the yolk of the man would spill out among the fragments.

'And Mr Hakesby?' she asked. 'How does he take this?'

'Your betrothed? Not well,' I said, too angry to be kind. 'They arrested him on Monday. He was in a bad way when I saw him yesterday.'

Cat turned away and plucked a shoot of willow herb growing from the floor of what might once have been a pantry.

'We must leave here,' I said. 'And we must leave now.'

She wheeled back to face me. 'Is that what your friend Lady Quincy told you to say? Have you seen her again, by the way?'

'She has nothing to do with this.'

'In any case, I won't go.'

'You will.'

Her eyes were bright with anger. It seemed to me that our wills were in balance, one against the other, so finely equal that the weight could not fall one side or the other.

'I've only your word for all this, after all,' she said with her nose in the air. 'And Brennan is made of sterner stuff than you think, and so is Mr Hakesby.'

'The last time I saw Hakesby, he was lying on his bed with his face to the wall and trembling like a child.'

She said with less assurance, 'I need time to consider what to do for the best. It's my safety at stake, not yours.'

With an effort, I kept my voice calm. 'It's not just your safety. It's Brennan's and Hakesby's, too.' I paused. 'Besides, you're wrong. If they find out what I've done to help you, I wouldn't give a groat for my safety, either.'

## CHAPTER TWENTY-EIGHT

THE JOURNEY TO London was exquisitely uncomfortable in more ways than one. At first I offered to walk, leading the horse, while Cat sat on it. She told me not to be a fool. Instead, we rode together. Fortunately it was a pillion saddle, uncomfortable in itself but capable of carrying more than one person. Mr Mangot gave us directions which led us across country and allowed us to avoid the high road.

Cat rode side-saddle behind me, with an arm around my waist. The horse plodded placidly along byways dense with the dusty, straggling vegetation of late summer. The animal was behaving better, probably because she was aware that Cat was on her back, and that Cat would stand no nonsense from her. I might be holding the reins, but that was a mere technicality.

My thighs ached with the unaccustomed exercise of their muscles. I was hungry and thirsty, but there was nowhere to buy food and drink. In any case, even on the high road, it would not have been wise to advertise our presence any more than we had to.

There were other reasons for discomfort – not least the fact that Cat and I were forced so close together, trapped in an unwanted intimacy, aware of each movement the other made. It seemed to me that since I had first met her a year ago, her body had lost its boyish contours and grown fuller and softer. The discovery unsettled me.

She was irritating me, too. Although we hadn't exactly quarrelled in the ruined farmhouse, we had come close to it. She had been unreasonable, I thought, in not following my advice immediately and in not appreciating the risks I had taken to track her down and warn her. As we rode on, I began to suspect that she hadn't wanted to be rescued at all, by me or anyone else, and that of course irritated me still further.

For several miles, we did not exchange a word, except to debate which way we should go. (We often disagreed about that, as well.) But we couldn't sulk in silence all the way to London. We had too much to discuss.

'We must talk about where you go,' I said over my shoulder.

'I thought you would have decided that for me too, sir,' she said.

'I suppose I'd better take you to my house. But you can't stay for long. It's too dangerous for both of us.'

'Then I'll find somewhere myself.'

'Don't be foolish. I want to help you. It's a question of knowing how best to do it.'

Her body seemed to relax against mine, and she said, with one of those sudden changes of mood that touched her sometimes, 'I know you do, Mr Marwood. Though God knows why. But truly I don't want to be a burden to you or to anyone else.'

We went on in silence, but a slightly more comfortable one than before. Nothing had been settled, but my mood was lighter, if only by a fraction of a feather's weight. But, for all the apparent thaw between us, I couldn't trust her.

'Do you recall a servant by the name of Gorse at your uncle's house?' I asked.

'Matthew Gorse? Yes – he used to serve at table sometimes.'

'Did you know he was working at Clarendon House?'

She shifted on the saddle. 'No.'

If only I could see her face, because so much hinged on this simple question. Gorse would have recognized both Cat and Edward Alderley. Any servant remembered the faces of the family he had once worked for, particularly one of such standing as the Alderleys had been. He might have told Edward Alderley that Cat was working in the pavilion – or he might have told Cat that Alderley was visiting Milcote at Clarendon House. It was even conceivable that he had told them both, and been paid twice for his pains.

It was vital that I find Gorse. If I was to negotiate a safe path through this thicket of intrigue, I must first establish the truth.

'Tell me,' I said suddenly, hoping to surprise the truth out of her, 'what happened on Saturday evening?'

I felt Cat move away from me. 'Was that when Edward was killed?'

'Perhaps. Because he was last seen on Saturday.' I misled her by omission. 'But, as I told you, he was found dead in the pond yesterday.'

'I wonder what he was doing up there? Was he robbed and murdered on the high road?'

'I don't know. But . . . But I am commanded by the King to investigate the circumstances.'

'You? Why?'

I shrugged. 'I'm not privy to the reasons of princes.'

She made a sound like breaking wind, puncturing my pomposity.

'All right.' I couldn't help smiling. 'I can speculate about the reason. I had some slight acquaintance with your cousin last year. Perhaps that was part of it. And the King can issue his orders to me by a private channel – through Mr Chiffinch and the Board of Red Cloth – and perhaps it's convenient for him to conceal his interest in this affair. These are uncertain times. There are changes afoot in the government and at court.'

'You have your fingers in so many pies, sir,' Cat said coldly. 'Lady Quincy. Mr Chiffinch. The King himself. These great affairs of state. Where does all this end? A knighthood, I hope, at the very least.'

'I make my living as best I can,' I said, my good humour gone. 'And I do my best to help you, as well.'

'Why?' Her voice was harsh, like a lawyer on the attack in a court of law.

It was a good question but I didn't reply. I knew guilt was part of it, for the dangers I had exposed her to in May. There was also the strange bond that links together the survivors of a great peril, particularly those who have been able to survive only because of the exertions of each other.

'On Saturday evening,' I said, 'you supped with Mr Hakesby and Brennan at the Lamb. Brennan walked back with you to Henrietta Street. But the porter said you went out again a little later.'

'What if I did?'

'He told me you said you were going to a friend, and that you might spend the night with her.'

'In fact I was doing exactly as you advised me to do when we met at the New Exchange last Saturday,' she said coldly. 'I'd turned your advice over in my mind and I'd decided to take it. And now you interrogate me as you would a criminal.'

'Then what did you do?'

'I made arrangements to leave Henrietta Street. I didn't tell Mr Hakesby – I thought it better not.'

'You asked Brennan instead.' I found I had raised my voice. 'I'm sorry. I didn't intend to – to—'

'To shout at me? To browbeat me, as if you were a judge and I before you in the dock?'

'I'm merely trying to establish—'

'Yes, I asked Brennan for help,' she interrupted. 'His Uncle Mangot had business in town, and he was going back to Woor Green early the next morning. Brennan took me to him – he lay at the stable of an inn, along with his horse and cart. We arranged the matter there and then.'

'A strange choice,' I said, without adding that what I found strange and unsettling was the fact that she had gone to Brennan, and he had helped her.

'Why? Going to Mangot's Farm? I went there because it seemed the best course available to me. A refugee camp, where people come who have never met each other before. Somewhere near London but not too far.' She turned her head. 'I didn't do it just because you advised it, by the way. I did it because I wanted to spare Mr Hakesby trouble.'

'In that case you were unsuccessful.'

Cat dug her elbow into me. 'That was unkind, sir.'

She was right, but I didn't give her the satisfaction of agreeing with her.

'Have you talked to Mr Milcote at Clarendon House?' she said after a pause. 'We deal with him over the pavilion and he must know all about Gorse, too.'

Was she trying to change the subject? I said, 'He and I have already talked a great deal.'

Her arm tightened around me. 'He's an able man.'

For a moment, I wondered if she entertained a liking for Milcote; a handsome fellow like that might catch the fancy of most young women; but Cat was not like the general run of young women.

'Anyway,' she went on after another fifty yards of plodding and swaying, 'Anyway, what's the point of all these questions? What are you trying to find out? If I killed my cousin?'

'Of course not.'

'Thank you for that, at least. How did you find me? Was it the letter?'

'What letter?' I said irritably.

'The one I sent Brennan.'

'Yes – that and the cloak and the wall-eyed pedlar.' I half-turned my head. 'Why did you write to him?'

Cat answered my tone rather than my words. 'He's not my sweetheart, if that's what you mean. No, it was because there was talk at the farm about my Lord Clarendon and his house. The tall man – the one you met – says the Duke of Buckingham intends some great attack on my lord that will ruin him utterly. I heard yesterday that the Duke's men are bribing disaffected men to march on Clarendon House. Men like those refugees, or at least some of the wilder ones among them.'

'What did you want Brennan to do about it?'

'Tell Hakesby, and persuade him to pass on the warning to Mr Milcote or my lord himself.' Cat paused. 'Lord Clarendon has been a good client to us, and I wouldn't like to see his house damaged. Or the pavilion we're working on.'

I almost laughed. She cared so much for someone else's house that she would risk betraying her own whereabouts to her enemies in the hope of preserving it.

'Do you think he passed the message on?'

'I doubt it,' I said. 'Mr Hakesby was already held for questioning when the letter came, and now they've taken Brennan too. He can tell the men who interrogate him, I suppose.'

'Well,' she said. 'You know everything, or at least everything I can tell you.'

I wondered if that were true. I knew that Cat was capable of lying to protect herself. We all are. But perhaps, I thought as we rode on in silence, she was also capable of lying to protect me. I was weary of the uncertainty. I must find other ways of uncovering the truth about what had happened to Edward Alderley and what it had to do with my Lord Clarendon.

In the meantime, I had a more pressing problem. I had found Cat, but what on earth was I going to do with her?

As we approached the city, the clocks that had survived the fire were striking eight in a ragged jangle that lasted at least three minutes. Time was running away with us.

'It's less than five days since I saw this,' Cat said, waving towards the ruins of the old city. 'It seems as many centuries.'

'Conceal your face as much as you can,' I said. 'Pull your

208

hat down. We mustn't linger. I'm due at Whitehall in two hours' time. Will you do me a service? Two men are watching for me – they don't wish me well. They would have taken me last night if Sam hadn't been there. One is very tall and thin, in a brown coat – it's a long one. The other is smaller but fat. They both wear swords.'

'Why are they after you?' she said. 'Is it to do with my Aunt Quincy, or my cousin's death?'

'Perhaps. But it doesn't matter why. Just keep a watch for them and tell me if you see them.'

We came into the outskirts of the city, took the road around the old Wall and threaded our way through the streets to the Mitre.

Cat dismounted in the street outside. I told her to wait while I returned the horse to the livery stable and paid what I owed.

Afterwards, despite the need for haste, I paused under the archway of the stableyard and watched her. She was standing in a patch of sunlight with her back against the wall and her hand wrapped around the handle of the knife in her pocket. On the other side of the road, a pack of small boys were tormenting a cat. The creature was all skin and bone, and spitting like a firecracker. It wriggled out of its captors' hands, scratched two of them, and bolted into an alley. One of the injured boys burst out howling. The other ran to his mother, who swatted him out of the way like a wasp.

She glanced at me. She was smiling. 'I knew it would end thus.'

'Aye,' I said. 'Cats are like that, I believe. Take my arm. Hurry.'

Still smiling, she chose to obey me. We walked swiftly

down to the Savoy, entered by the side gate, which was unattended at this hour, and made our way to Infirmary Close. I hammered on the door of my lodging.

There was a rattle of chains and bolts. Margaret opened the door. Her face lit up when she saw Cat. 'Mistress Hakesby, God bless me – how do you do?'

Cat pressed the older woman's hands in hers. 'Well enough. And you and Samuel?'

'Still here, mistress, as you see.'

'Get in the house and close the door,' I interrupted.

Margaret drew Cat inside. 'You look weary. Are you hungry? Thirsty? And what have you done to your face? Have you been too much in the sun?'

'Walnut juice to darken the skin,' she said. 'To make me seem a countrywoman.'

I closed and barred the door. 'Take Mistress Hakesby away and give her whatever she needs. Bring me some hot water in my chamber. Then come to me in the parlour.'

Margaret curtsied. So did Cat, though hers was an expression of mockery rather than respect.

'You are too kind, sir,' Cat said.

I closed the door of my bedroom. I was very weary. My limbs ached. I was tempted to lie on the bed. Just for half an hour, I told myself, and it will make a new man of me.

Instead, I forced myself to throw off my coat and sit at the dressing table. I lifted off the periwig and set it on the stand. It was dusty from the road. I stared at my haggard face in the glass.

Without the wig, the fire's scarring on the side of my head and face was as naked to my sight as a newborn babe to the midwife. What did it matter? In the schedule of my present troubles and discontents, it seemed an entry of minor importance.

Cat, I thought, then Chiffinch, then God alone knew what lay ahead of me. Unbidden, a vision of Lady Quincy's face rose in my mind.

There was a knock on the door, and the image of Lady Quincy vanished, to be replaced by Margaret with a jug of warm water. She set down the jug. She was about to withdraw when I stopped her.

'Close the door for a moment.' I waited until she had obeyed. 'Has there been a letter for me?'

'No, sir.'

I had hoped that I might hear from George Milcote about the missing servant, Matthew Gorse. 'You mentioned a friend of yours the other day – one who helps with the distribution of the *Gazette*. Martha, was it?'

Margaret smoothed her apron. 'Dorcas, sir. I hope there's nothing wrong – I'm sure she wouldn't—'

'The *Gazette* has a great lack of trustworthy distributors. You said Dorcas needs help, I think?'

'Why yes, sir, they all do.'

I put my finger to my lips. 'Can you trust her?'

She nodded. But her eyes were anxious.

'If she can keep her mouth shut, I can give her a chance to earn a little money and lighten her load at the same time. Does she share her bed with anyone?'

Margaret looked so alarmed that I burst out laughing. 'I mean her virtue no harm. I only want to know whether she lives alone.'

'She sleeps in a loft above a stable, sir. By herself, except when her boy has leave. He's in Tangier, with his ship.'

'Mistress Hakesby needs somewhere to stay for a few days,' I said. 'Her face isn't well known but there are people searching for her, and they may look for her here. Could she stay with Dorcas?'

'I can ask,' Margaret said doubtfully. 'She's not one to blab, I know that. And she'd starve if she lost her job.'

'Don't mention me. Make up some story with Mistress Hakesby – she could be a maidservant with the bailiffs after her, perhaps. Or she's run away from her master to preserve her virtue, and he's pursuing her.'

'Is it dangerous?'

'There should be no danger to Dorcas or you or anyone else. And if we can but change Mistress Hakesby's appearance a little more than she already has, I see no reason why she shouldn't go about the city, particularly if she had a role to play. For example, if she were hired to distribute the *Gazette*, to help Dorcas with her round.'

For a long moment Margaret and I stared at each other in silence. The best place to hide is under the light.

# CHAPTER TWENTY-NINE

SHORTLY AFTER TEN o'clock, I presented myself at the Privy Stairs. I had come in haste from the Savoy, and I was hot from the exertion as well as sore from the riding. I was brought at once to Chiffinch, whom I found on his feet already and not in the best of tempers.

'You're late, Marwood,' he said, interrupting my attempt to apologize. 'Come with me.'

He brushed past me and took me through a doorway I had never passed through before into a strange warren of half-finished building works. Here were the private lodgings of the most favoured courtiers, and the royal apartments themselves. Walking swiftly, never at a loss for his direction, he turned left and right, and left again, went upstairs and downstairs, across courts and into hallways. We passed a number of guards, who saluted Chiffinch and opened doors for us. It seemed to me that they did not meet my eyes. It was as if I were invisible to them.

In one apartment, two richly dressed courtiers were standing talking by the window, their heads close together.

Beyond them was the grey, sluggish river. In the failing light, the water was as dull as old fish scales. They glanced towards us as we entered. I recognized them. So did Chiffinch, who muttered something under his breath.

'Your grace,' he said, bowing. 'My lord.'

I bowed even lower. The Duke of Buckingham and Lord Rochester nodded to Chiffinch. For a moment the Duke's eyes lingered on me. He was a handsome man with dark, strongly marked eyebrows and a moustache so thin and fair it was barely visible. His face was cold and unsmiling. Then Rochester whispered in his ear. He burst out laughing, and they turned back to the window. Chiffinch and I hurried on.

Then at last we were back in the open. He had brought us to the bowling green beside the river to the south of the palace, towards Westminster. A small flight of stairs descended to a shallow jetty projecting into the river. The tide was high and the water lapped against it. I had seen these stairs from the river but I had never landed here, for their use was strictly controlled. They were rarely used, unlike the public stairs and Privy Stairs to the north.

A lantern burned there, and two manservants waited, not in livery, and both with swords by their sides. A boat with a pair of oars was moored alongside, with the rower waiting. There was a lantern at the stern but it wasn't alight.

A sense of foreboding crept over me. Chiffinch went forward, bowed and crouched to speak in a low voice to the man in the boat. One of the servants barred my way with his body. His face was impassive; there was no hostility in his bearing. Then, at a word from Chiffinch, he stood aside to let me pass.

'Sit in the stern, and be quick about it,' Chiffinch said to me. As I passed, he snatched off my hat, and that was when I knew for sure who I had to deal with.

It is never easy to climb gracefully into a small boat, and I lowered myself with caution, holding on to a bollard as I transferred my weight from the land to the water. Nevertheless the boat rocked violently under my weight, and almost pitched me into the water.

The rower chuckled.

Clutching the sides of the boat, I sat under the lantern at the stern. Chiffinch tossed my hat on to my lap and stepped back.

One of the servants cast off; the other pushed the boat away from the jetty. Dusk was falling but it was brighter on the water. The rower brought the bow round and set out towards the centre of the river with long, slow strokes. When we were fifty yards or so clear of the land, he raised his head. I recognized the dark and ugly features of the King.

'Your Majesty.' I bobbed my head in an apology for a low bow.

'Enough of that, Marwood,' the King said. 'If you're not careful you'll capsize us.'

I had seen him on the river often before, for sailing was one of his passions, and he and the Duke of York frequently raced their yachts against each other. But I had never seen him like this, without even a single attendant and looking no better than a common waterman. He was dressed not as a private gentleman but in a rough coat and breeches. He had taken off his periwig and pulled his hat low.

'Edward Alderley,' he said, using his oars to keep the boat's bows into the incoming tide. 'I hoped we had seen the last of that cursed family. Nothing but trouble in both life and death. I know what you've told Chiffinch about the discovery of the body and what came after, but I want you to tell it to me.' He paused, holding up his hand with a great ring on it. 'I want you to tell me everything. Think carefully. Not just what you told Chiffinch. Everything.'

Everything? I had no time to think what to include, and what to leave out, no time to calculate consequences and implications. I began to speak, trying to sort my thoughts as I went.

I told the King of my enquiries at Clarendon House and elsewhere into Alderley's death. I told him about Alderley's lodgings, his sudden wealth and his possible plans for marriage, and about the discovery of the broken box, which I believed Alderley had stolen from my Lord Clarendon. I told him of the man called the Bishop who had been Alderley's companion, and who appeared to be engaged in orchestrating the protests in Piccadilly against the former chancellor. I even told him that I feared the Bishop might be connected to the Duke of Buckingham.

I hesitated here, reluctant to continue because it meant inculpating myself. But the King stirred on the thwart and said with a touch of irritation that he had no time for fools who tried to keep secrets: he would thank me to tell him everything I knew.

Chiffinch, I said, had ordered me to move the corpse away from the grounds of Clarendon House. Accordingly, Mr Milcote and I had transported it to a field near Tyburn with the help of the servant who had originally found it in the well. But there was a problem: the servant had vanished yesterday morning. Milcote had found evidence that the man had previously been in Alderley's employ, though I could not begin to guess what this might mean.

'And so,' the King said, 'we come to the Lovett woman.'

Because I had no alternative, I told him about Cat: how she had been working for Mr Hakesby, the architect, on the pavilion at Clarendon House, and it was widely believed she had murdered her cousin. Mr Chiffinch had received an anonymous letter to that effect. Alderley's address had been discovered in her box. I paused and for an instant I was sorely tempted to make a clean breast of everything, to tell the King that I believed her innocent, despite the evidence against her, and that at this very moment I was sheltering her from the constables.

But I found I could not. The words stuck in my throat, awkward as a fishbone and perhaps as liable to lead to my being choked to death.

The more I talked, the more afraid I felt. Here was I, talking to the King of England, the two of us quite alone. I was discussing the private affairs of Lord Clarendon, until a few weeks ago his most powerful minister and his most trusted councillor. I was all but accusing the Duke of Buckingham of involvement in the case; the Duke was not only the cherished friend of the King's childhood but he was reputed to be his most favoured courtier, not least because he knew how to make the King laugh; he was also one of the richest men in the land.

The King heard me out until I stumbled into silence. To my surprise, I heard his soft laugh in the gathering gloom. 'Now, Marwood,' he said, 'before you dizzy me with speculation, tell me what Chiffinch doesn't know. You met my Lady Quincy the other day, in the Banqueting House while

I was touching the sick. Remind me what she wanted of you.'

I shivered, for it was growing colder and colder on the water, with the breeze stiffening as the light went. He must know already what Lady Quincy wanted. Perhaps he was testing me – or perhaps he was testing my lady.

I said, 'She asked me if I knew where to find Catherine Lovett, sir. She's her niece by her marriage to the late Henry Alderley, if you remember.'

I sensed his growing restlessness. The King was not a patient man. Perhaps kings rarely were, though I had seen another side of him when he was touching scores of people for the King's Evil: he had sat as still as a graven image on his throne, hour after hour, while the drone of prayers filled the air, repeating themselves for each sufferer.

'She desired me to warn Mistress Lovett that Edward Alderley had found out her direction and meant to do her great harm,' I went on. 'She advised Mistress Lovett to flee. I . . . I did as she asked.'

'Did you meet Mistress Lovett in person?' The words were as sharp as a falling axe. 'Or did you write to her?'

'I met her, sir, at the New Exchange early on Saturday evening, and I passed on my lady's warning.'

'How did she respond?'

'She was angry. She . . . was reluctant to leave Mr Hakesby, too. She is betrothed to him and helps him in his work. But she seems to have heeded the warning. Afterwards, I learned that she supped with Mr Hakesby and his draughtsman. She went back to her lodging and, later that evening, she went out again, alone, and did not return. When they came to arrest her on Monday morning, there was no trace of her.'

'Where might she go? Assuming she went of her own choice.'

I cleared my throat. 'It is hard even to form an opinion, sir. But she's a young woman of resource, I can vouch for that.'

'And more than capable of violence, by all accounts. Chiffinch has told me the evidence against her. She disappeared on Saturday evening. Alderley was last seen an hour or two earlier, at his lodgings.'

'Yes, sir.'

'So if Alderley was murdered, and he almost certainly was, then she's the obvious suspect.'

I bowed my head. Cat was not just the obvious suspect, she was also far and away the most convenient one. A murderous quarrel between cousins, neither of whom was of much importance, would be so much easier for everyone to deal with than a murky intrigue that touched the great ones of our world, such as Buckingham, Lord Clarendon and the Duke of York. That was why the King had wanted the body moved from the pavilion to a safely neutral spot. He was nothing if not pragmatic.

Then, like a fool, I said, 'Sir, I believe Mistress Lovett is innocent.'

'Why?'

'The evidence against her is circumstantial. There's nothing to say that she was in Lord Clarendon's pavilion with Mr Alderley, and it's hard to see how she could have entered it. Lady Quincy's warning to her explains why she fled.'

'That means nothing. My advisers believe her guilty, and they are men of experience who have examined the evidence.' The King glanced up at the sky. He dug an oar into the water and brought the boat round and began to row back to the palace. 'Tomorrow morning,' he said, 'you're to go to Cradle Alley at six o'clock.'

I stared blankly at him. 'And do what, sir?'

'You'll escort Lady Quincy to Cambridge and perhaps elsewhere.'

'But, sir—' I began, not to object (for I could hardly do that) but simply from surprise.

'You may be away for some days,' he interrupted. 'Follow her commands in all things. I shall wish for a most particular account of what passes, of what she does, where she goes, what she says. Find Chiffinch, and he will give you what you need.'

I dared not ask why Lady Quincy was going to Cambridge. There was a finality about the King's last words; he had finished talking to me.

We rowed the rest of the way to the Bowling Green stairs in a silence broken only by the lapping of the water and the creaking of the rowlocks. There were still three men waiting under the lantern on the jetty. But Chiffinch had gone. He had been replaced by a taller man wrapped in a dark cloak, who stood with his back to the water.

The King brought us alongside the stairs. 'Marwood,' he said softly, 'if you believe this young woman is innocent, despite everything that speaks of her guilt, you must bring me the evidence to prove it.'

The servants crouched and held the boat steady against the masonry while he climbed out. I followed less gracefully. One of the servants took my arm and urged me towards the entrance of the Stone Gallery, which was the public way to the Bowling Green.

On my way I passed the tall stranger. He was in the act of turning towards the King, just as I was bowing to His Majesty. The lantern was behind the newcomer and I glimpsed his profile, sharp as the face on a newly minted coin. It was James, Duke of York, the King's brother.

At the Back Stairs, I asked for Chiffinch and was brought up to his closet. He gave me a purse containing thirty pounds in mixed gold and silver for my expenses on the journey. 'I'll need a schedule of all disbursements,' he said, 'and if my lady offers to pay for anything, then well and good, you must let her.'

'Should I hire a horse or take one from the stables here?' The very thought of riding made my limbs ache even harder than they were already.

'Lady Quincy's people will see to all that. Just go to her house in the morning, and do as she tells you.'

He waved his hand to dismiss me.

'Sir – have the prisoners spoken?'

'Hakesby and Brennan, you mean?' Chiffinch snorted. 'No one's got a word of any sort out of Hakesby. I think he's gone mad – he'll spend the rest of his days in Bedlam, if he's not careful. As for Brennan – would you believe it, he's gone down with fever, and the difficulty is to stop him talking. But there's no making sense of anything he says.'

That was a stroke of luck. Brennan was one person who knew where Cat had gone.

'I'm told the fellow's complaining of cold,' Chiffinch said. 'Keeps asking if his cloak's arrived yet. Who does he think we are? His servants? Mind you, Marwood, it's certainly getting chilly in here. Tell them to send in another scuttle of coals on your way out.'

I left him and went back to my lodgings. I took a hackney, partly because I was so weary and partly because I was carrying so much money on my person.

Sam opened the door to my knock. Cat was no longer in the house, he told me – she had gone to Dorcas, Margaret's friend.

'All well, sir – she's glad of the help with the *Gazette* and gladder still of the money Mistress Lovett will give her.'

He seemed unusually merry – so much so that at first I wondered whether he had been drinking again. Even the news that he and Margaret would have to work half the night preparing my clothes against the journey tomorrow did not dent his good spirits.

But it wasn't ale that had elevated Sam's mood. It was the business with Cat, with its air of risk and secrecy. I had noticed this before about him: whereas any person of sense was made unhappy by danger, he by contrast tended to become more cheerful in times of peril.

I did not get to bed until nearly two o'clock in the morning. When I did, I found that I couldn't sleep. I lay on my back and stared up at the darkness. The King and Duke of York, Clarendon and Buckingham, were so far above me and my world that they might have been distant planets revolving in the night sky, quite beyond my terrestrial comprehension. So I thought about Cat Lovett and Lady Quincy instead until my head hurt and my heart ached.

# CHAPTER THIRTY

IT WAS STILL dark when I knocked on the door of the house in Cradle Alley. Sam had accompanied me in the hackney and waited with my portmanteau. A servant took my bag and showed me into the gloomy and plainly furnished chamber where Lady Quincy had interviewed me on my last visit. He brought biscuits and a draught of small beer. He would call me, he said, when my lady was ready.

I sat down and made myself eat and drink. I was neither hungry nor thirsty but I knew it might be a while before I had another chance of refreshment. Beyond the closed door, footsteps clattered down the stairs. There were snatches of conversation in muffled voices. Heavy objects scraped and bumped on the floor.

The servant reappeared, bearing a sword and a holstered pistol. He asked if I had brought my own weapons and, when I said no, he gave me the ones he had brought. 'My lady wishes it,' he said.

My next visitor was Lady Quincy herself, already in her travelling cloak. 'Thank you for agreeing to escort us, sir,' she said with unexpected civility. 'Would you sit with us in the coach?'

Nothing pleased me more. My limbs were still aching from my unaccustomed riding yesterday. I followed her into the hall, which was full of people. A coach drawn by six great horses, matched greys, was waiting in the street before the door. The coachman was already on the box, and the postillion mounted on the leading horse on the nearside. Another servant was standing behind, beside his horse. I saw to my relief it was a glass coach, with doors and windows, rather than the old-fashioned leather flaps that kept out light and let in draughts. It was heavy-built, for long-distance travel.

I had never travelled in anything like such style and comfort before. Lady Quincy was helped into the coach. I waited at the door until she had settled herself on the seat facing forwards. She beckoned me to join her and indicated that I should sit diagonally opposite her by the window.

For a wild moment I thought that perhaps we were to travel alone together in the swaying interior of the vehicle. Then I heard steps behind me. The servant helped in a thin-faced maid, who avoided looking at me. She sat beside her mistress.

Then the servant lifted up the small figure of the boy Stephen. The maid thrust him on to the seat beside me. He huddled into the corner, his face invisible in the gloom apart from the whites of his eyes.

The door closed and the servant raised the steps. The coachman cracked his whip. The coach twitched and then edged forward, gradually gathering speed. No one spoke.

We made good speed, for the roads were still dry after the heat of the summer, and the six horses kept up a steady pace that made short work of the miles. We had little conversation, for Lady Quincy was lost in her thoughts and spent most of the journey staring out of the window at the passing country. I had enough to think about myself. Cat Lovett was much on my mind. Would she be safe with Dorcas? Why had I been such a fool as to help her? What on earth would I do with her in the long run?

Stephen slept for much of the time, or at least closed his eyes and withdrew into himself. The great swellings on his neck threatened his delicate features: it was as if scrofula were a species of worm that was burrowing beneath the skin of the poor child and gradually reshaping him into a monster. My own scars seemed trivial by comparison, and I felt ashamed of my self-pity.

Cambridge was more than fifty miles from London, too far for the coach-and-six to carry us with ease in a single day. We lay at Puckeridge that night, where we took rooms at the Falcon. At the inn, the country people pointed and sniggered at Stephen, both for the colour of his skin and the swellings beneath it, until I put a stop to it.

Lady Quincy supped in her bedchamber. I was about to sit at the host's table downstairs when her maid came to ask me to join her mistress. The curtains were drawn and the candles were lit. She had changed her gown. We talked of trivial things while we ate. But when we were done, she sent the servants away.

'Well, sir,' she said, toying with an apple, rolling it about like a ball on the tablecloth, 'so you are sent to watch over me?'

'I'm here at the King's command, madam, and to do as you bid.'

'And to report to him where I go and what I do?'

'Yes, madam.'

She started to peel the apple. 'You're an honest man, at least.'

'You'd not have believed me if I'd said otherwise.'

'Then if not honest, at least intelligent.'

That was suspiciously close to flattery. I said, 'May I ask what your plans are?'

'Tomorrow we should reach Cambridge in the afternoon. I should like you to take a letter to a gentleman who lives there. At Jerusalem.'

Her mention of the name made me start. I said, as casually as I was able, 'Jerusalem, madam?'

'The college. The gentleman in question is one of the fellows there.'

'Of course.' I sensed danger; there must be more to this expedition than merely delivering a letter; the business must somehow be connected with Dr Wren's plan that I had found in Hakesby's notebook. I said, 'I hear that they plan to build a new chapel at Jerusalem.'

'Really?' Lady Quincy sounded weary. 'These colleges are always building something or other – it is surprising they find any time at all for learning.'


The following morning, when we left the Falcon, Lady Quincy gave me her purse and asked me to pay what we owed.

The landlord, who had profited handsomely from our visit, could not have been more civil. As he was counting out the money I gave him, he asked me if I had seen my friend.

'My friend? Who?'

'The gentleman who stopped for breakfast, sir. He's bound

for Cambridge like yourselves, but he was pressed for time and couldn't linger. I wasn't sure whether he would find you and my lady before he went.'

'I wonder who it could have been,' I said. 'So he's gone, has he?'

'He and his servant rode on when their horses were ready. They're travelling post so it won't take them long to get to Cambridge.'

My alarm was growing. 'What was he like?'

'Tall man – a northern gentleman by his voice. I can't rightly tell you much more than that. The servant was a big man, too. In more ways than one.' The landlord sketched a great belly with his hands. 'I pity his horse.'

'Does the man carry an old cavalry sword?'

'That's him, sir,' said the landlord. 'So you do know them. I told his master you were putting up at the Rose tonight so I daresay he'll call on you there.'

'I daresay.'

I went upstairs, wondering which of us the Bishop and his servant were following: Lady Quincy or myself. And why would the Duke of Buckingham have sent his men to follow either of us?

Lady Quincy had asked me to send the postillion ahead to command rooms at the Rose Tavern. We dined on the road and reached Cambridge in the early afternoon. Despite a few fine buildings, the town was of no great size, low-lying and poorly paved.

I had not told Lady Quincy about the Bishop – this I had decided to keep to myself until I knew more of what it meant. If she could have secrets, then so could I.

At the tavern, she called me up to her chamber while her maid, Ann, was unpacking her bags. Stephen was fetching and carrying as the maid ordered. He was a compact boy, neat in his movements.

She gave me the letter she had mentioned last night. It was addressed to the Reverend Mr Warley at Jerusalem College. 'Take great care of it,' she said. 'Don't give it to anyone apart from Mr Warley. And as soon as possible, if you please.'

Despite Lady Quincy's last words, I lingered in the taproom and called for a draught of beer, for my throat was dry from the dust of the road. That was not my only reason. I have a dislike of being used as a cat's paw, without understanding the business I am employed in. The King, Chiffinch and Lady Quincy expected me to serve them with blind loyalty, as a dog serves his master. Loyalty was one thing, I thought, but blindness was quite another, close kin to folly.

The landlord was at his table, reckoning up a set of accounts. It was a quiet time of day for the tavern, and he was happy enough to take a glass of beer with me. He was obliging, too, and for the same reason as his colleague at Puckeridge had been: our party was spending a great deal of money with him.

'I wonder if you could satisfy my curiosity,' I said. 'I'm to call on a gentleman at Jerusalem College, a man I've never met, and I'd be glad to have some idea of him beforehand. His name's Warley.'

'Mr Warley? Yes, indeed. A gentleman of high repute. I've known him since he was but a boy. Local man, sir. I can just remember his grandfather.'

'His family comes from Cambridge?' I asked.

'No – from the Fens, north of here. They have an estate

228

at Hitcham St Martin. It'll all come to Mr Warley one day, I suppose.'

I realized the landlord was a man who enjoyed gossiping, so I settled down to make the most of it. 'Mr Warley is the heir?'

'Yes – mind you, it's not a large estate and they say it's much embarrassed. His grandmother is living at the house, and has the benefit of it for her lifetime by her husband's will, as well as most of the income. But that's not likely to be long, as the poor lady is ailing. Lungs, probably. It's the damp air in the Fens, you see, sir. It kills off the old people.'

I drained my beer. The landlord, sensing I was about to leave, tried to delay me.

'It's possible, of course, that Mr Warley will put in a bailiff to run the place when he takes possession.'

'So he can stay in Cambridge?' I asked idly, looking for my stick. 'At Jerusalem?'

'Or elsewhere. He's in holy orders, of course, like all the college fellows are. So he may get preferment that takes him away altogether.' He paused and then added impressively, 'The family has connections who can make interest for him. A word in the right ear, and Mr Warley could end up a bishop with a coach-and-six and a seat in the House of Lords.'

'Connections?' I said. 'It's always useful to have connections. Who?'

The landlord gave me a wink. 'I don't know for sure, sir. It's just what they say. He was a very young man when they made him a fellow. A young man with friends in high places, perhaps.'

I probed further, but I could get nothing more out of the landlord on that subject. But the mention of bishops had reminded me of another thing. 'Would you tell me privately if anyone enquires about us while we're here?'

Suddenly wary, the landlord squinted at me. 'Nothing that will bring my house into ill-repute, I trust?'

'No,' I said shortly. 'A private matter that doesn't concern anyone else in the least. Now tell me the way to Jerusalem.'

# CHAPTER THIRTY-ONE

I LEFT THE Rose soon afterwards. The tavern overlooked the bustle of Market Hill, which was packed with
the stalls of traders. I had expected to find more students in
Cambridge, but I learned from the landlord that the
Michaelmas Term had not yet begun so the town was quieter
than usual.

I made my way through the crowd with some difficulty
and followed his directions into the streets on the far side.
Jerusalem was on the edge of the town. I entered the college
by way of an archway set in a line of railings, which led into
an open court with a collection of buildings on three sides.
They were largely of brick, old and soot-stained.

The porter at the gate asked my business, and I asked for
Mr Warley.

He stared up at me. He was a small, squat fellow with long
grey hair and beetling brows well-framed for frowning. 'Not
one of ours, are you, sir? I never forget the face of a gentleman
who matriculated here, however many years pass.'

'Indeed. Where can I find Mr Warley?'

He pointed to a doorway in the left-hand corner of the court. 'Through there. Mr Warley's chambers are in the court beyond, on the far side. Second door from the left.'

The porter's directions took me through a passage that smelled of cooking into another court, larger than the first, where somebody was talking in a loud, angry voice. I lingered in the passage, keeping to a patch of shadow. Two men were standing not far away, their backs to me. They were looking up at a low and dilapidated building to the left.

'. . . it's all very well but we can't take your word for it.' The speaker was a heavy, stooping man; he had sloping shoulders like a bull's; he wore a gown that had once been black and was now a dark and grubby shade of green. 'Besides, until the money's here, we can't tear the whole place down, just on your whim. We have chambers for undergraduates in there and—'

The other man, who was small and slight, said something in a softer voice.

This led to another explosion. 'I know they've been empty for a few years. Our admissions aren't what they were before the war. But numbers will improve one day, God willing.'

The smaller man shook his head and made another inaudible remark.

'Of course repairs will cost money,' roared the first man. 'But it would be folly to let the place fall down for want of a few pence. East Building has sheltered scholars for nigh on three hundred years. Your chapel will cost a hundred times as much, a thousand times, and it will give shelter to no one. If you ever see it built, it will do nothing but encourage ungodly rituals and Papist practices. Our founder must be turning in his grave.'

The other raised his voice at last. 'We shall have the money to build it. I have a promise of it.'

'From whom?'

'I can't say at present.'

'Then it's no more than fairy gold.'

'It will come. I have given my word.'

'You're hardly in a position to find the money yourself, I believe.'

The bull-man was smiling in a way that showed that his words were designed to taunt. The smaller man raised his arm, and for a moment I thought he was going to strike the other. But he restrained himself.

'So we must trust you, must we?' said his tormentor. 'We must tear this college apart simply because you say so? Well, sir, consider this: we may have been forced to accept you into our fellowship by royal mandate, but you can't expect us to take every word you say as gospel.'

'When you see the model that the architects are making, Dr Burbrough, you and others will understand. This chapel will make Jerusalem the glory of Cambridge.'

'The glory?' bellowed the bull. 'More likely the laughing stock.'

They glared at each other. I decided that I had heard enough. I left the shadows and came out into the sunshine.

'Good day, sirs – could you direct me to Mr Warley's rooms?'

The smaller man turned towards me. His face was flushed with anger, and he was breathing rapidly. 'I'm Warley,' he snapped.

'May I speak privately to you?'

Warley glanced at the other man. 'Of course,' he said in a tight, hard voice. 'I'm quite at leisure.'

233

Burbrough's colour darkened. 'By God, you've not heard the last of this.'

'I fear you're right, sir.'

Burbrough marched away, striding with heavy footsteps across the court towards a staircase in the far corner. Warley stared after him.

'My name's Marwood, sir. I come from Whitehall, and I've a letter for you.'

He turned to me, his head on one side, his eyes widening a fraction as he took in my scars. 'What's this?' he said brusquely.

'When you've seen the letter, you'll know.'

'Very well.' His dark eyes moved over me. 'You'd better come to my rooms.'

We walked across the court. Warley was a neat man with darting movements and a silk gown that fluttered as he walked. His lips were tightly compressed, perhaps with anger.

'From Whitehall, you say?'

'Yes.'

'You are employed there?'

'At the Board of Red Cloth.' Glancing back, I went on, 'You intend to build the chapel there, sir?'

Warley threw me a suspicious glance. 'Yes.'

'I understand that the architects are Dr Wren and Mr Hakesby.'

He stopped. 'But how can you know that? It's not public knowledge yet, or it shouldn't be.'

'I saw Mr Hakesby two days ago.'

'Where?'

'In London. I've also seen a sketch for the chapel's design.'

'He showed it to you?' The anger was gone, replaced by

234

an enthusiasm that was almost boyish in its intensity. 'It will be such a fine thing when it's finished. The most elegant in Cambridge. So you know Mr Hakesby. How does he do?'

'Not too well at present, sir,' I said. 'But I'm sure he will be better soon.'

'His ague is bad? Poor man – it comes and it goes, but he manages wonderfully. I know Dr Wren thinks very highly of him.'

'So the new chapel will fill the whole of that side of the court?'

'Not exactly.' Warley waved at the old building. 'Though we'll start by pulling down East Building over there. It's been standing empty for years, and in any case it was always mean and inconvenient. Look at it, sir – how that old fool Burbrough can think it worth saving is beyond all comprehension.'

I saw Warley's point. The low, steep-roofed range was propped up with buttresses. The brickwork was thick with ivy, dusty after the dry summer. Several tiles were missing from the roof, and the glass in some of the small windows was broken.

'In the place of that shameful ruin,' Warley went on, 'we shall have an open arcade the entire width of the court, with a fine new gallery for the Master above it, all faced with stone and with a pediment above. We shall have a clock, perhaps, and a cupola set on top to crown all. I would like a cupola myself but Dr Wren is not convinced. What do you think?'

'Definitely with a cupola,' I said, thinking that all this would cost a great deal of money, and that Burbrough's doubts were understandable.

'And through the arcade we shall be able to walk directly into our gardens, which lie behind. And then, here, in the centre' – Warley spread out his arms to show me – 'we shall have the chapel itself. But its entrance will be most cunningly set within the arcade so it does not break the run of it or the gallery above. Indeed, sir, it will be the neatest and most convenient thing you ever saw.'

'I couldn't help overhearing some of your conversation,' I said. 'Not everyone shares your enthusiasm for the scheme.'

Warley walked on, his excitement draining away. 'Dr Burbrough is the Vice Master. He's old-fashioned in all things.'

'In politics, too?' I suggested. 'Religion?'

'Yes.' Warley glanced at me, and I knew he had taken my meaning. He hesitated, prudence fighting a losing battle against his anger with Burbrough. 'He got his fellowship under the Commonwealth,' he burst out. 'If you ask me, he's a Presbyterian at heart, and with Calvinist and republican leanings. And he dislikes me intensely into the bargain.'

'Because of the royal mandate?'

'You've heard about that too? You're well informed. Yes. It's true that I wasn't elected to the fellowship in the usual way. There happened to be a vacancy and I was selected for it by royal mandate. In fact, the Master was brought in by royal mandate as well. The crown has a perfect right to do that, just as it has the right to vary our statutes or command the university to award honorary degrees. But Burbrough hates it when the King interferes with the university, and when it's his own college it's even worse.' Warley raised his chin and added defensively, 'The King is perfectly entitled to exercise his mandate if he wishes. Don't you agree, sir?'

'Naturally.'

'Jerusalem was a hotbed of Puritan dissent during the late

disturbances,' Warley went on. 'The university as a whole was. God be thanked, that's all changed since the King came into his own again. But there are still a few men like Burbrough that linger like a bad smell from Cromwell's time.'

Warley went into the staircase and led me up to a sitting room on the first floor.

'Smith?' he called as he went in.

The windows overlooked the court on one side and a secluded garden on the other. It was a pleasant, airy room, though the furniture was scuffed and old-fashioned. The floorboards were covered with rush matting. There was a solitary rectangle of Turkey carpet, faded and threadbare, before the fireplace.

'Will you take a glass of wine, sir?' Warley didn't wait for an answer but raised his voice again. 'Smith? The Madeira, if you please, and two glasses.'

There was no reply, apart from a soft, broken whimper, like an animal in pain.

Warley muttered under his breath. He flung open a door beyond the fireplace, which stood ajar. He stopped on the threshold. 'God's breath—'

I crossed the room and looked over his shoulder. The doorway led to a closet furnished plainly with book-laden shelves, a tall cupboard and a desk scattered with papers. An elbow chair lay on its side against the wall. An old man lay sprawled beside it.

'What mischief's this?' Warley said, clutching at the jamb.

I pushed past him and knelt down. The man's thin grey hair was matted with blood on the left-hand side of his scalp, and it had streaked the skin of his face. He moaned as I touched him.

'Smith!' Warley cried. 'What happened? Did you fall?'

The servant continued to whimper. I put my arms under him and lifted him into a sitting position on the floor. He was as light as a child; I felt the bones under his skin.

I glanced up at Warley. 'Pick up the chair.'

He obeyed. Between us, we picked Smith up and lowered him into the chair. He slumped into its embrace, with his head lolling to one side. Warley fired questions, a rapid and almost incoherent fusillade. Smith was incapable of replying.

'Find something to stop the blood.' I ordered. 'Linen. A shirt, perhaps.'

Warley stared wildly at me. 'What?'

'A shirt,' I snapped.

He left the room. I looked about me. The papers on the desk were disordered, and some of them had been pushed to the floor. I noticed a box tucked into the corner beyond the desk. It was askew, and a padlock lay on the floor beside it, partly concealed by the side of the cupboard. I picked it up. It was locked, and still attached to a hasp that was bent out of shape.

Warley came back with a shirt over his arm.

'Press it against the wound on your servant's head to stop the bleeding.'

He obeyed, glancing down at the padlock in my hand. 'By God, sir – have they opened the box?'

I tugged out the strongbox into the centre of the room. There was a metallic scraping sound as I did so. A poker had been lying on the floor behind it, and I guessed it had been used to lever off the padlock. The box was a simple affair bound with two strips of iron. The padlock had been its only security, enough to deter a prying servant but not a serious thief. I lifted the lid. There were papers inside and a leather bag.

'Can you tell what's missing?'

'Wait,' Warley said. 'We must find the Master, the Dean, and—'

'In a moment.'

He pushed between me and the box, forcing me to step back. 'I don't know who you are, and—'

'Then look at this letter,' I said.

'But for all I know, you're in league with—'

'Enough, sir,' I said, tiring of his objections. I took the shirt from him, folded it and held it against Smith's head, which was already bleeding much less. 'Forgive me if I seem rude, but there may well be more to this than simple theft. You must find out what's been taken. But first, read this.'

He took the letter and broke the seal. Lady Quincy's letter was short – no more than a few lines, though I couldn't read them from where I stood. I was taking a chance, for I had no idea of the contents. He read it quickly, folded it and thrust it into his pocket.

'So this lady, sir,' he said. 'My Lady Quincy – she says she travels on the King's business?'

'Yes. As do I.' I spoke with all the assurance I could muster. 'She asks me to call on her.'

'At the Rose Tavern. As soon as we can. But before we go, sir, we must help your poor servant. And I want to know if anything's missing from this box.'

Warley gave me the shirt. He knelt beside the box and emptied it. The leather bag was heavy, and its contents shifted as he lifted it. Almost certainly money – so this was not the work of an ordinary thief. I was reminded of the search at

Alderley's apartments in Fallow Street: the impression it had given of someone searching for a particular item, of someone who wasn't interested in the usual fruits of robbery.

'A folder of papers is gone.'

'What was in it?'

He shook his head. 'Forgive me, sir, but that's none of your business.'

'Sir,' whispered the servant. He was looking from his master to me, his face puzzled. 'Sir . . .'

'What happened?' Warley demanded. 'Who did this?'

'I didn't see his face properly. He knocked – I opened the door to him – and he hit me.'

'You must have seen him,' Warley said angrily.

'Only his gown. The sleeve was over my face when he dragged me in here. That's when he hit me again.'

Smith covered his eyes with his hands and began to weep the tired, helpless tears of old age. They mingled with the dried blood that had trickled from his scalp.

'Gown?' Warley said. 'What sort of gown?'

'MA, sir.'

'You're sure he wasn't a member of this college?'

'Yes, sir.'

'When did this happen?' I asked.

'While the gentlemen were having dinner in hall.'

I turned to Warley. 'Did you come back here after dinner?'

He shook his head. 'No – Dr Burbrough and I fell to disputing about the new chapel, and we went out to inspect the East Building after dinner. We had been talking – arguing, I'm afraid – for some little time when you came upon us.'

I felt an unwilling admiration for the stranger in the MA

gown. He had put his faith in his academic dress, knowing that the gown made him unremarkable in this setting. He had chosen his time with care, when the fellows were at dinner. He had been bold, too, entering in broad daylight.

'He can't have been one of us,' Warley said. 'All of us in residence were at dinner. The porter must have admitted him – I shall ask him at once.'

A man of impulse, he took a few steps towards the door. I laid a hand on his arm to detain him. 'Are there other gates in and out of the college apart from the main one on the other side of the hall?'

'Yes,' Warley said. 'Three others. But we pride ourselves on our security. The college and entire gardens are surrounded by a high wall.'

'Do porters watch the other gates?'

'Not usually. But they're kept locked. Only the fellows have keys.' He turned to the window and pointed. 'There's one down there.'

'And your key, sir?'

'Why, it's on the ring with the others. Smith, you had them while I was out – where are they?'

'On the mantelpiece, sir. Where you left them.'

Warley stepped quickly into the sitting room and went over to the fireplace. 'Still there,' he said over his shoulder.

At my suggestion, Warley gave the servant a glass of the Madeira intended for us. Leaving the man to recover, we went downstairs.

'Poor fellow,' Warley said. 'He isn't usually here at this hour, but he started late today.'

'In the normal course of things, your rooms would have been empty?'

Warley nodded. He looked worried. His temperament was mercurial, and his moods showed on his face.

'Which suggests,' I said as we walked across the lawn, 'that whoever did this knew the ways of this college.'

'This place seems so tranquil from the outside.' He glanced at me. 'Rational and benevolent in its ways, far from the troubles of the world beyond its gates. But believe me, sir, Jerusalem has its secrets.'

We made our way to the porter's lodge.

'Who has come through in the last few hours?' Warley asked. 'Anyone in an MA gown, for example?'

'This gentleman's the only one who's come into college since midday, sir,' the porter said, peering up at me through bushy eyebrows.

'Are you sure?' Warley said. 'Could you have been distracted? Or in the necessary house?'

'No, sir,' growled the porter, whose surliness was not confined to visitors. 'No one came through apart from him.' He jabbed his thumb at me.

'I've been robbed. If a stranger tries to leave, hold him here and send for me.'

I drew Warley aside. 'We should check the other gates.'

He looked sharply at me and for a moment I thought he would object. But he gave a nod and led me into the gardens behind the college buildings. There was a small gate set in the wall of the Master's Garden, but that was firmly locked and bolted. So was the second gate, which was on the other side of the college, beyond a large pond.

The third gate was in the separate Fellows' Garden. This was the one which Warley had shown me from the window of his sitting room. The garden was a pleasant place with gravelled walks set between low hedges, a shady arbour planted with vines, and another, much smaller pond shaded by a willow.

As we entered, Warley muttered under his breath and stopped sharply. 'That fool Burbrough's here.'

The older man was walking along a path. He was reading a book and appeared not to have noticed us. He did not look up as Warley and I crossed the garden to the gate in the wall. Like the other two gates had been, it was locked.

'The thief must still be here,' Warley said. 'Somewhere in college.'

'Perhaps.' Something black caught my eye at about shoulder level. I bent down. It was a scrap of cloth that had snagged on the head of the nail securing the latch. I lifted it off. 'Or perhaps not.'

As I spoke, I straightened up and turned. Dr Burbrough was standing by the pond and looking at us with his head lowered, like a bull about to charge.

'Doctor? A word with you, if you please.'

Warley walked quickly towards him, with me a pace behind.

'Changed your mind about that wretched chapel?' Burbrough said as we drew near. 'We are taught to believe in miracles.'

'Someone has broken into my rooms.'

'Really?' Burbrough sounded curiously unconcerned. 'When?'

'During dinner or afterwards, when I was talking to you.'

'Terrible. I blame the times we live in, sir – we've lost all sense of right and wrong in this country.'

'And Smith was attacked,' Warley said.

Burbrough's expression changed. 'What? Why was he there at dinnertime?'

'He was behind in his work.'

'What happened? Is he badly hurt?'

'He answered a knock at the door, and the intruder hit him — he lost consciousness, I believe. He's awake, but in a bad way. Bleeding from the head, and very shaken. It's a wonder he wasn't killed.'

'That is intolerable!' Burbrough said, his voice rising in volume with every syllable. 'A harmless old man, who's served the college loyally all his life. Why, he used to be my own servant. I must have known him for twenty years or more.'

He glared at us as if we had been responsible for the attack. He wheeled about with a flurry of his gown and stalked out of the garden.

I stared after him. How strange Burbrough's questions had been, I thought. Not merely the questions themselves, but the order in which they had been asked.

# CHAPTER THIRTY-TWO

I WATCHED LADY Quincy fail to work her magic on Mr Warley.

She was a woman who was aware of the men around her, and the men generally repaid the compliment, with interest. But Warley was different. He sat stiffly at the table in her sitting room at the Rose. He sipped his wine and nibbled a biscuit as if discharging a painful duty. The emotions he had shown so readily at Jerusalem – his anger with Burbrough, for example, his enthusiasm for the chapel plans – might never have existed. Perhaps he was still shaken by the events of the last hour. Or perhaps a man who did not care for the society of women.

Lady Quincy was sitting opposite him, while I was perched on a stool by the window, a witness but apart. She had sent her maid and the boy Stephen away, and the three of us were alone. I had had no opportunity to talk privately to her, so she had not heard about the stranger in the MA gown and the robbery at Jerusalem.

'Mr Warley,' she said, 'the care of a child was entrusted to your grandmother during the Interregnum.' Her voice had become crisp and businesslike. 'I have been sent to bring her to London.'

'Madam, it's true that my grandmother adopted a young cousin of hers into the family.' His own voice was chilly; I suspected he did not like being dictated to by a woman. 'She's perfectly happy with the arrangement, and so is the child. I see no reason to disturb it.'

'Really? On the contrary, sir, I hear that Mistress Warley is not in the best of health, and the child is becoming a burden to her. The child isn't well, either. She needs the sort of treatment you will not find in Hitcham St Martin or even Cambridge. Before we go any further, I advise you to read this.'

She took a letter from her pocket and slid it across the table towards him. He glanced at it. Frowning a little, she stared at him and he stared back. Then he took up the letter, broke the seal and unfolded it. The blood rushed to his face as he scanned the contents. He swallowed hard and looked up at her.

'This is from the King himself. It . . . It looks almost as if . . . as if it's in his own hand.'

'You hold your position at Jerusalem by royal mandate,' Lady Quincy said softly. 'In case you had forgotten.'

'I could hardly forget,' he said angrily. 'But my grandmother dotes on Frances. She will be distraught if she loses her.'

'I'm sure Mistress Warley wants what's best for the child.'

'We need time to consider. My grandmother will want to discuss whatever is planned with — with an adviser. She will want to write to him.'

'To Lord Clarendon, you mean?' she said. 'Oh, I think not.'

Yet again she had taken me by surprise. I could not help looking at her. She looked very handsome, I thought, sitting by the window with the late afternoon light on her face. I admired her poise, too, and the seemingly effortless way she was bending Warley to her will.

'It has nothing to do with him,' Lady Quincy was saying smoothly. 'It was the late Lady Clarendon who made the original request to your grandmother. The yearly payments for the child's maintenance came from her ladyship, and so did the promise of funds towards your new chapel at Jerusalem. But as you know, Lady Clarendon died last month. The arrangement concerning the child' – she hesitated – 'concerning *Frances* was a personal matter, between cousins, for your grandmother was born an Aylesbury, as her ladyship was. And Mistress Warley was well aware that her Lady Clarendon was acting on behalf of someone else.'

'Who?' Warley leaned forward, his face intent. 'I've often wondered.' He tapped the letter before him. 'Do you mean—'

'I mean nothing,' she interrupted. 'And you would be unwise to speculate.'

There was an awkward silence. God in heaven, I thought, what have I stumbled into? Is this child the King's bastard?

'All you need to know,' Lady Quincy went on, 'is that, in view of Lady Clarendon's death, Mistress Warley's health and Frances's condition, the King has decided that this would be the best time to make changes to the arrangement. He wants to bring the girl to London before winter sets in. And he has sent me to escort her.'

'Will she return to us?'

'That's not for me to say. Perhaps.'

Warley's nostrils flared. 'It seems we have no choice in the matter.'

'No, sir,' Lady Quincy said. 'You do not.'

Her last words were almost drowned out by footsteps thundering on the stairs and on the landing. There were raised voices and a frantic knocking on the door. Warley, nervous as a cat, spun round towards the noise. I stood up.

Lady Quincy looked at me and smiled. 'Thank you, Mr Marwood.'

I unlatched the door. A small boy darted under my arm and rushed into the room, bringing with him a faint but disgusting smell of rancid fat.

Lady Quincy's maid was red-faced with anger. 'Madam, I tried to stop him.'

Another servant, one of the tavern's maids, dropped me a curtsy. I turned and seized the boy by the shoulders.

'Sir,' he was saying in a high, excited voice to Warley, 'sir, the Dean says you're to come back to college.' His voice rose higher still. 'Dr Burbrough's drowned.'

# CHAPTER THIRTY-THREE

A N HOUR LATER, with the sound of water roaring in my ears, I stared down at Burbrough. The doctor was not drowned after all, though he had come within an inch or two of it. He had also sustained a number of injuries, including a blow to the head. He had vomited copiously after they had dragged him from the mill pond and now lay barely conscious on the grassy bank. Someone had covered him with a cloak.

Warley was with me, as well as another fellow of Jerusalem, an elderly, desiccated man who had been introduced to me as the Dean, together with the small boy who had brought us the news at the Rose Tavern.

'Who exactly is this gentleman?' I heard the Dean whisper to Warley. The Dean was a trifle deaf, and his whispers were louder than he realized.

'Mr Marwood?' Warley glanced at me. 'He comes with the King's authority, sir.'

'The King? This is most irregular.'

'So is your Vice Master in a millpond, sir,' I said, tiring of eavesdropping. 'You may see my warrant if you wish. First, though, have you sent for a physician?'

'Yes, sir.' The Dean was trembling with shock. 'We must make the poor fellow more comfortable. There's an inn nearby . . .' He turned to the kitchen boy. 'Your uncle works there, does he not? Run over and order them to prepare a chamber and light a fire for us.'

The boy ran off. I glanced at Warley. He shuffled uneasily under my gaze.

'I – I wish Burbrough no harm, you know,' he murmured to me, too low for the Dean to hear. 'Not personally. It's just that we disagree about everything.'

The miller and his two sons were standing a little apart, giving us sullen, suspicious glances. I guessed that there wasn't much love lost between the university and the ordinary folk of the neighbourhood. The miller was probably scared he would be blamed for the accident, if it had been an accident.

The afternoon had shaded into a golden evening. The sun dappled the water of the millpond. The great wheel was no longer turning, for the miller had locked it as soon as he heard what had happened. But the stream surged through the wheel race, relentless and unceasing, as unstoppable as time.

The stone coping at the sides of the millpond was mossy and wet from the spray. A narrow millstream channelled the water towards it with considerable force. The wheel itself must have been nine or ten feet in diameter with paddles projecting from its circumference to catch the power of the water and use it to turn the wheel. It was set in a narrow race lined with old stone. It looked centuries old. For all I knew, it had been built by the monks. Below the millpond, a tailrace carried the water back to the river.

The mill building was on the other side of the wheel, reached by a footbridge that crossed the mill race. It had a lower storey of stone and two upper ones made of wood. House martins ducked and dived into nests tucked under the eaves.

By a fluke of the current, Burbrough's hat was bobbing serenely on the water against the further bank. As for the man himself, he had been found half-submerged, wedged between the wheel and the bank of the millpond. The miller and his sons had managed to drag him out. He was lying on his side on the grass.

In this broken, bedraggled state, Burbrough seemed half the size of the man I had met earlier, quivering with passion in Jerusalem. He wore his own hair, and it trailed around his head in an indefinite halo. Some of his gown's dark material had been shredded when it was dragged underwater in the mill race. There was a long, bloodless gash on his right cheek from the corner of the eye to the base of the jaw.

He must have fallen into the water upstream, I thought, and been dragged by the current under the wheel. It was a miracle he had survived.

'You,' I said, beckoning the miller. 'Come here.'

The man shuffled towards me. He was heavily built, not unlike Burbrough himself, with muscular arms from shifting the sacks of grain.

I ignored the muttering behind me. 'What's your name?' I asked the miller.

'Cutlack, master,' he said. 'Listen, we didn't see anything. Didn't hear anything either. Then my boy Tom came out for a piss and saw him. God's body, sir, I'd have given all I have to prevent this.'

'When did he fall in?'

He shrugged. 'He wasn't there dinnertime, I know that. As soon as I saw him, we pulled him out, and I sent Tom to tell them at Jerusalem. But he can't have been there long or he'd have drowned.'

'How did you know who he was?'

'We know the doctor well enough, sir. He often comes up here. College owns the mill.'

Warley cleared his throat behind me. 'The Master is infirm, so Dr Burbrough generally deals with the properties that the college owns. As Vice Master.'

'Where's his horse?' I asked.

'He was a great walker,' Warley said. 'He probably came out here this afternoon to have a word with Mr Cutlack. The way to the mill is by the footbridge. I assume he was walking along the bank of the mill race and was taken faint. It's been a warm day . . . I can only imagine that the heat and the exercise had fatigued him, and perhaps he stumbled . . .'

I knelt by the doctor and pulled away the cloak that covered him. He must have left Jerusalem almost immediately after we had seen him in the Fellows' Garden. A dreadful sense of familiarity swept over me: it was only five days since I had examined another waterlogged body – Edward Alderley's, in the basement of Lord Clarendon's pavilion.

I went through his pockets. The Dean stared pop-eyed but didn't challenge me. All I found was a clay pipe with a plug of sodden ash in the bowl, a tinderbox, a purse and a ring holding three keys.

I covered up Burbrough again and stood, slipping the keys

discreetly into my pocket. I gave the other items to the Dean. I beckoned the miller, who regarded me with small, shifty eyes. 'Have you seen any strangers recently?'

He gave a bitter laugh. 'There are always strangers here, sir. And half of them are thieving devils, I can tell you.'

'Why here? What do you mean?'

'The main road's on the other side of the river. There's a post-house not a quarter mile away, so travellers pass to and fro everyday.'

'That's the inn where we'll take him,' said the Dean.

'I shall leave you to it.' I touched Warley's arm. 'I must get back to Cambridge. Would you come with me?'

Warley and I left the Dean to deal with the constable and walked back to Cambridge. I had been tempted to go to the inn first, for I wondered whether that had been Burbrough's destination, rather than the mill. But I had more urgent things to do in Cambridge, and I did not want to risk further questions from the Dean.

'The poor man,' Warley muttered as we went. He gave a sigh. 'Such a dreadful sight.'

After that, we went on in silence. I was turning over in my mind the last words I had heard Burbrough say, in the Fellows' Garden at Jerusalem. When Warley had told him about the intruder at his rooms and the attack on the college servant, Burbrough's first impulse had not been to ask how Smith was, or whether anything had been stolen, or whether the intruder had been caught. Instead, he had wanted to know why the servant had been in Warley's rooms in the first place.

Smith's presence there had been exceptional. Burbrough would have expected the rooms to be empty while the college was dining in hall. Add to that the fact that he himself had been talking with Warley about the projected chapel over dinner and had delayed him afterwards in the court, where I had come across them this afternoon. I put that together with his presence in the Fellows' Garden, the stranger in the MA gown whom Smith had seen, and the shred of black stuff caught in the latch of the Fellows' gate to St Andrew's Street. An unexpected picture emerged.

We were approaching the chimneys of Cambridge. The buildings of Jerusalem College came into view above the trees lining a field where cattle grazed.

'Mr Warley? I should like to see Dr Burbrough's rooms before we go back to the Rose.'

His dark brows drew together, rising where they met in an arch of disapproval. 'That would be most irregular. I couldn't condone it without consulting the Master.'

God save us from the scruples of scholars, I thought. 'I'm afraid, sir, that I must insist in the name of the King.'

'But I don't see what possible relevance this could have to the business on which you're employed.' He compressed his lips. 'Whatever that may be precisely.'

'I don't propose to enlighten you. But if you wish, you may accompany me.'

'You will have a difficulty over the keys,' Warley said. 'For all we know they are at the bottom of the mill race. The Master has a spare set but he will take some persuading before he hands them over. That's assuming that he is well enough to receive us. He suffers terribly from the stone and was too ill to dine in hall today.'

'The keys won't be a difficulty.' I took out Burbrough's set and showed them to him.

'You removed these from . . .?'

'How else could I have them?' I said, suddenly impatient. 'Three keys. What are they for?'

'The door of his rooms. The Fellows' Garden gate. And the Fellows' Parlour.'

We used Burbrough's own key to enter the college by way of the gate into the Fellows' Garden. His rooms were in the same building as Warley's, but further to the east and on the ground floor. They were laid out on the same pattern – a large sitting room, a small study, a smaller bedchamber and a cell-like closet, little more than a cupboard, which was the servant's domain. From the latter, however, a private door led directly into the Fellows' Garden.

With Warley at my shoulder, I moved from room to room. There was very little furniture and a great many books. Rushes were strewn on the floor. The grate had been swept but there was no fire laid in it. Two mugs and a jug stood on the table in the sitting room. They were empty and smelled of small beer.

There was also a roll of paper on the table. I unfurled it and found a map of the county, hand-drawn in ink. The county was divided into its hundreds. It seemed a sparse, watery place, intersected by rivers, dikes and causeways, and dotted with meres. Cambridge, near the bottom, was the only town of any size.

'I believe it's a copy based on the Blaeu map,' Warley said. 'Twenty years old, and the best we have. We had a sizar here a few years ago who supplemented his scholarship by making such things. Probably Burbrough bought one.' He bent over it, perhaps glad to be diverted from the grim reason for our presence here. 'Look – there's Hitcham St Martin.'

'Where your grandmother lives with Frances?'

'Yes,' he said. 'Where my estate is.'

I stared at the map. Hitcham St Martin lay north of Cambridge, not far from Ely. I peered more closely. On the map, the village was no more than a blob with a tiny church tower poking out of it. To the immediate left was a tiny hole. I looked more closely. Someone had pricked the name with a pin.

'How far is it from here?' I asked.

'About seventeen miles. Why do you ask?'

I shook my head. A possible pattern was beginning to emerge. But I could only see some of its outlines. 'Dr Burbrough had a visitor,' I said. 'When do you think that was?'

'Probably during the morning. Or else his servant would have tidied this away.' Warley turned aside and stared into the garden. 'This is becoming a nightmare,' he said in a muffled voice. 'He must have fallen in by accident, mustn't he? Surely?'

I ignored his question and asked another. 'What was in the folder? The one that was stolen from your box?'

Warley said nothing. He continued to stare into the garden.

'You must tell me,' I said. 'This is a dangerous business, whatever it is, and if I'm to help you I must know.'

'Letters,' he said at last, so quietly I had to strain to hear him. 'Lady Clarendon's letters to my grandmother, and copies of the ones that she had sent to her ladyship. And, latterly, some correspondence between all three of us that touched on the same affair. Lady Clarendon did not write directly to my grandmother, for fear of prying eyes at Clarendon House. Since I've been at Jerusalem, their letters have passed through me.'

The pattern was growing clearer in my mind, and so was the need for urgency. We couldn't afford to linger in Jerusalem any longer.

Warley was turning to face me at last, and his face was distraught. 'Whoever took this knew exactly what they wanted. Now they've found it, they must know everything about Frances. The poor child.' He hesitated and then something – perhaps the scholar in him that knew the value of precision and the cost of truth – made him add, 'Almost everything, that is. They can't have learned who she is. None of us knows that, even my grandmother.'

# CHAPTER THIRTY-FOUR

A FEW MINUTES later, as Warley and I were walking through the college's hall passage, a thought struck me. 'Sir – this post-house near the mill. Do you know it?'

'The Duke's Head? Yes, of course. Everyone knows it.'

'If I had time, I would go there and make enquiries about travellers who have passed through today. In particular, whether two men have been seen at the inn. One is a tall man with a northern accent. The other his servant, a gross fellow who carries a sword. They would have been on horseback.'

'I would go there myself if it was really necessary, but I can't be in two places at once.' Warley sounded irritable, as men often do when frightened and under pressure. Suddenly he stopped in his tracks, and his face brightened. 'I shall tell Jeremiah to ask.'

'Who?'

'Our kitchen boy – the lad who brought the news of Dr Burbrough's accident to us. He knows the Duke's Head well. His uncle's an ostler there.'

'An excellent plan, sir.' Ostlers were aware of every traveller who passed through their yard. 'Can you arrange it for me when the boy returns?'

The light was fading by the time we reached the tavern. I would have liked to send Warley ahead to Hitcham St Martin this evening to make sure that his grandmother's house was secure. But it was too late for that. I could only hope that the Bishop and his servant would be reluctant to ride seventeen miles in the gathering darkness on an unknown road across the Fens.

We went up to Lady Quincy's chamber, where the candles were already lit and the curtains drawn. It was a large, low room with sloping floors whose boards creaked at every step. I explained what had happened as fully as I could in the presence of Warley. She listened calmly, without interruption, sitting tranquilly with her hands folded in her lap as though listening attentively to a sermon.

'I believe we must go to Hitcham St Martin as soon as we can, madam,' I said. 'I can't be sure but it's possible that others are already on their way.'

'The Fens are not hospitable at night to those who do not know them,' Warley said solemnly. 'Even if they find a guide, which is by no means certain at such short notice.'

Lady Quincy nodded. 'In that case, let us hope they haven't,' she said briskly. 'We must leave as soon as we can in the morning. Mr Warley, we shall need to have a warrant signed by a justice if we are to travel unhindered on a Sunday. Can you apply to a magistrate on our behalf this evening? It would be foolish to allow some petty-minded official to delay us in the morning. A man of your standing in Cambridge could arrange the matter so much more easily than a stranger like Mr Marwood.'

He bowed, rising to the flattery, and said he would attend to it immediately.

'Another thing,' I said. 'Would it not be wise if Mr Warley rode ahead tomorrow to warn them at Hitcham St Martin? They will want to prepare the house for us and—'

'I'll send a servant with a letter,' Warley said. 'He can leave at dawn. Then I can escort you.'

'I think it would be better if you went yourself, sir,' I said.

'But why?'

'In case these two men are on the road before us. Mistress Warley should be warned. And she may need a gentleman's protection sooner than we think.'

An hour later, I went downstairs to give orders for our departure to the landlord and Lady Quincy's servants.

'Hitcham St Martin?' the landlord said. 'Not sure if you'll get there in that great coach of yours. You wouldn't in winter, sir, I tell you that.'

'Are the roads that bad?'

'All roads are bad in the Fens,' he said with melancholy pride.

We heard raised voices at the entrance of the tavern. One of the maids was trying to prevent Jeremiah from entering. The kitchen boy was squeezed between her and the wall, screeching as if he were being murdered.

'Let him pass,' I called. 'I sent for him.' I turned back to the landlord. 'He comes from Jerusalem with a message.'

The boy followed me upstairs and into Lady Quincy's chamber. He had added the smell of fresh horse manure to his kitchen odours so I made him stand by the door.

'Well?' I said. 'You may speak freely before this lady. First, how is Dr Burbrough?'

'He's awake, sir, but in much pain from a broken leg and the wound in his head. He said he slipped and fell as he was passing the mill. He was on his way to see the miller.'

'And the two strangers?'

'They was at the Duke's Head today, master,' Jeremiah said in an accent so broad I found it hard to follow him. 'My uncle reckons the tall one's a Yorkshireman, he knows what they sound like on account of him serving at Marston Moor, and they was all Yorkshire folk up there. Mean devils, he said, him and his servant, close as misers with their money, but you wouldn't want to cross them.'

'When did they get there?' I asked.

'This morning. The master went out on foot as soon as he got here. The servant dined early and then he went out too. But they came back together, late this afternoon, and they called for their horses.' The kitchen boy grinned unexpectedly, revealing very white teeth with a gap where he had lost one of the upper ones. 'My aunt died last winter, and Uncle's courting the maid who does the tables in the taproom. And she said she heard them talking about whether they could reach Stretham before nightfall.'

'Where's that?' asked Lady Quincy.

'On the high road to Ely, mistress,' the boy said, with a hint of surprise in his voice as if he had thought that everyone in the world must know where Stretham was.

His report was another piece of evidence to lend weight to a theory that was growing like a canker in my mind. I paid the boy for his trouble. He looked down at the silver coins in his dirty palm as if they were a miracle on a par with the loaves and fishes, which I suppose they were, for miracles are relative to circumstances: they depend on the context in which they occur.

'Go,' I said gently.

He snapped out of his trance and ran from the room. I closed the door behind him.

'What did you give him?' Lady Quincy said.

'Two shillings.'

'He's only a kitchen boy.' There was a hint of disapproval in her voice. 'One shouldn't spoil such people with kindness.' Then she gave me a smile that made me feel suddenly, foolishly, breathlessly happy. 'Will you sup with me, Mr Marwood? We have so much to discuss.'

A table was set up for us by the fire in Lady Quincy's chamber.

Ann, her maid, tried to stay, but her mistress sent her away. Stephen, the little African, remained to pour the wine and preserve decorum, but for most of the time he sat almost invisible on a low stool in the shadows in the far end of the room.

Everything was in readiness for our departure in the morning. Mr Warley had sent Jeremiah back to us with our Sunday travel warrant, signed by a justice. He enclosed a note to me, saying that Dr Burbrough's leg was badly broken in two places, and that he appeared confused, perhaps because of the blow to his head. The coachman and the postillion had made their preparations in the stables, and Ann had packed everything that could be packed before morning.

I helped myself to a dish of jellied eels. 'Do you recall a servant by the name of Matthew Gorse, madam? At Barnabas Place.'

She wrinkled her forehead. 'The name's familiar.' She

clicked her fingers. 'Yes, I know. A sturdy fellow? With freckles all over his face?'

'Yes. That's the man.'

'He attended my stepson for a while, I think. And sometimes he waited at table. Why?'

'I met him the other day. He serves Lord Clarendon now.'

'Had he anything to do with Edward's murder?'

'I don't know,' I said, which was true enough as far as it went. 'He's disappeared.'

'You said there's a warrant out for my unfortunate niece. Do you think he helped her murder Edward? I fear it's all too likely that she had help. After all, Edward was not a weakling.'

I wondered if Lady Quincy were right. I had assumed that if someone had bribed Gorse, it must have been Alderley. But in theory it could just as easily have been Cat. I said, 'Do you remember anything between Gorse and your niece at Barnabas Place? Did he make himself useful to her? Run errands, perhaps?'

She shook her head. 'I hardly remember him at all. We had so many servants there.' She paused. 'I wonder where Catherine is hiding herself.'

'Who knows?'

'Nothing would surprise me. She is such a strange, odd girl.'

'And a resourceful one, too,' I said drily.

We ate in silence for a moment. I watched Lady Quincy surreptitiously. Candlelight and firelight played on her face and made her skin shimmer.

She said abruptly, 'Is Gorse allied to these men who have followed us to Cambridge?'

Her voice dragged me back from my folly. 'I think it possible,' I said. 'Likely, even.'

She lowered her voice. 'Do they mean to do us harm?'

Prudence urged me to ration the information I shared with her, however much I wanted her to think kindly of me. I settled on a compromise with my wiser self. 'I believe they mean mischief to Lord Clarendon. More than that I cannot say for sure.'

'But they cannot be the principals in the matter, surely? Who are they working for?'

I shrugged. 'His lordship has many enemies.'

'Including the Duke of Buckingham, I think,' she said.

I looked sharply at her. There was an innocent expression on her face.

'This is just the sort of mad, fantastical scheme that would appeal to him,' she went on. 'He's hated Lord Clarendon for years. I remember them in Bruges. They circled each other like dogs.'

'In Bruges – during the exile?' The King had lived in the Netherlands for a year or two before the Restoration, I remembered, under the protection of the Spanish authorities. He had held a threadbare court in Bruges. His brother had been there too, and the Duke of Buckingham for a time as well. All three men had been unmarried, and tales of the court's licentiousness had circulated widely in England. 'Were you there too?'

There was a momentary pause, and the flames trembled in her eyes as if she had jerked back her head in shock. 'For a while. My first husband, Sir William, served the King on several diplomatic missions before the Restoration.' She moistened her lips. 'The Duke of Buckingham did not linger long in Bruges.' She smiled at me, narrowing her eyes like a cat calculating its next move. 'He could not see the profit in it, so he turned his coat and went to England to ingratiate himself with Cromwell and marry Fairfax's daughter.'

'Why does the King cherish him?'

'Who knows? The King keeps his own counsel. He always does.' She took a sip of wine and turned towards the fire. 'But enough of this. I'm not sleepy yet, for all we must make an early start tomorrow.'

'Madam,' I said, 'I could serve you so much better if I knew more of what this matter is about.'

She smiled at me. 'Mr Marwood, you serve me very well as it is, and I am quite content.'

'But what is it about this child – Frances, is it? Who has sent you to bring her to London? The King?'

'It's safer for you to know only what you need to know.' She waved her hand, dismissing my concern, dismissing the King. 'Shall we play cards? A hand of cribbage? Piquet?'

'Forgive me, but I don't know these games.' My voice sounded sulky even to me. 'I wasn't permitted to play cards when I was younger, and since then I haven't found the time to learn.'

'I had quite forgotten you come from Puritan stock, sir. Then I shall teach you. You will grasp the rules of piquet in a trice.' Lady Quincy raised her voice. 'Stephen – rouse yourself and come here.'

The footboy detached himself from the shadows near the bed. Like a dusky ghost, he walked uncertainly towards us, rubbing his eyes.

'Take that candle and fetch me the cards from the travelling case on the dressing table,' she ordered. 'Be careful not to knock anything over or drop wax on them.' She added to me, 'He's dreadfully clumsy, you know, especially in the evenings.'

'The boy's tired,' I said. 'He should be in bed.'

'You're pleased to be droll. Stephen should stay awake when I need him. He is here to serve me, not to sleep when he feels like it.'

I said nothing. She burst out laughing. 'You look so serious, sir.' She leaned forward and added teasingly, 'It makes you look like a child yourself. A child in a sulk.'

The words were insulting. But the way that she said them was a backhanded intimation of intimacy, simultaneously an insult and a caress.

The footboy laid the pack on the table in front of her and withdrew into the shadows. She sorted the cards into two piles.

'Don't be cross with me, sir. Mr Chiffinch tells me you are quite the rising man, and he is an acute judge of such things.' She smiled at me, and I was dazzled yet again. 'So I shall treat you with great respect from now on. Let us play.'

# CHAPTER THIRTY-FIVE

W E WERE ON the road by six o'clock in the morning, rumbling north from Cambridge. The landscape changed around us as we went, becoming progressively flatter and more watery. The coach swayed and bumped over potholes and ruts. Once we were stuck in the mud; we had to empty the coach and remove the luggage, before the six horses, the coachman and the postillion succeeded in getting us underway again.

'What a wretched place this is,' Lady Quincy murmured as she settled herself back in her corner. 'It's worse than the Low Countries.'

We set off once more, and I stared out of the window. The high road ran above the level of the Fens themselves, which were a waterlogged wasteland made up of pools of brown water, muddy-looking bushes and the occasional islet. There were few signs of life apart from waterbirds, whose melancholy cries and screeches made me long for the racket of London. We passed several farms; these were on higher ground or on land that had been drained by the digging of long straight ditches. The peasants were squat and sullen-faced. The worst of it was the sky – a grey dome that stretched for miles to the distant horizon in all directions. Clouds crawled slowly across its vault.

It had been cool when we started our journey, but the sun rose higher, so did the heat, and so did a closeness of the air that presaged a storm. We met no trouble on the way, apart from the mud, but I was glad when we came to Stretham, a small village built upon a low hillock. It was nearly ten o'clock, for the mud had delayed us. Warley had sent his bailiff to greet us at the only inn.

He eyed Lady Quincy's coach with a doubtful air. 'It will have to stay here, my lady. It's too heavy and too wide for the road to Hitcham.'

'Then we shall ride,' she said calmly. 'I shall enjoy the exercise. Is there a parlour where I may sit while you arrange the horses?'

A maid showed her into a gloomy room at the side of the house, with a window overlooking a farmyard. Ann and Stephen stayed with her. Meanwhile, I went to see about the horses and about transferring our luggage from the coach to a pair of carts, which the bailiff had commandeered for us.

Lady Quincy's postillion came over to me in the yard. 'They're mighty curious here,' he murmured. 'They want to know who my lady is, what we're doing here, and how long we'll be here . . .'

'More than you'd expect?'

'It's their way of showing it as much as anything, sir. As if . . .'

'Someone had put them up to it?'

He nodded, and then shrugged. 'Could be nothing. But maybe the mistress should know.'

'Have they had other strangers passing through since yesterday evening?' I asked. 'I'm interested in a tall man, a Northerner by his voice, with his servant, a fat, greasy fellow.'

'No, sir.' He paused. 'Or that's what they said.'

The trouble with this underhand business, I thought as I went back into the inn, was that it made you suspicious of everything and everyone. Distrust breeds distrust. But the postillion was worth taking seriously. Like all Lady Quincy's menservants, he seemed competent, even formidable. Given that Lady Quincy enjoyed a discreet connection with the King, it would not have surprised me to learn that her menservants had been appointed on the recommendation of Mr Chiffinch.

That led me to the uncomfortable thought that we might have an informer in our midst. After all, I had been charged to inform the King about Lady Quincy's doings. Why should not Chiffinch have set someone to inform on me?

If our journey from Cambridge to Stretham had lowered my spirits, then those last few miles to Hitcham St Martin lowered them still further. The road was much narrower, often no more than a cart track and a muddy one at that – so much so that in two places I feared that our horses would sink to their bellies.

Lady Quincy had left the coachman to guard the coach and our own horses in Stretham. There were now five of us in our party, together with the bailiff. He led the way; then came her ladyship, followed by the postillion with Ann up before him. I rode last, with Stephen before me, clutching the saddle. With the boy so close to me, I realized how frail he was. The tumours of his scrofula seemed the most vital part of him.

Along the way I was relieved to meet Mr Warley, who had ridden out to escort us into the village. Lady Quincy greeted him, and straightaway asked him if there had been any strangers seen in the village in the last day or two.

'No, madam,' he said. 'You must not trouble yourself about them. I shall hear at once if anyone is seen. They will not catch us unawares.'

We rode on, with Warley riding beside Lady Quincy. The clergyman and college fellow were less obvious in him than before: the land-owner was in the ascendant, and his pride in his land – and his water – burst out of him in a stream of plans he had for when the estate was finally his.

'I shall cut a drain, madam, to run along here' – flushed with enthusiasm, Warley pointed with his crop – 'to here, which will drain another fifty or sixty acres. And when the land dries out, there will be no matching it for the richness of its soil in the length and breadth of England.'

At one point the path ran along the bank of a stretch of water, a shallow mere where gnats danced in dense clouds. The insects began to bite, seeming to find particular delight in the white flesh of Lady Quincy, who swore at them in a most unladylike fashion.

From here a causeway led to the village. The tower appeared, as squat as one of the inhabitants of these barbaric and waterlogged parts. Villagers stared at us through the open doorways of low cottages with thatched roofs made of reeds. Some of them pointed out Stephen to each other.

'They have never seen an African,' Warley explained to

Lady Quincy. 'Most of our peasants are what we call breedlings, which signifies that they were born and bred in these parts. Why, some of them have never ventured as far as Stretham, let alone Ely or Cambridge.'

We approached the church, which was raised on the mound of graves surrounding it. Opposite it was a larger house, built mostly of brick. To one side was a wall with a gateway set in it. We rode through and entered a stable yard beside the house. The ground sloped down to a group of farm buildings.

'Nothing much has changed here since my grandfather's time,' I heard Warley saying to Lady Quincy. 'When it is mine, I shall pull the place down and rebuild it on the higher ground beyond the church, removed from the smells of the midden. Mr Hakesby has agreed to draw me a plan of a gentleman's house, a mansion both elegant and modern. Do you know of him, madam? He's one of the architects we have working on our new chapel at Jerusalem.'

She inclined her head, a gesture which meant nothing. Warley dismounted and helped her from her horse. I summoned the postillion and lifted Stephen down to him.

I sensed that someone was looking at me. I turned towards the house. An old woman dressed in widow's black was standing in a doorway. She was scrutinizing us with a look of distaste on her face. Her hand was resting on the shoulder of a small girl.

Lady Quincy swept into a curtsy, as graceful as a swan. 'Mistress Warley. Your servant, madam.'

I heard a gasp. I glanced down. Stephen was staring at the girl, and she was staring at him. They were much of an age probably, I thought, no more than eight or nine. The girl's features were teasingly familiar, but I could not understand why.

Both children raised their hands at the same time, as if they were reflections of each other, and touched their swollen necks.

The manor house at Hitcham St Martin was damp and inconvenient. The family took their meals in a stone-flagged hall that was open to the rafters and smelled strongly of damp. The windows were small, the fireplace was huge but lacked a fire, and the rats rustled and scrabbled behind the fraying tapestries on the wall.

Our dinner was a fish stew with yet more eels, which were found everywhere in the Fens. There was nothing to wash it down but small beer. While the five of us ate, the house was alive with invisible movement – with footsteps crisscrossing the rooms overhead, with raised voices and the scraping and bumping of furniture. The arrival of Mr Warley with two guests and three servants had thrown the household into confusion.

We were waited on by a single maidservant, little older than Frances. The latter sat at the old woman's elbow, her eyes on her plate and her presence inhibiting conversation as perhaps Mistress Warley intended. Warley was on her other side.

Even before the King's Evil had blighted her appearance, Frances could not have been a pretty child, being chubby and clumsy, with regular features, small watchful eyes and a sallow, spotty complexion. I knew nothing more about her – she had curtsied clumsily to us when Mistress Warley had told her to, but I had not heard her say a single word to anyone since our arrival. I could not rid myself of the curious idea that I had seen her somewhere before.

It was not a sociable meal. The only one who talked at length was Mr Warley. The old lady listened to his account of Dr Burbrough's accident, though with little appearance of interest. She had lost most of her teeth; as a result she sucked rather than ate her stew, and the sounds of this punctuated her grandson's story.

After this, Warley went on interminably about Jerusalem and about the Warley estate at Hitcham St Martin. It was only towards the end of the meal that I wondered whether he talked to fill the silence or because he was on edge. Perhaps Burbrough's escape from near death and our presence here in his home had unsettled him more than I realized.

Lady Quincy was unusually silent. I noted how her eyes would drift time and again towards Frances, and then veer suddenly aside as if an invisible force had repelled her interest. At least, I thought, I now knew the reason for her interest in scrofula, the reason for our meeting at the Banqueting House while the King was touching the sufferers, and for the presence of the African boy in her household. It hurt me that she had not confided in me earlier – even yesterday evening – but had left Frances's condition to reveal itself to me directly. She was a woman, I suspected, for whom secrecy was a habit of mind; perhaps it had become its own justification.

There was a lull in the conversation and I asked whether the causeway was the only way to approach the village.

'Yes,' Warley said, 'and we become an island when a flood sweeps it away, as sometimes happens in the storms. We are quite cut off.'

'You exaggerate, Richard,' said his grandmother. 'We still

273

have punts. We always have punts in the Fens. I don't hold with this foolish mania for drainage. It brings those wicked foreigners here, those Dutchmen. Besides, God made the Fens as they are for a purpose. Would you argue against our maker's design for us?'

He smiled, bobbing his head, though his expression made it clear he did not like being contradicted. He gave me a sharp look. 'Strangers rarely take us unawares.'

Afterwards, Warley murmured a few words to Mistress Warley. She nodded and told the maid to clear the table and then leave us to talk.

'You too, Frances. Go and learn the Collect for the day. I shall hear you recite it after Evensong.'

'May she find the blackamoor?' Lady Quincy said suddenly, breaking a long silence. 'A child of her own age might amuse her . . .' She turned and spoke directly to Frances, 'If you like him, my dear, you shall have him for your own, as a present from me. He is a slave boy, you see, and I may give him to whomever I wish.'

For the first time, I think, the child looked directly at her. There was a spark of emotion in her face, instantly repressed.

'A slave boy would not be a suitable gift for a little girl,' Mistress Warley said. 'Far too expensive and most impractical. And, Frances, I've told you time and again that a spoilt child is not pleasing in the sight of God. Still, you may thank Lady Quincy for her kindness. Then leave us.'

Frances gave Lady Quincy another wobbly curtsy, made another to Mistress Warley, muttered her thanks and withdrew. When the four of us were alone, Mistress Warley turned to Lady Quincy. The old woman seemed not entirely human; she put me in mind of a lizard, for she had a narrow head with a long jaw and skin marked with smallpox. She moistened her lips with the tip of her tongue, which was surprisingly pink in comparison with the yellowy, wrinkled face that surrounded it.

'When I wrote to Lady Clarendon,' she said, 'I wrote only to inform her of the child's illness, and to seek assistance for it, whether from a physician or from the King himself.'

'You knew it was scrofula then?' Lady Quincy put in.

'I've seen the King's Evil before. It's common enough in the Fens.'

'Then why should you object if we take Frances to London? There are the best physicians in the country there. And of course – most importantly of all – there is the King himself. He is God's anointed. God himself has granted him the divine power to cure this affliction.'

Mistress Warley shook her head. 'I explained all this to Lady Clarendon. I begged that the King would permit us to bring Frances to him when he is next at Newmarket for the horse races. It is not far from here, and it would distress the child less – and it would also make it possible to manage the matter far more discreetly. I'm sure if my lady were alive, she—'

Warley cleared his throat. 'Madam, forgive me, but it would hardly be fitting for us to oppose the King's wishes in this. Lady Quincy brought me a letter in his own hand commanding us to surrender Frances to Lady Quincy. Her ladyship has come all this way to fetch her, and at great expense. It shows the King's great kindness for Frances – and it's surely a sign that he has her best interests at heart.'

Mistress Warley threw him a glance, and the tongue appeared once more. 'Just as you have yours, Richard. You would not be at Jerusalem if it were not for the King. Since

Dr Burbrough is so ill, I wonder who will act as Vice Master there? A man who has the King's support, perhaps?'

Her grandson flushed and looked away.

'Madam, pray don't distress yourself,' Lady Quincy said. 'Your concern does you much credit. Frances may well be back with you in a week or two, or perhaps a little longer. While she's gone, she will write to you, and so will I to tell you how she does.'

'The child has a delicate constitution,' Mistress Warley said, spitting out the words as if they were missiles. 'She is not accustomed to strangers, or to strange places. We are all the family she has ever known. To snatch her away from everything she knows would be cruel. She was entrusted to me, madam, and I will not permit her to be removed from this house. You may tell the King that I would be obliged to him if he would heal her at Newmarket. As I originally asked.'

She snapped shut her mouth. With sudden vigour, she pushed back her chair. She rose to her feet, leaning on the table and pushing away Warley's hand when he tried to help her.

Warley and I stood up. With her stick tapping on the flagstones and her skirts brushing the rushes underfoot, she made her way towards the door. She didn't lean on the stick. She merely used it to make her presence felt.

No one spoke. I opened the door and bowed to her as she passed. She did not look at me. It was a withdrawal, not a capitulation.

# CHAPTER THIRTY-SIX

AFTER DINNER, WARLEY detained me for a moment in the hall. 'I regret my grandmother's obduracy, sir,' he said. 'You will tell the King it was none of my doing, won't you? I've done everything I can to assist you.'

'This house is yours, sir,' I said curtly. 'Aren't you master here?'

His mouth twitched uncertainly. 'Of course.'

'Then why can't you insist?'

'My grandmother has ruled the roost here for so long that it is difficult to cross her, either in the house or in the village. She's a law unto herself. She is determined to keep the child with her, and you would need a court order and the King's sergeant-at-arms to change that.'

'This is an absurd position,' I said. 'We've come all this way, and at so much expense; the King desires only to help the child, and God knows she needs help – only for us all to be thwarted by the whim of an old lady.'

I had spoken bluntly and he winced. 'If I could change matters, sir,' he said, 'believe me, I would.'

'What if you told her about the robbery in your rooms and the attack on your servant? Other people are concerned in this matter, and they don't come from the King. Their interest is hostile; they won't be as polite as us. That might change her mind.'

He shook his head unhappily. 'You don't know my grandmother, sir. She won't listen to reason. Not where Frances is concerned.'

On these unsatisfactory terms we parted. I went up to my bedchamber, a garret under the eaves which I was to share with Stephen. I sat by the open window, looking down on the garden, scratching the more accessible of my gnat bites and trying to collect my thoughts. It was a sunny afternoon, warm for the time of year. The window overlooked an orchard, and the scent of apples drifted into the room.

This journey had become a nightmare. First the robbery at Jerusalem, then Burbrough's accident, and now the further complication of Mistress Warley's obstinacy. The old lady was in her own place, and surrounded by her own people. We could hardly take her to court to force the issue. Besides, we lacked the authority; the King had chosen to make a request to the Warleys, not given them an order. Frances's ambiguous status didn't help. She was a nobody who had arrived at Hitcham St Martin by the agency of Lady Clarendon; and Lady Clarendon was dead.

At least the wider picture was clearer. The King had sent Lady Quincy to collect Frances. The child had originally been entrusted to Mistress Warley by Lady Clarendon, presumably acting on behalf of the King, who in return had advanced the career of Richard Warley, and who to some extent was still acting as Warley's patron. The identity of the child remained a mystery, though I thought it most probable that she was an unacknowledged bastard of the King.

Given Frances's age, and what Lady Quincy had told me last night, her conception or birth must be linked to the court's stay in Bruges during the King's exile on the Continent. Lord Clarendon, then Sir Edward Hyde, had been at his side, his chief adviser. The Duke of Buckingham had also been there, at least for part of the time; he must have known of the affair, I thought, and he was seeking to use it to gain political capital, particularly in relation to his continuing campaign to crush Lord Clarendon. To that end, the Duke had sent his two hirelings after us, the man known as the Bishop and his servant.

That was, if not clear, at least visible in shadowy outline. But there was much I did not understand. Did Buckingham intend to harm the child, even to have her killed, or did he merely want control of her? What had been the role of Edward Alderley in this? Could his murder have somehow been connected to the sad, clumsy girl I had seen at dinner? What had the Bishop been looking for in Alderley's apartments? What of Gorse and his disappearance? To make matters worse, Alderley's murder was tangled up with Cat Lovett, and I didn't know how. Questions and theories, fears and doubts swirled in my mind like those wretched Fenland gnats.

I heard distant laughter and looked up. For a moment I couldn't work out where it came from. Then a movement on the other side of the orchard caught my eye. I looked more closely. More movement, and then a glimpse of brown, a glimpse of white.

The two children burst out into the clearing. Frances in her brown dress was pursuing Stephen, who had lost his coat and shoes. She was half a head taller than he was, and more strongly built. I thought how pleasant it was to see the children playing together, particularly two such as these.

Then Frances flung herself at Stephen. Her weight threw him to the ground, on the bank of the stream that formed the border of the orchard on that side. She knelt over him, pinning him down and pushing his face into the earth. Then she scooped up a handful of mud and rubbed it into his hair.

Not as pleasant as I had assumed. Frances shrieked with laughter – where was the grave and silent girl I had watched at dinner? – and dug up two more handfuls of mud. Stephen wriggled from under her and tried to stand. This threw her off balance, and most of the mud ended up on her skirt.

Stephen scrambled up and ran into the trees, pursued by Frances. I listened to her cries of rage until a woman called angrily, and she fell silent.

If Frances were indeed the King's bastard, I thought, why in God's name did he not acknowledge her as he did all his other bastards? After all, what was one more among the crowd?

I could think of only one reason for his silence, and for all this secrecy: because Frances's mother was married to someone else.

Both children were soundly whipped – Frances by Mistress Warley's maid and Stephen by Lady Quincy's postillion. It was partly because of the mud, Mistress Warley said, and partly because of so much unseemly mirth on the Lord's Day.

Mistress Warley asked Lady Quincy and myself whether we would attend evensong with the family. Both of us declined, which earned us a disapproving look. Frances did not have the luxury of choice. The maid took her away and dressed her in a thick grey gown that hung on her like a sack.

Mr Warley escorted them to the church on foot. I hoped that their absence might mean that Lady Quincy and I could talk together. But she retired to her room with her maid to attend her, leaving me to my own devices.

I walked about the garden for nearly an hour instead, half-heartedly slapping the gnats as they sucked their fill of me. At the back of the house, the ground sloped down to a stretch of brackish water, with the empty fen stretching beyond. Waterfowl were on the wing, and their cries were unearthly.

The more I thought about yesterday's events, the more convinced I became that Burbrough had not fallen into the mill race by accident. For some reason he had cooperated with the Bishop or whoever had broken into Warley's rooms at Jerusalem. But the news of the attack on Smith, his old college servant, seemed to have angered him: he had gone to remonstrate with the men at the inn by the mill; perhaps he had threatened to expose them; and he had been mangled by the mill wheel for his pains. I could prove nothing but the scraps of evidence pointed towards this sequence of events.

If I was right, it showed beyond doubt the ruthlessness of the Bishop and his colleague. But they would not find it easy to reach us here. The Warleys – or rather Mistress Warley – dominated Hitcham St Martin, and the only way to the village was by the causeway. This was not a place that people passed through on the road to somewhere else. Strangers would stand out.

By chance, I found Stephen in the orchard, idly throwing twigs into the stream. I had forgotten about him – and so, it seemed, had everyone else. He was an anomaly, poor child, a lady's toy who did not belong with the rest of the servants, any more than he belonged with the rest of us. He was like a little dog, designed for petting or showing off to one's friends, but of no practical value. Now his charm was spoiled: no lady of fashion would want a pet with scrofula.

The swellings clung to his neck like giant barnacles on a scrap of rock. Would Lady Quincy keep him? If she did, what sort of life would he have in her household? I hoped for his sake he wouldn't find himself under the same roof as Frances for very long. If the scene I had witnessed in the orchard were any guide to her character, his life would be a misery.

When Stephen saw me, he rose to his feet and bowed. He had been well trained by his previous owner, the lady who had discarded him when the King's Evil had made him a pretty boy no longer.

'Stephen,' I said, 'I want you to be on your guard. I believe that two men may be following us. They are dangerous. I don't think they mean us well, or Mistress Frances.'

He caught his breath. 'Who are they, sir?'

His voice took me by surprise. It was a clear, high treble. If you closed your eyes, he could have been any English boy.

'There's a tall man – middle-aged; the last time I saw him he was wearing a brown coat. And his servant, who is fat. They both wear swords. They are almost certainly travelling on horseback. I don't know either of their names.'

He glanced about us, his face suddenly fierce. 'Have they followed us here?'

'I don't know. It's possible. They followed us to Cambridge.'

'I'll keep a watch, master, I promise.'

'I know you will.' A thought struck me. 'Have you eaten?'

'No, sir. Only an apple.'

I felt a sudden surge of anger. No one had troubled to wonder whether Stephen might be hungry, including myself. 'Come. We must find you some food.'

# CHAPTER THIRTY-SEVEN

A FTER EVENSONG, THE vicar came back for supper. He was a wiry, nervy man with hunched shoulders and eyes that were never still. His name was Dawson. Perhaps Lady Warley invited him to prevent the conversation returning to Frances. Lady Quincy and I were introduced to him as travellers from London, who were acquainted with Mr Warley.

Dawson had once been a fellow of Jerusalem and Warley's tutor. When his term as a fellow had come to an end, his position had been desperate indeed, for he came from a humble family and had no resources of his own. The living of Hitcham St Martin happened to fall vacant at this time. Warley, who had the right of presentation, had offered it to him, and Dawson had accepted with gratitude. The income was only £40 a year and the house was not in perfect repair. But with prudent management, he told us, and through the constant benevolence of his patron and his patron's grand-mother, he had contrived very well on this, and even managed to marry a wife and support a family.

I learned all this and more in the first ten minutes. The man could not stop talking. The Warleys encouraged him to some extent, partly because Dawson harped so constantly on their generosity to him, partly because it stopped us talking about Frances and our reason for being here. He and his patrons had in its way a perfectly balanced relationship, with symmetrical benefits on either side.

The candles were lit. Frances was sent to bed, curtseying precariously to each of us in turn. Again, only for a moment, I had that curious sense of familiarity when I looked at her. After she had gone upstairs, the five of us sat in the gloomy hall where we had dined earlier in the day. Mr Warley was at one end of the table, his grandmother at the other, with the vicar on her right. I was next to the vicar.

Lady Quincy sat opposite Dawson and me, her head slightly bowed. I had noticed before that candlelight became her, giving her skin a soft, smoky quality, like the bloom on a piece of fruit. I had to force myself not to stare at her.

'That was a most instructive sermon, sir,' Mistress Warley said graciously to Mr Dawson, as if encouraging a backward child. Her eyes flickered towards Lady Quincy. 'If only our guests had been able to attend evensong. They would have found much meat in it, much to digest.'

'What was your text, sir?' I asked, as the conversation showed signs of foundering.

'"And there came a fear on all,"' Mr Dawson said sternly. '"And they glorified God." From today's Gospel,' he added in his ordinary voice. 'The story of the widow of Nain and her dead son from St Luke, chapter seven.'

In his excitement, he wriggled on the chair beside me, and I felt his foot brush mine. I moved my foot away.

'It is an affecting story, which shows Our Lord's compassion to widows,' Mistress Warley said. 'Mr Dawson gave us a most learned account of why it meant we should all fear God, and why widows in particular should bless Him and the infinite mercies He bestows.'

Was this a sly taunt directed at Lady Quincy? The vicar nudged my foot again. I drew away and glanced at him. To my surprise I saw that he had turned to face Mistress Warley. Unless the laws of anatomy had changed, it could not have been his foot.

'When the widow's son rises up from his bier at Our Lord's command,' Mr Dawson said, 'it signifies that Our Lord brings us all the blessed possibility of redemption in the name of His Father.'

The pressure on my foot returned. A pulse began to beat in my temple. I looked across the table. Lady Quincy was peeling an apple, the coils of its skin winding like a snake on to her plate.

For an instant she looked at me and parted her lips. She gave me the ghost of a smile. Then the pressure withdrew and she returned to her apple.

They kept early hours in Hitcham St Martin.

After supper, the vicar had departed, a stream of thanks pouring from his lips into the dank evening air, and the front door was barred against the outside world. We withdrew to the parlour, where Mr Warley read prayers to the assembled household. The dog was loosed in the yard. Mistress Warley ushered us all to the foot of the stairs, where the maid waited with a tray of lighted candles.

'You will be leaving us tomorrow, I imagine?' she said to

Lady Quincy. 'And I know Richard needs to get back to Jerusalem as quickly as possible – the college must be in a sad way after Dr Burbrough's unhappy accident. Shall I send someone to call you early?'

'Thank you, no. I haven't quite settled my plans.' Lady Quincy inclined her head. 'Goodnight, mistress.'

The Warleys lingered at the bottom of the stairs, talking in low voices, perhaps about their unwelcome guests. Lady Quincy paused at the head of the stairs. I joined her on the landing. The Warleys were out of sight round the turn of the stairs, though their voices were still audible below.

'Would you come to my chamber a little later, sir?' Lady Quincy murmured. 'In twenty minutes or so – I wish to ask your advice.'

I bowed, and she wished me goodnight in a firm, clear voice which showed me that the invitation was a private matter. Not, I thought hastily, that there could be anything improper in my visiting her in her chamber, for Ann would be there to make her mistress ready for bed.

I went up to my own room, which was on the floor above. There was no light in it, apart from the candle in my hand. Stephen lay asleep on a truckle bed between my own bed and the wall. He didn't wake as I entered. I saw the outline of his body under the covers, somehow smaller in sleep, and heard his slow, almost soundless breathing.

I sat down on the side of my bed and tried to argue a little sense into myself. Why should Lady Quincy have meant any more than her words had said? There was a matter she wanted to discuss confidentially with me. That was all.

However, I removed my coat and wig, laid them on the bed and washed my hands and face in the basin on the table. I took a toothpick to my teeth. I had not shaved for three or four days but it was too late to worry about that. I put on my coat and tugged down the sleeves. I set the wig on my head and straightened it as best I could without a mirror.

I had felt that pressure on my foot under the table at supper. It hadn't been the vicar or Warley. It must have been Lady Quincy.

'You're a fool,' I whispered to myself. 'You're a fool.'

Lady Quincy's bedchamber was directly under mine. The air was chilly and damp, for Mistress Warley had not ordered a fire to be lit for her guest. The room was lit by two candles, one on the night table by the bed, and the other on a dressing table, with a mirror behind it that doubled the light it threw into the room. There was a smell of perfume – musky, with a hint of something earthy underlying it.

Lady Quincy was already in bed, propped against the pillows. I looked about for Ann, her maid, but she was nowhere to be seen.

'Close the door,' she said softly. 'And put the bolt across.'

I obeyed her. My fingers shook as I pushed the bolt into its socket.

'It's so cold, isn't it?' she said. 'Damp, as well. I wonder when this room was last used.'

I turned to her and said abruptly, 'Why do you want to speak to me, madam?'

She patted the bed. 'Come and sit here, Mr Marwood. I can hardly see you over there. And it would not do for us to raise our voices.'

When I sat down, she moved to make room for me on the

bed. Her bedgown fell open, showing the smock she wore beneath it and the swell of her breasts.

Dear God, I thought, must she tease me so? It was either that or she considered me essentially harmless, a creature without carnal desires, someone like Ann or Stephen. It was a form of humiliation, however I looked at it.

'This is a dreary place, isn't it?' she said, smiling. 'I believe that foul old woman would drown us both in the mud if she thought she could get away with it.'

I found myself smiling back, drawn into her humour. Her white hand lay inches away from my leg. Her fingers picked at the coverlet.

'I don't know how I could have managed this journey without you,' she said.

'I'm sure you would have managed perfectly well, madam.'

'You value yourself too low, sir. The King was determined to send someone with me, you know, so I asked for you. And he commended my choice.'

I like flattery as much as any man, but I was wary of it in this context.

'And here,' she went on, 'we have a difficulty where I least expected to find one.'

'Mistress Warley, you mean? We must go back to London empty-handed, I suppose. Unless we stay a night or two in Cambridge and you write to the King for instructions from there.'

'There's another way. If the foolish old woman won't give us Frances, we simply take her.'

'But we can't do that. Think of the scandal, madam.'

'I'm sure we would be able to find a way to contain it. It would hardly help Mistress Warley if the news got abroad, would it? After all, she has no legal right to the child. And her grandson will do what he can to suppress the story, even if he dares not cross her to her face, in this house. He is ambitious. He knows whom he must please if he is to find preferment.'

'We can't simply call Frances to us and walk out of the house with her,' I said. 'Even if the child obeyed, Mistress Warley's quite capable of using force to stop us. What do you suggest? That your servant and I draw our swords and fight our way out of here?'

The unexpected humour of the situation caught us both off guard, and we smiled at each other, suddenly as complicit as children in their shared naughtiness.

'I think the old lady would almost enjoy a battle,' Lady Quincy said.

'And she might well win. Swords or no swords, there are any number of servants or peasants in this barbarous place who will do her bidding. What if someone were hurt, or even killed? Remember, we have no standing here.'

She shifted on the pillows, and her eyes met mine. 'Then we must find a way to prevent her from raising the village against us.'

'How would we do that?' The conversation had taken such a bizarre turn that I was still smiling, still willing to indulge this flight of fancy. 'Break into her chamber? Tie her up and gag her? Lock her door, and then leave in a hurry, before anyone can stop us?'

She nodded. 'That might answer very well.'

'I spoke in jest, madam, as well you know.'

'And as well you know, sir, many a true word is spoken in jest.' She turned towards me, and the contours beneath the smock shifted. 'Mistress Warley has been most discourteous to us, and I don't mind causing her a little discomfort. I have come here for Frances, and I will leave with her.' She paused. 'If you will help me.'

'I can't. It's a reckless scheme. Mistress Warley may have no legal right to the child, but we have no right to confine her in her own house. Imagine the scandal if it got out. I can't think that the King would approve.'

'I'm not talking about the King. I'm talking about me.'

She lifted her hand from the coverlet. She held it up, parting the fingers, and the candle flame made five shadows on my leg. Then she picked up my own hand and carried it to her breast.

If I were a knave or a courtier, a strutting soldier or a lewd apprentice, I would boast of my conquest, embellishing the story to make my lusty qualities shine like a beacon. But I'm none of these things, though sometimes I wish I were: instead, my conscience ambushes me when I least expect it. For all I might wish to take these things lightly, I cannot. To do so would cut against the grain of who I am and who I was. Even when we reach man's estate, we never quite escape our childish selves.

So, back to the matter of Olivia, Lady Quincy, and myself, and what happened that night. The first time was rushed – on my part not hers – for it was not within my power to delay for an instant what I had desired for so long.

Without warning, it was over.

The candles were still burning. I was still half dressed. The very touch of her, the sight of her, had been enough to catch me unawares. Then disappointment. Was this all there was and ever would be, this quick, unhappy fumble?

I drew away from her. I felt ashamed of myself. I had allowed myself to succumb to her charms, knowing that she could not desire me. All I wanted was to retreat into the welcoming darkness.

But she said – from pity? from policy? – 'It's cold. Snuff out the candles and come to bed.'

I undressed to my shirt and climbed into the high bed. She and I lay side by side in the tolerant, enchanted darkness, only our hands touching. The sheets were warm with the heat of her body.

For a while neither of us spoke. I wondered if she despised me as I despised myself. But a bargain was still a bargain. I could not renege on it, for that would be another thing that would go against the grain. I had committed myself to help her in her mad scheme. I wondered at myself, too, for agreeing to do what she wanted, and for so strange and unsatisfactory a reward.

At her request, I had closed the bed curtains. The darkness was absolute. I felt, rather than saw, her head turn towards me on the pillow. Her breath touched my cheek, soft as a whisper.

'You must think me mad,' she said, 'even to entertain such a plan.'

'Not mad. Reckless, certainly. Either that or . . .'

'Or what?'

'Or there's something I don't yet understand.' I turned my own head. Our faces could be no more than six inches apart. I abandoned all caution, for after what had happened between us there was no reason not to speak my mind. 'You don't strike me as reckless. Quite the reverse. So there must be a reason for your determination to take Frances away, and to take her now.'

'Go on, Marwood.'

'Who wants her so badly? You or the King? Or possibly both?' I thought of Stephen and his scrofula. 'Is it to do with the King's Evil?'

She gave a snort of laughter. 'You could say that. Light the candle. I want to see you.'

I swung my legs out of bed and tugged back the bed curtain. I fumbled in the darkness for the tinderbox on the night table. It took me at least a minute to light the candle there, and I was glad of the chance to think. The flame caught at last. I watched it grow on the wick, wavering in a draught.

'Perhaps the disease must receive swift treatment if it is to be cured,' I said. 'Though it can't be as urgent as that, for a few days could not much matter either way. But perhaps you aren't certain of the King's wishes?' I paused and then said casually, 'Is she his daughter?'

'I can see why you might wonder that,' Lady Quincy said.

I waited but she said nothing more. If Frances were the King's bastard, why had she been tucked away in this godforsaken place? I remembered my speculation earlier today: that perhaps the child's mother was married to someone else, and the bastard had been spirited away to avoid the husband learning of his wife's infidelity.

I climbed back into bed and turned to look at Lady Quincy's head next to mine on the pillow. The light of the candle flickered over her face, turning it into an unfamiliar landscape: it created valleys and hills, it turned her eyes into golden pools. And yet—

The landscape was not so unfamiliar after all. I had seen

a similar face, and seen it very recently. I had been a fool. 'Madam,' I said. 'Is Frances your daughter?'

I sensed her body stiffening beside mine.

All she said was, 'Would you still help me if she were?'

'Yes. I said I would.'

I heard her letting out her breath. We lay together without speaking for a moment, our own breathing the only sound in the room. Somewhere outside, an owl hooted. A dog barked twice, and then fell silent. I tried to imagine Frances as a young woman, her plumpness gone, her scrofula cured, her body no longer a child's. Yes, it was perfectly possible that the adult Frances would make a copy of her mother. A crude copy, perhaps, but still one that derived unmistakably from the original beside me in the bed.

'She's your child,' I said. 'I'm sure of it.'

Lady Quincy's hand moved from the sheet between us and rested on my leg. She lifted the hem of my shirt. I thought, what does it matter?

This time it took longer. Towards the end, however, something unexpected happened. As the rhythm speeded up, as our double urgency reached its peak, my mind filled with an incongruous image. I thought of Catherine Lovett on the pillion saddle we had shared when we had ridden back from the refugee camp three days earlier. I thought of how she had changed since I had last seen her in May, and the touch of her body bobbing up and down behind me, and her breath on my cheek when I turned back to her.

Cat Lovett? God help me, I thought, surprised into childish superstition, what witchcraft is this?

And then, in a rush of sensation, it was all over.

# CHAPTER THIRTY-EIGHT

WHILE IT WAS still dark, I went back to my own room. I fell asleep almost at once.

I woke an hour or two later, when the dawn light was fingering its way between the curtains of the bed. Despite having had so little sleep, I felt refreshed. I needed the pot so I got up and pulled it from under the bed. As I relieved myself, I glanced down at the pallet where Stephen lay.

He wasn't there.

I flung open the curtains over the window. Light poured into the room. His covers were thrown back. He had been there when I came up to the bedroom before going to see Lady Quincy. But I hadn't noticed him when I returned. I hadn't looked. At some point in the night he must have gone, but I had no idea when.

I felt the sheets on his bed. They were cold. I pulled on my breeches, pushed my feet into shoes and put on my coat and hat, without troubling with the periwig. I left the chamber and went down to the first floor. Everything was quiet, but below me I heard a rattling and scraping that suggested the maid was lighting the kitchen fire.

Perhaps, I thought, Stephen had been hungry and had gone downstairs to see if he could beg a crust.

I followed the sounds to the kitchen. The maid, the one who had served us at dinner, started violently when she saw me.

'Have you seen Stephen?' I asked. When she looked blankly at me, I added impatiently, 'The African boy.'

She shook her head.

'He's not in his bed. Where could he be?'

She found her voice at last. 'I don't know, master.' Her eyes slid away from me, towards the back door. 'It was unbolted when I came down. I thought it was my mistress. Sometimes she can't sleep, and goes out early.'

I crossed the kitchen and opened the door. It led to a kitchen yard with a handful of chickens squabbling in a coop in one corner. I went outside. An arch led to the stables and the gateway to the road outside the house. Underneath the arch, there was a perfect print of a small, naked foot.

The maid had turned her back to me and gone back to riddling the ash from the fire. I swore under my breath. I went down past the stables and into the gardens. I called Stephen's name but he did not reply. I walked round the end of the house and entered the orchard, which lay on the other side from the stables.

The dew lay silver and cold on the ground. Two hogs rooted for late windfalls under the trees. I glanced up at my window, which was a leaded casement squeezed under the roof, with the larger window of Lady Quincy's chamber directly below it. I thought I could make out a trail of ragged, darker patches on the grass among the trees, following a wavering path towards the stream. Stephen's footprints or my imagination?

I followed them. Almost at once I saw a shadowy shape huddled on the bank near the water. Sweat broke out on my forehead. I swore and ran towards it, my shoes slithering on the wet grass.

Thank God, I thought as I drew nearer. It's not Stephen.

There was brown fur on the grass, not dark skin. I staggered to a halt over the body. The dog lay on its side with a dribble of white foam at its mouth. Its eyes were open.

Panting, I knelt beside it. It was a big animal of no particular breed. It wore a wide collar set with spikes. I touched its flank. It was cold. There was no sign of a wound.

There was no sign of Stephen either. But there were more footprints in the grass, and they led towards the misty waters of the Fen.


'Poison,' Mistress Warley said in a tone that brooked no argument as she prodded the corpse with her stick. 'If Grimball were prone to fits, we should have known it.'

'But where's Stephen?' I said.

'The blackamoor? Ten to one he did this. Some witchcraft of his own. I hold you responsible, sir.'

I had found the old lady in the kitchen when I returned to the house. When I told her what had happened, she had glared at me as if it were my fault and sent the maid upstairs to rouse her grandson. Mr Warley had hurried down, still with his nightcap on and with a cloak flung over his bedgown, and we had walked into the orchard.

As we were trooping back to the house, Ann arrived with

a message from her mistress. Lady Quincy sent her compliments to Mistress Warley and begged to inform her that she and her party would leave Hitcham St Martin this morning. The message made no mention of Frances.

'We can't leave until we've found Stephen,' I said to Mistress Warley. 'He must be somewhere.'

'What's happened?' Ann asked, too surprised to be respectful.

'The boy slipped out at night. I don't know when. His bed was empty when I got up.'

The maid was staring at me. Usually she would have expected to sleep with her mistress, as she had done in Cambridge and Puckeridge on the way here. If she didn't know for sure about my nocturnal visit to Lady Quincy, she certainly must suspect it.

Mr Warley turned slowly around, making a complete circle, as if in the hope of spotting Stephen sitting in a tree or strolling towards us. There was a frown on his thin, dark face.

'A fit of madness? Moonstruck – there was a moon last night? Africans are not as we are, sir. The rational faculty is not as developed, and there's some debate as to whether in fact they have souls as we do, or are closer to the horse or the dog in that respect. One thing is certain, they are in thrall to ungodly superstitions. My grandmother is right about that.'

'Stephen's not mad,' I said. 'He must have had a reason to go outside.'

'He's not here, sir,' Warley said. 'He can't have left the house and gardens. That wall is nigh on ten feet high, and topped with spikes.'

The old woman ground her stick into the mud. 'If the boy's not on the earth, he must be on the water. Or in the water.' She stared out at the Fen, grey and ghostly in the first light of the day. 'Perhaps he's drowned himself,' she went on with an air that suggested that, taken all in all, this would be a happy outcome for everyone concerned. 'After all, he's unlikely to know that self-murder is a mortal sin.'

'Then let's look for him,' I snapped. 'You must have a boat of some sort.'

'We rely on punts in this part of the country, sir,' Warley said, adapting the didactic manner that seemed to come naturally to him. 'Not the most elegant of conveyances, but appropriate to this setting, owing to their shallow drafts. Every Fenman has his punt.'

'Is there one missing from here?' I asked.

'No,' Mistress Warley said, pointing with her stick. 'Our own is there – moored at the foot of the orchard.'

While we had been talking, the light had been growing stronger and the mist was beginning to lift. Beyond the Warleys' punt was a stretch of open water fringed with islets, reeds and stunted saplings. A dark shape was moving among them, which a moment later resolved itself into a smaller punt with a man poling in its stern.

'Someone eeling or fishing,' Warley said.

'Ragfield,' said his grandmother crisply. 'Cottage by the cattle pound. Lives with his mother.' She frowned. 'Something's upset him. Call him over.'

We walked to the landing stage, with Ann trailing behind the two Warleys and me. Ragfield was punting as if his life depended on it, driving his pole into the muddy water with unmistakable urgency, splashing himself with water. He had seen us and was coming in our direction. The unwieldy craft was incapable of speed, and it wallowed from side to side.

'What's he doing?' Warley said. 'Has the fellow gone stark mad?'

'He looks scared out of his wits,' Mistress Warley said.

'Mistress!' Ragfield cried as he approached. 'Master!'

He drove the punt into the bank with such force that he almost lost his balance. He scrambled on to the land. I seized the painter and made it fast. The punt was small and crowded with baskets. There was a powerful smell of fish.

'Mistress, we need vicar!' His accent was so hard and broad I could hardly distinguish what he was saying. 'There's a marsh imp out there, black as sin, and he cursed me when he saw me, and I'm damned as sure as hellfire if vicar don't come quick.'

'An imp?' Mistress Warley demanded. 'Do you mean a blackamoor?'

'No, an imp, mistress, an imp, and I could hear him shrieking his spells at me.'

'Where exactly?'

'Prior's Hump.'

'It must be Stephen,' I said. 'Let me fetch him.'

'But how did he get there?' Mistress Warley said suddenly. 'Someone must have taken him.'

'The dog . . .?' I said.

She glanced at me, and I saw she understood me perfectly. 'We have a trespasser, it seems. First he came here, killed our dog somehow, and then he took the boy to Prior's Hump.' I raised my eyebrows, and she went on, 'It's a rocky outcrop.' She pointed again. 'About two hundred yards away over there, behind that big reedbed. It's part of the Warley estate.'

'Where is he now?'

'The rogue could be still there. But why would he kidnap a boy like that? Unless the boy went of his own accord.'

'I doubt that,' I said. 'I must go there at once.'

'Ragfield will take us,' Mistress Warley said.

I stared at her. 'Us?'

'I shall come too, sir. I don't care for trespassers on my land.'

'Madam, it's hardly suitable that a gentlewoman of your —'

'Suitable, sir? Who are you to tell me what's suitable in my own garden?'

'Perhaps Mr Warley should come in your place.'

She threw her grandson a glance that spoke volumes for her opinion of him. 'I want to see for myself if we have poachers. We set our own traps there.'

I shrugged. 'As you wish. You should fetch a thicker cloak though, madam, and I shall bring a pistol.'

Warley cleared his throat. 'Very wise, sir, if I may say so. I would of course come with you, but as a man of the cloth I fear I should be more of a hindrance than a help.'

'Ragfield? While you're waiting, bail out that punt of ours. It's larger than yours and a good deal cleaner.'

'Must I go with you, mistress? The imp will—'

'Don't talk nonsense,' Mistress Warley snapped. 'Whatever the imp can do to you, I can do worse, I promise you that.'

I beckoned Ann as I walked back to the house. 'Tell your mistress what's happened.' The merest hint of a plan was beginning to form in my mind. Anything was worth trying. 'Have her dress as soon as she can, and pack her things. Tell the postillion to saddle our horses.'

She stared up at me with wide eyes. Without my wig, the scarring on that side of my head was more obvious.

'Make haste.' I lowered my voice. 'And wake Mistress Frances, too. Tell her ladyship that this may be her chance.'

The maid gave me a startled glance, but she didn't argue or question me. I suspected she knew her lady's business here already.

We went into the house by the back door. I went up to my room and found my cloak. The pistol was still in a holster that had been attached to my horse's saddle. I took it out, checked the priming and stuck it in my belt.

On the landing below there were already sounds of hasty movement in Lady Quincy's chamber. I went downstairs and into the yard. Mistress Warley was walking back to the place where the punts were moored. Her grandson was beside her, gesticulating, and I guessed he was trying to dissuade her from going. I hoped he wouldn't succeed.

Ragfield was waiting by the Warleys' punt. It was no more than a flat, open box: a crude rectangle of planks, with more planks below, coated with pitch both inside and out to repel the water. I helped Mistress Warley into it. She moved stiffly but calmly to the single seat, which was another plank placed across the craft about halfway down. She sat in the middle, her stick across her lap, in a way that made it impossible for me to sit beside her. I crouched in front of her in the bow.

'It's cold, isn't it?' Warley said from the bank. 'I'll rouse the village. And I'll make sure they light the fires downstairs. You'll need breakfast, too, and a warm drink.'

He retreated towards the house. Ragfield began the laborious process of turning the punt about. I looked round. Mistress Warley was staring after her grandson.

'Mr Warley is better off in his college,' she said abruptly. 'He's a fish out of water here, though that's an odd thing to

301

say in a watery place as full of fish as anywhere in the kingdom.'

She turned away, drawing her cloak tightly around her. It was indeed very cold on the water. Ragfield was punting more efficiently than before. The mud, only a foot or two below the surface, sucked ceaselessly at the pole. Using it as a primitive rudder, he steered a course that took us round one end of the reedbed. I took up a paddle that lay in the bottom of the punt, and did my best to help.

The journey didn't take more than ten or fifteen minutes. Once we were past the reeds, Prior's Hump lay before us. The island was about thirty yards long, too small to serve any agricultural purpose. At one end there was the hump that gave it its name. It was covered with scrubby trees, except at the lower part, where a tangle of bushes grew untidily in the mud.

'Moor there,' Mistress Warley said, using her stick yet again as an extension of her index finger.

I craned my head round as we approached. 'Stephen's there,' I said, unable to keep the relief from my voice. 'I can see him on the hump. He's waving.'

Frowning, she peered in that direction, her head hunched forward on her shoulders. 'Can you see the poacher?'

'No, madam.' I guessed that she was short-sighted. In a flash, I glimpsed a method of solving the problem of how to remove Frances from Hitcham St Martin. I launched into a lie. 'No – I'm not sure . . . Yes, I believe I can – I think someone's over there.'

'On the other side of the hump? I knew it. That's where our traps and nets are.'

The punt bumped against the stump of a tree on the edge

of the island. I scrambled off the punt and made the painter fast. Stephen had seen us and was moving towards us.

Mistress Warley rose to her feet, steadied herself with her stick and moved cautiously towards me. 'Take my hand.' She climbed on to the bank and glanced back. 'You too, Ragfield. Let me take your arm.'

'But, mistress——'

'That's not an imp, you numbskull. That's just a boy with a dark skin. Come here at once. If there's a poacher on my land, I want him caught and brought before a magistrate.'

Ragfield obeyed. He was more afraid of the old woman than of poachers or the black imp of Prior's Hump.

I shaded my eyes. 'Yes, I'm sure there's someone over there . . . There's movement among the trees. The fellow's punt must be on the other side of the island.'

'Quickly then. We shall need your pistol.'

Stephen stumbled towards us. He was trembling with cold. I took off my cloak and draped it over his shoulders.

'Get on the punt. Sit in it.' I gave him a little push towards it and raised my voice. 'To the side there, madam. Do you see him? If we hurry we can cut him off.'

I took her arm and guided her further away from the punt, leading her towards a path winding between tussocks of coarse grass among marshy puddles. Ragfield was on her other side.

I glanced back. Stephen was on board the punt. Mistress Warley forged ahead.

I released her arm, turned and ran as fast as I could back to the punt. She cried out behind me but I couldn't make out her words. I tore the painter free, pushed the punt into the water and tried to leap aboard. I managed one leg in but the other trailed in the water. The mud sucked at my foot. With a mighty effort I hauled myself dripping into the bottom of the punt.

We were about six feet away from the bank, drifting slowly over the water. Mistress Warley had realized what was happening and was walking back as fast as she could, clinging to Ragfield. I seized the pole and pushed it into the water. The mud gripped it. I pushed hard. The punt shot away from me, and my body extended itself over the water, one hand still holding the pole.

Mistress Warley was shouting, and so was Ragfield. I felt a pair of hands gripping my free wrist, the one that was not attached to the pole.

For a moment the issue was in doubt. Then Stephen's extra weight drew me back into the punt. I twisted the pole and pulled free from the mud.

Mistress Warley's shouting continued. With Stephen paddling vigorously in the bow, I poled the punt slowly and uncertainly towards the reedbed and Hitcham St Martin.

# CHAPTER THIRTY-NINE

'THANK YOU FOR your hospitality, Mr Warley,' Lady Quincy said. 'And pray give my compliments to your grandmother when she returns.'

The six of us were on horseback in the yard of the Warleys' house. Frances sat on the pillion behind Lady Quincy; Stephen shared my saddle; and Ann, a disapproving expression on her face, was behind the postillion.

Lady Quincy rode out into the lane. The postillion followed. I lingered a moment. I heard shouting from the bottom of the garden. The stableboy and one of the peasants had gone to assist in the rescue.

'I regret it had to be like this,' I said. 'I hope Mistress Warley comes to no harm from her adventure.'

'So do I.' Warley was looking desperately worried, as well he should. 'She will miss Frances.'

'I know. But she would be unwise to try to get the child back. She has no grounds for it. And you yourself, sir – you have seen the King's letter. I'm sure you will discourage Mistress Warley from acting imprudently.'

I nodded to him and rode after the others. Warley was in awe of his grandmother, but time was on his side, and her power over him diminished as soon as he left the village. Besides, as I had hinted none too subtly, it was in his interests to restrain her: he was an ambitious man and, if he wanted preferment, he would be a fool to risk losing the King's favour.

We didn't linger in the Fens. We made good time to Cambridge, where we dined at the Rose and hired fresh horses from the livery stable. I enquired after Burbrough. He was fully conscious and in his right mind; but he remained in great pain; he had told his attendants that he had slipped on the bank and fallen into the mill race while on the way to see the miller.

In the afternoon we rode on to Puckeridge, where we put up again at the Falcon. Both children were exhausted, and Frances was weeping silently. I wondered if she had ever been away from Mistress Warley and Hitcham St Martin since she had gone to the Warleys as a baby.

While Lady Quincy and I were eating supper in her chamber, the news was brought up that her coach had arrived.

'Thank God,' she said. 'At least we shall travel more comfortably tomorrow.'

We went to bed early. Nothing was said because there was nothing to say. She had been courteous to me – grateful, even – but I knew that there was no question of my going to her in the night. I wasn't even sure that I wanted to. She had never desired me for myself, only for what I could do for her. What had occurred at Hitcham St Martin had been in the nature of a transaction. Each party had rendered the other a service, and the invisible contract between us had been fulfilled.

I told the landlord that my Lady Quincy was of a nervous disposition. Frances and Ann the servant slept in her bedchamber. I made sure the window was shuttered and barred, and I set the postillion on the landing outside her door with a pistol and a cudgel. I was in the neighbouring room.

Stephen was still awake when I came up to our chamber. I had not tried to question him during our ride – he had dozed, or at least pretended to doze, for most of the way, closing his eyes and wrapping himself in silence as if it were a blanket. I crouched down by his mattress and gave his shoulder a gentle shake. He stared at me with wide eyes. He was breathing very quickly.

'You've done nothing wrong,' I said. 'But I want you to tell me what happened last night.'

He swallowed. 'I couldn't sleep, master. I – I heard you go out somewhere.'

I nodded, as if my absence had been nothing out of the ordinary. 'Yes. And?'

'I got up and looked out of the window in case . . . in case you were outside. I thought I might see you.'

Scared of being alone in the dark? Nothing strange in that. I had feared the night and its monsters myself at his age.

'There was a moon, sir – enough to see a man in the orchard. It could have been you, but I wasn't sure, and you'd told me to keep a watch for strangers. So I went down to see.'

He was sitting up in bed and the candlelight picked out the whites of his eyes and his teeth. His courage humbled me, and so did the thought that he had wanted to please me so much that it had outweighed his fears.

'When I was in the orchard, I tripped over the dog and the man seized me, and took me away and into the boat. He said he would cut my throat if I cried out, and he carried me to the island where there was the other man.'

'But why?'

'They wanted to question me. They wanted to know where Mistress Frances was. Which chamber she was lying in, whether she was alone. But I couldn't tell them.'

'Two men. Did you see them properly?'

He shook his head. 'The moon had gone in. Big men, I think. The one who brought me was fat. The other one was the master. He said it was too late to do anything, it would soon be growing light, and they should leave me here.'

'Did they hurt you?' I asked.

'No. The fat man asked if he should try persuasion, but his master said no, it would not answer as I was as much a stranger here as they were, and he believed I was telling the truth. So they left me in that place and went away in their boat.' He began to tremble. 'It was so cold, sir. I thought I would die.'

I patted his arm. 'You did well. Go to sleep.'

Stephen must have been bone-weary. He fell asleep almost at once. I built up the fire and sat before it, wrapped in my cloak. My body was tired but my mind was as restless as a dog with fleas.

The Bishop and his servant were probably on their way back to London, but I could not run the risk of their making another attempt to seize Mistress Frances. Their abortive foray last night had been reckless in the extreme. I guessed that the Bishop's servant had intended to waylay the kitchen maid when she came down to light the fire at dawn, and force her to show him Mistress Frances's chamber. Then the sudden appearance of Stephen in the garden had forced him to retreat.

I wondered how Cat was faring in London, and prayed that she was safe.

Next day, we climbed into her ladyship's coach and set off for London. There were five of us – Lady Quincy, her maid, the two children and myself – and we had a silent journey in its swaying interior. Frances's eyes were red, and she looked as if she had had little sleep. Her mother, sitting in the opposite corner, glanced at her from time to time, her own face as revealing as a shuttered house.

At first, Lady Quincy tried to engage Frances in conversation. She talked of the wonders of London, of the King's court, the shops, the theatres, and the outings on the river. Frances nodded occasionally and made the shortest possible answers when her mother appealed to her directly. Frances, I thought, had become more than a pawn in a political intrigue: Lady Quincy also wanted the girl for herself; she had suddenly discovered that she was a mother in need of a daughter.

It was the middle of the afternoon when the coach turned into Cradle Alley and stopped at Lady Quincy's door. There was a bustle outside as the servants made ready for their mistress. I climbed out and handed Lady Quincy down. She smiled at me as she took my hand. Frances, Ann and Stephen followed her up the steps to the house.

Lady Quincy paused in the doorway. Frances was beside her, and her mother's hand rested on her shoulder.

'Thank you for escorting us, Mr Marwood. I am much obliged to you. Goodbye.'

The door closed. The servants were unloading the luggage from the coach. As it was still broad daylight, I hired a boy to carry my bag and walked with him behind me through the ruins of the city to Fleet Street, and thence to the Savoy. After the confinement of the coach, I was glad of the exercise at first, for my muscles were still aching from the riding.

The sky was grey, pressing down on London, heavy with the promise of rain. I felt like a man who had emerged from a bout of fever. As I walked through the streets, the city around me seemed provisional and transitory, neither what it had been nor what it would become. It was broad daylight, so there were plenty of people among the ruins and temporary shelters and half-made houses. But even the most respectable and wealthy of them had an impermanent air, like gypsies and beggars and other men who lack a settled home. The Fire had left its mark on the inhabitants of London, as well as on its buildings.

My spirits were depressed. It was not until I reached Cheapside that I allowed myself to admit the reason. For nearly a year I had carried round with me the thought of Olivia, Lady Quincy. She had been the focus of my desires and, on another level, in my barely acknowledged dreams, the heroine in the drama of my future life.

All that was gone, partly by my own wish. She hadn't made a fool of me. She hadn't twisted me around her little finger so that I would commit any knavery for her that she cared to ask. I had done that for her all by myself.

No more. The spell was broken. But there was an absence within me. Nothing filled the place where she had been. I had lost something, as surely as if a surgeon had sliced me open and cut out a vital organ. Here, among the ruins of London, I was like a newborn child, naked in the bright light of day and alone in the company of strangers.

I smelled the ale on Sam's breath when I entered the hall of my house. He pushed the door shut with his crutch. I dropped my bag on the floor and tossed my cloak to him.

He caught it nimbly, draped it over his shoulder and executed a clumsy bow. 'A gentleman called to see you, sir. Twice. Name of Milcote.'

'Did he leave a message?'

'No, sir. Only to say that he called. He was quite put out you weren't here.'

That sounded ominous. Perhaps there was news about Clarendon's missing servant, Matthew Gorse. I toyed with the idea of going immediately to Clarendon House in search of Milcote. But if there was news, it was probably bad and it would surely keep until the morning. So too would my inevitable meeting with Mr Chiffinch at Whitehall.

'Anyone else? Or anyone showing signs of interest in my house? Asking questions? Watching?'

'No one,' he said with a hint of disappointment.

'Tell Margaret I'm back. I'll have supper early. Light a fire in the parlour. And bring up a bottle of the Rhenish wine from Mr Newcomb.' I changed my mind about the last item, not wishing to trust Sam with the key of the closet where I kept my wine. 'On second thoughts, I shall bring it up myself.'

He gave me an injured look, perfectly understanding my change of mind, and hobbled away.

I felt better when I had eaten. When I had finished,

Margaret came to clear the table. I beckoned her over to where I was sitting by the fire with the last of the wine at my elbow.

'Mistress Hakesby?' I said softly. 'How does she do with your friend Dorcas?'

'All's well, sir. Though God knows, Dorcas's lodging is no place for one such as her.'

I suspected that in Margaret's estimation, no one's lodging would have been good enough for Catherine Lovett. 'And is she helping with the *Gazette*?'

She nodded. 'Aye, master, she helped Dorcas with yesterday's round. You wouldn't recognize her, with her face all dark, and a ragged old cloak and a shawl over her head.'

'I want to talk to her as soon as possible.' There was a chance that Cat could tell me more about Gorse and the events leading up to Edward Alderley's death. Also, if I were entirely frank with myself, I was curious to discover if I felt differently about her since her unexpected intrusion into my mind while I was in Lady Quincy's bed. My curiosity was purely academic, for if all went well she would soon be married to Master Hakesby.

'She and Dorcas will be at Mr Newcomb's tomorrow morning, sir, to collect their bundles.'

'On a Wednesday?' I said. The usual *Gazette* days were Monday and Thursday.

'It's because Mr Newcomb's having a new press installed on Thursday. They had to change the day.'

Mr Newcomb was the government printer whose work included the lucrative *Gazette* contract; hence the present of Rhenish wine he had given me. I had lodged with him for a few months when my father was still alive. On *Gazette* days his apprentice distributed the bundles early in the morning to the women who took them about London. The process was supervised by his journeyman, who at the same time paid the women for the distribution of the last issue.

I briefly considered telling Margaret to send a message to Dorcas, asking her to call with Cat at Infirmary Close after they had collected their bundles. Then I had another thought.

'What time do they fetch their bundles?'

'Six o'clock, sir. Mr Newcomb likes them to be prompt.'

'We have had our difficulties with distribution, as you know,' I said. 'Mr Williamson is most concerned. I shall make an unannounced inspection tomorrow morning on his behalf. There's no need to mention that to anyone.'

Margaret stared at me, screwing up her features as she often did when she was thinking. She was a long way from being a fool. I waved her away.

# CHAPTER FORTY

C AT WAS RUNNING late. Yesterday, Dorcas had sprained her ankle when she had stumbled into the gutter that carried the refuse down the centre of Carter Lane near St Paul's. She had also spoiled the remaining sheets of Monday's *Gazette*, which were wet and foul from the gutter. By this time, they had distributed the newspaper over most of their assigned round. Cat had helped Dorcas back to her lodging in an alley off Fenchurch Street. After that, it had been too late for her to collect fresh copies from the Savoy and complete the round by herself.

She was doing it today, leaving Dorcas to rest. But the task had taken much longer than she had expected. It was nearly half-past four by the time she reached the Green Dragon Inn, or rather what was left of it after the Fire. The landlord was running the business as best he could in the ruins of his establishment, with a temporary roof over the ordinary, which had a long table where anyone might sit and dine on the dishes of the day if they had the money.

Cat gave the landlord his copy, and he swore at her because

it was late. She dodged a predatory ostler and went into the street. The Green Dragon was on the corner of Thames Street and Botolph Lane. Her next destination was Botolph's Wharf below Mary Hill.

She glanced up the lane and felt a stab of emotion, fear probably. There was Mr Milcote, Lord Clarendon's gentleman, walking towards her.

It was a piece of ill-luck. She ducked back into what remained of the inn's stable. Much as she would like to ask Milcote a few questions, she couldn't afford to let him see her.

He strode past, not giving her a glance. Her relief was tempered by the strangeness of his appearance. His clothes were dark and shabby. He wasn't wearing his sword. Even his bearing was altered, she thought, for his shoulders were bowed and his eyes cast down. He wore a deep, wide hat, and under the brim she glimpsed his profile as he passed. His face looked paler than usual and perhaps worried, even miserable. She wondered what business a man like Milcote could possibly have in this mean and ruinous part of the city?

The following morning Cat had another shock, another unexpected encounter, this time at Mr Newcomb's printing house. She and Dorcas were among the crowd waiting to be paid for the last delivery, and to receive the next.

There was Marwood standing in the doorway. Cat ducked her head at once. She watched him from the corner of her eye. She saw him sniff. The air smelled strongly of ink, wet and newly applied to paper. A printing house must be familiar territory for him, she realized, dense with childhood memories.

At the sight of him, noise and movement ebbed away,

leaving an uneasy silence. The room was packed, mainly with women. They were of all ages, most of them swathed in shawls and cloaks against the early morning chill. They looked at him, then rapidly away. They stood more stiffly than before, as if afraid a sudden movement might break something.

This was power, Cat thought, or at least power of a sort; and she didn't much like it. Marwood was Mr Williamson's clerk and the man who gave Newcomb the printer his orders; he had the power to take away their livelihoods with the snap of his fingers.

In the silence, he glanced about the room, as if savouring his control over them. 'Carry on,' he said, and his voice sounded harsh in her ears. 'There's no time to be wasted.'

A wooden counter stained with ink was set at right angles to the door, with Mr Newcomb's journeyman and his apprentice behind it. The journeyman was paying the women for Monday's round. The women signed their names – or more usually made a cross or a thumbprint – on his list to record the receipt of their wages.

The apprentice had another list in front of him, which recorded the various routes around London, the numbers of copies and the names of those who carried them. Beyond him, at the end of the counter nearer the door to the print shop itself, was a small, inky boy, one of Mr Newcomb's brood, who brought out the bundles of newspapers and gave them to each woman as the apprentice ticked them off.

Mr Marwood and Mr Williamson insisted that everything be done in a certain way, Dorcas had told her, and that proper records be kept of the *Gazette*'s production. Each sheet of paper was kept, and every six months they were bound into a book, together with a detailed account of the monies disbursed on behalf of the King. Dorcas had told Cat this with pride, as if the record-keeping connected her directly with the King, as if he personally inspected each sheet, each entry in the accounts.

Marwood went behind the counter. He made a show of inspecting the lists and checking the amounts of money the journeyman was disbursing.

'Continue,' he said. 'I wish to study the procedure.'

He leaned against the wall and watched. The women shuffled up to the counter in ones and twos. At last it was the turn of Cat and Dorcas, a little woman with skin like a walnut shell. Cat kept her eyes down. She watched the journeyman counting out the money from his leather pouch. Dorcas signed for it with a scrawled cross. Cat scratched a pair of illegible initials, unlike her usual handwriting, which was notably well-formed and clear.

The two women moved along to the apprentice and finally to the printer's boy. As he was handing them their bundles of the *Gazette*, Marwood rapped his knuckles on the counter. The boy froze.

'I shall inspect one of those bundles,' he said. 'They look slim to me.' He glanced down at the apprentice's list. 'There should be fifty in each. We shall see, won't we?'

The journeyman cleared his throat. 'I swear they're all there, sir, down to the last copy. Mr Newcomb's most particular.'

'There's no harm in making sure,' Marwood said. 'You don't disagree with me, I take it?'

'No, sir, beg pardon, I'm sure.'

Marwood glanced about, pretending to survey the room

317

before making his choice. 'This one.' He indicated Cat with his finger. 'You. It's too busy here – come into the passage and I'll watch you count your bundle.'

Cat felt her colour rising. Beside her, Dorcas stiffened and sent Marwood a hostile glance before lowering her head. The old woman probably attributed Marwood's motive to lust rather than attention to business, and so would almost everyone else in the room.

Cat followed him into the passage. He told her to close the door. That was when she lost her temper. What a vain coxcomb Marwood was, strutting about in the printing house as if he owned it and everyone it contained, including her. She glared at him.

'They'll think you're stealing kisses from me and fumbling at my clothes,' she hissed. 'How dare you?'

'Better that than the truth,' Marwood said. 'I got back to London yesterday evening. I need to talk privately with you before I go to Whitehall. Untie the bundle in case anyone comes.'

Her fingers fumbled at the twine, tugging viciously at the knot.

'How are you faring?' he said quietly.

'Well enough.' She stared at him. 'I can't say I've much enjoyment in life at present, but no one's troubled me.' Her lips tightened. 'Apart from you, of course. Where have you been? I thought you'd forgotten me.'

'After we came back from Woor Green, the King sent for me. The very same evening.'

'Dear God – he knows about me?'

'Not that you're here. He still believes you're responsible for your cousin's death, I think, though it's hard to tell what's truly in his mind. But he didn't summon me about the murder. He commanded me to accompany Lady Quincy down to Cambridgeshire. We left London at dawn on Friday.'

She blinked. 'Is this somehow to do with Edward's death?'

'I'm not sure. I think it must be but I can't for the life of me see how. Your cousin was involved in an intrigue that was bigger and more dangerous than he realized. And he paid for it with his life.' He looked away. 'Unless . . .'

Unless, Cat thought, the intrigue had been incidental to Edward's death. She could read what was passing through Marwood's mind as clearly as though it were written on his forehead: unless, he was thinking, Cat herself had killed her cousin as she had sworn to do. He knew better than anyone that she was not afraid to fight back with any weapon at her disposal. He had watched her push Edward's father from the tower of St Paul's to his death. He knew that she had tried to kill Edward himself after he raped her; and she had left him maimed for life. The first time she met Marwood himself, she had bitten his hand to the bone when, as it had turned out, he had been trying to help her. Like the cat she had watched outside the Mitre last week, when she was threatened, she hissed and she scratched. And why should she not?

She frowned at him. 'What did my aunt want in Cambridgeshire? And why did she want you with her?'

'It was a family matter,' he said awkwardly. 'This isn't the time – I will tell you later.'

She sensed he was embarrassed, and pressed him harder: 'And why *you*?'

'I believe the King trusts me to be discreet.'

She snorted. 'Presumably my Aunt Quincy trusts you as well.'

He was silent.

'And what of Mr Hakesby?' she said. 'How is he? Is he free?'

'I've heard nothing. That's one reason I'm going to Whitehall now, to make enquiries.'

'You must help him.' Cat came a step closer and stared intently at him. 'He's not well. And he's done nothing wrong.'

'If I can help him, I shall.'

'Tell him I'm safe, and that I think of him. And when you've seen him, will you send word to me by Margaret?'

Marwood nodded, and turned his head away. She fought back panic. What if Mr Hakesby was dead? The thought opened up a prospect of desolation to her.

'I wish to God this was over,' Cat said suddenly. 'I can't abide this skulking in corners. I want employment. What's happening at Clarendon House? Have they stopped work on the pavilion?'

'I'm not sure. I have to see Mr Milcote — I'll ask him. Lord Clarendon has his troubles at present, so he may not have much time to think of his garden.'

'I saw him yesterday afternoon. Mr Milcote, I mean.'

'Did he see you?' Marwood said, alarmed.

Flustered, she shook her head. 'He was in a hurry, and it was raining.'

He stared at her, his eyes narrowing. 'Where was this?'

'In Botolph Lane, the Thames Street end.'

'There's not much left down there, is there?'

'Plenty of temporary shelters,' Cat said. 'They've cleared most of the cellars. The Green Dragon's reopened. And the Botolph's Wharf is nearly as busy as ever.'

'Why were you there?'

She stared, disliking the interrogation. She wished she hadn't mentioned Milcote. 'Why are you so interested all of a sudden? They take the *Gazette* at the Green Dragon, and so does the man who manages the wharf.'

'And Milcote? What was he doing down there?'

'How should I know?' She paused, but Marwood said nothing. 'I didn't recognize him at first,' she went on suddenly. 'He looked different.'

'In what way?'

'Usually his clothes befit his station. But yesterday he looked like a lawyer's clerk, and a shabby one at that, with his hat pulled down. He wasn't even wearing his sword.'

Marwood was looking fixedly at her, and his gaze made her uncomfortable. 'Cat,' he said, and the use of her name surprised, and even shocked her. 'Cat, before I go, I want—'

The door to the printing shop opened, and a tide of women carrying inky bundles flowed into the passage.

'Very well,' he said to Cat in a loud, harsh voice. 'Tie up your bundle, woman, and go on your round.'

# CHAPTER FORTY-ONE

M EN HAVE STRANGE reservoirs of strength. One cannot plumb their depths, or even suspect their existence, until circumstances draw them out. I would never have thought Brennan had such a store of resilience as he must have shown when he was imprisoned in Scotland Yard.

'They let him out on Monday,' the sergeant at the prison said. 'Best thing to do with him. They couldn't get a word out of him, even when the fever went down, and there was nothing against him.'

'What about Mr Hakesby?' I asked, jingling the coins in my pocket.

'I kept an eye on him, sir, like you said. Indeed, I watched over the poor gentleman like a mother watches a baby.'

'How is he? Has he eaten?'

'He's taken a little broth, though not enough to keep a sparrow alive.' The sergeant's hands rested for a moment on his great belly as if to emphasize the contrast between his own appetite and Mr Hakesby's. 'Mind you, sir, his teeth are chattering so much he could hardly get a word out even if he wanted to. A doctor came to see him on Tuesday. Young Brennan sent him. Not that it helped. I could have told him it would be a waste of money. If a man's prone to ague and he comes here, the damp will bring on the shaking fits, and the fits won't go away until he does.'

'Has he been questioned?'

The sergeant nodded. 'Several times. Not a chatty gentleman, is he?'

I wondered why Chiffinch had kept Hakesby here so long. Perhaps there was other evidence against him. More likely he had simply been forgotten. I took out some change. 'Would you take me to him?'

The sergeant's vast hand swallowed the silver coins. I followed his swaying rump down the passage to the cells, past the cries of the unfortunates penned in the common chamber. The pervasive stench of excrement and despair filled my nostrils.

I found Hakesby where I had left him, lying on his cot with his face to the wall. But when I said his name, he turned slowly towards me. I was shocked by his appearance – his face resembled a skull covered in grubby linen, and his clothes had acquired the grime of the prison. He had not been shaved, and the grey stubble gave him a shaggy, feral look, like one who has walked too long in the wilderness with nothing but his own thoughts for company.

'Bang on the door when you want to leave, sir,' the sergeant said.

When we were alone, I bent down and brought my lips close to Hakesby's ear. 'She's safe, sir. She asks after you.'

A shudder ran through him. He struggled to sit up. I put my arm around his shoulders and helped him to sit against the wall.

'Do they still—' he broke off and tried to moisten his chapped lips. 'Do they still believe she—?'

'I think so. I'm not sure, though – I've been away these last few days.' I hesitated, remembering the plan I had found in Hakesby's notebook on my last visit. 'I went to Jerusalem College.'

He looked confused. 'About the chapel? You?'

'I had other business with Mr Warley there.'

Hakesby nodded. 'Lady Clarendon's cousin. She most kindly suggested my name to him.' He veered back to Cat. 'Are you sure she's safe?'

'Yes.' I looked about me. There was an uncovered jug with a little beer in it on the floor. A fly floated on the surface. Beside it was a platter containing nothing but a rat dropping. 'You must eat, sir, and drink, to restore your strength. I shall tell them to bring you something on my way out.'

His hand shot out. Long, bony fingers wrapped round my wrist. 'Are you leaving me?'

'I'll return, sir. I promise.'

I left him and walked through Scotland Yard to the more elegant surroundings of Whitehall itself. Hakesby looked worse than he had when I had seen him last week, but at least he was talking to me.

I went through the public rooms of the royal apartments and sent a message to Mr Chiffinch. As I had expected, he kept me waiting. Waiting was the principal activity of Whitehall, and it was almost midday before a servant brought me to him. We went into the Privy Garden and walked up and down the gravelled paths under the windows of the Privy Gallery.

'The King was asking only last night whether you'd returned,' Chiffinch said. 'When did you get back?'

'Yesterday evening.'

'And what happened with you and Lady Quincy?'

I could hardly reveal the whole truth on that subject, but I told him the rest of what had happened at Cambridge and at Hitcham St Martin, including my inconsiderate treatment of Mistress Warley. Afterwards, we walked in silence for a while.

'You think this man Burbrough was attacked?' Chiffinch said abruptly.

'I think it probable, though he did not want anyone to know, even though he nearly died as a consequence. He must have been to some degree in league with this man they call the Bishop. But they fell out.'

Chiffinch grunted. 'It's possible. Burbrough was appointed to his fellowship under the Commonwealth, when Cambridge was a different place from what it is now. And the Duke of Buckingham still has friends in that quarter, many of them old Commonwealth men who'd bring back Cromwell if they only could.'

That at least could not happen, not on this side of the grave: Cromwell's head was stuck on a pole above the Palace of Westminster. But Buckingham was very much alive. It was becoming clearer and clearer that I had stumbled into something much more dangerous than a child with the King's Evil.

We turned at the end of a path, which brought us round to face the windows of the Privy Gallery range on the north side of the garden. The sun was out and reflected back to us from hundreds of panes of glass.

'And the child?' Chiffinch said. 'Mistress Frances?'

'At my Lady Quincy's.'

'What about the Warleys? Should we look for trouble in that quarter?'

'Not from Warley himself, I think. He has an eye to prefer-ment. But Mistress Warley is another matter. She's attached to the child.'

'I think we can deal with her. If the old woman wants the King's pension to continue, she'll not make trouble, despite your behaviour to her, and despite the child. The estate's mortgaged, and they owe money everywhere. She couldn't have managed without the pension these last ten years or so, and nor could young Warley. They barely survive as it is.'

I wasn't surprised to hear that – the signs of the family's reduced circumstances had been plain to see, both in Warley's rooms at Cambridge and in the house at Hitcham St Martin. But it was interesting that Chiffinch thought the Warleys' pension would still be paid, even after the removal of the child from their care, presumably to ensure their continued silence.

It was at that moment, as we paced on down the path, that I realized Mistress Frances must indeed be the King's daughter. Nothing else could explain the continued expense of maintaining her, and the extraordinary efforts that Chiffinch was making on behalf of his master. Nothing else could explain Buckingham's interest in her. But what had the Duke in mind? After all, the child was just another royal bastard, and not even a boy.

'On another matter, sir,' I said hesitantly, 'is there news of Mistress Lovett?'

'Eh?' He dragged his mind away from Mistress Frances. 'No. The bitch has gone to ground. But we'll dig her out sooner or later.'

'I'm not sure she's guilty.'

'You must convince the King of that, not me.'

'Another fact has come to light that may have a bearing on Alderley's murder. About Lord Clarendon's servant – the one who found Alderley's body in the well. His name's Gorse. He's disappeared. As far as I know, he's not been seen since he helped us move the body.'

Chiffinch stroked the wart on his chin. 'You'd better go to Clarendon House and find out if he's turned up since you were away.'

'Yes, sir. And there's another thing. It turns out that Gorse once worked for Alderley at the family's old house, Barnabas Place. It's possible that he and Alderley were conspiring together.'

'To what end?'

'Against Lord Clarendon.'

'The Lovett woman lived at Barnabas Place too,' Chiffinch pointed out. 'So it's equally possible that the servant was conspiring with her against Alderley.'

I bowed my head, as if accepting the argument. 'And Mr Hakesby, sir?'

'By all accounts he knows nothing. He's practically in his dotage, trembling like a leaf in a storm. The woman wouldn't have been so foolish as to trust him.'

'In that case, sir, would it not be better to release him?'

Chiffinch frowned. 'Why?'

'Because at Scotland Yard he can do nothing for us. But in his own house he may act as bait.'

'You mean his presence may persuade the Lovett woman to break cover?'

I spread my hands. 'It's possible, sir. She has a kindness for him. He gave her a roof over her head, and employment she finds congenial.'

He shrugged. 'You may be right. I'll consider it.'

I looked up at the windows in front of us. Whitehall has

327

thousands of windows and thousands of watchers and thousands of secrets. And there, at the centre of the gallery, a tall, richly dressed man was standing at an open casement on the first floor and looking down at the garden. The sun fell on him. His periwig shone like gold. Perhaps he had been there the whole time as we strolled up and down the paths.

I touched Chiffinch's arm. 'The Duke is watching us, sir.'

'What?' He wheeled round to face me. 'Which duke?'

'Buckingham.' I let my eyes drift towards the Privy Gallery. 'The bay window.'

'He's a clever man,' Chiffinch murmured, glancing up at him. 'I give him that. Sometimes too clever for his own good.' He paced on, with me just behind him. 'Talking of whom: have you heard the news?'

'About . . .?'

'Buckingham. On Monday the King restored him to his old offices – both in the Bedchamber and to the Privy Council. He's high in favour, and is seen everywhere at court. The King finds him amusing. So be careful what you say in that quarter, at least in public.'

'And Mr Hakesby, sir?' I said.

'Say we release him. How do we keep a watch on him? And on the other fellow – Brennan?'

'I could talk to the porter at his Drawing Office in Henrietta Street. I think he will be our friend in this – I could make him a present of money and give him the promise of more. He won't want to offend us, either. Hakesby lodges elsewhere – off the Strand. If you wish, I'll see what I can do with one of the servants there, as well.'

'Do it. At once. I will see he is a free man by the end of the day.'

I bowed. I noted that Chiffinch had the authority to command Hakesby's release. It was an indication of the power he wielded at the discretion of his master. The King did not care to be troubled with such details.

I never fully understood Chiffinch. He was as venal as any man I knew, and as faithless as the serpent. Yet the King trusted him as much as he trusted anyone, and Chiffinch repaid him with absolute loyalty.

I ate a solitary dinner in an ordinary in King Street. I had originally intended to walk across the park to Clarendon House afterwards, but Chiffinch had made it clear that he wanted me to bribe the porter at Henrietta Street at once. It was a good sign, I knew. If all went well, Hakesby would sleep in his own bed tonight.

The tide was high, and on the ebb, so I decided to take a pair of oars from Whitehall to the Savoy, call in at my house and walk up to Henrietta Street from there. Whitehall Stairs was crowded, as I had expected at this time, for it was the public landing place for those who went up and down the river.

As it happened, I had to wait, for there was a shortage of available boats. I lingered at the southern side of the jetty and stared upstream at the long river frontage of the palace. I was in no great hurry. I had taken a pint of wine with my dinner and, now the interview with Chiffinch was over, I felt more relaxed than I had for days.

At the edge of my attention, I was aware of people coming and going around me. I heard a shuffling of feet among the crowd and turned my head. More men were crowding on to the stairs. I gazed down at the turbid water, which was lapping against the river frontage of the palace and swirling around the piers that supported the landing stage.

A man at my shoulder cleared his throat. I sensed that he was edging closer, trying to find an excuse to enter into conversation. I ignored him. I wanted my own company. I did not want to exchange banalities about the weather or hear an account of last night's cockfight.

'Mr Marwood. At last.'

The Bishop was standing there in his shabby brown coat, his hand resting casually on the hilt of his sword.

Someone brushed my arm on my other side. I turned my head quickly. The fat man was beside me, and a little behind. He too was armed, with his old cavalry sword. I had no weapon at all, not even a stick. In front of me was the Thames. I had no means of escaping them.

'You're a difficult man to meet, sir,' the Bishop went on in his hard voice. 'You've given us a deal of trouble.'

'I don't know you, sir,' I said coldly. 'Forgive me, I'm pressed for time.'

I tried to walk away, but both the Bishop and the fat man moved closer to block me.

'There's no hurry, sir,' the Bishop said. 'We must all bide our time. God knows when we shall find a boat.'

I moistened my lips, cursing the wine I had just drunk. 'I'll shout for help if you don't leave me.'

'I don't think so. Mr Chiffinch and his master wouldn't want the world to know where you have been these last few days, and with whom, and what you did there.' He stooped, bringing his mouth close to my ear. 'You and the lady and the child. The doctor who nearly drowned and the unfortunate old woman. It would make an interesting subject for a broadsheet, would it not? We could have it about town by the morning.'

'Who are you?'

'My name's Veal, sir. And this is my servant, Roger.'

'What do you want?'

'A word or two in private. Is that so very difficult? I tried to talk to you last week – if you remember, I sent Roger to you as you were coming back from your evening with your friend Mr Milcote. Poor Roger was most distressed that you would not come with him. Still – never mind that.'

Two boats were approaching Whitehall Stairs, bringing passengers across the Thames. I raised my hand and called out. 'Here – a pair of oars, if you please.'

'All in good time,' someone shouted from the end of the landing stage. There was a rudimentary queuing system, jealously guarded, at Whitehall Stairs. 'Wait your turn or you can swim for it.'

'Don't disturb yourself, sir,' Veal said. 'We shall find you a boat in a moment. But first you'll be so good as to come with me. There's someone who would very much like to talk to you.'

'Your master?' I said. 'Would that be his Grace of Buckingham?'

'Hush, sir. Come along with us. You won't be the loser, I promise you. No man is so happy in his work that he would not better himself if he could.'

As Veal spoke, his servant nudged against me with his great belly, pushing me towards the doorway into the passage that led to the palace. He allowed his cloak to fall open, allowing me to see the glint of a dagger, a more discreet weapon than a sword. Did they mean to murder me?

I looked wildly in front of me, at the water below. It wouldn't be deep, so close to the bank, though it was muddy and foul with the rubbish from the palace. If I jumped in, I wouldn't drown. I wouldn't even need to swim. All I would lose was my dignity. But Veal and his servant would still be here, waiting to help me out.

A boat bumped against the nearest pier. An elderly lawyer was clambering on to the landing stage. Men clustered around him, ready to take his place.

I acted on impulse, without thought to the consequence. I pushed Roger aside and jumped from the jetty. I landed in the boat, which rocked violently, nearly pitching me into the river. Water splashed over me. The waterman swore and raised an oar. There was chaos on the stairs, with men milling about like angry wasps, and shouting.

'I'll kill you, bumfodder,' the waterman said. He swung his oar at me to knock me into the river.

I crouched, just in time, and caught the blow on my arm. I clutched the gunwale of the boat. 'A pound for you,' I gasped. 'I have gold. Take me downstream.'

He paused in the act of raising the oar. I fumbled in my pocket and drew out my purse. Something hard – a stone, perhaps, or even a coin – hit my cheek and made me yelp with pain.

The waterman shrugged. He pushed off with his oar, swung the boat round and rowed towards the middle of the stream.

'If you don't give me that pound now,' he said in a confidential voice that barely reached me because the breeze off the river snatched at the words, 'I swear to God I'll drown you.'

# CHAPTER FORTY-TWO

CLARENDON HOUSE HAD changed since I had last been there. It had acquired a forlorn air, as though for all its grandeur it no longer mattered very much. No one had swept up the leaves in the forecourt. Even the crowd in the street had deserted it.

A distant clock was striking four when I arrived. The servants recognized me at the front gate. I mentioned Mr Milcote's name and they waved me through, though without the civility they had shown on previous visits. I entered by the side door and asked the porter to send word to Milcote.

A footboy walked off with the message. The porter retired to his alcove, leaving me to stare at the busts of emperors and the paintings of the gods that decorated the hall. I paced to and fro beneath them. It was colder inside the house than out. There was a dead mouse in the empty fireplace. Above the mantelpiece the emperor Hadrian stared down at me with a disapproving expression on his face.

There were footsteps on the stairs, and Milcote appeared on the half-landing. He shook my hand warmly and led me to a closet on the ground floor. He closed the door, making sure it had latched securely. We stood by the tall window, looking down at the leaves chasing each other over the fore-court.

'I am so glad to see you, sir,' he murmured. 'I've been at my wits' end. It's as if we're standing on quicksand.'

'Is there news of Gorse?'

'Pray keep your voice down. There are eavesdroppers everywhere. And the Duke's upstairs.'

'The Duke?' I stared stupidly at him, thinking that Buckingham had suddenly turned up in his enemy's house.

'The Duke of York. He's in conference with my lord. They saw you arriving. You are to go to them, so we must hurry.'

'And Gorse?'

'He's been seen in Leadenhall Street. My servant tells me he encountered a man he knew in the street, and treated him to wine. He said he had a new master, and that he was more prosperous than ever before, and like to be more so in a month or two. Apparently he was wearing a new beaver hat that must have cost at least fifty or sixty shillings.'

'Who is this new master?'

'He wouldn't say.'

Leadenhall Street. The name set off an echo in my memory. I said, 'When was this?'

'Saturday. I tried to find you at once, but your servants said you were out of town. Where have you been?'

'An errand for the King,' I said. Leadenhall Street was not that far from Botolph Lane, where Cat had seen Milcote. It was in the eastern quarter of the walled city, near the Tower, and was one of the few streets that had escaped the Fire. 'Did you go there to look for Gorse?'

He shook his head. His handsome face was haggard. 'I thought it better to wait for you. Besides, I hardly know that part of town at all.'

'Is there talk about Gorse here, in the house?'

'Less than you would think. The servants have other things on their mind. A score of them have left, and no doubt there will be more.'

At that moment, with a sinking sensation, I remembered why Leadenhall Street was significant.

Milcote glanced towards the door. 'Come, sir, we really must go. They're waiting for us.'

The Duke of York was a tall man, like his brother the King, though better looking. But I found it hard to imagine him laughing. There was a marmoreal quality to his stiff, regular features and upright bearing that fitted well with our austerely tasteful surroundings in Clarendon House.

He received me in the Earl's private closet, which was uncomfortably warm from the fire. I bowed low to His Highness and then to his father-in-law, Lord Clarendon. Both men were seated. Clarendon had his bandaged legs up on a cushioned footstool. His face was drawn with pain.

The Duke glanced up at Milcote with something approaching a smile on his face. 'Leave us for a moment, George. But stay within call.'

Milcote bowed and left the room. I remembered that he and the Duke had served together in the French wars.

'Well, Marwood,' the Duke went on, 'so you are safely returned from your errand in Cambridgeshire. What happened?'

I was in a quandary. I could talk frankly on this subject

only to the King and Chiffinch. But I could hardly refuse a direct request from the King's brother.

'I accompanied my Lady Quincy to a village named Hitcham St Martin, sir. We brought back a child to London. Mistress Frances.'

His hands fluttered about his neck, sketching swellings. 'She has . . .?'

'Yes, sir. Scrofula.'

'Is it very bad?'

'I've had little experience with the condition, sir, but it is certainly noticeable.'

Clarendon stirred in his chair. 'Was there any difficulty? Either with the Warleys or on the road? Any . . . undue attention?'

I hesitated. Without the King's leave it might be unwise for me to mention the details of what had happened in Cambridge. I said, 'Mistress Warley was reluctant to be parted from the child.'

'She had no right to have an opinion on the subject,' the Duke said, glancing at Clarendon. 'She has been paid handsomely enough for her services.'

'And we were followed, sir, by two men,' I went on. 'They tried to find out where the child slept in the Warleys' house, and I believe we foiled an attempt to kidnap her.'

'It's as I feared,' Clarendon said.

The Duke glanced at him. 'He can do nothing without . . .'

Clarendon nodded and pressed his lips tightly together.

*He can do nothing without* . . . Did they mean Buckingham? But what was this thing he could do nothing without?

'Where's the child now?' the Duke asked.

'At Lady Quincy's, sir, as far as I know.'

'She'll be safe enough there,' he said to Clarendon. 'My brother will see to that. He has his own reasons to make sure that the house is secure.'

He glanced at me and frowned, as if he wished he had not spoken so frankly in front of me. There was silence in the room, broken only by the settling of the coals on the fire.

'But it's not the child that really matters, is it?' the Duke burst out as if he could no longer restrain himself. 'It's—'

'Hush, sir,' said Lord Clarendon. The old man winced, as if from a sudden stab of pain. 'The child is nothing as she is, or very little. But . . .'

'She could be everything,' the Duke of York said. 'If . . .'

If what? Something clicked in my mind, as if a cog had turned by some internal mechanism, permitting a new line of thought. I remembered the mysterious box I had found broken open in Alderley's rooms. Perhaps that was where the answer had lain.

After my interview with the Duke of York and his father-in-law, I asked Milcote if I could have a word with him in private. He escorted me downstairs and through the huge reception rooms on the ground floor to the terrace overlooking the garden, where there would be no danger of eavesdroppers.

'I noticed that the protesters are gone from Piccadilly,' I said.

'For the moment.' Milcote shrugged. 'But I'm sure Buckingham still has spies watching who comes and goes here.'

'Talking of Buckingham's men,' I said, 'have you seen any more of the two who were there before among the protesters? The ringleaders?'

'The tall one in the brown coat and his fat friend? No. Not for a few days.'

'Will you send word to me if you see them?' If Veal and his servant reappeared in Piccadilly, I thought, perhaps I could persuade Chiffinch to speak to the King and have them arrested. To be frank, they had terrified me this afternoon: not only their actions there, but the fact that they had been so confident in their powers that they had tried to kidnap me in Whitehall itself. 'It's a matter of some urgency.'

Milcote must have heard an unusual note in my voice, for he frowned and glanced at me. 'Of course, sir. You may depend on me.'

As we walked along the terrace, I glanced at the pavilion where we had found Edward Alderley's body. One of the windows in the upper room had been left open. Outside the door, the canvas covering a pile of old bricks had worked its way loose and was flapping in the breeze. A wheelbarrow had been abandoned on a heap of sand, now sodden with rain.

Milcote read my mind. 'It's hard to believe it will ever be finished, isn't it? It would have grieved my lady to see it in such a condition.'

'What was Lady Clarendon like?'

'Formidable in her time. But age and illness had done cruel things to her.'

I nodded, thinking that the description could also be applied to her ladyship's cousin, Mistress Warley.

Milcote added softly, 'As they do to my lord.'

I glanced at him. 'I know Lord Clarendon is pained by the gout — but is he ailing in other respects?'

'No — or not in body. His mind seems as vigorous as ever,

but he has had so many trials in these last few months and he has lost so much ground with the King that I cannot help wondering if he will ever be the man he was. His friends abandon him on all sides. If Buckingham and his other enemies in Parliament have him impeached, then what's left for him? Unless the King intervenes, even his life may be forfeit.'

'And you, sir?' I said. 'If the worst happens to Lord Clarendon, what will you do?'

Milcote gave me a smile of singular sweetness. 'Me? I've no fears on that score. The Duke of York has promised me a position in his household, and I know he will keep his word to an old comrade. I saved his life at the siege of Arras, and he does not forget those who have done him a service.' We walked on for a moment and then he added, in a softer voice: 'But I fear for my lord.'

When I left Clarendon House, I walked in the park for half an hour or more, trying to tease apart the tangled threads of this business. Of this at least I could be sure: it was all somehow connected, from Alderley's drowning in Lord Clarendon's well to the child hidden away in the Fens, from the robbery at Jerusalem College to the King's Evil. Veal – why was he known as the Bishop? – was clearly acting as someone's agent, and that someone was almost certainly the Duke of Buckingham. Both Lady Quincy's daughter and the missing contents of the silver box were crucial elements in this intrigue.

But the nature of the intrigue continued to elude me. What did Buckingham and Veal desire to gain from all the dangers and the expense of this? Veal was pursuing me, though I didn't know why. Did he hope to corrupt me and bring me to their side? Or did he merely mean to silence me for ever?

I paced up and down, my spirits sinking lower and lower. It was bad enough that the King expected me to do so much in the affair for his own interest. What made it infinitely worse was the fact that I was secretly sheltering Cat Lovett from the authorities. If it all went wrong, I faced more than losing my clerkships and my income for failing to carry out the King's wishes. I faced arrest, and perhaps a prosecution that might lead me to the gallows.

In the end, I decided I must do something – anything – or my own thoughts would drive me mad. I walked to Charing Cross and went by water into the city, as far as Old Swan Stairs by London Bridge. It was a place that brought back unhappy memories to me, and I was glad to hurry into the streets of the City, or rather what was left of them.

The quay and the docks that lined the river were crowded with shipping, and their spars and rigging made broken spiders' webs against the grey sky. Thames Street was almost as busy as it had been before the Fire, despite the temporary nature of so many of the structures.

I was going east, in the direction of the Tower. I passed the entrance to Pudding Lane, where the Fire had started last year, and then came to Botolph Lane, which ran parallel to it, as did Love Lane beyond. Between the two was a network of ruined buildings with deep, brick-lined cellars roofed over with scraps of canvas and timber.

There were people everywhere, milling about, carrying on their business, or simply staring at the world around them and the wide grey river on the far side of Thames Street. Most were men – building labourers at work or men employed at the docks or merely the idlers and vagrants that pass endlessly to and fro through the streets of London.

By and by, I realized that there was another category, too. Little knots of sailors, many in their best clothes and as drunk as a man could be. I also saw more respectable citizens – some were clerks or artisans on a holiday; others might have been merchants, or belonged to one of the professions. Most of these men weren't drunk, but they had a furtive air.

I passed a doorway. A woman was standing within, her bosom exposed. Her cheeks were pockmarked but she was comely enough, and handsomely built. 'God bless you, your honour. Looking for a little amusement?' She touched my scarred cheek. 'Ah – I like a gentleman who's been in the wars. I wager you know a thing or two about gallantry and brisk assaults.'

I shook my head and hurried on, but her wheedling voice pursued me down the street, promising me a foretaste of heaven's raptures for a mere trifle. I was still enough of a puritan, still my father's son, to find such trade in flesh both repulsive and enticing. The Fire had burned Fleet Alley, where so many of the pimps and brothel keepers of London had congregated, and most of their other haunts nearby. They and their whores had been forced to ply their trade elsewhere. Where better to buy and sell this shabby apology for love than among the ruins of Love Lane?

At least that was one small mystery solved: the reason for Milcote's presence in this part of town and his desire to conceal it. He was not the first gentleman to take his private pleasures in such places, and he would not be the last. Lord Clarendon was reputed to be a prude: he would not approve of lecherous behaviour in a senior member of his household.

I turned up St Mary's Hill, quickening my pace. I was tempted to tell Cat what I had discovered. But, with my transaction with Lady Quincy so fresh in my memory, who was I to set myself up as a judge of morality?

In Leadenhall Street I walked up and down, looking into coffee houses, alehouses and taverns. According to Milcote, Gorse had been seen in Leadenhall Street. But I had another reason to be here. Among the taverns was the Golden Ball. On the last day of his life, Alderley had sent Bearwood's boy, Hal, here, with a letter for the Bishop, Mr Veal.

I strolled through the public rooms but saw no one I recognized. Not that it meant anything – there were private rooms here, as there were in most taverns of any size. Besides, since the Fire, the untouched streets around Leadenhall were more populous than they had ever been.

Was it really so much of a coincidence that Veal had dined in a tavern here, and that Gorse had been seen nearly two weeks later in the street? By any rational yardstick, I knew, and in normal circumstances, it was the sort of coincidence that happens every day. But there had been nothing normal in the circumstances of my recent life. There was nothing rational about my dry mouth, my clammy skin and my overwhelming need to keep looking over my shoulder. Since Veal had waylaid me at Whitehall today, I was scared.

# CHAPTER FORTY-THREE

CAT WAITED IN the kitchen yard at Infirmary Close. Margaret had tried to persuade her into the house, but she would not come inside. She preferred to loiter by the water butt, sheltering under a projecting roof from the rain drifting from the darkening sky.

By the time Marwood returned, it was almost dark. She heard him knocking on the street door and later his voice drifted down from an open window. He sounded angry, which did not surprise her. When he came into the yard, she was waiting for him with the newspapers under her arm. His face was white and strained. He looked anything but pleased to see her.

'Thank you,' Cat said.

The words took the force from his anger, as a sudden calm makes a sail hang loose and useless on the mast. Gratitude, she thought, was the last thing he had expected from her. In this past year she had learned that men were such children that it was often possible, with a little care, to manage them, or at least to steer them away from the worst consequences of their own folly.

'What are you doing here?' he said. 'For God's sake, are you mad?'

'I've an errand. That's my excuse for being here. I brought you these.'

'What's that?'

'Spoiled copies. The press had been badly inked towards the end of the run. There were complaints. Mr Newcomb's house is empty and the door is barred. So I came here.' She held the newspapers out to him. 'After your performance this morning, I know how important the conduct of the *Gazette* is to you.'

Automatically Marwood took them from her, ignoring the irony in her voice. The paper was damp from the rain. It was true that the women who delivered the *Gazette* were meant to bring back spoiled copies, but they usually left it until the following morning. He beckoned Margaret, who was standing in the doorway to the kitchen, and gave the newspapers to her.

'For Sam,' Marwood said. 'He can take them to Mr Newcomb's in the morning.'

When they were alone in the yard, he turned back to Cat. 'What's this really about?'

'I told you. I want to thank you.'

'Why?'

'For securing Mr Hakesby's release, of course.'

'Who told you?'

'Brennan.'

He frowned. 'You've seen him?'

'Why not?' she said. 'Oh, don't worry – I'm not a fool. I know his routine. I approached him when he was walking back to his lodgings. No one saw me, I'm sure. Anyway, I wanted to find out if he was all right himself. It was my fault he was arrested.'

'Are you sure he didn't tell them what he knew?'

She shook her head. 'First he was ill. They questioned him when the fever went down. But he said he was only a draughtsman, that he knew nothing worth knowing about the rest of his master's business, or about me. And in the end they let him go.'

'He could be lying. Have you considered that?'

If she hadn't known better she would have suspected that Marwood was jealous. 'You shouldn't think so unkindly of him.'

'I don't think unkindly of him. I don't think of him at all if I can help it.'

She suppressed a desire to laugh. 'I want to see Mr Hakesby. Can you contrive it?'

'See him? You really have lost your wits, haven't you? Have you forgotten there's a charge of murder hanging over you? Or that he's only just been released from prison?'

'And have you forgotten I'm betrothed to him?' Her meekness vanished. She glared up at him and then forced her anger under control. 'I know it's dangerous, sir,' she said in a low voice, 'and we must take every possible precaution, but I still want to see him – to find out how he really is, what help he needs. He's at Three Cocks Yard.'

With an effort, Marwood tried to match her reasonable tone. 'It's impossible at present. For a start, I've been ordered to set a watch on him in case you try to see him. You must wait. Perhaps in a few weeks, when everything's settled down, and he's back in the Drawing Office. And now you must leave here at once – you mustn't come here again.'

'Wait. You searched my cousin's lodgings?'

He nodded.

'Was there much there in the way of valuables? He must have saved something from my uncle's ruin.'

He shrugged. 'Yes – it's hard to be sure – but what he had must be worth a few pounds – hundreds, even – if it's still there.'

'I need money. Besides, they cheated me. Whatever's left should belong to me.'

'No doubt. Unless Alderley left a will leaving it to someone else. But you can hardly go to law and claim it, can you? Not as things stand at present.' Marwood hesitated. 'But when I was there, I picked up a few things in case you needed money. A pocket clock, some silver forks, things like that. They're in a satchel in my closet upstairs. You can have them at once if you want.'

His forethought, and the kindness that must have prompted it, took her by surprise. Her eyes filled with tears. She bit her lip.

'Will you keep them for the moment?' she said. 'They will be safer here.'

'And of course he owned the freehold of the building itself,' Marwood rushed on as if anxious to be rid of the subject. 'He'd cleared the mortgage on it. But the question is, how to prove your title to it.'

'But—'

She broke off. Someone was running along the alley on the other side of the high wall at the side of the yard. No – two people, perhaps three. There were the sounds of a struggle, short and brutal, then the scrape of metal on stone, and a long, whimpering cry that tapered into silence.

Footsteps receded down the path. Her mouth was dry, and

her skin was clammy. She and Marwood stared at each other. He went inside the house, calling for Sam and telling him to bring a lantern.

Cat followed the two men upstairs, their shadows leaping ahead of them. By the time they had armed themselves and unbarred the hall door, there was just enough light to see that the alley was empty.

'What's that?' Sam said, stamping his crutch down on the flagstones.

Marwood stooped. When he stood up, he was holding a beaver hat with a broad brim. He stared at it by the light of the lantern, turning it around in his hands.

Sam reached out and stroked it. 'A fine hat.'

Marwood said nothing.

'Looks good as new. If no one else cares to have it, sir, I'd take it off your hands.'

Cat was peering at Marwood's face. 'What is it?'

'Gorse was last seen in Leadenhall Street. He was wearing a new hat. A beaver.'

'It sounded like someone was coming to the house,' Cat said. 'And someone stopped them, and dragged them away. Do you think it was Gorse——?'

'We don't know.' Marwood stared into the darkness at the end of the alley. 'We don't know if Gorse was the victim or the attacker. We don't know how many attackers there were. We don't know if the victim is living or dead. We don't know why he was on his way here.'

'We don't know anything, master,' Sam said cheerfully. 'That's plain enough. Nothing new there, eh?'

'Into the house,' Marwood said. 'There's nothing we can do out here.'

They retreated inside. Marwood called for supper to be brought up to the parlour, where a coal fire smouldered in the grate. He and Cat shared a cold mutton pasty. Neither of them had much appetite. After a few mouthfuls, Marwood pushed aside his plate.

'You must go back to your lodging in a hackney,' he said. 'Sam and I will escort you, just in case.'

'There's no need.'

'It's best to be on the safe side. This business grows worse by the day. I believe I may be in danger too. Two men tried to waylay me at Whitehall Stairs today. In broad daylight. They're in the employ of the Duke of Buckingham.'

'Why?' Cat said. 'What's at the root of all this?'

'I wish to God I knew.'

'And Edward? How did he fit into it?'

Marwood shrugged and left the question unanswered. When she had finished eating, he called for Sam to bring their cloaks.

'I'm sorry about this morning at Newcomb's,' he said while they were waiting. He turned aside from Cat and poked the fire viciously. 'I should have thought of how it would appear when I singled you out in the printing shop, in front of everyone. How they would gossip and sneer.'

'It's nothing,' Cat said, thinking of the satchel upstairs and the kindness that had prompted Marwood to bring it from her cousin's lodgings. 'There are worse things.'

He threw down the poker. For a moment their eyes met. He smiled at her and began to speak. Then the door burst open and Sam staggered into the room with their cloaks over his arm.

\*\*\*

348

The following morning, Cat woke early. Dorcas was still snoring on the other side of the loft. It was a Thursday, which for Dorcas would normally have been a *Gazette* day, and hence a day for early rising. But not this Thursday, because of Mr Newcomb's new press.

Cat lay on her back and watched the dawn light make cracks in the tiles above her head. She listened to the animals in the stable below as they stirred and began to go about their business. The air was full of their rich, pungent smells.

She had an almost physical desire to be in the Drawing Office. She wanted to be standing before her slope in the growing light and poring over the plan that lay there. She missed her work as a starving person misses food.

Instead, she knew, she would have to spend the coming day skulking in corners and scrabbling to make a few pennies to pay her share of their expenses to Dorcas. Blessed are the poor in spirit, Cat's father had told her when she had shied away from a beggar, and he had felt inclined to instruct her on the subject, for theirs is the Kingdom of Heaven. That wasn't much help at present. Had God been an architect, Cat thought with a touch of blasphemy, he would have ordered things more wisely.

Vitruvius and Palladio never left you wondering about their intentions and by and large they achieved what they set out to do. Besides, now that Cat was a woman, and no longer rich, she felt that the promise of a distant heaven was little consolation for poverty on earth. In the last year, since she had left the Alderleys, she had had ample opportunity to discover what the lives of the poor were like.

Later, Cat went out to the baker's for their rolls. While she was there, a boy rushed in with the news that a man had been found murdered in the river, and was lying at Botolph's Wharf by Billingsgate. No one knew who he was. On her return to the stable, Cat told Dorcas.

'A body?' The old woman began the laborious business of standing up. 'We must go and see it. Murdered, you say? Help me up, will you – quick, before they take him away.'

Her eyes were brighter than usual. For many Londoners, a body – especially a murdered one – was a form of entertainment, the cause of ghoulish fascination.

'Besides,' Dorcas went on, 'maybe there'll be scraps for us on the foreshore.'

There was no gainsaying her. Cat helped Dorcas down the ladder. The two of them walked to the river under a sullen grey sky, eating their rolls as they went. Botolph's Wharf was downstream from the bridge, where the Thames began to change its character as it flowed to the estuary. The water was dense with shipping, with smaller craft darting among the lighters and merchantmen moored midstream.

When the tide was low, Dorcas often went down to the foreshore to watch the children picking their way among the mud and the rubbish in search of anything that might retain a scrap of value. The Thames was capricious. Though it sucked away so many things, Dorcas said, you never knew what it might leave behind. The scavengers knew her; some of them would bring her their finds, and if she thought she could make a profit from a sodden rag or a worn shoe, she would buy them.

The stalls on the quayside had a strangely deserted look. Fewer people than usual were out on the foreshore. But on the quay fronting the river, a clamouring crowd had gathered, peering inwards and downwards.

Dorcas touched the arm of an apprentice. 'Where did they find him?'

The boy turned a freckled face, alight with glee. 'In the lee of that lighter over there – he got tangled in the anchor chain last night.'

'How was he killed?'

'I heard he was stabbed.'

'Who is he?'

'Don't know. Maybe he's a Papist, and that's why they killed him. Look – there.'

The crowd had shifted for an instant, as a harbour official pushed his way among them. Cat glimpsed among a forest of legs and skirts the body of a man lying on his back on the quayside. He was naked. Someone had already stolen his clothes, before or after death. His limbs were splayed at unnatural angles, and there was a deep gash across his chest, washed clean by the water. She glimpsed bone. She swallowed, fighting back the urge to retch.

The dead man's eyes were open, looking at the sky. His mouth gaped, pink and toothless. He had his own hair, and it splayed about his head like pale ginger seaweed. His skin was colourless apart from a generous sprinkling of freckles.

Freckles, Cat thought, freckles? Oh lord God almighty save us, surely it can't be Gorse?

The crowd eddied again and the body on the flagstones vanished. The constable and his officers were making their way purposefully down to the quay.

Cat turned her back on them. She took Dorcas's arm and urged her away.

# CHAPTER FORTY-FOUR

THEY CAME FOR me at last when I least expected
trouble. After all, it was broad daylight and I had taken
precautions. I had gone to dine at the Goat at Charing Cross,
where I had met George Milcote for supper just over a week
ago. Before I went into the house, I had made sure that no
one in the street was taking an undue interest in my
movements.

I sat at the common table, but among the shadows at the
back so I could see who came in and out. Milcote often came
here to escape the oppressive atmosphere of Clarendon House
for a few hours. I hoped I might encounter him, to see if he
could throw any light on Gorse's abortive visit to Infirmary
Close last night. If it had been Gorse.

I treated myself to a venison pasty washed down with ale.
I avoided conversation with my neighbours by pretending to
be absorbed in the contents of the Goat's *Gazette*. I enjoyed
the meal and felt I had taken a brief holiday from my troubles.
Afterwards, I was comfortable and a little hazy with drink,
but no more than that. For upwards of an hour in this crowded

public place, the almost physical heaviness of fear had lifted from me. It had been part of my life for the last ten days and, until it had gone, I had not realized how much it oppressed me.

When I had finished the meal, I paid the bill and went out to the privy, which was in a noisome outhouse in the yard. I did my business there. That's where they were waiting, the Bishop and the fat man, when I came out. The Bishop – I still thought of him as that, though I now knew his name was Veal – appeared in front of me, his body blocking my path. Simultaneously, I heard a step behind me, from beside the privy, and the sound of laboured breathing. A pistol prodded my side, digging deep into my waist. I grunted with pain and jerked away. The jamb of the doorway brought me up short.

I heard the cocking of the pistol.

'It has a delicate mechanism, sir,' Veal said in a quiet, flat voice. 'Temperamental. I would advise no sudden movements. Roger might act before he thinks, as he so often does, I'm afraid. Nobody wants an accident.'

'If you kill me, you'll suffer for it,' I said in a voice that sounded thick and not quite my own.

'But who would know, sir? Besides, what's all this about killing? I am merely giving you a friendly word of caution about the danger of accidents.'

The pressure on my waist increased.

'This way, sir.' Veal laid his hand on the hilt of his sword. 'There's a coach waiting.'

They pushed me towards the passageway that led from the yard to the street. Too late, I began to struggle, and they closed in, squeezing me between them. The fat man's breath was hot on my cheek. It stank of beer and onions.

'Be prudent, sir,' Veal urged. 'We are two to one. We mean you no harm, and on my honour we shall have you back within the hour.'

I tried to slip back inside the building, but Roger fumbled at my periwig, seized my right ear and twisted it until I squealed. They pushed and pulled me through the passage to the street, where the coach stood. I had time to note that it wasn't a hackney. It was a small vehicle, for town use, plain and unremarkable. Once we were inside, it moved off with a jerk, its iron-shod wheels grating over the stones. The noise of the street surrounded us like earth around a coffin. The entire process must have taken no more than a minute.

Roger tied my wrists behind my back together with cord. He worked with brisk efficiency, his fingers surprisingly nimble for so large and clumsy a man.

'Just a precaution, sir,' murmured Veal. 'Pray don't alarm yourself.'

'Shall I gag him, master?' asked Roger.

'What do you think, Mr Marwood? I would enjoy a little conversation if you would promise me not to be foolish.'

'You'll do as you please, whatever I say.'

I tried to work out where we were going. Into the Strand, perhaps, in the direction of the City? The coach made so many twists and turns, so many stops and starts, so much noise, that it was hard to be sure of anything.

'I know our manners may seem rough,' Veal said. 'I'm Yorkshire-bred, sir, as you may have realized, and we don't beat about the bush. But all my master wants is a word or two with you in private. And you must own, sir, you have made my task so difficult. This is the third time I have invited you to see him, and you force me to be less gentle than I would like.'

'Spare me this drollery,' I said. 'I know who your master is, and I know what you've done in his name. If he wishes to see me so badly, why couldn't he ask me to wait on him like an honest man?'

'I hear your friend Mr Hakesby is a free man again,' Veal went on as if I hadn't spoken. 'You wouldn't want any more accidents to befall him, would you? And that young woman, his maid – is that really what she is? What a curious piece of work she must be, the Regicide's child. Like father, like daughter? They'll find her soon enough, and I wouldn't give tuppence for her chances of avoiding the hangman. Unless . . .' He paused and glanced at me. 'Unless, of course, she found a friend at Court who would put in a good word for her.'

I turned my head from him and stared at the heavy curtain that separated me from freedom. The leather was stained and cracked. It was almost as hard as wood after years of exposure to the weather. My mind fastened on a mark that seemed to my disturbed mind to mimic the line of a hog's back.

The stick, then the carrot. Veal had threatened me, then offered to bribe me. The audacity of his behaviour took my breath away. I was no longer wholly insignificant at Whitehall. Not quite. I had powerful patrons. The King knew my name. Undersecretary Williamson was my master. I was clerk to the Board of Red Cloth, where Mr Chiffinch held sway.

Yet Veal's master, the Duke of Buckingham, cared nothing for all that. He was too rich to care, too sure of his own power, too arrogant. If Edward Alderley had been killed on his orders, he would hardly baulk at having me murdered. I didn't even know why.

355

I thought of trying to escape before we reached our destination. But Veal was beside me on the seat, his thigh nudging mine, and his long legs stretching across the right-hand opening. We were facing the horses. Roger was opposite us, his body angled so that it formed a barrier between me and the left-hand opening. He and his master had long legs and long swords. My hands were tied behind my back, forcing me to sit slantwise on the seat and limiting my possibilities of movement. My captors had boxed me into this confined space, just as they had in the yard.

For a while, we rode in silence – or, to be more precise, with the noises of the street mingling with Roger's stertorous breathing and the tapping of Veal's restless fingers on the guard of his sword. They were both old soldiers, I thought, probably the Commonwealth army – not that that necessarily meant anything about their current loyalties, for most of the country had changed its allegiance at the King's Restoration as easily as a man changes his coat. But there was another quality to Veal that was harder to pin down. He was no gentleman, and he didn't pretend to be, but he talked like an educated man.

'Ugly devil, ain't he, sir?' Roger said as if I were not there. 'Seen his ear on that side, and his neck?'

'Hush, Roger,' Veal said drily. 'You must not insult our guest: it is not seemly.'

My mouth was dry and my breathing fast and shallow, however much I tried to slow it down. I had long since lost track of where we were. Did I face torture, or even death? In a flash, there passed through my mind the consequences of my death for others, for Margaret and Sam, who would lose their livelihoods and the roof over their heads, for

Hakesby and, most of all, for Cat. I seemed to have acquired dependants without even noticing it, though I doubted Cat would accept that description of herself.

'You're very quiet, sir,' Veal said to me. 'Which a wise man knows is always a good policy. A word of advice, sir. When you meet our master, talk only if he asks you a question.' He moistened his lips. 'He's a great man in all respects, but liable to fly into a passion if he thinks you're trying to cross him.'

I looked at him in the swaying gloom of the coach. His face was barely eighteen inches away from mine. 'I believe you're afraid of him,' I said.

Veal turned his head. 'Blindfold him now, Roger. Make sure it's tight.'

# CHAPTER FORTY-FIVE

'HURRY,' CAT SAID. 'Hurry.'
Her urgency communicated itself to Dorcas. The two women walked quickly up from the crowded riverside to the safety of the stable off Fenchurch Street.

'What is it?' Dorcas whispered, when they were safely in the loft.

'I must tell someone about this.'

'The body? Why? The whole town will know before dinnertime if it doesn't already.'

That wasn't the point. The point was that the nameless, naked man lying on the wharf was Matthew Gorse. Marwood needed to know that as soon as possible. If the beaver hat was anything to go by, Gorse had come to the Savoy the previous evening, but at the last moment someone had prevented him from talking to Marwood.

The old palace had a long river frontage, and the tide had been high yesterday evening. Cat bit her lip, as she worked out the implications. It was probable that Gorse had been killed soon after he had knocked at Marwood's door. He had perhaps been stripped at that point, to make him as anonymous as possible, and dumped into the river.

The Thames at night was a lawless place, where only the tide wielded much authority. If the murderer had been luckier, what was left of Gorse would have been washed down the estuary towards the sea, a prey for rats and birds and the other predators of the river. It looked as if the tide had taken the body under London Bridge. That was what had probably done most of the visible damage to the body – the broken limbs and the gash on the chest. After the bridge, the murderer's luck had changed. When the water was ebbing strongly, the debris that had passed through the piers of the bridge sometimes found its way to the north bank by Billingsgate, with the deeply recessed harbour at Botolph's Wharf, and the Customs House stairs downstream.

'Did you know him?' Dorcas whispered.

Cat nodded.

'Best keep your mouth shut.' The old woman laid a brown, dirty hand on Cat's arm. 'Not your business, my dear. That's the way to look at it. Least said, soonest mended.'

'There's a man I must see. He needs to know.'

Dorcas withdrew her hand. She seemed to compress herself into a tighter bundle of flesh and bone. 'Leave it.'

'I must.'

'Is it Mr Marwood? The man who wanted you yesterday morning?'

'Yes.'

'Is he . . .?'

'My lover?' Cat snapped. 'Of course not.'

Dorcas shied away from her anger. 'Send him a letter then. If you must. We'll buy a sheet of paper. You've got a pencil.'

'It would be better to talk to him if I can.'

Gorse's murder could change everything, Cat thought – not just Marwood's investigation but also her own position. Someone at Clarendon House had known more about her cousin Edward and his presence in the garden pavilion on the night of his death than they were prepared to say. Almost certainly that person was Gorse. He had once been Edward's servant, after all.

'It's too dangerous,' Dorcas whimpered. 'This could bring the constables to us. This could end at Tyburn.'

'I don't know where master is,' Sam said, draping Marwood's second-best cloak over the line across the kitchen yard. 'He never tells me anything.'

'When he comes back, give him this.' Cat thrust the folded paper into Sam's hand. 'At once.'

'All right, mistress, all right.'

She had found Sam leaning on his crutch in the yard at Infirmary Close in the Savoy. Margaret was at the market, he had told her. He was alone, ostensibly cleaning shoes and brushing clothes.

'And what are you doing here?' he said, lowering his voice to a throaty whisper. 'Margaret says it's too dangerous. She nearly had a fit of the Mother when you turned up last night.'

'It'd take more than me to drive Margaret to hysterics,' Cat said tartly, thinking that Sam had been drinking strong ale with his dinner again. 'Is Marwood at Whitehall?'

'God knows where he is these days. He's not much at his office, I tell you that. He's a fool, mistress, if you ask me, dabbling in matters that don't concern him.'

'I didn't ask you,' Cat said.

'Mixing with noblemen and gentlefolk never pays,' Sam said, waving the clothes brush at her and waxing philosophical. 'Not for the likes of him. It's against nature.' He studied the brush in his hand. 'As is this. It's not a job for a grown man. The master should get a maid or a boy to do this sort of job. It's not right for a full-grown man who served His Majesty by sea to be put to such tasks. It's downright disrespectful to the King. I shall tell master so when he comes back.'

'You'll lose your place if you do.'

'Master might be in the Goat,' Sam said, returning abruptly to the question of Marwood's whereabouts. 'You know the place? Charing Cross? Mr Milcote's having his dinner there again – I saw him going in when I went out to fetch a little refreshment – and master's seen a lot of him lately. Or Mr Milcote might know where he is.' He dropped the brush into the basket of clothes and shoes he had brought from the house. 'Tell you what, mistress, I'll go and ask him, shall I?'

'No,' Cat said firmly, her mind filling with a vision of a drunken Sam staggering into the Goat with a discreet message for the fastidious Mr Milcote. 'You will do no such thing.'

Besides, it was safer not to involve Milcote. She smiled at Sam, which took him unawares and made him frown, and slipped out of the yard.

The more she thought about it, the stronger the argument for enquiring at the Goat became. If Marwood were at the tavern, she would send in an unsigned note to him, telling him that Gorse's body had turned up in the river by Billingsgate. She wouldn't go inside, of course, for fear of Milcote seeing her.

At the door of the tavern, Cat asked the porter if Mr Milcote was dining with a friend named Marwood inside, as she had a message for him. The man said he didn't know, but he would enquire. As ill-chance would have it, however, just as he was beckoning his boy, Milcote himself came down the stairs. The porter bowed and stood aside to allow him to pass out into the street.

'This young woman's asking after your friend, master,' he said, nodding towards Cat. 'If you dined with him today.'

There was nothing she could have done to avoid the meeting. Before she could move, Milcote's eyes met hers. Despite her changed appearance – the shawl, her walnut-stained skin, the shabby cloak – he knew her at once; she saw the flicker of recognition on his face. In that instant, a sense of her own folly welled up inside her. She had brought this danger on herself.

She turned to flee. It was too late. He caught her wrist. She swung back, her hand diving into her pocket, searching for her knife.

'God's body, sir,' the servant said. 'What's this?' He seized Cat's other arm. 'A thief?'

'It's nothing,' Milcote said. He drew the struggling Cat an inch or two closer to him. 'It's all right. I need to talk to this woman.' He stared down at Cat and said softly, too low for the porter to hear, 'I mean you no harm.'

Her fingers closed on the knife. She could try to stab him but he was probably fast enough and strong enough to prevent her. Even if she succeeded, what then? The porter was watching, and so was his boy. The street was crowded. There were soldiers at the gates of the Royal Mews. They would raise a hue and cry in seconds.

362

'Pray believe me,' Milcote said.

He tossed a coin to the porter, who ducked back into the tavern with a leer on his face. It was clear how he interpreted what was happening.

Cat felt the blood rising to her face. 'Why should I trust you? You of all people?'

Milcote ignored her. He urged her up the street, taking her up St Mary's Lane and then into one of the smaller streets west of Covent Garden, where there was no one around.

'You're a fool to show yourself in the street, Mistress Hakesby,' he said, stopping outside a shuttered shop. 'There's a warrant out for you.' He frowned. 'What was that the porter said? That you were asking if I was dining with a friend. Who?'

She said nothing.

'It must be Marwood.' He took her by her shoulders and shook her. 'Why? Do you know him?'

Her right hand was still in her pocket. She eased the knife from its makeshift sheath. She said, 'I hear that he has the King's authority to investigate Mr Alderley's murder.'

Milcote released her. He looked puzzled. 'But that doesn't make any—'

She ripped out the knife and jabbed it at the front of his left thigh. It penetrated less than an inch but for an instant the shock paralysed him. She ran past him, into an alley on the left. He shouted with pain. She swung right into a larger street.

They were not far from Covent Garden and she knew the area well. The knife was still in her hand but concealed under her cloak. Milcote's footsteps were pounding after her. She darted into the yard behind a bakery, opened a door, ran through a kitchen full of startled faces, through the shop and outside by the street door into the lane beyond.

She didn't stop until she reached the decorous environs of Lincoln's Inn Fields. She stood beside one of the gravel paths, panting, a stitch in her side. Two fine ladies were approaching on foot, with their footmen behind. Suddenly, Cat bent double and vomited not ten yards away from them.

'Another drunken whore,' the elder lady said in a shrill voice. 'Why don't they keep them out of here?'

# CHAPTER FORTY-SIX

THE COACH DREW up. I heard the coachman jump down and the clatter of him lowering the steps. The door opened. Veal scrambled out, his sword knocking against my leg. Then, with no warning, Roger pushed me out of the coach. In my blindness I missed my footing and stumbled. Veal caught me.

'Steady, sir.' His arms held me up. He was all bone and muscle; there was nothing soft about him; his coat felt like good quality broadcloth but my finger snagged on a hole. 'Roger, you must be gentler. Come, sir, I shall take one arm and Roger shall take the other.'

They manhandled me across a muddy, stone-scattered surface which smelled of fresh manure and a cesspit; perhaps a stable yard. I heard the crack of whip, the jingle of harness and the diminishing clatter of hooves. Afterwards, there were few sounds apart from our own footsteps, the distant noise of the streets and Roger's heavy breathing – until, with sudden, piercing sweetness, a missel-thrush burst into song.

Judging by the acrid smell in the air, we must be somewhere in the fire-damaged ruins. But probably in an area where the rebuilding had not begun, and where the refugees hadn't planted their shelters.

There was the clack of an iron latch.

'Steps down, sir,' said Veal. 'A little narrow, so I shall lead the way, and Roger will bring up the rear.'

As we slowly descended the stairs, a smell of damp, drains and old fires rose up to greet us. There were sixteen steps and, at the bottom, another door; this one required a key.

Once inside, I stood there, arm in arm with Roger. There came a scrape of flint and steel, and the sound of Veal blowing gently on the tinder until he succeeded in coaxing a flame. The stink of a tallow candle filled the air.

'Roger, tell Mr – ah, Mr Pearson that we await his pleasure down here, would you? I'll stay with Mr Marwood. But first, tie him to the ring on the wall, just in case.'

There was nothing gentle about Roger, and when he tightened the knots about my wrists and dragged my arms further back, I almost cried out with the pain of it. A moment later the door closed behind him, and I was alone with Veal.

'Well,' he said, 'we have the chance of a little private conversation. At last.'

He untied the blindfold. The wavering flame of the candle made me blink.

I swallowed, trying to bring moisture into my mouth. 'What does your master want from me?'

'I shall leave that for him to tell you. But I can't tell you how glad I am to have you here at last. You've led us a merry dance, you have indeed, and my master's been growing impatient.' Then, without any warning, he switched tack: 'Where's the little girl you brought back from the Fens? Still at my Lady Quincy's?'

'I don't know. Why do you want her so badly?' When he didn't reply, and as I felt I had nothing to lose, I threw other questions at him: 'Did you kill Edward Alderley? Did you throw Dr Burbrough in the millpond?'

'Of course not,' Veal said. His harsh Northern voice was well-adapted for outrage. 'What do you take me for?'

'A kidnapper, for a start. And you broke into Alderley's lodgings after he died, and God knows what you stole from there. You—'

'I took nothing that was not my own or someone else's.' His voice had grown passionate. 'As for Ned Burbrough, he is my friend. Or rather he was. He came to the mill to talk to me about my – ah – my visit to Jerusalem, and I admit we had a disagreement, sir, as friends sometimes do, I don't deny that. But nothing more. But as the doctor made his way back, Roger said, the poor fellow slipped on the stones and fell under the mill wheel. Roger saw it all.'

Dear God, I thought, there's no fool like a holy fool: had it not occurred to Veal that Roger might have pushed Burbrough under the mill wheel to shut his mouth, and Burbrough had survived only by a miracle? Roger would not be the first servant to play a different game from his master's.

Veal's features were working with anger, which he suppressed with an obvious effort of will. 'And that you should accuse me of trying to murder him, sir!' he went on in a quieter tone. 'That's unjust. I would not wantonly take the life of a fellow man. I'm a clerk in holy orders, I'd have you know, not a hired assassin.'

367

I gaped at him. 'You? A clergyman? But you wear a sword, not a parson's coat, and you—'

He drew himself up. 'Sir,' he said, 'my present occupation is not of my choosing. It has been forced on me by circumstance.' Frowning, he took a step or two, kicking viciously at a stick that lay in his path. Then the need to explain made him burst into speech. 'I had no thought of holy orders at first, mind you. I was intended for the law. But after the university, I joined the New Model Army. That's where I learned to use a sword, and where I met poor Roger – he served under me, and when he was wounded at Marston Moor all those years ago, I prayed with him. Then God called me to serve Him in other ways. So I was ordained and became an army chaplain. Under the Commonwealth, I was presented with a living in Yorkshire. But when the King returned, I was most unjustly deprived of my benefice.'

'Ah. I begin to understand. That's why you hate Lord Clarendon.'

There were hundreds of these dispossessed clergymen about the country. Since the Restoration, Parliament had insisted on passing a series of penal religious laws, which were designed to strengthen the grip of the Church of England on the country, and to weaken the influence of Roman Catholics and the non-conformists, who were considered politically dangerous. As a result, many Church of England clergy who clung to their old puritanical ways had been ejected from their parishes. The legislation was known collectively as the Clarendon Code, as his lordship was believed to have been behind it.

'Hate him? You wrong me, sir,' Veal said. 'As a Christian, I must oppose Lord Clarendon and all he stands for. It's true that, for the good of the country, I would cheerfully see him in his grave. But I don't hate the unhappy man. Indeed, I pray for his immortal soul, though I doubt my prayers will be heard.'

I shrugged, unwilling to debate the point. I sensed that Veal's need to justify his actions was his weak spot so I gave the sore place another poke: 'And that's why they call you the Bishop, I suppose. Because you are, or were, a clergyman.'

He looked sternly at me. 'The name is intended satirically, sir. I don't much care for bishops.'

Despite my plight, I almost smiled. I had known so many men like Veal – rigid, honest as the day according to their lights, convinced of their own rectitude and confident that they were serving their God as He wished; yet so strangely devoid of humour.

'Burbrough and I matriculated at Sidney Sussex College in the same term,' Veal said. 'We were inseparable. He was ordained long before me, but he chose to take up a fellowship at Jerusalem, which was then a very godly place, and stay at the university. Why, he might have been vice chancellor by now, had it not been for those men with their harsh laws and Papist ways. But he knows his days are numbered in Cambridge. Warley and his allies are working to have him expelled. That's why he was willing to help me.'

A blasphemous thought came to me. Religion brought poison into politics. The last twenty-five years had proved that, time and again. Would not the business of government be so much more straightforward and pleasant if one could purge religion from the country? England might well become an earthly paradise, and there would be no need of heaven at all.

'We must not despair,' Veal said, his voice growing louder as if he stood in a pulpit. 'The Lord does not abandon his servants, and He finds new tools for their hands. The righteous shall prevail.'

'And me?' The cords were chafing my wrists, and I had shooting pains in my arms. 'Am I such a tool, sir?'

'You will find out in due course.' He cocked his head, and I guessed he was listening for footsteps. Then he added a remark that mystified me: 'You would be wise to remember the parable of the Prodigal Son. We should make the most of it if we're offered a second chance. It happens so rarely in life.'

Roger returned. I begged for a pot to piss in and something to drink. Veal agreed to both requests, and even ordered Roger to free my hands that I might better deal with my needs. Roger brought me a pot and a jug of small beer. Veal stood with his back to me while I did what I needed, but Roger watched me while his hand caressed the butt of his pistol. I massaged my aching shoulders and arms.

Afterwards, Veal ordered me to be tied to the ring again. He held a whispered conference with Roger, then bid me be patient and said they would leave me alone with the candle.

'Wait,' he said, pausing with his hand on the door. 'Perhaps you would care to pray with me first?'

'Thank you, sir, but no,' I said. 'I am not in a prayerful state of mind at present.'

He shook his head sorrowfully. 'In a time of affliction, a man should always open his heart to God.'

I turned my face to the wall and waited for him to leave.

The man who came down to the cellar was tall and well set up. He was dressed in a lawyer's robe, which concealed his clothes. He wore a black hood over his head, in which holes for the eyes and the mouth had been cut. He carried a candle. He was alone.

He was like a figure of Death in a masque, needing only a scythe to complete the resemblance. The effect could have been theatrical rather than sinister, had he not also been carrying a sword.

He levelled the blade at me. I backed towards the wall until I could go no further. The tip of the sword darted forward and nicked the skin of my throat, just below the jawbone on the right-hand side. It happened so quickly that I had no time even to flinch.

I cried out. The man slowly lowered the sword. The wound smarted. A trickle of blood zigzagged down to my collar. I was trembling. I had come, literally, within an inch of death.

Buckingham, I thought, or someone closely connected to him. After all, Veal and Roger were his servants. Most likely, though, it was the Duke himself. The height fitted, and he was said to be proud of his swordsmanship. Moreover, Whitehall was rife with stories about the pleasure he had derived from disguising himself earlier in the year, when he had been charged with treason and on the run.

'I'm wondering whether to have you killed outright,' he said, turning the sword towards me and then raising it in a salute, presumably to himself. 'It might be simpler. You've caused a great deal of trouble.'

The voice was Buckingham's, too. But if the Duke were pretending to be anonymous, it would be better for me to go along with it.

'I serve the King, sir,' I began, 'and if—'

'Naturally we all serve the King,' Buckingham interrupted.

'When I want you to speak, Marwood, I shall ask you a question. Do you remember a silver box? Small, and with a monogram on the lid.'

'Yes, sir.' Of course I did. I had found it in Alderley's apartments in Farrow Lane; he had probably stolen it from Lord Clarendon's closet. Everyone seemed interested in it, and I didn't know why. I didn't even know what the monogram's letters were.

He swung the sword, cutting at the air from side to side; he was like a schoolboy with the switch in his hand. 'Where is it?'

'Mr Chiffinch has it, sir.' I hesitated. 'The lock's broken. Someone had forced it open.'

'Who?'

I shrugged as well as a man can with his arms attached to a ring on the wall behind him. 'I don't know.'

'I want the contents.'

'It was empty when I found it in Alderley's lodging.'

'Are you sure of that? Quite sure? Would you take your Bible oath on it?'

'Yes, sir.' I was telling the truth but somehow it sounded like a lie. 'I don't know what it contained, either. I know nothing at all.'

Except, of course, I knew this: that all the great ones of the land wanted whatever had been in that box: the King and the Duke of York, Lord Clarendon and the Duke of Buckingham. For some reason it was mortally important: it was probable that whatever was in that box had caused the deaths of three men, and that it was somehow connected with Frances and her scrofula. I had assumed that Veal had broken open the box when he searched Alderley's lodging, and taken whatever it had contained. But if Buckingham didn't have it, who did?

'Is this why I'm here?' I asked. 'Is this why I'm tied like a dog? Because of whatever was in that box?'

Buckingham said nothing. The two candle flames wavered, and his shadow danced on the damp walls. 'Are you content?' he said suddenly.

'Sir?'

'With your lot in life, Marwood.' He waved a beringed hand, taking in my immediate circumstances. 'Not just with your present condition, of course, which cannot be agreeable. But in general. You are your father's son, after all. Isn't it hard for you to serve men who are destroying all he stood for? They would make every honest Presbyterian a criminal. They hound every Christian who won't bow and scrape to their bishops. Why, I believe they would hand England over to the Pope in Rome if he made it worth their while.'

Remember the parable of the Prodigal Son, Veal had said. Be grateful for second chances. Was this what he had meant?

I swallowed. 'I do what I must, sir, to put food on my table and a roof over my head.' I thought of Chiffinch and his devious ways. 'I'm a poor man. I admit that what I have to do is not always to my liking. Or what my masters do.'

Without warning, the blade leapt at me again. The tip outlined an invisible figure of eight barely an inch from my nose.

'And does that include murder, Marwood?'

'I don't understand, sir.'

'I have reputable witnesses who will testify that you swore to murder Edward Alderley, and that a day later he was found drowned in that well. I have other witnesses who saw you

373

enter Lord Clarendon's garden by the gate from the fields on the very afternoon of Alderley's death.'

'Then those witnesses lie,' I said angrily.

'That's not the point. These are men who will be believed. One is a clergyman, in fact.'

So Veal would have no objection to seeing me hang for a crime I had not committed if it served his cause. I tried to remain calm. 'And what possible reason could I have to kill Alderley?'

'Because you lusted after his cousin, the Regicide's daughter, and you wanted to protect her. Alderley was threatening to bring her to the gallows.'

'There's not a word of truth in that, sir, and you know it.'

'You are not a fool,' the Duke said. 'What I know and you know has nothing to do with it. What matters is what men can be led to believe about you.'

'I'm not without friends.'

He laughed. 'Do you really think men like Chiffinch or Williamson would raise a finger to help you if you were accused of murder?' He paused, watching me. 'Or even the King. Especially not the King.'

I turned my head away. A moment passed. I heard the sound of Buckingham sheathing his sword.

'There's another way open to you,' he said, his voice gentle, almost coaxing. 'You know as well as I do that the King and his ministers cannot order things entirely as they wish. The King envies his cousin of France, who rules his kingdom absolutely, with no check on his power. But here we do things differently. Parliament holds the purse strings and I – that is we, or rather our cause – command much support in the Commons and even in the Lords. The common people sympathize with the Presbyterians, not the bishops. They are with us, not the Court. The King is perfectly aware that I could raise the City with a click of my fingers.'

He paused. We both knew that his identity was no longer a secret. But he kept his face disguised, as if the play-acting itself gave him pleasure; and I was wise enough to know that my role in this play was to be the audience.

'Work for me instead,' he said softly. 'For myself and Veal and others like us. For our shared beliefs, our common interests. Keep your present employments, and act as my eyes and ears. Then, when we have gained our ends, you shall have your reward, in this world and the next.'

I hesitated, turning his words over in my mind. There were shooting pains in my arms, and in the sockets of my shoulders. I felt suddenly very tired. If I said no, what were my chances of leaving this cellar alive? And was there not something in what Buckingham had said? Where indeed did my best interests lie?

'Sir,' I said. 'Nothing would give me greater joy than to do my duty to God and to serve you.'

I wasn't proud of what I had done. But how else could I have managed it? I had time enough to brood, for Buckingham left me alone to think.

In a while, Veal and Roger returned. They untied me. They offered me food and wine.

'May I go?' I said – speaking with my heart in my mouth, hoping that the Duke had believed my acceptance of his offer, and that his words had not been part of a game for him, a game whose rules I had no chance of knowing.

'Of course, sir,' Veal said. 'Whenever you wish. Roger will

fetch a coach. But you will have to be blindfolded again, I'm afraid. My master insists.'

'Why?'

'Because he chooses that it should be so, and that's enough for me. This place has many uses for him.'

They left me in the cellar again, but free to roam and to stretch my aching limbs. Perhaps half an hour later, they returned, covered my eyes and led me up the steps to the yard. The air smelled wonderfully sweet. I felt the warmth of the sun on my cheek.

Veal took my right arm and Roger my left. I was not a prisoner as before, but my movements were circumscribed. We walked across the yard. I heard the chink of harness ahead.

'I understand we shall see you again, sir,' Veal said politely. 'It will be an honour, I'm sure. A step up here, and you're into the coach.'

'I wish to go to the Strand,' I said.

'Indeed.'

I knew at once that this vehicle was no hackney, or even a simple private coach like the one in which I had been brought here. I touched a door as I climbed in, not the usual leather curtain. There was a strangely familiar perfume in the air, a hint of musk and freshly watered earth. With a sinking heart, I discovered that I had fallen from one danger into another.

'Do sit down, sir,' said Lady Quincy. 'Allow me to help you to remove your blindfold.'

# CHAPTER FORTY-SEVEN

'I TOLD BUCKINGHAM you would agree.' Lady
Quincy sat back and looked at me sitting opposite
her. She smiled. 'He didn't believe me at first. He said his
men were going to teach you a lesson, teach you not to
poke your nose into his business. But I said no, he misun-
derstood you and your motives. You could be an ally not
an enemy. Besides, I told him you were my friend. I vouched
for you.'

In an instant, everything had changed. Nothing could be
taken for granted.

The coach moved away. This was not the huge vehicle in
which we had travelled down to Cambridgeshire, but the
lighter, more elegant coach Lady Quincy used in town. We
were the only occupants. I recognized our surroundings. We
were rumbling down Snowhill, away from the City. We passed
the remains of St Mary Woolnoth on the right.

'The Duke came to me this morning, quite unexpectedly,
with a proposal. We talked tête-à-tête for hours – I told him
you were so kind and so obliging with Frances.' She looked

away, perhaps affecting modesty. 'And . . . and in other ways, though of course I did not mention that to him.'

Dear God, I thought, she thinks I'm still besotted with her. I said, 'A proposal, madam? And how could it concern me?'

Lust blinds a man to everything that does not feed it. Once it is stripped away, one sees more clearly. But Lady Quincy did not yet understand that since that night at Hitcham St Martin I was no longer drawn to her as the moth to the candle. That was the one thing I knew and she did not. It was my one advantage.

'I know you,' she said, with a faint but deliberate emphasis on the verb, to remind me that we had known each other that night in the biblical sense of the word. 'You are like me, Marwood. In the end you follow the dictates of duty.'

I inclined my head. 'One goes where one must.'

For the moment, my safest policy was to echo what she said, or to agree with it. The coach swung sharply round a corner, throwing her skirts against my leg. She took her time disentangling herself. We trundled over Holborn Bridge and began to climb the hill beyond.

'That is very true,' she said, a little breathlessly. 'We both of us let duty be our guide. I'm not disloyal to the King – of course not, how could I be? – any more than you are, my dear Marwood – but when Buckingham came to me and showed me where the path of my duty lay, the true path, I realized that an alliance with him was my best way to serve the King.' Her eyelashes fluttered. 'And in doing so, to serve others. Including, as it happens, Frances.'

I nodded and smiled, hoping my face did not show the confusion I felt. 'Was it only today you discovered this?'

'Yes.' She looked innocently at me, her eyes wide and

candid. 'That's why he came to see me. It's not as if we're strangers. I've known Bucks for years, since the Court was at Bruges in fact, and we're old friends.'

Bruges, I thought, that place again. At a time when the King, the Duke of York and the Duke of Buckingham had all three been unmarried. Any of them could have been Frances's father.

'He wished to see Frances for himself, so I presented her to him. He was charmed by the child, and I'm persuaded that he has her best interests at heart. He agrees that she should have what is hers by right, and that it will be better for the country if she does. And he's convinced the King will agree too, once he knows all. He must.'

How old was Frances, exactly? Nine years of age? Ten?

'Then I was right, madam,' I said.

'Right?' she gave me a sideways look, a half-smile. 'In what way?'

'When we talked at Mistress Warley's.' I watched her. 'In your chamber.'

She turned away, pretending an embarrassment I doubted she felt.

'In supposing that Frances is your daughter.'

'Yes, you were right, sir. She was born before my first marriage, when I was a waiting woman to my Lady Hyde – my Lady Clarendon, as she later became. I was young and foolish and easily impressed. Easily tempted, too, perhaps, and easily fooled. I had no one to advise me. My father was dead. My mother had remarried and had no time for me.'

'What happened when she was born?' I asked.

After a pause, she looked at me again, and for once her face seemed stripped of artifice and calculation. 'Frances was taken from me directly. Lord Clarendon and his wife saw to everything. They gave me no choice – I was young, and I had no one to speak for me, nowhere to turn for help. She was put to nurse and then taken to England, to the Warleys. I had not seen her since then. Not until the day when you and I went to Hitcham St Martin. But blood tells, does it not? A mother has a duty to her daughter.'

'So has a father.'

'Exactly.' She leaned forward and tapped my hand with her gloved finger. 'That is the heart of the matter. Which is why, my dear Marwood, if you will be so kind, you will escort me to see my lawyer. I believe you called on him once before, but he was not at leisure to see you.'

I stared at her. 'You mean Mr Turner?' I said. 'Of Barnard's Inn? Your attorney.'

I had called on him in his chambers over a week ago and shown his clerk, Frankley, my warrant. Frankley told me that Alderley, newly rich, had called there to discharge Lady Quincy's mortgage on his Farrow Lane house – and that, while he was there, he had taken the opportunity to mention something to the attorney about a marriage contract. At the time, I had assumed Alderley was contemplating offering his hand to a lady. But I now realized that the marriage in question had not been his own. In that case, whose?

The coach drew up outside the Holborn entrance of Barnard's Inn.

'Will you ask Mr Turner to step out to me?'

The coach waited, an impediment to traffic, while I passed into the inn and crossed the front court to the staircase by the hall. The clerk recognized me at once. His confusion was written on his face.

'My master is engaged, sir, so—'

'Tell Mr Turner that my Lady Quincy is waiting for him in her coach.'

Frankley shot me a startled glance. He went into the inner room without knocking. I heard the murmur of voices, and then the stout and untidy figure of Mr Turner emerged, straightening his periwig. He was the red-faced, bright-eyed man I had glimpsed on my previous visit. 'Mr – ah – Marwood?'

'Your servant, sir. Allow me to take you to her ladyship.'

We clattered down the stairs together. Turner said nothing as we crossed the court, though he couldn't help glancing surreptitiously at the scars on my face and neck. He was uncertain how to treat me. I opened the coach door for him and he bowed clumsily to Lady Quincy. She told him to sit with her. He clambered inside and squeezed himself into the corner opposite her, trying to make himself as small as possible.

'And will you join us, sir?' she said to me, to my surprise. 'You had better sit beside me.' She gave the lawyer a swift, sly smile, which made him smile nervously and twitch on the seat. 'Mr Turner needs a little more room than either of us.'

The lawyer's colour darkened still further, and he spluttered an apology. I climbed into the coach. When I sat down, my hip rested snugly against Lady Quincy's thigh.

'I have a question for you, sir,' she said to Turner. 'A hypothetical question. Let me put a case to you. On foreign soil, an English gentleman offers marriage to a lady, also English. She accepts. They exchange a verbal contract of marriage in presence of witnesses, and also give each other a gold coin as a token of betrothal. The next day, a clergyman of the Church of England marries them in the presence of the same witnesses, but without a licence or banns being called. The groom gives his bride a ring, a plain gold band. Being young, and hot for each other, they consummate the marriage at once. The following day, the gentleman writes a letter to the lady, referring to her as his beloved wife and referring both to the contract of marriage they have made and to the fact that they have lain together. My question is this: would such a marriage be valid now, in England?'

Turner stirred uneasily. He glanced at me and then back at Lady Quincy. 'Yes – and no.'

'Come, sir,' she snapped. 'It must be one or the other.'

'Then probably it would be considered valid. Can the witnesses sign affidavits in support of the—?'

'Unfortunately they are both dead. As is the clergyman. In the same outbreak of plague, as it happens.'

'And the gentleman . . .?'

'Is not inclined to admit his part in the affair. There was a certificate signed by the clergyman, but the gentleman kept that and he has probably destroyed it. Apart from the lady's testimony, the evidence consists of the letter he wrote in his own hand on the day after the contract of marriage. And the ring, together with the coin he gave to the lady. The coin bears his teeth marks, for he bit and bent it as a token of the betrothal.'

'My lady, the ring – if it is plain and lacks any inscription, is neither here nor there. It proves nothing. The teeth marks might be more interesting, if unusual. Perhaps it could be offered as evidence – assuming the gentleman retains the teeth in question, and they could be shown to correspond with the marks. But the letter could be far more important than all the rest. That he would find difficult to dispute, so long as the writing can be proved to be his. Does it mention the lady by name?'

'Yes.' Lady Quincy permitted herself a small smile. 'The letter was enclosed in a cover addressed to the lady by her maiden name, because the marriage had been in secret. But the letter itself was addressed to the lady in her married name.'

May God and all his Angels save us, I prayed. At last I saw where this was tending, and I could not see how it could lead to a happy ending for anyone, save perhaps the Duke of Buckingham.

Turner pursed his lips and considered. There was a sheen of sweat on his forehead. 'As I said, the ring is neither here nor there, nor probably the coin . . . But the lady would certainly have a case. It is a great pity that the witnesses and the clergyman are dead, but the gentleman's letter, if it can be produced in court, might well prove a compelling piece of evidence.'

'Would the marriage be upheld?'

'I can't say whether it would be considered good in law. Partly because the law itself is not entirely clear on the subject of marriages and their validity. Indeed, all three branches of the law – ecclesiastical, common and equity – are sometimes involved in cases involving a disputed marriage. What makes matters worse, is that they do not always agree on what constitutes a legally binding marriage. That means that their verdicts may be contradictory. The case such as the one you postulate would definitely need to be heard in a church court, where the rules of marriage are governed by medieval canon law, in their revised form as laid down by the Canons of 1604. If there are considerations of property involved, however, then that would also be the province of civil law so—'

Lady Quincy held up her hand. 'Enough, sir. One last question. What if the parties in such a case had contracted subsequent marriages?'

There was no mistaking the look of shock on Turner's face. 'Then, madam,' he said slowly, 'there would be yet another complication, particularly if one party chose to sue the other: bigamy is a statutory penal offence, so it must be a matter for the criminal courts.'

# CHAPTER FORTY-EIGHT

'YOU CAN'T BE too careful,' Brennan said. 'Best not show your face in Henrietta Street. I think they've bribed the porter.'

'Who has?' Cat asked.

'How do I know? Probably those rogues at Whitehall. But other people have been sniffing around too. Asking questions of the neighbours . . .'

After a frustrating afternoon, she had found the draughtsman in the garden of an alehouse in Long Acre where he sometimes stopped to refresh himself on his way back to his lodgings. Since she had given Milcote the slip, she had spent hours criss-crossing London in the hope of tracking down Marwood. Now she was footsore, hungry, thirsty and close to despair.

'Do you want a drink?' Brennan said, reading her mind. 'You look half-starved. Bread? Cheese?'

She nodded, wordlessly, and sat down on the bench in the sun while he went to the hatch to order. No one gave her a second glance. Brennan came back, and she fell on the food and the ale with a ferocity that made him stare.

After a couple of minutes, she said with her mouth full, 'How is Mr Hakesby?'

'Not too bad. He's moved in to the new lodgings. Landlord said he could come a week early. That makes it easier for him.'

'What?' She stared at him, and then remembered. Hakesby had taken a lease on the apartments below the Drawing Office. He had been due to take possession of them at Michaelmas, the Quarter Day on 29 September. This was where she and Hakesby would live when they were married. The thought caught her off guard. It made her feel nauseous. He was old enough to be her grandfather. The arrangement seemed distasteful and faintly ridiculous. Such alliances belonged to other people living other lives, not to her and Hakesby.

'The old man keeps talking about you,' Brennan went on. 'He misses you. So do I.' He flushed suddenly and rushed on, 'I mean, the work's mounting up. They want the final drawings for Dragon Yard by the end of the month, and we should really make a site visit and check the foundations before we sign them off.'

The words were not meaningless but they had lost most of their significance. The Dragon Yard commission was their biggest yet, giving Mr Hakesby the responsibility for the design and construction of a small street of houses north of Cheapside. One way or another, it had dominated her life for the last few months. But now it seemed unimportant.

Cat finished the rest of her ale and stuffed the remains of the bread and cheese in her pocket. She stood up. 'Thank you.'

'Where are you going?' he said, scrambling to his feet. 'Where are you living?'

'Better you don't know.'

Brennan held out a hand, trying to detain her. She swerved away from it and slipped through the back gate into the street.

Cat recognized the coach by the widow's lozenge on the door. She had seen the arms before, often, on a set of silver gilt plates that her Aunt Quincy had brought to Barnabas Place when she married Henry Alderley, Edward's father and Cat's uncle. The plates had been a wedding present from the King on the occasion of her first marriage to Sir William Quincy.

The lozenge displayed the arms of her aunt's family quartered with those of Quincy. Her aunt had enlisted even heraldry to support the fiction that her second marriage, to Henry Alderley, a man who died a bankrupt Regicide, had never taken place. Here, Cat thought, was a woman who believed that truth should not be allowed to stand in the way of a more convenient alternative.

The coach drew up on the south side of the Strand, by Arundel House. The footman jumped down to open its door, forcing Cat to step into the gutter, which fortunately was dry. She had been waiting among the crowd in the Strand for nearly an hour, hoping to catch a glimpse of Marwood.

Marwood climbed out. Cat turned her head, concealing her face. His face was hot and flushed as if running a fever. He looked back into the interior of the coach. A hand in a grey glove appeared. He took it in his own hand and bowed over it.

The rogue, she thought, the damned rogue. Yet another fool who kept his brain between his legs.

He set off towards the Savoy. The footman closed the door and scrambled up. The coach inched its way into the traffic.

This changed nothing, though. She still needed to talk to

Marwood, and for her sake as much as his. She followed him down the Strand to the great gateway of the Savoy. She waited until they had both passed under the archway and into the broad cobbled way beyond.

Once inside the palace precinct, the noise of the Strand receded to a bearable level. The lane sloped down to the river, with the walls and chimneys of the Savoy on the left-hand side. She put on a spurt of speed, drew level with Marwood and touched his arm.

He spun round as if she had stabbed him. 'Why, what the devil—'

'I must talk to you.'

'Here? In broad daylight? Where anyone might see you.' He glared at her. 'And see me with you, as well. Have you thought what that could mean? For me as much as you?'

'I've been trying to find you all day. While you've been dallying with my aunt like a moonstruck fool.'

A flush stained Marwood's face. 'It's not what you think. I've—'

'Have you heard that Gorse is dead?' she interrupted. 'They fished him out of the Thames this morning.'

His eyes narrowed. For a moment he said nothing. Then: 'How did he die?'

'I heard that he'd been stabbed. When I saw him, he was laid out on the quay at Botolph's Wharf with a great wound in his chest.'

Marwood frowned. 'But he was here yesterday evening, if the hat is anything to go by.'

She nodded towards the river, towards the Savoy stairs. 'Then perhaps that's where he went into the water. And the tide carried him down under the bridge.'

She watched his eyes widening as he worked out the implication: that he and Cat had heard the killer's footsteps yesterday evening outside his house in Infirmary Close; that only the width of a wall had separated them from a murder.

'The news will be all over town by now,' he said.

'Only the news of a murder. When I saw the body, no one had identified it.'

'Do you mean that we may still be the only ones who know that Gorse is dead?'

'It's possible.' Cat hesitated. 'I went to look for you at the Goat today, to tell you the news. But Mr Milcote saw me.'

'For God's sake—'

'I couldn't avoid it. He tried to seize me.' She looked away from him. 'I stabbed him in the leg and ran.'

Marwood glared at her. 'God save us all,' he said. 'You fool. Will he live?'

'It was only a pinprick.'

The tension burst like a bubble. They both smiled, and then both looked away, as if guilty of a foolishness.

'What are we going to do?' Cat said.

'There's not a lot Milcote can do. You should go back to Dorcas, and pray no one has seen us together.' Marwood glanced up and down the lane. 'But first I had better tell you this while I can. Buckingham and your aunt are intriguing against Clarendon and possibly against the King himself.'

'My aunt? Then you were not—?'

He overrode her, speaking rapidly. 'Lady Quincy has a daughter, Frances. The girl has never been acknowledged – she's been living in seclusion with a connection of Lady Clarendon's. That's why she wanted me to escort her to Cambridgeshire, to fetch the girl.'

'My aunt has a child? But why wouldn't she acknowledge her?'

'Because her first husband wasn't the father. She had the girl before her marriage, when she was living in Clarendon's household in Bruges. She was one of her ladyship's waiting women.'

'Why now?' Cat said. 'Why has she brought the girl to London?'

'She went to see a lawyer this afternoon to ask him about the validity of marriage contracts. So perhaps . . .'

'She believes that she was married to the father after all?'

Marwood nodded. 'If the man is still alive, that would mean her marriages to Sir William Quincy and your uncle were bigamous. And it—'

She was there already: 'And it would also mean that if Frances's father had married someone else, that would be bigamous too and—'

'And therefore any children of the second marriage would be illegitimate,' he finished. He looked ill, she thought: he was hunched forward, shoulders slumped, his skin clammy and his breathing rapid, like his speech. 'They were all in Bruges then, when the Court was in exile. The King, York, Buckingham and Clarendon. And your aunt.'

She forgot everything else, as the implications of what Marwood had said sank in. 'What do they want, my aunt and Buckingham?'

'The Duke wants power and glory.' Marwood glanced down at her. 'And your aunt? I think she's suddenly discovered that she wants her daughter. I'm not sure that the girl returns the compliment and wants my lady as her mother. But of course the real question is—'

'Who is the girl's father?' Cat said.

\*\*\*

George Milcote was so much in Cat's thoughts that it seemed almost natural that she should see him again. He came walking down Botolph Lane and turned into Thames Street. It was early evening, and Thames Street was busy. Cat and Dorcas were on their way to the cookshop for food. Cat had money in her pocket – Marwood had been generous with the boat fare – and she was determined to buy their supper.

Milcote was near the Green Dragon Tavern, where she had seen him two days ago. He was dressed as he had been then, in dark, shabby clothes. His shoulders were bowed, and he walked rapidly, without looking from side to side. She turned aside, pretending to read a handbill on the tavern door. He passed them without a glance. He threaded his way through a group of sailors and turned up Love Lane.

If she were wise, Cat thought, she would thank God for a lucky escape and run back to the safety of Dorcas's stable. But what the devil was a man like Milcote doing in this area, and dressed so meanly? She touched the older woman's arm. 'Humour me. I want to see where that man goes.'

Dorcas looked aghast. 'Do you know him?'

'I've seen him sometimes.'

'Why do you want to follow him?'

'I'm curious.'

'Who is he?'

Cat didn't answer. She took the older woman's arm and urged her along.

Dorcas smiled at her. 'You're a sly one. Who'd have thought it?' They turned into Love Lane. Milcote's tall figure was twenty yards ahead of them. 'But . . . you do know why men usually come here, don't you?'

'No. Why?'

'It was always called Love Lane. But since the Fire, it lives up to its name. It's where the whores are now. Convenient for the river trade.'

'But he's not like—'

Cat broke off. Milcote had stopped outside a house which had lost its upper storeys to the fire. The blackened stone walls of the ground floor remained, and a makeshift roof had been constructed over it. Without a word, the two women stopped.

Dorcas caught her breath. 'If you're sweet on him, I think you're making a mistake.'

Milcote glanced up and down the narrow street and knocked on the door. It opened almost at once. Cat couldn't see who was inside. Milcote slipped into the house. The door closed.

As they stood there, two men passed them and walked quickly up the lane away from the river. The sword of the taller one brushed Cat's skirts, and his colleague nudged Dorcas out of his way. Cat watched them with dislike. They stopped for a moment and looked up at the house that had swallowed Milcote. The taller man spoke to his companion, who nodded, looking up at the frontage. They continued up the lane at the same rapid pace as before in the direction of Fenchurch Street. The smaller of the two was as fat as a barrel. They were soon out of sight among the crowd.

'We should go,' Dorcas said, anxious and urgent to be gone. She took Cat's arm and tried to draw her away. 'I'm hungry.'

Cat pulled her arm free. 'Wait.'

Those two men had brought to mind Marwood's request last week, as they were riding into London on their return from the refugee camp at Mangot's Farm. He had asked her to watch out for two men who wished him harm, one tall and thin in a long brown coat; the other smaller but fat; and both carrying swords. She had asked if they were connected with her cousin Edward's death or with Lady Quincy, and he had not given her much of an answer. Were these the same men? Did they wish Mr Milcote harm as well?

'Let's walk past the house first.'

Ignoring Dorcas, Cat started up the lane. A man accosted her, recoiling when she bared her teeth at him and spat at the ground. Dorcas caught up with her and took her arm.

'Don't be foolish. Please. It's dangerous here. Let's go home.'

Cat shook her off. They reached the house which Milcote had entered. A rag had been draped over a hook above the door. It looked like the remains of a gown. Dorcas tried to hurry past it.

'What is this place?' Cat asked, her heart sinking. 'Do you know?'

Dorcas grimaced. 'Can't you tell?'

'It's a brothel-house, isn't it?'

'Yes.' Dorcas hesitated, and then whispered, 'But my son says it's worse than the rest. One of his shipmates used to go there on leave sometimes, and when they found out they hanged him from the yard arm.'

Cat stopped. 'But why?'

'Because it's where the sodomites go, my dear. And that's what sailors do to the foul beasts if they catch them. They hang them. Or worse.'

# CHAPTER FORTY-NINE

T HE KING DID not share my sense of urgency.

It shouldn't have come as a surprise, but it did. Before leaving the Savoy, I had given Cat the fare for a boat back to the City and returned to Infirmary Close, where I washed my face and changed into my best suit of clothes. It was a little after six o'clock by the time I stepped out of the sedan chair outside the Court Gate at Whitehall. I had taken a chair to preserve my finery from the mud and the dust. I went through the suite of public rooms to the door of the King's private apartments. The guards refused to let me enter because my name wasn't on the list for the evening.

I sent a message to Mr Chiffinch, begging him to vouch for me, and telling him that I sought an interview with the King. In a while, he came out and drew me aside to an alcove. His face was flushed with wine – his skin habitually grew darker as the day advanced until by midnight it reached a shade approaching puce.

'This had better be important, Marwood.'

'It is. I must see the King.'

'The King's engaged,' he said. 'And I doubt he'd see you, in any case. You'd better tell me what it is. If it's important enough, I'll tell him when there is a chance for a word in private.'

'I beg your pardon, sir,' I said, 'but I must speak to him myself. It's a most delicate matter.'

'If you've any sense at all, you'll let me be the judge of that,' Chiffinch said, scratching the great wart on his chin. 'Very well. If it's that delicate, as you say, you had better come to my closet. You can tell me privately.'

'Sir, you will remember that the King did me the honour of talking to me on the river last week. He chose to do it there – just the two of us, in the middle of the water – because this is a matter where discretion is essential.' I took a liberty with the truth. 'He commanded me to report directly to him when I had further intelligence on this particular subject. He was quite clear about that. I cannot disobey him.'

It was a gamble. I wasn't sure how far the King had taken Chiffinch into his confidence. To my relief, though, he shrugged his heavy shoulders.

'He may not be at leisure. But I suppose I can let you come in and wait in case he has a moment for you.'

'Will you let him know I'm here, sir?'

Chiffinch scowled. 'You grow impertinent, Marwood. It doesn't become you.'

'Forgive me, sir. It is my desire to serve the King.'

He sniffed and led the way to the door of the private apartments. He whispered to the guard and we went through.

The King spent a great deal of money on the public apartments of Whitehall, because it was important that their magnificence should provide a worthy setting to enhance his

395

own. The private apartments were equally dazzling, but they had a careless, luxurious extravagance that was absent elsewhere: the gilded French furniture and the bright carpets, the pictures and clocks and sculptures reflected the taste and personality of their owner.

Chiffinch led me to an anteroom. He told me to stay there and not to make a nuisance of myself among my betters. He went through the adjoining withdrawing room. As the door was opened for him, I glimpsed the scene within, caught for an instant within the frame of the doorway, fixed like a Dutch picture. The room was a blaze of candlelight, which cast a shifting glow over the courtiers, who were standing and chatting in their finery, and over the large table where the King sat with a group of men and women. They were playing cards. Piles of gold shimmered on the table.

One tall figure drew the eye: the Duke of Buckingham was standing at the King's shoulder, leaning forward, smiling as he gestured towards the gold. The door closed, and the picture vanished.

The anteroom was equally crowded, but with men and women with restless eyes and whispering voices. This was where attendants gathered to await the pleasure of their betters, and where people waited in the hope of an audience with one of the great ones in the next room. I drew back into a corner beyond the marble fireplace. I prayed that the Duke of Buckingham would not pass through the anteroom and catch sight of me.

Time passed, first minutes and then hours. Courtiers came and went through the door to the withdrawing room, but I was not sent for. After a while I found a seat on a bench against the wall. Every time the door opened, the chink of glasses and the hum of conversation rolled out, bringing with them a heady smell of candles and perfume. Servants went to and fro with wine and food, but none was offered to us in the anteroom. At one point, the Duke of York emerged, his face grim, and marched across the anteroom, ignoring the bows of those who waited there. He appeared not to notice me.

At last, Chiffinch returned, a little darker in the face than before. 'Why are you hiding away in a corner, Marwood? The King will see you. Wait on him in the Red Room.'

A servant took me there. The King was sitting at a table, eating a leg of chicken and drinking a glass of wine. His features, always strongly marked, seemed heavier than usual, the lines on his face more deeply scored. He acknowledged my bow with a wave of his hand and told me to open the window. 'God's fish,' he said, 'it's as warm as a furnace in here.' He glanced up at the servant who attended him. 'Leave us.'

When we were alone, he helped himself to a dish of turbot. 'Well, Marwood? You went down to Cambridgeshire with my Lady Quincy. I hear she's pleased with you.' His voice hardened. 'And what of the killing of Edward Alderley? Have you found any trace of the Lovett woman?'

'Not as yet, sir,' I lied. 'But there's other mischief afoot.'

'Ah.' He dropped his fork on the plate and wiped his mouth with his napkin. 'You had better tell me.'

'There's been another murder. One of Lord Clarendon's servants, a man named Gorse, was stabbed and thrown into the Thames last night. It turns out that he used to serve the Alderleys before he went to Clarendon House. There must be a connection with Alderley's murder, but I don't know how.'

'Perhaps he recognized Lovett, and she had him killed to shut his mouth.'

'There is another matter, sir. Were you aware that Lady Quincy brought back a child from Cambridgeshire? The child suffers from scrofula, and Lady Quincy wishes to have her touched by Your Majesty.'

He nodded and tore off a piece of chicken from another dish.

'I understand that when the child, Mistress Frances, was born, my Lady Clarendon arranged for her to be brought up in seclusion by a cousin of hers. But the girl's mother is Lady Quincy.'

The King waved impatiently. 'Yes, yes. You'd be wise not to repeat that outside this room.'

'The question is, who is the Mistress Frances's father?' I took a deep breath, for suddenly the King was frowning. 'And whether there was a contract of marriage between that person and Lady Quincy.'

He was sitting very still, the chicken leg forgotten between his fingers. He was watching me.

'I believe that there was such a document, sir, and that Lord Clarendon kept it in a silver box in his closet. The box was locked. Edward Alderley stole it from my lord's private closet, shortly before his death.'

'How? Lord Clarendon is a man who guards his privacy carefully.'

I bowed, acknowledging the point. 'In the days of his prosperity, Alderley knew Lord Clarendon's gentleman, Mr Milcote.'

'Milcote? Yes, I know. The soldier. My brother speaks highly of him.'

I bowed again. 'Alderley renewed the acquaintance. Mr Milcote is a benevolent man. He lent Alderley money and invited him to Clarendon House on several occasions. On one of them, Alderley was discovered in my lord's closet, though he had an excuse to divert suspicion. All this is certain, sir.'

'So you think that was when Alderley stole the box.' The King paused and then pounced on the inference that I had already drawn for myself. 'Ah – I see. This was not a random theft. Someone had told him what to look for.'

'Yes, sir. After Alderley's death, I found the box in his lodgings and gave it to Mr Chiffinch. By then the box had been forced open, and the contents removed. The lodgings had already been searched by a man named Veal, who is in the employ of the Duke of Buckingham.'

The King cleared his throat but did not interrupt.

'Veal and his servant followed Lady Quincy and me into Cambridgeshire. They tried to capture Mistress Frances, but we foiled that. This afternoon, though, they carried me away by force, and held me in a cellar somewhere in the ruins. I was interviewed there by a man who I believe was the Duke himself. He wanted to recruit me to his cause, for me to be his informer. I pretended to agree – what else could I do? But—'

'You believe it was Buckingham? But you must know what he looks like. Why don't you know if it was him, one way or the other?'

'He was masked, sir.'

'Go on. Are you saying that the Duke has this document in his possession?'

I shook my head. 'I understood from him that he is still

looking for it, whatever it is. Which means that Veal must have failed to find it in Alderley's lodgings.'

'Then where the devil is it?'

'I think Alderley broke open the box and hid the document before he died. It's even possible that he planned to renege on his bargain with Veal. Perhaps, when he saw what the document contained, he thought he could get more for it than Veal had offered. He hoped to sell it to the highest bidder.'

'You mean he intended to approach me? Or——?'

The King broke off and drummed his fingers on the table. He pushed back his chair so violently that it rocked on its legs. He rose, went to the window and looked out on the Privy Garden. 'But then that damned cousin of his killed him, for quite a different reason.' He turned back to me, and to my surprise I saw he was smiling. 'Chance. We can't escape it, Marwood. Our lives are governed by the roll of the dice whether we like it or not.'

'There is one more thing, sir,' I said. 'Lady Quincy has thrown in her lot with the Duke of Buckingham. She is ambitious for herself and her daughter. She asked me to escort her to see a lawyer this afternoon. She wanted to enquire about a certain letter from a man she claims became her husband in Bruges, to discover whether such a letter would constitute a legally binding contract of marriage. She——'

The King hammered his fist on the table with such force that the cutlery rattled. 'This is a parcel of lies, Marwood. Why in God's name would she trust you? Because Buckingham has bribed you?'

I forced myself not to flinch from his rage. 'More than that, sir. She trusts me because she believes that I will do anything she wishes in the hope of pleasing her. Besides, they may have calculated that they would lose nothing if I did tell you.'

He considered that. Then: 'Is that true then?' There was a flicker of mockery on his face. 'That you love Lady Quincy?'

'No, sir. Never that. Though there was a time . . .'

The King stared at me and looked away. The muscles in his cheek quivered. 'Damned fool.' He glanced back at me. 'Not you. Anyone can make a fool of himself over a woman, and I can't blame a man for that. I mean my Lord Clarendon. He should have burned what was in that box years ago. He told me that he had. These lawyers – they can't bring themselves to destroy documents. Scraps of paper are meat and drink to them.'

His face hardened. He sat down and commanded me to ring the handbell that stood on the table. I dared not raise the question of the identity of Frances's father or the possibility of bigamy. The King would not thank me for pointing out what he must already know and fear.

When the servant came, he called for writing materials. I stood before him in silence while he wrote a letter – only a few lines. He folded the paper. He took up the nearest candle and melted the end of the sealing wax. A soft red pool formed on the letter. He stamped it with his ring.

He took up the letter and looked at it for a few seconds. He tossed it on the table towards me. 'Take this to my Lord Clarendon,' he said. 'At once. Rouse him out of bed if necessary. Put the letter in his hands and watch him opening it.'

Clarendon House was in darkness. The only lights were the watchmen's lanterns by the gates in Piccadilly and the lantern over the front door in the centre of the house.

The watchmen admitted me when they saw the King's warrant. One of them took me to the side door on the west side of the house. Here a porter waited in the side hall. It was lit only by a single candle and the porter's lantern. Our footsteps on the marble floor set off echoes among the shadows in the corners. The bright figures on the painted ceiling were reduced to spectral shapes.

The porter rang a bell and eventually a servant came. 'My lord left orders he shouldn't be disturbed.'

'I insist on seeing him.' I held up the letter. 'This is from the King. And I have his warrant here.'

The servant became less surly. 'Of course, sir.' He conducted me up the shallow stairs to the private apartments. 'His lordship isn't alone, by the way,' he said at the turn of the stairs. 'His Highness is with him.'

'Is Mr Milcote here this evening?' I asked.

'I believe not, sir. But I will enquire if you like.'

I wished the King had not sent me. I was not looking forward to seeing Lord Clarendon but I had not expected his son-in-law, the Duke of York, to be there as well. No one likes the bearer of bad news, and I had no desire to make an enemy of a man as powerful as the King's brother and heir.

They were in the earl's closet. The servant bade me wait in the antechamber. He knocked and went in when his master called. I heard the voices of the men within, and caught the King's name and mine. The servant returned, bowed to me and held the door open.

The closet was stuffy, warm and bright with candlelight. The Duke and his father-in-law were sitting by the fire. Lord Clarendon was in his wheeled chair. The Duke ignored my low bow and did not look at me.

'Well, Marwood,' said Clarendon. 'You have a letter, I understand?'

I gave it to him. 'The King bade me wait while you open it, my lord.'

Clarendon raised his eyebrows. 'To make sure I read it?' Despite his age and infirmity, his voice was strong and sardonic. 'He need not have troubled.'

He broke the seal and unfolded the letter. I stood at a distance and watched. He put on a pair of glasses and held the paper close to his eyes. He lowered it and pursed his lips. The Duke stared at the fire.

Clarendon beckoned me to approach him. 'Pray hand this to His Highness.' He gave me the letter without troubling to fold it.

The Duke read it quickly. He looked up. 'This is intolerable.'

Clarendon said, 'It's no more than I expected. And I am concerned for you, of course.' He glanced at me. 'Enough of that for the moment. Marwood, you may tell the King that I have read his letter, and so has the Duke. Tell him that I am in a strange country, where I know nobody, and where there are very few who remember that they ever knew me.'

The Duke of York stirred uneasily in his chair.

Unexpectedly, Clarendon gave me a thin smile. 'But pray remind him that I am not altogether friendless, and that I will not allow villainy to triumph.'

I was dismissed. The manservant was waiting for me in the anteroom. He conducted me down the dimly lit staircase.

'I've sent a footman to enquire after Mr Milcote, sir,' he murmured.

There were agitated voices in the hall below, rising and

falling and stumbling over one another. I recognized the porter and the house steward, whom I had met briefly when I had dined here with Milcote. There were also two other footmen and one of the watchmen from the gates. Finally, a sixth man, dressed in black, stood by himself with a paper in his hand.

When they heard our footsteps on the stairs, the men stopped talking. Their pale faces looked up at us.

The steward stepped forward. 'Mr Marwood – you're come from my lord and His Highness?'

'Yes,' I said, glancing from one to the other. 'What is this?'

He ignored the question. 'And they are still in my lord's closet?'

'Yes.'

'I must go to them, I suppose.' He waved at the man in black, who looked like a clerk. 'You'd better come as well in case they want to question you.'

I drew the steward aside. He was an old man and was in his gown and with a cap on his head. He had been preparing for bed when they sent for him.

'I'm here on the King's business, sir,' I said. 'What's happened?'

He looked wildly at me. 'It's Mr Milcote,' he said. 'He's been arrested.'

## CHAPTER FIFTY

THE FOLLOWING MORNING, I went early to Whitehall. I found that the news of Milcote's arrest had travelled before me. In the Matted Gallery, it was the subject on everyone's lips.

Chiffinch received me in his closet. He was still in his bedgown, with a plate of rolls and a cup of chocolate at his elbow. His barber was stropping a razor by the window. He greeted me cheerfully, which was unusual, and told the barber to leave us.

'First things first,' he said. 'How did my lord take it? Did he give you a message for the King?'

'He said to tell His Majesty that he felt he was in a strange country, where few people knew him any more. But he also said he had friends, and he could not allow villainy to triumph.'

'Strong words. But I thought he would come out fighting.'

'The Duke of York was with him, and my lord gave him the letter to read. He was angry.'

Chiffinch shrugged. 'Without the King's support, what can the old man do, even with the Duke at his side? And the

405

Duke's not a fool. He's the King's heir, and he will not venture to go against him in this.'

He paused to dip a fragment of roll into the chocolate. He popped the morsel in his mouth, leaving a trail of drips on his gown.

'Have you heard about Mr Milcote's arrest?' I said. 'And the charge?'

'Oh yes.' Chiffinch wiped his mouth with a napkin. 'We heard late last night. The Duke of Buckingham made sure of that. The news was probably known at Whitehall before it reached Clarendon House. The timing could not have been better for Buckingham and his party. Sodomy, eh?' He whistled. 'Who would have thought it? And Milcote — such a brave gentleman, by all accounts. Is there no doubt?'

'I believe not, sir. I talked to the magistrate's clerk last night.' I hesitated. 'When the constables broke in, they found Milcote in circumstances that . . . that made doubt impossible.'

'How did it happen that they went there in the first place?'

'Two men laid information against Milcote, and said that they had seen him enter the house, and that they believed he intended to commit sodomy on a man within.'

Chiffinch scratched his nose. 'Disgusting. Still, it's an ill wind that blows nobody good. Filth of this nature smears all it touches. It will damage Lord Clarendon greatly, for example. People will probably whisper that he knew all and condoned all. Perhaps he did — he certainly trusted Milcote — cherished the man, even. He had him living under his own roof and dining at his table. At best it will be seen as a terrible error of his lordship's judgement, and at worst — well, you can imagine what will be said. Believe me, Marwood, this will do my lord no good at all.'

'Both the witnesses are in the service of the Duke of Buckingham, sir,' I said. 'One is a clergyman named Veal, who was deprived of his living.'

'Still – a clergyman? That will go down well with the judge, I'm sure.'

'He's the man who followed Lady Quincy and me into Cambridgeshire, the man known as the Bishop. He was friendly with Alderley and searched his lodgings after his death. He was looking for the silver box. He and his servant were also the men who incited the protesters outside Clarendon House.'

Chiffinch considered. 'I shall pass on what you have said to the King. I suspect he will decide that the Duke of Buckingham's connection with Mr Veal has nothing to do with this matter, not in its essentials. After all, sodomy is both a grievous sin and a capital offence.' He smiled up at me with an unprecedented display of pleasure. 'You've done well, Marwood, all in all. I shall tell the King so. Go back to Mr Williamson and your duties at Scotland Yard. I've nothing more for you at present.'

Taken aback, I stared at him.

He waved me towards the door. 'Send the barber to me on your way out.'

After leaving Chiffinch, I went directly to Scotland Yard. I felt strangely adrift. The investigation into Alderley's death and its unexpected ramifications had taken up my entire life. Now the matter had been removed from me. But there was still so much I did not know. And Cat remained a fugitive. Unfinished business leaves a sour taste.

After the distractions of the last fortnight, I was woefully behind in my usual work. Mr Williamson was not in the office, which was a relief. There was much sorting and filing for me to do. The *Gazette* had gone out during my absence, but Williamson's confidential letters to his correspondents up and down the kingdom had been largely neglected; the task of copying and dispatching these was usually mine.

I set to work. The other clerks tried to discover the reason for my absence but I evaded their questions. They were wary of me, I knew, because I had more than one master and spent too much time on business that had nothing to do with the office.

In the middle of the morning, Williamson arrived. He summoned me to his private room and told me to close the door.

'You're back at last,' he said. 'You will have to work twice as hard to catch up.'

'Yes, sir.'

'I know you have been looking into Edward Alderley's death,' he said. 'Have you heard the latest news about it?'

'I've heard nothing at all, sir.'

'The sodomite Milcote has just confessed to his murder.'

'Milcote? But – I don't understand. I—'

'He made a voluntary deposition to the magistrate,' Williamson interrupted. 'He admitted that he pushed Alderley into the well that night. He lured him to the pavilion on the promise of gold, expressly with that in mind.'

'But why, sir?'

'Because Alderley was blackmailing him, that's why. He found out about Milcote's sodomical ways and threatened to expose him. Milcote had given him almost all the money he had in the world. Then something must have snapped.

Even the meanest worm will turn if you tread on him hard enough.'

The evidence reshuffled itself like a pack of cards and created a different order. The blackmail, presumably, was the reason for Alderley's apparent intimacy with Milcote, which had always puzzled me, for the two men had had so little in common. The Duke of Buckingham had not been responsible for Alderley's sudden affluence after all, or rather not for the whole of it. Alderley had blackmailed Milcote – and he had also sold Milcote's unhappy secret to Buckingham. This was how, at Buckingham's bidding, Alderley had gained access to the most private apartments in Clarendon House and been able to steal the silver box.

Gorse must have been part of it, I realized suddenly. He must have known about the sodomy. That explained the flashes of insolence he had shown to Milcote, and also Milcote's willingness to employ him in moving Alderley's body. Had Milcote tracked him down and killed him too?

'We must be careful how we handle this,' Williamson was saying. 'How much we make public, how we present it. I shall advise with my Lord Arlington.'

'Why did Milcote confess to Alderley's murder, sir?' I said suddenly. 'There was no need for him to do that. There's no evidence against him.'

'Even a sodomite must have an immortal soul. Perhaps he wants to make his peace with God before he dies. Why not? After all, what does it matter to him now? A man can't be hanged twice.'

# CHAPTER FIFTY-ONE

N EWCOMB'S BOY SAID, 'He says you've got to go there.'

'Where?' Cat said.

'Printing office. You're to come with me directly.'

The boy had caught up with them near the end of their round. Dorcas was watching and listening, shifting from one foot to the other.

'Is something wrong?' Cat asked.

The boy looked slyly at her. Like all printer's devils, he was a patchwork of inkiness, fresh ink and ink faded with age over weeks and months. It had soaked into his skin and his clothes and probably into his very soul. 'I heard the order came from Mr Marwood.'

Cat turned her back on him. 'Don't worry,' she whispered to Dorcas, though she could not see how this could end well.

She followed the boy back to the Savoy. In the printing office, she found Newcomb supervising the installation of his new press. He drew her aside and told her to go to Infirmary Close. His eyes lingered speculatively on her as she left.

Marwood wasn't at his lodging, but Sam and Margaret were. Sam had a letter for her.

'Master didn't want to leave it with Newcomb,' he said. 'There's gossip enough already.'

'That's not my fault,' she snapped. 'It's his, and he's just made it worse. Tell him I don't like being considered his mistress.'

She tore open the letter. There was no salutation.

*The warrant for your arrest has been cancelled. You are free to go back to*

*Mr Hakesby whenever you wish. JM*

She crumpled the note and thrust it in her pocket. 'The warrant against me has been cancelled. I don't understand.'

'Haven't you heard, mistress?' Sam grinned broadly at her. 'The sodomite Milcote killed Alderley. He's confessed it all.'

The Drawing Office was at once familiar and strange. It didn't match the place in Cat's imagination, the place she had hungered for during the two weeks of her exile. Hakesby and Brennan greeted her with a mix of wariness and enthusiasm.

Hakesby was sitting by the fire. He told her to sit on the stool beside him and took her hand in his. 'This is a warning to us,' he said. 'The sooner we are married, the better. If you are my wife, I can protect you.'

Cat bowed her head in submission. The idea of Hakesby protecting anyone seemed faintly ridiculous, but she knew there was value in being his wife: she would no longer be a stray young woman living under a name that was not her own: she would acquire a place in the world.

'We have much work on hand, even without Clarendon House,' he said. 'Dragon Yard, of course, and the Jerusalem chapel. Dr Wren was asking after you yesterday when he called to see how I did. He said you have a remarkably steady hand for the finer detail. I said, is it so strange? Women have a delicate touch as part of their birthright. Think of the embroidery they do.' His grip tightened convulsively. He looked at her with hunger in his face. 'Think, my dear. Think what we can achieve when we are married and living together under this roof.'

In the evening, Cat went back to Infirmary Close in the hope of catching Marwood there. She was fortunate. He had returned from Whitehall to change his clothes before going out to the playhouse. She found him in the parlour.

'What is this about Mr Milcote?' she demanded as soon as she entered.

He rose. 'You've heard then? He confessed to Alderley's murder. He made a voluntary deposition to the magistrate.'

Tears pricked her eyelids. She turned away, fighting for control.

'Are you well?' Marwood asked.

She felt a spurt of anger. She swung round. 'I'm quite well, thank you. Merely surprised, and a little sad. There was much to like about the gentleman.'

'It appears that your cousin was blackmailing him, and that led to his murder. I applied to have the warrant against you lifted immediately, and there was no difficulty about it.'

'Thank you,' she said coldly.

He looked at her, his eyes narrowing. 'It was honourable of Mr Milcote, was it not? Despite everything.'

412

His stare made her uncomfortable. She said, 'And the other matter, sir?'

'The other matter?'

'Concerning my Aunt Quincy.'

'I have nothing to do with that now. Or with her.' He paused. 'Will you and Mr Hakesby marry soon?'

'Yes, sir.' She refused to look away. 'We discussed it only this afternoon. He is a most benevolent man. He's not concerned that I lack a dowry.'

'I daresay you bring him something in return, one way or another. Anyway, perhaps you will have a claim on Alderley's estate, if it's worth anything.' Marwood's face suddenly changed. He tapped the table beside him. 'And you also have those trinkets I found in your cousin's lodging.'

He opened the door and shouted for Sam. When the servant arrived, Marwood gave him a key and told him to bring down the satchel hanging at the back of the locked closet in his chamber. In silence, they listened to Sam's irregular progress: despite the crutch and his missing leg beneath the knee, he managed stairs with marvellous speed and agility. A series of thumps above their heads revealed that he had reached the bedchamber.

Gratitude is not an easy emotion, Cat thought, and nor is pity. She wondered whether Marwood was grieving, for the fool might well have nursed hopes of Lady Quincy's hand.

'No doubt you yourself will marry soon, sir,' she said. The words came out more curtly than she intended.

'I doubt it.'

'Why? It is natural for a man to want a wife.' Unless, she thought, the man is like George Milcote. 'You have the means to marry.'

'I have disadvantages, too.'

Sam was slowly descending the stairs.

'You mean this?' she touched the side of her own face. 'The scars?' Suddenly, and mysteriously, she felt furious with him. 'You're a fool, sir. They are barely noticeable, except to your mind's eye.'

Marwood turned his face, presenting her with his undamaged right profile. Sam entered the room and laid the satchel on the table in front of his master.

'This is yours,' Marwood said, pushing the satchel towards her. 'It doesn't add up to much, but at least you won't be entirely penniless when you marry Mr Hakesby.'

She unstrapped the satchel and picked through the contents. There was a fine gold bracket clock that she remembered from Barnabas Place. It had belonged to her uncle. A purse containing three pounds, ten shillings. Her aunt's set of French forks, which had been imported from Paris and used only on special occasions. A pocket watch without a key to wind it. In a pretty wooden box, a quantity of nutmeg worth five pounds or more. And then this—

The portrait of her mother, with Coldridge, the house that should have come to Cat, in the background. But the eyes of the face had been mutilated. She looked up. Marwood was watching her.

'It was hanging on the wall of Alderley's lodging,' he said. 'He must have poked at the eyes with a dagger. Is it your mother?'

She nodded, unable to speak.

'She was beautiful.' He hesitated, and then said, 'I – I daresay a skilled painter could repair the damage if you wished. They can do such marvels nowadays.'

Cat swallowed and said, 'I'm glad to have it, sir; thank you. My father had the likeness made on his marriage. It is in fact a double portrait, and painted on wood, as you see.'

She ran her fingers around the frame until she found the two catches, one on the right, one on the left. They moved easily. The frame separated into two, the front lifting away from the back. She took out the wooden panel within. She turned it, bringing the reverse to the fore.

There was the companion portrait: her father, Thomas Lovett, as a young man; soberly magnificent in his wedding finery; every inch the wealthy stone mason of the City of London.

There was something else: a folded paper that fluttered to the floor. Marwood stooped to pick it up. She held out her hand for it. But, to her surprise, he turned away and carried it to the window.

'Sir,' she said. 'What are you doing?'

He had already unfolded the paper. He glanced at the contents. He looked not so much at her as through her. His face was blank. 'I must go back to Whitehall.'

# CHAPTER FIFTY-TWO

IT WAS NEARLY midnight by the time I saw the King. On this occasion he summoned me into the drawing room where he had been playing cards the previous evening. Others were playing at the same table, with piles of gold in front of them. Their faces seemed flushed and ill-tempered. Perhaps the game never stopped.

'What is it, Marwood?' The King sounded dreadfully weary. He beckoned me to whisper in his ear.

'Sir, I have found something you must see.'

He looked up at me, and my expression must have convinced him of my urgency. He stood up. 'Follow me,' he commanded.

He took me out through his private apartments to the river. It was like a building site in this part of the palace, for he was engaged in remodelling his own quarters. A servant set a lantern beside us and withdrew. The wind was blowing upstream. I shivered. For the first time I sensed the approach of winter.

I took out the paper I had found in the damaged double portrait. 'This, sir. I believe this was in the silver box stolen from my Lord Clarendon. Alderley hid it in the frame of a picture in his lodging.'

The King took it from me. He laid it on the parapet and read the contents by the light of the lantern. There was music from the palace behind us, and before us were the sounds of the night and the river. He turned it over and read the direction on the back.

'Has anyone read this but you?'

'No, sir. Apart from Alderley, that is.'

'Can you be sure of that?'

'I can. No one since he stole it.' And before Alderley, I thought, probably no one, even the King, had seen it since my Lord Clarendon, with a lawyer's circumspection, had confiscated the letter and silver box from Lady Quincy in Bruges.

'Until a few weeks ago, I thought it had been destroyed.' The King dug his fingers into his waistcoat pocket and brought out the silver key that fitted the lock of the silver box. He held it up so the light of the lantern shone through the fine filigree of the monogram. 'Have you worked out what these entwined initials are?'

'I believe there is a J, sir. And an O.'

The King sighed and put the key back in his pocket. 'Well done. Do you understand whom they signify?'

James and Olivia. Ever since I had known Lady Quincy, I had assumed that she had once been the King's lover. But I had been wrong. James, Duke of York, had been her lover. The bond that now existed between her and the King was one of mutual interest: she had cooperated with His Majesty in the matter of his brother's indiscretion, and made herself useful to him in other ways ever since.

'Do you understand?' the King repeated.

'I believe so, sir.' My voice shook a little, and not from cold. The King had known that his brother and Olivia Vauden, Lady Quincy as she now called herself, had been lovers in Bruges, and that Frances was their child; he had known that the Clarendons had sent their bastard daughter to live with the Warleys and he had authorized the payment of a pension for her support. But he hadn't known of the continuing existence of this letter until Clarendon had found it missing, and had been forced to tell the King.

*Had that tipped the scales against Clarendon? Was that the reason that he had finally lost the King's backing?*

The letter had been written in the Duke of York's own hand in Bruges in 1657. It was addressed on the outside to Mistress Olivia Vauden. Inside, however, the Duke had made it abundantly clear that he was addressing his wife, in the eyes of God and of the law. He wrote of their marriage the previous day, and of the night they had spent together in each other's arms. He referred by name to the priest who had married them according to the rites of the Church of England.

It was a letter that made the Duke of York a bigamist, by his later marriage to Lord Clarendon's daughter, and therefore his children by her illegitimate. A good lawyer – Mr Turner, for example – might even argue that the letter effectively legitimized little Mistress Frances and made her next in the line of succession to the throne after her father the Duke. And, by concealing its existence, Lord Clarendon had committed a felony.

*And of course that was why the King had ordered Frances to be brought to London, to keep her safely under his eye. The child's scrofula had been a convenient excuse. But he hadn't bargained for Lady Quincy's switching her loyalty to Buckingham.*

'Open the lantern,' the King commanded.

I obeyed. The flame flickered and almost went out. I turned the lantern to shelter it from the wind. The King folded the paper into a spill and fed it carefully and slowly to the insatiable flame. At the end he burned his fingers. He swore and shut the lantern.

I waited, as one usually does with a king. Thank God, I thought, it's over at last. Clarendon had become a political liability – his unpopularity in the country and his habit of lecturing the King had already seen to that. Now he had also lost any lingering chance of regaining royal favour, and he was even more in danger of impeachment than he had been before. The winner was Buckingham. Without Clarendon, the King would have to rely increasingly on the support of the Duke and his allies in Parliament if he was to govern the country effectively. But at least the King had destroyed the letter, which meant that Buckingham had lost the biggest prize of all: the chance of using Frances to destabilize the Royal Succession and to weaken the position of the Duke of York, thereby increasing his own influence still further.

'Marwood,' the King said. 'I understand that this child has scrofula.'

Taken unawares, I could only bow.

'You had better take her to have the disease certified by the Surgeon General. If he confirms it's scrofula, then you will bring her and my Lady Quincy to me, and I will touch the child in a private ceremony. Tell Chiffinch when you have the certificate, and he will make the arrangements.'

'As you wish, sir. But . . .'

'What?' The King was already moving away.

419

'There's another child with scrofula in Lady Quincy's house. An African she keeps as a footboy. Would you allow me to bring him to be touched as well?'

He stopped and looked back at me. 'Why?'

I scarcely knew the answer myself. 'It would be a kindness to him. And he was useful to us when Buckingham's men tried to kidnap Mistress Frances in the Fens.'

'Very well. As long as one of my surgeons certifies that he has the disease.'

'Mr Knight has already done so, sir.'

The King gave a low laugh and clapped me on the back with as much familiarity as if I had been one of his intimate friends. 'You're a strange devil, Marwood.'

# CHAPTER FIFTY-THREE

THE FOLLOWING MONDAY, the last day in September, Lady Quincy and I paid a second visit to the Surgeon General, this time with Mistress Frances as well as Stephen. Lady Quincy did not wear a veil, and she was happy for the servant to announce her by her own name. If Mr Knight found anything curious in this, he was too well-bred to mention it.

He examined Frances. When he pronounced that the girl did indeed suffer from scrofula, the consequences took us all by surprise. Mistress Frances stamped her small feet and cried that she could not have the same disease as a nasty little blackamoor. She wailed loudly and tried to bite her mother's hand. Meanwhile Stephen watched her with great eyes.

'A good whipping and a diet of bread and water for a day or two,' Mr Knight said above the racket as he was writing out the certificate. He looked up and smiled benevolently at Frances. 'That's the preliminary treatment I would recommend in this particular case. I think you'll find it will answer.

Would you like me to write you a ticket of admission for her as well?'

'No, thank you,' Lady Quincy said. 'The King has agreed to a private ceremony for her.'

Mr Knight raised his eyebrows. 'I see. How gracious of him.' He glanced at Stephen. 'And your footboy?'

'The next public ceremony, I suppose. But we mustn't keep you from your patients any longer, sir.'

It was clear Lady Quincy had no interest in Stephen. She had used him as a stalking horse to conceal the real reason for her interest in scrofula and its cure.

Somehow we got Frances into the coach while Mr Knight wrote out Stephen's ticket. When I came back from settling his bill, the girl was relatively calm, though she keened continually as the coach rumbled slowly through the streets. Her mother seemed helpless in the face of her daughter's tantrum.

'I want to go back to Hitcham St Martin,' Frances wailed suddenly. 'I want to live with Mistress Warley.'

She buried her face in her hands and repeated the words over and over again like an incantation. Gradually, as the coach found its way back to Cradle Alley, the sounds subsided.

Lady Quincy touched my arm and smiled wearily at me. 'My dear Marwood,' she whispered, 'whatever would we do without you?'

'You'd do very well, madam, I'm sure.'

'I want to ask your opinion about another matter. I believe I shall dismiss Stephen.' She nestled a little closer. 'Even if he's cured, he's too old to be a footboy – look, his features are coarsening already. Tell me, how does one get rid of a blackamoor, especially one with such blemishes? Does one sell them in the usual way? Pray, do advise me.'

The two children were sitting opposite but apart. They were both watching us, both listening. I turned my face towards Lady Quincy. It is one thing to desire a woman, I thought, another to love her, and yet a third to like her.

'Would you let me have the lad, madam?' I said.

'You? Why do you want a slave boy?'

'My servants need someone to fetch and carry for them.'

'Of course you shall have him. I'll give you his scrofula certificate, too, and his ticket of admission to a public ceremony.'

I had not yet told her that the King had agreed to touch Stephen privately as well as Frances. I said, 'For whatever is the usual price for such a boy, of course. I'll enquire.'

'I think not.' Lady Quincy tapped my cheek with a gloved finger. 'Stephen will be my present to you. A token of my friendship.'

At Whitehall, friendships and enmities are made and broken in the blink of an eye. Mr Chiffinch appeared to have forgotten his former dislike of me. On Tuesday he ordered me to call on him after dinner at his lodging. He gave me wine and congratulated me on serving the King so well and so discreetly.

'His Majesty knows,' he added, 'that he can trust me to choose my subordinates with care, so I take some small share of the credit.'

I took advantage of this unexpected approval to ask how the King intended to deal with Buckingham and his hirelings, Veal and Roger.

Chiffinch smiled tolerantly at me. 'You are still an innocent,' he said. 'The King shows the Duke every mark of favour imaginable – he enjoys his company – they are seen everywhere together – he listens to his advice in the Privy Council.'

'But . . .'

'But what? A King does not have friends and enemies as we mere subjects do. And a wise man makes a friend of a foe, because if one keeps an enemy close he has less room to cause harm. Besides, there's no proof against Buckingham. When he talked to you, he was masked, wasn't he, so you can't swear it was him who talked to you, can you? As for this man Veal and his servant, they are remarkably popular in the City at present – did you know that? They rooted out a nest of sodomites. They have earned London's gratitude.'

We sipped our wine.

'Mind you,' Chiffinch added, 'if I were you, I would not expect any favours from the Duke of Buckingham. He does not forget.'

# CHAPTER FIFTY-FOUR

GEORGE MILCOTE WAS lodged by himself in Newgate. He was lucky in this, if in nothing else, for they would have done terrible things to a sodomite if he had been placed in the condemned hold among the worst men that London had to offer. I didn't know who paid for this small mercy, and nor did he when I asked him. Perhaps Lord Clarendon or even the Duke of York, though neither man gave him a scrap of public support.

Much of the prison was still in ruins after the Fire last year, when the stones along the eastern wall had exploded in the heat. Milcote was housed in a part that had been hastily refurbished as a stopgap until the rebuilding could be completed. The walls of his cell were black from the flames, and the wood of the door was charred, though still sound. The air smelled damp. The barred window was less than a foot square. It was unglazed. The sounds and smells drifted up from the yard below.

Apart from the bed, there was nowhere to sit, so we stood and talked. The change in Milcote shocked me. He still wore his periwig, but its curls were tangled and matted. There was a bruise on his cheek. He was pale, unshaven and grubby. His clothes were creased and stained.

'You're my first visitor,' he said. 'Perhaps my only one. Why have you come? It must be to bring bad news.'

'I came because I want to talk to you,' I said. 'How do you fare in here?'

'I survive. They bring me food twice a day. I expect they spit in it. But they leave me alone most of the time, and that's a great deal.'

'Tell me,' I said, 'did you kill Gorse as well as Alderley?'

'I was desperate.' He sounded uninterested, as if answering a question of no importance that related to someone else. 'I was coming to call on you that evening to tell you that Buckingham's pair of rogues were outside Clarendon House again. I'd almost reached your door when I realized someone was following me. So I laid an ambush. When I found it was Gorse, I . . .'

'You killed him to shut his mouth,' I said. 'Once and for all.'

Milcote frowned at me. 'What else could I do? I had to. He was the main witness against me. He wanted more money, or he swore he would write to my lord about me. So I stabbed him and took him down to the river. It was easy enough – I'd ridden over, so I put him on my horse. It was almost dark by then. If anyone had asked, I would have said my friend was drunk and I was taking him home. But I didn't meet anyone.'

'You ran a great risk when you put the body in the river. Anyone might have seen you.'

'I didn't take him to the Savoy stairs – I went to the Somerset Yard wharf next door. At that time there was no one about. The tide was high, and it was on the ebb.'

'Still, you were fortunate.'

'Fortunate?' He gestured around him. 'You call this fortunate? No, I was desperate, and I did the only thing I could. All this happened because of Gorse. Everything. He saw me one night in Love Lane and he realized what I was about. He sold the information to his old master, Alderley. He was hand-in-glove with him from the start. That's how he came to work at Clarendon House.'

'Ah,' I said. 'So they made you recommend him. I wondered about that. Once you said Lady Clarendon had recommended Gorse. But later you forgot – you contradicted yourself and said it had been you.'

'I'm not sorry Gorse and Alderley are dead,' he said. 'They were evil. They made me . . .'

Milcote ran out of words and turned to face the wall.

Blackmail, I thought – was not that a worse crime than sodomy? I said, 'What did they make you do?'

'Alderley wanted that silver box from my lord's closet – I never found out why. Both of them wanted money, too.' He screwed up his face. 'More and more. I even had to steal from my lord . . .' He turned back to me. 'Alderley said that once he had the box, that would be the end of it. He swore it, on his honour. But he had no honour. The devil lied.'

'Because he'd seen Mistress Hakesby working at the pavilion,' I said. 'And he realized that there was something else you could do for him.'

'It was the straw that broke the camel's back.' Milcote put his head in his hands. 'Alderley wanted his revenge on her. He told me to lure her to the pavilion on the Saturday after the workmen had left. I was to make some excuse about needing to talk about the work and her master's health –

whether Hakesby was well enough for it. And he said I should make sure the well wasn't covered and the pavilion door was left unlocked, and the wicket gate in the garden, too. That's . . . when I realized what I had become.'

Silence settled over the room. The sounds rose up from the yard below, the shouts, the screams and the laughter.

'I couldn't let him do that to Mistress Hakesby.' Milcote looked up. 'I wanted no part of it, sir. So I pretended to agree. But I said nothing to her and I laid in wait for him myself. But the devil guessed what I was about and came at me with his sword. And I threw him down the well, and good riddance to him. I left him there and let Gorse find him on Monday morning. Afterwards I feared that my guilt would be obvious to everyone. I panicked and wrote that cowardly letter to Chiffinch, accusing Mistress Hakesby of killing him. I cannot forgive myself for that.'

The effort of telling me this had exhausted him. He sat down abruptly on the bed, a narrow straw mattress on a stone shelf that ran the length of one wall.

'That letter was a mistake,' I said. 'Because you sent it to Chiffinch. Not many people knew his role in this.'

Milcote groaned and slumped against the wall of his cell. I could not understand him. He was a mass of contradictions. He was the same man as before, who had earned the respect of all who knew him – the soldier, the loyal servant, the gentleman. Yet his strange desires ran through him like knots in a plank of wood, as much part of him as his courage and his courtesy. Fear of exposure had driven him to act as he had, not those desires in themselves.

I remembered when we had supped at the Goat on the day that Gorse ran off. Milcote had drunk himself within sight of oblivion. Now I knew why: because Gorse knew his secret. That evening, before he had lost consciousness, he had seized my arm and asked me when this nightmare would end. We had both learned the answer to that question, almost to the day, and we knew how it would end, too. For him, at least, it would end on the scaffold.

He sat up straight, making an obvious effort to compose himself. 'Is Mistress Hakesby back in the Drawing Office?' he asked.

'Yes. She marries her master soon.'

'That old man.' Milcote grimaced. 'It's unseemly.'

Though I felt sick in my stomach at the thought of the marriage, I forced myself to speak levelly, as if the subject barely interested me: 'I understand that it's a contract between them, not a love match. Both parties gain by it.'

'Will you give her a present for me? As a wedding gift. Or perhaps a token of apology.'

'What?'

'That sword.'

'Alderley's Clemens Horn?' I said. 'I thought—'

'I couldn't bring myself to throw it away. I know I should have done but . . . I had his crest ground away from the blade, and I intended to get a new sheath because the old one was ruined by the water . . .' He shrugged. 'It seems so trivial now. They have it here. I will write a note saying you can take it. It is the only thing of value I have left. Anyway, if she's Alderley's cousin, it's hers by right.'

He scribbled a note in pencil on a flyleaf he tore from his Bible. Afterwards, we lapsed into another uneasy silence.

'Do you know when?' I asked at last.

'When I will be hanged? No. No one tells me anything. I

don't mind dying, Marwood, but I wish this was over. It's the waiting that's the worst of it.'

The day after I saw Milcote at Newgate, I called at Lady Quincy's house during the afternoon. I was shown up to the drawing room on the first floor, where she was sitting by one of the windows and sewing a piece of lace on to a shift; she made a pretty picture of femininity, as perhaps she intended. There was no sign of Mistress Frances.

'You are punctual, sir,' she said as I bowed to her. 'I like a man who knows the value of time. Stephen is ready for you, but perhaps you will talk to me for a while first.' She laid aside the sewing and smiled. 'In fact, why not stay and sup with me? I am quite alone today.'

It was an invitation that said one thing and suggested others. I replied that I was pressed for time and could not stay; like hers, my words said one thing and suggested others. Her smile vanished. It was then, I think, that she grasped that it was over. Each of us had served our turn for the other, and there was nothing left between us.

Lady Quincy bade me ring for the maid. She ordered Stephen to be made ready and brought down to the hall. While we waited, she handed me four documents: the paper that had come with the boy, which confirmed her ownership of him; a letter signed by her transferring him to me; his certificate of scrofula from Mr Knight; and the ticket of admission to a public ceremony that the surgeon had written at the end of the last visit.

'So that is that, sir,' she said coldly, taking up her sewing again. 'I daresay we shan't meet again.'

'I think we shall, madam. The King has commanded me

to escort you and Mistress Frances to the private ceremony, whenever that will be. And Stephen.'

'Stephen? *Stephen?* What nonsense is this?'

'The King has agreed to touch him as well, on the same occasion.'

She sucked in her breath but did not dare object. We exchanged cold farewells and I went down to the hall. Stephen was waiting with his few belongings wrapped in a cloth bundle.

We walked up to Moorgate, where I found a hackney to take us to the Savoy. I asked him two or three questions, but all he would say was yes or no. We spent most of the journey in silence.

When we reached Infirmary Close, Sam let us into the house. He whistled at the sight of Stephen. 'An African, eh? We had one of those on my last ship. Nimble as a cat, I give him that, and he could sing a psalm as well as any Christian. Can you sing a psalm, boy?'

Stephen stared at him.

Sam clouted him gently. 'I asked master for a boy to be my legs for me. I suppose you'll do well enough when you find your tongue.'

I took Stephen down to the kitchen. Margaret looked askance at him. 'Are we having him in the house?'

'He's staying,' I said. 'He can be a kitchen boy. Whatever's needed.'

'A pagan? Is he safe?'

'Give him work to do. He can chop the kindling and carry in the coal. Sweep the floor. Run errands and turn the spit.'

Stephen was looking around, his eyes wide.

'First of all, though,' I said, 'give him something to eat.'

431

# CHAPTER FIFTY-FIVE

L ATE IN THE afternoon, Hakesby and Cat were alone in the Drawing Office. Brennan was away in the City, overseeing the digging of the new cellars at Dragon Yard.

Cat was measuring the height of an arch when there was a knock at the door. James Marwood came in with a long bundle under his arm. She threw him an irritated glance, for he had thrown out her calculations. She hadn't seen him since he had given her Cousin Edward's satchel last week and almost immediately rushed away to Whitehall.

Once he had greeted Mr Hakesby, he came over to her. He laid the bundle on the table and unrolled it. The covering was an old cloak. Inside was a sword.

'What's this?' she said, putting down her pencil. 'Can't you put that thing somewhere else?'

'Mr Milcote gave it to me for you,' he said. 'A sort of wedding present. It used to be your cousin's. It's an old sword, but it was made by Clemens Horn, it seems, which makes it desirable.'

'It is,' Hakesby said, raising his head at the name. 'And valuable too.'

'I don't find it desirable at all,' Cat said. 'My cousin was proud of it.'

'Then sell it,' Marwood said.

Hakesby struggled to his feet. He shuffled towards his closet, unbuttoning his coat.

Cat touched the sheath. 'It's still damp from the well. It's almost wet.'

'Milcote said it needs a new one. The leather's decayed.' She shivered. 'I don't want it anywhere about me. Will you take it away and dispose of it for me, sir?'

'If you wish.'

'You've been kind,' she said, her voice curt as if reprimanding him. She was suddenly aware of how much she took Marwood for granted, and how much he had done for her. 'I'm grateful.'

'It's nothing,' he muttered.

Hakesby closed the door of the closet behind him. Cat heard the scrape of the bolt. Her future husband did not like to be disturbed when he was trying to persuade his bowels to move.

She drew nearer to Marwood. 'Did you actually see him? How was he?'

'Milcote? As well as might be expected. They keep him away from the others, which is a blessing. He's waiting to hear when he will die.'

'He's a good man in his way,' she said. 'A decent man, too, and a brave one. He served his master well, and the King. He needn't have confessed to the murders, either.'

'He's also a sodomite,' Marwood pointed out in a flat, hard voice.

His tone enraged her. 'My cousin Edward was a rapist. A bully. A blackmailer. A thief. He would have killed me if he could. Do you honestly believe that Milcote is worse than he was?'

'Perhaps not. But you can't deny what Milcote did was against God and nature and the laws of man.'

'How do you know?'

'Sodomy's a sin. A crime. Everyone knows that.'

'Why – if it harms neither party and both want it?'

'Are you saying the Bible is wrong?' Marwood hesitated. 'And the laws of England, too?'

'Perhaps I am. Would that be so very strange?' She sensed that he was less sure of his ground. 'Besides, it's not the Bible that's wrong necessarily, it's the men who interpret it and use it to justify bad laws.'

'Milcote killed your cousin and Gorse. Doesn't he deserve to hang for that alone?'

'That's beside the point,' she snapped.

'You're mad.' Marwood turned aside to roll up the sword in the cloak.

'You're like them all, aren't you?' she said. Somehow they were no longer talking about Mr Milcote. 'I thought you were different, but you're not. You intrigue and plot with the best of them. It's all Mr Williamson, and Mr Chiffinch, and how they both need your services, and what each of them can do for you in return. It's my lord this and the duke of that and whispering secrets in people's ears. It's what the King said to you when you saw him last. It's your house in the Savoy and your servants and your cursed new periwig. I can't even trust your kindness to me. I wager it has some purpose behind it.'

She paused for breath. The intensity of her anger had taken her by surprise.

'Why are you marrying Hakesby?' he said.

'What's that to you? I conduct my life as I please. I've decided to marry him, and I shall. And I do it for the two best reasons in the world: I esteem him greatly, and it's a prudent step for both of us.'

'Prudent?' Marwood had paled, which threw into relief the scars on the left side of his face.

'Yes. And speaking of prudence, have you seen my aunt lately?'

'Yes.' He took a step back as if she had threatened to hit him. 'But that has—'

'You should stay away from her.' She wanted to hurt Marwood. She also wanted to help him. 'Don't you understand? That whey-faced bitch poisons everything she touches, sooner or later. She'll poison you if she hasn't already.'

He winced. 'Thank you. But you needn't concern yourself. Pray make my farewells to Mr Hakesby.'

He picked up the bundle and bowed. At the door, he paused and looked back. 'You said the sheath was still damp from the well. But how did you know he was wearing that sword when he died, not one of his others? How did you know the sheath had been in the well in the first place? How . . .'

His voice faded. Noises drifted up from the street. From Hakesby's closet came a low moan that might have been caused by pain or pleasure.

Cat's anger deflated. She said: 'I thought . . . I thought – I assumed – that Edward must have been wearing it when . . .'

For a long moment she and Marwood stared at each other. Marwood turned away without a word and raised the latch. After he had gone, Cat went into the closet where she slept. Words were dangerous. So were memories. She lay on her bed and stared at the wall. Her eyes filled with tears. She willed her mind to become as near as possible to a perfect blank.

## CHAPTER FIFTY-SIX

GEORGE MILCOTE WAS hanged on 7 October, along with eight other condemned felons. It was a Monday, which was the usual day of the week for hangings. The administration of justice cost money. All things being equal, the authorities preferred to make economies of scale, so it was sensible to hang as many felons as possible on the same occasion. Moreover, each public hanging attracted substantial and often rowdy crowds, which clogged the streets of London even more than usual and which in turn had its effect on trade.

In the middle of the morning, the prisoners, all men, were taken to Tyburn in a cart. Their shackles had already been struck off at the prison, where the hangman would have shaken the hand of each man. This was not entirely a courtesy: it enabled him to estimate the heights of the men and the individual lengths of rope he would need for them.

I saw the cart from afar, for I kept my distance. Some of the prisoners were in their Sunday best; some were attended by their families and friends. But Milcote had no one beside him, and he still wore the filthy clothes I had seen last week. He had lost his hat and wig. He stood apart from the others, clutching the rail. But he was straight-backed and calm-faced. He was going to his death like a soldier.

The procession wound its way slowly over Snow Hill and across Holborn Bridge. At St Giles-in-the-Fields, the cart stopped, and each of the prisoners was given a quart of ale to ease their journey to oblivion. Milcote poured his ale on the ground, and the crowd booed.

At Tyburn, the Triple Tree was waiting, the three posts supporting a horizontal wooden triangle from which more than a dozen felons could be conveniently hanged at any one time. I went ahead of the procession and pushed my way through the foot of the gallows, where the hangman was checking his ropes and bantering with the women among the spectators. He broke off when I gave him a sight of my warrant with the King's signature.

I drew him aside. 'You hang a man named Milcote today, I believe?'

'Aye.' He spat on the ground. 'A sodomite and a murderer.'

'How much would it cost to make it short?'

He looked me up and down. 'People won't like me doing that. Especially for someone like him.'

'How much?'

'Ten shillings, sir, and I'll tug his legs and break his neck. Once he's danced on the rope for a minute or two.'

I tapped the warrant. 'Do it as soon as he's up there and you shall have a pound in gold. Ten shillings now, and ten shillings afterwards.'

Once we had struck our bargain, I withdrew into the crowd as the cart approached the gallows. The men were hanged

437

from the cart in groups of three. Some of them exercised their right to address the crowd; others prayed to their Maker. But Milcote said nothing. He stared up at the sky, standing as if on parade. I could not but admire his courage.

After their speeches, the condemned men were blindfolded. The horse was led forward, drawing the cart under the scaffold. The hangman placed the halters around their necks. Then the horse pulled the cart from under the gallows and the men were left dangling and kicking and pissing themselves in the air.

Milcote was in the second batch. He raised his head while he was waiting for the blindfold. It seemed to me that his eyes roved over the crowd, looking for a friendly face. While he was looking in my direction, I raised my arm, and he nodded: perhaps he saw me standing there and knew he was not quite alone; I hope so. He had done Cat a kindness that perhaps she did not entirely deserve. But I honoured him for it.

When the three men had been blindfolded, the hangman gave a signal, and his man led the horse and cart away from the gallows. There was a sudden silence, as if the entire world were holding its breath. Then three more men were dancing on air.

The hangman stepped forward and wrapped his huge hands around Milcote's ankles. He pulled sharply. It was over.

After I had paid the hangman's fee, I walked slowly to Henrietta Street to tell Cat what had happened and what I had done. God knows what I hoped for in return. Not praise, certainly, not from her. But perhaps her acknowledgement that I had valued Milcote's good qualities, as she had, though not for the same reasons.

As I walked, I turned over in my mind the other matter that lay there, which had festered like an untended sore for the last three days. The sheath of the Clemens Horn sword had been damp. Cat had known that it had been in the well. But only Milcote, Gorse and I had been aware of that. I had not told her, and she could not have learned it from Milcote or Gorse.

Gorse, who claimed he had found Alderley's body there on the Monday morning, could not have seen the corpse unless he had lowered a lantern down the shaft. Milcote had told me that Alderley had commanded him to lure Cat to the pavilion on the Saturday evening. He had also told me that he had not done as Alderley had ordered, that instead he had thrown Alderley into the well to end the blackmail once and for all.

Then how could Cat have known that the sheath had been in the well? How could she have known even that Alderley was wearing the Clemens Horn that evening, rather than one of his other swords?

Unless . . . Suppose, I thought, Milcote had lied to me?

Suppose Cat had gone to the pavilion on Saturday afternoon after she had met me at the lace shop in New Exchange? 'I have a meeting with one of our clients in less than an hour,' she had said to me as she rushed off. 'I must go.' Had the client been Milcote? Had she gone to the pavilion, believing she would find Milcote there, and found Alderley waiting for her instead?

'One day,' she had said a few minutes earlier, 'I shall kill my cousin.'

How else to explain that discrepancy about the sheath of the Clemens Horn? In theory, it should have been an unequal

439

struggle – a grown man with a sword facing an unarmed young woman taken by surprise. But the woman had been Cat, and I had just put her on her guard against her cousin, so perhaps the odds had not been as weighted against her as they seemed. Then, that very evening, long before the news of Alderley's death was known, she had fled from London, despite telling me earlier at the New Exchange that she would not run away from her cousin. But running away from a possible murder charge was another matter.

Suppose Milcote had returned to the pavilion to find Cat gone and Alderley drowned in the well? Even if he had wanted, he could hardly have accused her of the murder without revealing his own part in arranging the affair. Everything followed quite naturally from that, including this last act: his decision to take the blame for Alderley's death on his own shoulders when he no longer had anything to lose. He had been thrust into the part of a villain by Alderley's blackmail. The role had not come naturally to him and this, perhaps, had been his attempt to make reparation to Cat.

Should I say something of this to her, if only to make her aware of Milcote's last kindness to her? Or should I hold my peace?

In Henrietta Street, I knocked at the door at the sign of the Rose. The porter recognized me, and was instantly affable. Mindful of Cat's good name, I asked if Mr Hakesby was within.

'You've missed him, master,' he said. 'Indeed, you've missed them all.' There was an unusual excitement to the man's manner, and I wondered if he were drunk. 'The Drawing Office is empty.'

'Where are they?'

'Up at the church.' He pointed across the road at St Paul's. 'Mr Hakesby's marrying his cousin today. Mr Brennan's one of the witnesses, him and Dr Wren.'

'But they haven't called the bans yet,' I said. 'I thought the wedding was at the end of the month.'

'Bishop's licence.' The porter gave me a leer, one man to another. 'Mr Hakesby couldn't wait.'

Cat lay on her back, dressed in her shift and nightcap. The bed curtains were open. A dozen or more candles burned around the room; a reckless extravagance.

'I want to see my bride on her wedding night,' Hakesby had said at supper, nuzzling closer to her and slurring his words a little, though whether from wine or his illness she could not tell. 'Have I not earned this?'

Until then, she had assumed that their marriage would be essentially a business arrangement for their mutual benefit, and that the usual conjugal duties of the bed would have no place in it. Hakesby had implied as much when he had made his offer to marry her the previous May. He was old and infirm, and there had been no hint of love-making from him then or later – until now.

For the moment, God be thanked, she was alone. She listened to the sounds of the night. Henrietta Street was rarely silent. Its proximity to Covent Garden saw to that. In the colonnades around the piazza, and in the neighbouring streets, you could find a whore or a beggar or a man to dice with at almost any hour.

It was before midnight, and the shouts and singing drifted up from the street, mingling with the clatter of hooves and the grating of wheels on the roadway. Cat wished she were on the floor above, in her little closet off the main Drawing Office in the attic. It was quieter there, nearer the sky, and she would have been alone. Instead she was in her new bedchamber. Hakesby had leased the entire floor, which meant that her new home consisted of a parlour or withdrawing room and four closets, as well as the room in which she lay. At least he did not expect her to maintain a kitchen – their food would be prepared below or ordered from a cookshop or tavern.

'It's all most convenient,' Hakesby had said when he had shown her the apartments. 'It will suit me very well to be so near to the Drawing Office, and you will be glad to be mistress of your own establishment at last.'

Cat had said nothing. She had made a bargain with Hakesby and the terms he had given her were more than generous. After the events of the last three weeks, she knew that she should be grateful that she was not dead or imprisoned. Instead, here she was – the mistress of her own establishment. During the day she would be able to do work that interested her. She had the legal protection of a man's name. Her husband had given her a place in the world. What was there to dislike?

As if in answer, she heard a low moan from the closet. Earlier in the evening, they had gone by coach to the Lamb. Hakesby had made a better supper than usual, and taken more wine. She suspected that he was paying the price for his self-indulgence. But he would not stay on his close-stool for ever. Soon he would emerge from the closet and demand what was his by the authority of both church and state.

But it could not be as bad as when Cousin Edward had laid an ambush for her in her chamber and raped her. Cat clung to that knowledge. In his way, Hakesby had shown her nothing but kindness. But Edward—

Her mind lurched sideways, slipping into the nightmare that haunted her, perhaps always would. Time and effort of will had allowed her to dull the memory of the rape. But this new memory, no more than three weeks old, was still raw and bleeding. It was waiting every time she closed her eyes.

'One day,' she had told Marwood when they met at the New Exchange, 'I shall kill my cousin.'

A mere form of words, she told herself, an expression of hatred, not a statement of intent. Truly, she had planned nothing on that Saturday evening. When she had left Marwood in the Strand, her mind had been heavy with his news that her cousin had tracked her down. But that had been no reason to ignore her responsibility to Mr Hakesby and his clients. In the morning, Mr Milcote had asked her privately to meet him at the Clarendon House pavilion to discuss the sensitive subject of Mr Hakesby's ability to complete the commission he had accepted; he was concerned, he said, about Hakesby's declining health, and also about the state of progress so far. For Hakesby's sake, and hers, she had not wanted them to lose the commission.

Milcote had asked her to come to the pavilion by the wicket into the garden. He would leave it unlocked for her. 'I'm afraid tongues would wag if we were seen together without your master,' he had murmured. 'Our meeting in private might reach his ears, and he would naturally want to know why. Also, it – ah – might compromise your reputation. You know what people are. So pray be discreet, and I shall be the same.'

She had been touched by his consideration and flattered

that he valued her opinion. She dismissed the idea that he might try to seduce her – he was too much the gentleman, and too conscious of his reputation. He had seemed almost embarrassed that he had been obliged to ask her to meet him in private. Now she understood why. Edward had known Milcote's secret and used it to blackmail him into luring Cat into a trap.

So she had left Marwood; she had almost run up the Strand to Charing Cross and along Piccadilly to Clarendon House for fear she would be late. The daylight was fading. No one had seen her enter the garden, for the gardeners had stopped work by then.

The door to the pavilion was unlocked. She let herself in, closed the door and called Mr Milcote's name. She heard an answering shout from the basement kitchen. She went downstairs. The door was open. A lantern burned on the shelf above the fireplace. The basement was full of shadows.

'Sir?'

Cat advanced into the room. The door slammed shut behind her.

'Bitch,' a man's voice said. 'Unnatural punk. Devil's whore.'

She swung round. Edward was standing with his back to the door. In his hand was a drawn sword. The eyepatch he wore gave him an air of unreality, half-nightmare, half-clown.

'Scream if you want,' he said. 'No one will hear. The garden's empty at this hour.'

Cat backed away from him, fumbling for her knife in her pocket. But the knife had snagged slantwise, wedging itself in the material. She tugged desperately at the handle but she could not free it.

Edward was advancing slowly towards her, the tip of the sword dancing in the air, and its slender sheath swaying from his belt. He was larger than she remembered, heavier and more bloated. She remembered the suffocating weight of him pressing down on her. The stink of him. The pain.

Still facing him, she retreated, step by step, further into the room. On the far side of the well was a pile of planks, part of the dismantled scaffolding they had used when repointing the masonry of the well shaft. In the corner was the hoist. No tools, unfortunately – the workmen had taken them away.

Her shoulder touched the wall. She could retreat no further.

Edward laughed. 'There's nowhere for you to go.'

'Haven't you done enough?' she said, her voice little more than a whisper.

'I could bring a charge of attempted murder against you for your attack on me,' he went on as if she had not spoken. 'I could see you hanged. But where's the pleasure in that, in seeing the law take its course? I'm the one who deserves revenge, not the court.' He touched his eye patch. 'An eye for an eye, says the Bible.'

Cat ran her hand along the wall behind her, hoping for a loose brick that might make a weapon, hoping for a miracle.

'Besides, I have a mind to throw up your skirts first and teach you the sort of lesson I taught you once before. Indeed, Cousin, you look riper now, fitter to be plucked than you did then.'

She was cold and sick. Her left hand felt a current of air. She was near the opening of the fireplace, with the stone shelf running above it.

The tip of the sword was no more than a yard away. 'Then,'

445

he said, 'when I have finished with you, the well can have what's left. How fortunate for you, Cousin. They say its water is the purest in London. But it won't be pure much longer once your foulness mingles with it.'

There was no time for calculation, no time for anything except a flurry of movement. Cat flung her arm up to the shelf. Her hand jarred against the lantern. She hooked her fingers between it and the wall. She flung it in his direction with all her might.

The lantern was made of iron and heavier than she had expected. She had hoped it would reach him, but instead it fell with a clatter to the flagged floor at his feet. But for the instant it was in the air, it distracted him. His blade dropped. He took a step back.

The candle went out.

Even before the flame died, Cat was moving along the wall, away from the fireplace, towards the corner beyond the well. The basement was very nearly dark but memory guided her. The scaffolding and the hoist were there. Perhaps she could find a weapon of some sort. Perhaps—

It was too late. Edward had recovered himself. He plunged towards her, herding her against the wall. His face was no more than a shadow. He drew back, the fencer's move, preparing for the thrust. Then, with a grunt, he lunged, the blade darting towards her shoulder.

'God's—'

Edward's oath was cut off before it was out of his mouth. As she tried to scramble away from that murderous sword, he fell forward. The sword clanged on to the flagstones. There was a crack as his head hit the well's coping. Then a miracle: her cousin no longer existed.

She took a perverse pride in the fact that, when Marwood had told her of Edward's death, she had not lied to him. 'I never touched him,' she had said to Marwood. 'That's God's literal truth.' More than pride: relief as well; she found that she did not want to lie to him.

After Edward vanished, there had been a cry, followed by the sound of frantic splashing, amplified and distorted by the cylinder of the well shaft. Trembling, Cat had knelt by the side of the well and peered over the edge into the utter darkness below.

'Help me.' Edward's voice had been as high as a woman's. 'For the—'

The splashing continued, gradually losing its force until at last the only sound was Cat's own breathing.

She wriggled away from the well and stood up. Her limbs were shaking as Hakesby's did when the ague was upon him.

She knew that she must go before anyone found her here. It was vital to leave the place as it had been when Hakesby locked up for the day. She glanced at the nearest window. It was almost dark. There was no time to think, to act. At dusk they would release the mastiffs into the garden.

Cat's foot jarred against an object on the floor. She looked down. She could just make out the shape of the lantern on the floor. She picked it up. It was still warm. She had lobbed it into the well and listened to the sound of it hitting the water. She crouched by the wooden cover and tried to drag it over the well. It had been too heavy for her. A muscle in her back had shrieked with pain.

Panic had conquered her, swiftly and suddenly. She would have to leave the cover where it was. There was nothing left to do but run away.

A door creaked open, dragging her into the present, to Henrietta Street, to her wedding night.

Hakesby shuffled out of the closet and crossed the floor towards the bed. 'Ah,' he said as he drew nearer, 'still awake, I'm glad to see.'

He pulled back the covers. She was lying on her back, her legs together, her arms close to her side, like a stone figure on a tomb chest.

Hakesby climbed laboriously on to the bed. He knelt over her, his nightshirt ballooning about him, and stared down at her. His nightcap was askew, which gave him an incongruously rakish look. He laid a hand on her belly, where it lay like a large, pale spider. She closed her eyes. A bargain was a bargain. She willed herself not to shrink away from him. Perhaps she could pretend her husband was someone else, someone younger, someone more like – for the sake of example – James Marwood, on those rare occasions when he was amiable to her and not puffed up with pride.

'Ah,' Hakesby said again, and this time there was a sadness in his voice.

The hand was no longer resting on her belly. She opened her eyes. Hakesby moved clumsily away from her. He laid himself down and turned his back on her. He pulled up the covers and drew up his legs towards his chest.

'Draw the curtains, Wife,' he said in a muffled voice, 'and blow out the candles.'

## CHAPTER FIFTY-SEVEN

MR CHIFFINCH HAD leased a house conveniently close to Windsor. We travelled there by coach, one of the unmarked ones kept at Scotland Yard for the private use of the royal household. The weather was bad and the tide was against us, so we could not go by river as originally planned.

It was the Feast of All Souls, the last day of November. It had not been convenient for the King to command us to attend him at an earlier date. I sat facing forwards with Lady Quincy. Stephen and Frances were opposite. Two horsemen escorted us. Like the coachman and the postillion, they were armed because of the risk of highwaymen.

The coach swayed and rattled and jolted, throwing the four of us against each other. Sometimes the rain found its way inside. There was little conversation until London had fallen behind.

Lady Quincy had not been pleased when I had told her that the King had agreed to touch Stephen as well at the same ceremony. But she was doing her best to suppress her irritation.

'Have you heard?' she murmured in my ear. 'My Lord Clarendon fled abroad last night. To think of it.'

'Yes, madam.'

That drama had at last reached its ending. If Clarendon had stayed, he would have been impeached. One charge was corruption, with Clarendon House itself a great argument in stone against him. There were charges of high treason, too, with some of his enemies claiming that he had cost us the victory in the war against the Dutch, and betrayed us to the French into the bargain. Had the case gone against him, he would have lost his head on the scaffold.

'So great a fall,' she said. 'And from so high a place.'

There was a hint of a question mark in her tone, inviting me to play my part in the conversation. I ignored it. After half a mile or so, she tried again.

'I hear that the King uses Mr Chiffinch's house for private meetings.' She turned her head and I felt her breath on my cheek. 'Of one sort or another.'

There was no mistaking Lady Quincy's meaning: the King could meet people there in more discreet circumstances than Whitehall or Windsor Castle allowed.

I bowed my head towards her in the gloom, acknowledging her words but not replying.

She tried once more. 'Mr Chiffinch tells me that my niece is married,' she said. 'What a surprise. Given her circumstances, Catherine is indeed fortunate. Even if her husband has one foot in the grave.'

'I believe Mr Hakesby is kind to her,' I said.

'That's something, I suppose.' She drew away from me.

'Frances, my love,' she said. 'You look cold. Come and sit by me. Mr Marwood will take your place.'

At Chiffinch's house, the ceremony took place after the King had dined. It was the middle of the afternoon. Dusk was already creeping into the rooms and filling their corners with shadows.

We were shown up to the long gallery on the second floor. The rain pattered on the tall windows, and the air smelled of the river. The four of us waited at one end. At the other end, the candles were lit, and two servants carried in a heavy, old-fashioned elbow chair of carved oak. One of the King's surgeons – not Mr Knight – inspected the children's certificates of scrofula and pronounced them valid. One of the royal chaplains took us through the order of the ceremony.

We waited for over an hour before the King and his attendants arrived by a separate staircase from the great chamber below. They paced solemnly along like a procession of clergy in Westminster Abbey, their shoes clattering on the bare boards.

The King paid no attention to us. He commanded the ceremony to begin. The chaplain intoned the familiar readings from the Book of Common Prayer. At a signal from Chiffinch, Lady Quincy led Frances up to His Majesty.

Everything was done according to the pattern I had seen nearly three months earlier in the Banqueting House at Whitehall. There were fewer players and surroundings were humbler, but the service was the same in its essentials. A ritual is a ritual, I thought, and it must be followed in every particular or it will not work. The form was as important as the substance, perhaps more so. The truth or otherwise of the ritual was a different question.

When they returned, Frances was staring at the floor and Lady Quincy's face was wet with tears. Chiffinch nodded to me. I led Stephen up to the silent figure on the great chair.

The King laid his hands on either side of Stephen's swollen neck. The boy's body stiffened, and he began to tremble.

The chaplain read on, stumbling over the words in his haste. The King raised his eyes and stared directly into mine. His face was still, as if carved from dark-stained wood. In this light, the brown eyes looked black. There was no expression in them, only the candle flames reflected like flickering pinheads. The eyes were empty of understanding, empty of feeling.

Did the King believe in this himself, I wondered as the words filled the silence around us and rose to the smoke-stained plaster ceiling, did he believe he truly was a channel for God's grace, divinely appointed to cure the King's Evil by a miracle he had repeated thousands of times? Or did he know himself as a mortal man acting a part purely for his own advantage on this royal stage?

Or did the truth lie somewhere between?

THE END

READ ON FOR A SNEAK PEEK OF *THE LAST PROTECTOR*,
THE NEXT BOOK IN ANDREW TAYLOR'S ACCLAIMED SERIES
FOLLOWING JAMES MARWOOD AND CAT LOVETT

# CHAPTER ONE

The Walls Run With Blood
Friday, 13 November 1665

THE REVEREND JEREMIAH WHITE TOOK the Lincoln road from Peterborough, riding north through watery sunshine. He was a tall, narrow man, stiff and twig like, dressed in black. The horse he had hired from the inn was a small, brown creature. White's feet were too close to the ground for dignity.

He had set off in good time, not long after eight of the clock. The journey was no more than six or seven miles, but it took him longer than he had expected. The roads were treacherous after the recent rains, and the mare proved to be a sluggish, sour-tempered jade. He did not reach Northborough until the middle of the afternoon - well after the dinner hour, as his stomach reminded him with steadily increasing insistence.

The gates of the manor were standing open. He clattered under the arch of the gatehouse into the courtyard beyond. Ezra the stableman came out of the coachhouse, knuckling

455

his forehead with one hand and taking the horse's bridle with the other.

'Does she still live?' White asked.

'Aye, sir.' Ezra looked up at him. 'Though it will be a mercy when God takes her.'

White dismounted. There was a bustle at the main door of the house. Claypole came out with two servants behind him.

'Thank God you're here,' he said. 'Mistress Cromwell has been asking after you all day. She's working herself up to one of her fits. What kept you?'

'The roads were treacherous. I—'

'It doesn't matter now. Come in, come in.'

In his urgency, Claypole almost dragged White into the house, taking him into the great hall to the left of the screens passage, where logs smouldered in the grate. He guided White to a chair. One servant took his cloak. Another knelt before him and drew off his travelling boots.

'Will you see her directly?' Claypole said.

'A morsel to eat first, perhaps,' White suggested.

Claypole glanced at the nearest servant. 'Bread, cheese, whatever there is to be had quickly.' He turned back to White, rubbing his eyes. 'She . . . she was in great pain during the night again, and she was not in her right mind, either.' His mouth trembled. 'She says – she keeps saying . . .'

White took his host's hand. 'She says what?'

Claypole stared at him. 'She says the walls are running with blood.'

'Perhaps she has a fever. Or perhaps God has vouchsafed her a vision of the world to come, though I hope not for her or for you or me. But for now, my friend, there is nothing we can do except try to make the poor lady as comfortable as possible. And, above all of course, we must pray for her. Do you know why she wants me? Is it the will again?'

'I don't know — I asked her, but she wouldn't say. She can be close and suspicious, even with us, her family.'

The servant brought cold mutton and a jug of ale. White ate and drank a few mouthfuls, but his host's urgency had suppressed his hunger.

'The food must wait,' he said. 'I'd better see her ladyship now.'

The two men went upstairs. On the landing, a maidservant, her face grey with exhaustion, answered Claypole's knock at one of the doors.

'Mistress knows you're here,' she whispered to White. 'She heard you below.'

'Is she in a fit state to receive him?' Claypole said in a low voice.

The maid nodded. 'If it's not for too long. God send it will ease her mind.'

To White's surprise, the bed was empty, though a fire burned on the hearth. The air smelled of herbs and sickness.

'She's in the closet,' the maid murmured to him, pointing to a door in a corner of the room. 'She made me move her there when she heard your horse in the yard. Come, sir.'

Claypole made as if to follow them but she stopped him with a hand on his arm. 'Forgive me, master. She wants to see Mr White alone.'

She held open the door no wider than necessary to allow White to pass through. As soon as he was inside, he heard the clack of the latch.

The closet was tiny – no more than two or three yards square – and crowded with shadowy objects. The walls were panelled. The room had been built out over the porch and it faced north. The windows were small, their lattices set with thick green glass that let in little light. The air was stuffy with the smells of age and sickness. It was very cold.

For an instant, he thought the maid had played a trick on him and the closet was empty. Then, as his eyes adjusted, there came a rustle in one corner. The old lady was there, propped up against pillows and swathed in blankets.

'Mr White,' she said. 'God bless you for coming all this way again. I'm obliged.'

He bowed. 'My wife sends her service to you. She prays for you.'

'Katherine is a good girl.'

'How are you, my lady?'

Mistress Cromwell drew in her breath and whimpered like a dog. He waited; he knew better than to say or do anything. In a moment, when the pain had subsided a little, she said, 'I'll be in my grave by the end of the month.'

'God's will be done.'

'The workings of God's will seem mysterious indeed, these last five or six years.'

'It is not for us to question Him.' White paused, but she said nothing. 'Is it about the will? Should I send for the lawyer again?'

'No. Not that. Call for a candle, will you? It grows darker and darker.'

He opened the door a crack. Claypole had gone, but the maid was still in the chamber beyond. She had already lighted the candles and she brought him one.

'Will mistress take her draught now?' she asked as she handed it to him.

The old woman's ears were sharp. 'No, I will not, you foolish woman,' she said. 'Afterwards.'

He closed the closet door again and set the candle on a bracket in the wall. Mistress Cromwell watched him. It seemed to him that her face was markedly thinner than it had been in the summer, and her body beneath the coverings was no bigger than a child's. She had been a sturdy woman in her prime, with a plump, round face and a brisk, bustling air as she went about the tasks of her household. In the eight years since Oliver's death, she had slowly changed. It was as if time itself was devouring her.

'Sit down, Mr White.'

There was a low stool beside a chest, the only other furnishing in the closet beside the daybed on which she lay. When he sat down, his knees rose towards his chin. You could hardly see the floor.

'I don't care for candles,' she went on. 'It's when I see the blood on the walls. Smell it, too, sometimes. Fresh blood, you see.'

'It is the fever, madam, I assure you. There is no blood.'

She made a low, rattling noise that might have been a laugh. 'No, sir. There is always blood. There has been too much blood altogether. But enough of that for the moment. Will you do something else for me, as well as act as my executor?'

He bowed his head. 'Anything, madam. Anything I can.'

'You and Katherine will not be the losers. There will be something for you when I am gone.' A hand appeared from the blankets, small and wrinkled as a monkey's paw. 'Take this.'

It was an iron key, three inches long and warm to his touch with heat borrowed from its owner.

'Unlock the chest, sir. You will find a bundle of papers inside, on the top. Have the kindness to give them to me.'

He obeyed. The papers were tied together with a broad black ribbon. He glimpsed a dark, rich fabric underneath them; the candle flame glinted on the gold thread that brought the sombre material to life. A relic of the Whitehall days, he thought sadly, wondering what else the chest contained, what other mementoes of other places, of other, better times.

She slipped the ribbon from the papers. 'Hold the candle higher.'

She peered at the papers, one by one. Some were letters – White saw fragments of wax on some of them; on one of them he recognised the familiar hand of the old lady's late husband, the Lord Protector himself, Oliver Cromwell of blessed memory. She paused at this one, stroking the paper as if to give it pleasure and comfort. Her lips mumbled rhythmically like a Papist telling the beads of her rosary. Words, then phrases, then whole sentences emerged from the muttering:

'Thou are dearer to me than any creature; let that suffice . . . My Dearest, I could not satisfy myself to omit this post, though I have not much to write; yet indeed I love to write to my dear who is very much in my heart. It joys me to hear thy soul prospereth; the Lord increase His favours to thee more and more . . . I love to write to my dear . . . dearer to me than any creature—'

She was wracked with a second spasm of pain, worse than the first. White sat there, still holding the candle, watching the agony twist her features beyond recognition. Automatically

460

he found himself praying aloud, imploring God to ease her suffering in this world and the next. The pain slowly retreated.

'Madam,' he said. 'You're tired and you suffer much. Shall we continue later? I should ask your servant for your draught. It will help you sleep.'

'No,' she said with sudden vigour. 'I shall sleep long enough later.' Her hands went back to the papers. She shuffled through them. 'Ah! This one, Mr White, this is what we need.' She held it up so he could see. The paper was folded like a letter, but there was no name on it. She turned it over, showing him that the folds on the back were secured by three large seals. He made as if to take it, but she snatched it away and clasped it to her breast.

'What would you have me do?' he asked.

'This is for my son,' she said. 'It must reach him with the seals unbroken. Promise me you will guard it with your life. My husband trusted you, and I shall too.'

'You have my word, my lady. If you wish it, I shall set off for Spinney Abbey tomorrow.' Old women, he thought, made such a business out of nothing. But he was relieved to know that the task was as straightforward as this; it would be tedious and tiring, but once it was done, he could find his way home to Katherine without returning here. 'What is it? No more than forty or fifty miles from here across the Fens. It may take me more than a day at this time of year, but—'

Mistress Cromwell waved the letter, cutting him off in mid-sentence. 'No, no, Mr White. You misunderstand me. You must wait until I'm dead and in my grave. And this letter is not for my son Henry. It's for my elder son Richard.' Her mouth twisted. 'Tumbledown Dick. Poor Dick. It wasn't his fault.'

He stared at her. 'For Richard? But—'

'He is in France or Italy now, I think.' Now her mouth split wide, revealing pink gums: either a smile or a grimace of pain. 'Think of it – the second Lord Protector, as he would be still, if God had so wished it, in succession to his dear father; but now he has not a roof to call his own or a gold piece in his pocket.' The pain stabbed her again. He prayed silently while he waited for it to subside. After a few minutes, she went on: 'You must wait, sir – months, if necessary. They watch us, you know, especially Henry and me, and also Richard's wife. They may search this house when I am dead.'

He thought, dear God, all this will cost a deal of money. He was also fearful for himself. Of all the surviving Cromwells, Richard was the one whom the King's spies would watch most closely. He said, 'How do I find him?'

'You don't.' Mistress Cromwell gave him another glimpse of the pink gums. 'Someone will find you, and you will give that person the letter. With the seals intact.'

White leaned forward. Despite the cold, he felt sweat breaking out on his forehead and under his armpits. 'How will I know him, my lady?'

'Or her. Because the person in question will say these words to you: *The walls run with blood*. And you will say, *Aye, fresh blood*.'

She drifted away from him. Her eyes closed. She rubbed the blanket between forefinger and thumb, slowly and carefully, as though assessing the quality of the material. In a moment or two, even that movement stopped. Her breathing steadied. When he judged she was asleep, he rose and tiptoed to the door.

At the sound of the latch, Mistress Cromwell stirred and said something.

'Madam? What was that?'

'Bid him be kind to poor Ferrus.'

'Ferrus?' he repeated, unsure that he had caught the name correctly. 'Who is Ferrus?'

'I only gave him a penny. I should have given him more.'

Mistress Cromwell murmured something else as she glided into sleep or unconsciousness. It might have been 'Ferrus will help him.' Or it might not.

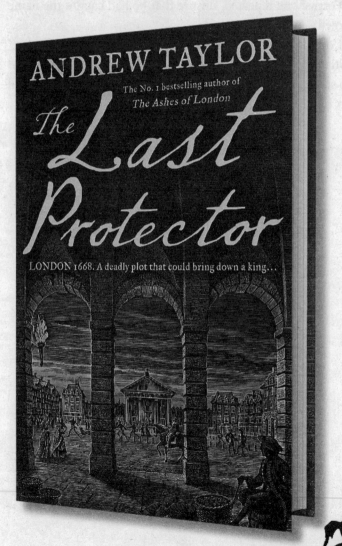